Emperor's A

ALEX GOUGH

EMPEROR'S
AXE

CANELO

First published in the United Kingdom in 2020 by Canelo

Canelo Digital Publishing Limited
Third Floor, 20 Mortimer Street
London W1T 3JW
United Kingdom

A CIP catalogue record for this book is available from the British Library.

Print ISBN 978 1 78863 830 2
Ebook ISBN 978 1 78863 700 8

Look for more great books at www.canelo.co

Printed and bound in Great Britain by Clays Ltd, Elcograf S.p.A.

Chapter One

Heavily bruised from repeated beatings and the impact of stones thrown during a riot, arms aching from the impact of a sword fight, bone weary after a race across the city to save the life of the Emperor, Silus looked at the chaos in front of him and said, 'Fuck.'

Atius nodded. 'I couldn't agree more.'

They had been making their way slowly from the Praetorian camp, where they had left the now sole Emperor Antoninus Caracalla heavily guarded by his most loyal bodyguards and Praetorians. The scent of smoke wafted across the city, and the air was full of distant cries and screams. Only hours before, Rome had been ruled by the two brothers, Caracalla and Geta. Since then, Geta had tried to kill Caracalla, and with the help of Silus, freshly escaped from prison and torture, Caracalla had slain his brother and taken the throne.

Now Silus and Atius were heading back towards Silus' lodgings in the Subura, where they hoped to recuperate from their injuries and their fatigue with a long drink and a longer sleep.

But interfering with this simple plan was a detachment of Praetorian guards who were sprawled across the Vicus Patricius, which linked the Viminal hill to the Subura. The Praetorians were normally pristine in appearance, metalwork polished like mirrors, leather buffed, boots spotless. But these soldiers, set loose on the city by Caracalla's orders to go and reward their loyalty by looting the temples and treasuries, sported uniforms covered in dust, blood and vomit. Buckles were undone, belts hung loose, and they laughed, cheered and sang with drink-slurred voices.

The reason for their celebrations, apart from the huge bribe in the form of cash and increased rations that Caracalla had given them, was that they had just looted a small temple. In the temple courtyard, in front of the steps leading up to the colonnaded building, half a dozen soldiers surrounded a priest. The young lad, barely old enough to have started shaving, was on his knees, blood and snot dribbling from his nose, begging for them to stop while the soldiers laughed.

A centurion sat on the steps of the temple with his optio, a small chest open, counting silver coins with the look of a child who has been given a bag full of honeyed treats. Some of the soldiers were drinking wine from silver goblets, heads tilted back and pouring into open mouths so it overflowed and ran down their chins.

Silus and Atius exchanged weary glances.

'This isn't going to be pretty,' muttered Silus.

'You'll fit right in, then,' said Atius.

'Come on.'

They approached the drunken soldiers cautiously, hands away from their swords, attempting to appear unthreatening. They were half a dozen yards away before one of the Praetorians noticed them and stood up abruptly, swaying slightly. He had a mop of curly red hair, exposed as his helmet was nowhere to be seen.

'What the fuck do you want?' he slurred.

'No trouble,' said Silus. 'We just want to pass through.'

'This road is ours,' said the soldier.

'The road belongs to the Emperor, and the Senate and People of Rome,' said Silus.

'Rome is ours tonight,' put in another soldier, his bushy black beard damp with wine. 'The Emperor told us to go and take what we wanted. And he said no man should stop us.'

'I was there,' said Silus. 'And he said to take what he has granted you. He didn't say anything about owning the streets. Or beating up priests.'

The redhead looked over to the priest in time to see one of the guards give him a hefty kick in the abdomen, making him curl up, hands around his head, knees drawn up, sobbing quietly.

'He tried to stop us taking the money,' said the redhead. 'He deserves it.'

'He is no concern of ours,' said Silus. 'Although isn't that the Temple of Mephitis, goddess of the foul smells of the earth? I would imagine her revenge for the desecration of her place of worship and her priest will be... unpleasant.'

The two Praetorians confronting them looked at each other uncertainly. But others had noticed their presence now, and were shouting at their comrades.

'Why are you mucking about? Break their heads.'

The centurion handed the chest to his optio and walked over, his face showing irritation.

'I suggest you two fuck off back the way you came, sharp,' he said. His voice was hoarse, likely from a combination of cheering, shouting orders and smoke inhalation.

'Centurion, we have had a long, long day. We just want to go home.'

'Are you deaf? Fuck off!'

Silus sighed. 'We don't want to hurt you.'

The centurion looked at them in surprise and let out a barking laugh. He gestured to the soldiers.

'I have twenty men here. Trained fighting men.'

'Fighting men?' said Atius. 'I thought you were Praetorians.'

The centurion growled and drew his sword. Atius made to do the same, but Silus put a hand on his wrist, making him keep the weapon sheathed.

'Centurion, your men are drunk. And they are celebrating, they aren't in the right frame of mind for serious combat. You

3

may have the numbers on your side, but we are ready to fight, and if we do, many of your men will die. You first. Now think carefully what you are going to do with that sword.'

The centurion was not used to being spoken to in this way by anyone who was not his superior in the Praetorians. He looked over to his optio uncertainly, who had stopped counting the coins and was watching with interest.

'Who the fuck are you?'

Silus knew his role was supposed to be secret, not bandied about idly. But he had had enough. Of this argument, of this day, of fighting and killing. He stepped forward, pushing the centurion's blade out of the way with the back of his hand, and pushed his face up close to the centurion's face.

'Have you heard of the Arcani, centurion?'

The man paled, eyes widening.

'Are you…?'

'Order your men to stand aside. Now.'

The centurion swallowed and nodded.

'Let them through,' he called out.

The soldiers made a corridor and Silus and Atius walked through, backs straight, too tired to feel anxious. The Praetorians glared at them and muttered curses under their breath, but none of them tried to impede the two Arcani. Moments later they were through, and on a clear road, leaving the Praetorians to their looting and rioting.

They walked on through a city of houses locked and barred, of streets emptied of their usual traffic. Carts and wagons were abandoned, overturned, some aflame, filling the air with the scent of smoke flavoured with the contents of the transport – corn, vegetables, herbs, cloth. A scant few frightened citizens scurried down the streets, heads down, casting glances around them as they rushed to safe destinations.

Silus contemplated the damage this magnificent city was taking. He knew fire was a constant danger, even though more buildings were constructed from stone these days than in centuries past, and the Roman infrastructure had suffered much worse damage from floods, fires and invasions, and it always survived. But there would be suffering on a grand scale this night.

They rounded a corner and almost stumbled into a member of the Urban Cohorts lounging against a wall, watching two colleagues having sport with a woman. She was wearing a toga, heavily made up, dark kohl-stained tear streaks down her cheeks. The two Urban guardsmen were making her walk on her hands and knees and howl like a wolf. One poked her backside with the tip of her sword.

'Growl, lupa,' he said. The pathetic woman bared her teeth and attempted a snarl, which broke down into a sob. The guards roared with laughter.

The soldier leaning against the wall clapped Silus on the shoulder.

'Funny, huh?' he said, wearing a broad grin.

'I don't think so,' said Silus.

'Oh, you aren't from Rome,' said the soldier. 'Let me explain. Lupa means both she-wolf and prostitute. The lads are making this whore act like a wolf.'

'Utter genius,' said Silus, unsmiling. 'What do you think, Atius?'

'Marvellous. It could have been written by, what's the name of that fellow who wrote that funny play we saw. Pluto?'

'Plautus,' said Silus. 'Yes, he would be proud of such a work.'

The guardsman's eyes narrowed, looking from one to the other. 'Are you mocking me?'

The stench of strong wine wafted over them as he breathed, and Silus knew that he was probably genuinely struggling to follow their irony.

'That's enough, I think. Let her go now.'

Now the Urban guardsman realised the two newcomers weren't joining in the fun. He put his hand on the hilt of his sword.

5

'What the fuck has it got to do with you?'

'Nothing. Doesn't mean we have to walk by and ignore it though, does it?'

'Silus,' said Atius. 'He is right. This is nothing to do with us. And what are you going to do, patrol the streets all night and rescue every woman in distress?'

'Listen to your friend,' said the guard confronting them. 'Leave us to our games and get on with your night. I won't warn you again.'

A scream came from the woman. Silus looked over the guardsman's shoulder to see that she had curled up into a ball, and one of the soldiers, a short man with broad shoulders and curly black hair, was kicking her, hard and repeatedly.

Silus thrust his forehead into the guard's face. The cartilage in the nose of the finely dressed guard crunched, and blood immediately began to stream down his face, staining his uniform. He staggered back, clutching his face, and Silus followed up with an uppercut to his jaw. The soldier's eyes rolled up into his head, his legs folded and he crumpled to the ground.

The other two soldiers looked up, noticing Silus and Atius for the first time now, and took a step towards them, ignoring the shaking woman lying curled up in the dirt.

'What have you done to Sulinus?' asked one, sounding genuinely confused.

'They've messed him up,' said the other, the one who had been kicking the woman.

'That one is mine,' said Silus, pointing to the shorter man who had just spoken.

Atius sighed. 'Let's try not to kill them?'

'I'm making no promises.'

'What are you two talking about?' asked the taller guard. 'Why don't you piss off and find somewhere to bum each other, or I'll rip your cocks off.'

'Suddenly I feel like I'm going to enjoy this,' said Atius.

The guards looked at each other uncertainly. Their swords were drawn but they hesitated, drunk, leaderless and without a plan.

The two Arcani took any decisions out of their hands. Moving forward swiftly as one, they paired off against their chosen opponents. Silus' opponent swung his weapon round towards Silus' midriff, but Silus stepped back easily, the sword carving only empty air. The black-haired guard grimaced, pushed forward and swung again. Again, Silus let the blade pass harmlessly. A smile came to his face. This actually felt good. After all the betrayal, torture and murder, a good, honest, one-on-one fight was just what he needed.

He toyed with his opponent, watching his eyes to predict his actions, side-stepping, ducking, retreating. The guard grew increasingly infuriated, his swings becoming wilder and less accurate. Silus saw the man's breathing coming harder and faster. He waited for the right moment.

It came soon. The guard was not only inebriated, but unforgivably unfit. A hefty swing missed by the best part of a mile, and the tip of the sword sagged at the end of the arc, slow to return. Silus took a swift step forward and gripped the wrist holding the sword tightly. He smashed the opposite forearm into the guard's face, and as the man staggered back, he twisted the wrist painfully, so the sword fell from his fingers.

The guard scrabbled for him, attempting to grip him in a bear hug, but Silus ducked his head and punched him twice in the gut. The guard doubled over, and Silus gripped his hair and thrust his head down while bringing his knee up sharply. The force of the impact reverberated through Silus. He threw the guard away from him, who fell in a crumpled heap on the floor.

Silus looked around. Atius had his foot on the chest of the other guard, his sword pressed to the terrified man's groin.

'What took you so long?' he asked Silus.

Silus shrugged. 'You don't rush a fine meal, do you?'

'These two hardly count as a fine meal. More of a rotten meat pie.' He looked down at the man below him. 'Didn't you say you were going to take my cock?' He pressed the sword harder against the guard's groin.

'Please,' gasped the guard. 'We were only having a laugh. The Emperor himself said we could.'

Silus shook his head. It seemed all the Praetorians and Urban Cohorts guardsmen had interpreted Caracalla's command to take their reward direct from the treasuries and temples as a licence to rob, harass, rape and kill. He turned to the woman, who had shuffled to the side of the road and was sitting, chin on her knees, hugging her shins.

Silus offered a hand. She looked up at him with wide, scared eyes.

'What are you going to do to me?' she said in a whisper.

'Not a thing,' said Silus. 'Except maybe escort you home. Where do you live?'

'At the Venus Lupanar.'

'Is it somewhere you want to return?'

'I'm a slave, sir. Where else could I go?'

Silus nodded. 'Very well, let's at least get you home safe.'

The woman hesitated, then took his hand as he helped her upright. She winced as she put her weight on one leg, and Silus offered an arm for her to lean on. She took it gratefully.

'Thank you, sir. It's not far.'

'What shall I do with this one?' asked Atius. 'Shall I cut his cock off?'

'No, please,' cried the guard.

'Let him go,' said Silus. 'These idiots are only doing what thousands of other soldiers are doing across Rome. It's not our place to punish them.'

Atius paused just long enough for the guard to begin to tremble, then he took his foot off the man's chest.

'Let's get this woman safe, and then get off the streets,' said Atius.

Silus nodded, and they followed her directions. It was only two blocks, and they avoided any major confrontations in that time. The Venus Lupanar was a small brothel, a painting of the naked goddess on the front wall, and above it a drawing of a large phallus. The door was firmly shut and Silus pounded on it. There was no reply, and he heard no movement inside, so he thumped it louder.

'Open up.'

Now he heard steps and a croaky, tremulous old man's voice came from the other side. 'We're closed. Go away.'

'I have one of your girls here. Let her in.'

There was a pause. Then the old man said, 'Are there any Praetorians or Urban guards out there?'

'No,' said Silus. 'But I don't know for how long that will be true.'

Another pause. 'How do I know this isn't a trick? To get my money and my girls.'

Silus shook his head. He turned to the woman. 'What's your name?'

'Agathina, sir.'

'Tell him you are safe, and that there are no soldiers here.'

Agathina spoke loudly.

'Master, it is Agathina. The man tells the truth. He saved me from the soldiers.'

There was a moment's silence, then the sound of a bar being removed and a chunky key turning in a lock. The door swung open a crack, and a sharp-nosed face peered through. Patience lost, Silus pushed the door wide, and the slight old man staggered back. Silus and Atius entered the brothel with Agathina. Atius closed the door behind them and barred it.

'Agathina!' said the old man. 'Where have you been?'

'You ordered me to the house of Onesiphorus the merchant, remember?'

'I should have you beaten, staying out this late, risking your life, my property in this way.'

'I think she has taken enough beatings for tonight,' said Silus.

The man looked at him through narrowed eyelids, then gave an unctuous smile. 'Of course, of course. I am Karpos, the owner of this establishment and the girls in it. And you are…?'

'Silus. This is Atius.'

'Well, I thank you for bringing my girl home safely. I'm afraid I have no coin with which to reward you, but I will remember you in my prayers next time I sacrifice. Have a safe trip home this dark night.' He made to unbar the door.

Atius put a hand on his arm. 'Are you kidding?'

Karpos looked at Atius with an expression of genuine puzzlement. 'I don't understand what you mean, sir.'

'We rescued your slave, your property, at considerable risk to ourselves, and you don't so much as offer us a cup of wine for our trouble?'

Karpos hesitated, torn between his desire to get these rough-looking men off his premises, and avoid giving them offence. 'Certainly. I just thought you would be in a rush to get home to your loved ones on a night such as tonight. But you are of course welcome here for as long as you wish it.'

'Excellent.' Atius walked in and sat down on a grubby couch, putting his feet up. 'Make it a decent vintage.'

Silus found a seat. Although he had been looking forward to his own bed, it made more sense to take shelter.

'I think we should stay here for the night,' he said.

'Silus spending a night in a brothel?' marvelled Atius. 'What a day this has turned out to be!'

'It's just sensible.'

'It may be sensible, but that doesn't mean we can't enjoy the experience.'

'Sirs,' said Karpos, 'the beds are all occupied by my girls, and they are resting.'

'I'm sure they could be woken up,' said Atius.

'He'll pay,' said Silus. 'Won't you?'

'I suppose,' grumbled Atius. 'But the wine is free, right?'

Karpos considered the compromise, and nodded. 'Would you like me to waken one of the girls for you now?'

'Give me a moment to get my breath back, man. I'm not a god! Where is that wine?'

Karpos poured them each a cup of wine which was strong and sour. Silus took a deep drink, then lay back on his couch. He suddenly found it impossible to keep his eyes open. He placed the cup on the floor, turned onto his side, and in moments was fast asleep.

–

The next morning there was a stench of burning and fear hanging over the city. Silus and Atius made their way along streets brimming with uncertainty and anxiety. The Praetorians had mostly returned to their barracks, with the ones that weren't still lying drunk propped in shop doorways or slumped in the refuse in alleys, or broken as a result of picking the wrong citizen to bully. The populace were trying to return to normal – those who could. They walked past a furious cobbler nailing planks across his broken door, a child weeping as she cuddled the bloodied corpse of a small dog, a baker who was clearing away the mess of smashed pottery and broken benches in his shop so he could start baking loaves for his waiting customers. There was an atmosphere of tension – people seemed to be wondering whether it was over, or worse was to come. Silus didn't know the answer.

By the time they reached Oclatinius' office, Silus felt thoroughly miserable. All the tension and uncertainty of the past year, the conflict between Caracalla and Geta, it should have ended with the death of one of them. Rome should be stable now. So why did he feel like this was just the beginning of something worse?

Oclatinius obviously sensed their mood from their demeanour, although Silus thought he wasn't looking particularly happy himself.

'Come on lads, perk up. It's not the end of the world.'

'Tell that to Geta,' said Atius.

'Atius! When will you learn to keep that stupid mouth of yours shut? Thank the gods you work for me, otherwise I would have to have you executed for treasonous remarks like that.'

'Just trying to keep it light, sir,' said Atius.

'How about you just be quiet and listen?'

Atius pursed his lips together and nodded.

Oclatinius shook his head despairingly.

'I've got a job for you. I think you might like this one.'

Silus could see Atius itching to make a quip about hoping it involved wine and whores, but he had committed to silence. Silus just listened respectfully.

'You both realise that the Emperor must now consolidate his position. It's a very dangerous time, the start of a rule, especially if the rule began in violence. Look at the five emperors who contested the throne with the divine Septimius Severus. Pertinax and Didius Julianus dead within a year, Niger dead the next, Albinus dead within four years. Or further back, after Nero died...'

'We get it, sir,' said Silus. He was tired, sore and fed up. He was in no mood for history lessons.

Oclatinius narrowed his eyes at the interruption. He sat down behind his desk and looked from one Arcanus to the other. There was a moment of silence, which Oclatinius drew out uncomfortably.

'Do we have a problem?' he asked.

'Problem?' asked Silus. 'No, sir.'

Atius shook his head.

'Do you need reminding of your oath?'

'No, sir.'

'I think you do. You swore loyalty to the Emperor and to the Arcani. I am the leader of the Arcani and I serve the Emperor. Is there any part of that that is unclear?'

'No, sir.'

'What is your word worth, Gaius Sergius Silus, Lucius Atius?'

Both Arcani now looked indignant.

'Sir,' protested Atius. 'I have done nothing to make you doubt my loyalty!'

'And you, Silus. You have disobeyed an order, and you have killed a fellow Arcanus. Do you only keep your word when it is convenient?'

Silus flushed and looked down. He tried to find words to justify his actions, but they didn't come to mind. Instead, he stuttered, 'The Emperor forgave me.'

Oclatinius shot to his feet, pointing a finger at Silus. 'Because you blackmailed him!' he roared.

'I saved his life!' Silus shouted back.

Oclatinius put his hands on his desk, breathing heavily. Then he swallowed.

'Yes, yes you did. And I believe that will keep you safe in the days and weeks to come, when all those of suspect loyalty will be purged.'

'Purged?'

'You told me you got it, but you clearly don't. Rome is ruled by an Emperor who has recently lost his father, has just killed his own brother, who is in a complex relationship with his stepmother, has had his wife murdered and is now in fear of his position and his life. There will be blood, and lots of it. And you will be shedding much of it. So I ask again, do you need reminding of your oath?'

'No, sir,' muttered Silus and Atius together.

'Louder!'

'No, sir!'

Oclatinius sat back down. 'Good. To business. As I said, I have a job for you. I know how much you like revenge, Silus. You are to go to the house of Gaius Septimius Severus Aper, the Emperor's cousin, and kill him. He was a Geta follower and helped run a network of spies, including Bek, who were working against Antoninus.'

'Just him, sir?. Not his wife or children.'

'Just him,' confirmed Oclatinius.

Silus nodded, relieved. 'You said he helped run a network of spies, sir. Who else was involved?'

Oclatinius frowned. 'That is not something you have to concern yourself with. Forget I said that.'

Silus thought Oclatinius looked uncomfortable, and wondered if he had let something slip he hadn't intended. Had the seemingly infallible spymaster made a mistake? He was an old man, he had been imprisoned, tortured, and wounded. He supposed even Oclatinius could not be perfect all the time. He filed the loose piece of information away in his mind for later use.

'So how do you feel about taking care of the man who ordered Bek to capture and torture us?'

'I am an Arcanus, sir. I obey.'

Oclatinius sighed. 'Fine, take that attitude, just get it done.'

–

'What are your orders, sir?'

The man who spoke was short and lean, but well-muscled. His skin was light brown, the colour of a semi-ripe olive, and he spoke with an eastern accent.

Aper was stuffing gold plates and cups into a large cloth sack. Slaves were hurrying around his domus, ferrying the most portable and valuable pieces of furniture out of the house onto waiting carts, collecting tapestries and statues. One slave, hastily clearing out the lararium, dropped one of the bronze household gods. The Lar crashed to the ground, and an outstretched arm holding a libation bowl snapped off.

'You idiot,' cried out Aper. 'Do you want to curse us all?' He set his sack down and scurried over to grab the broken statuette off the terrified slave.

'You're lucky time is so short or I would have the skin whipped from your back for this, slave. Get out of my sight.'

The slave disappeared at a run. Aper tried to force the broken arm back onto the statue, but he knew it was hopeless. It needed a blacksmith and a hot fire to repair it. 'Gods of the household, I will sacrifice richly to you to atone for this insult. But... not now. Forgive me.'

'Sir,' said the man, more urgently. 'What am I to do?'

Aper whirled on him. 'Run for your life, Aziz,' he hissed.

Aziz took a step back. 'Sir, Caracalla cannot be allowed to rule unchecked. He will not honour the gods of the East. He will persecute the Syrians who supported his brother. Just because we failed with Geta, it doesn't mean that we can't still...'

'It's over, you fool. Get out while you can.'

'It can't be over. There are others...'

'Enough! I have given you sound advice. Run, or wait for Oclatinius' men to find you.'

'No one knows about me apart from you and Festus.'

'Then you had better hope that neither Festus nor myself are tortured to reveal the names of those who were working for Geta. Because I am sure that neither of us are brave enough to take those names to the grave with us once Oclatinius starts using his talents on us.'

Aziz hesitated, watching the household, the frantic activity reminding him of an ant's nest that had been poked with a stick. Then he appeared to make up his mind.

'This is not the end. Just because you do not have the courage to stand for the cause does not mean that others feel the same.'

Aper turned to him. 'Courage? Watch your tongue. And call me sir.'

'No. You have given up the right to respect. I will find Festus. I will fight on.'

'Do what you want, then,' snapped Aper. 'Just get out of my way. I intend to get out of this damned city and survive.'

Aziz sneered. 'I should put a sword through you now. But I suspect Oclatinius will arrange that for you soon enough. Goodbye.'

Aziz whirled and strode from the domus, pushing an inconveniently placed slave out of his path as he left. Aper watched him for a moment, then shook his head and went back to filling his sack.

–

Silus and Atius marched into the domus of Gaius Septimius Severus Aper, first cousin of Caracalla, without any opposition or even at first any attention. The household slaves were too busy with their tasks, rushing about as the steward shouted directions and orders and swore at those slow to obey.

They walked through the vestibule and through the atrium, swords sheathed, shaking their heads at the chaos. Slowly they were noticed, and slaves abruptly stopped what they were doing and stared. The steward continued to shout orders, his back turned to the two Arcani until Silus tapped him on the shoulder. He whirled around, a curse dying on his lips as he saw the two armed assassins. He took a step backwards, his hands coming together before him in supplication.

'Please, sirs. Don't hurt me. I am at your service.'

'Where is your master?' asked Silus.

'In the peristylium,' said the steward, voice shaking, gesturing behind him but not taking his eyes from Silus' sword.

'Thank you. You may continue about your business, although I fear you are wasting your time. You will be serving a new master soon.'

The steward blanched, backing away, head bowed.

They walked through into a beautifully designed and cared-for garden, surrounded by a colonnaded walkway. A few doors led off the walkway to bedrooms, and at the far end was a staircase leading to a second floor of rooms. Two slaves were attempting to lift a large marble statue of a half-naked Venus while a tall man wearing a red cloak fastened with a gold brooch shouted exasperated commands at them.

'Take the weight. Tilt it. Tilt!'

'Gaius Septimius Severus Aper,' said Silus.

Aper turned and stared at the two intruders. The slaves froze, the statue unbalanced, resting on one side of its base, one of the slaves straining to stop it toppling over. For a moment Aper looked like he was about to speak. Then he turned and ran, with the speed of a cat pursued by a pack of hounds.

Silus cursed and sprinted after him, elbowing the slave supporting the weight of the statue out of the way. Atius began to follow, but the statue crashed in front of him, shattering into a thousand pieces on the flagstones, causing him to jump back as shards of stone sprayed him.

'Silus, you idiot,' he yelled after his colleague, then ran after him.

Aper ran straight for the stairs at the far end of the peristylium, Silus on his heels. As he leapt up them three at a time, he ripped his cloak from his shoulders and threw it behind him. It wrapped around Silus' face, and, unable to see his feet, he tripped and pitched forward, scraping his knee painfully on the edge of a step. Silus tore the cloak away, picked himself up and continued to race up the staircase.

Aper had reached the top, and he charged along the open walkway above the garden. Silus yelled after him as he followed.

'Aper, stop. It's useless. You're trapped.'

'Go to Hades, assassin.' Aper yanked open a door at the far end of the walkway and ran inside the small room. It was dark, in contrast to the brightness of the garden, and when Silus peered inside, he could see little except for a shaft of light filtering through the street window. Silus drew his sword and entered cautiously. He blinked, waiting for his eyes to adjust. Atius caught him up and Silus held out a hand, gesturing for him to wait. He moved further into the room, then lunged forward, slamming the door closed so he could see behind it.

Aper leapt out from behind a cupboard, roaring, a bronze statuette raised over his head. He brought it down just as Silus turned. Silus threw up an arm, and managed to deflect the blow just enough so it missed his skull and thumped painfully into his shoulder. He cried out, and Aper leapt away towards the window. For a moment, his frame blocked out the incoming sunlight. He turned back to Silus.

'Curse you, and curse that foul Emperor you serve.' Then with a cry, he jumped.

Silus rushed to the window and looked down. Atius threw the door open and rushed in, sword drawn, searching for danger. He saw Silus at the window and peered out over his shoulder.

'Oh,' he said. 'That didn't go as planned.'

A jump from a first-floor window was not a suicide attempt, Silus knew, but an escape. Unfortunately, although the height was not a fatal distance, bad luck and old bones had not favoured Aper. He lay in the dirt on the cobblestones of the road, clutching his leg. The shin bone had an unnatural angle in the middle, and a spiky white point protruded through torn and bloodied skin.

Silus sighed. 'Keep an eye on him from here. I'll go round.' He left the room, jogged down the stairs and walked briskly through the house, watched by slaves who had now completely abandoned their tasks and hovered uncertainly. As he marched through the atrium towards the front door, a woman came flying towards him. He lifted his sword, preparing to defend himself, but she dropped to her knees and clutched the hem of his tunic.

'Please, sir. Spare him. He is a good man.'

Silus tugged the hem out of her grip, but she grabbed his leg tight, weeping hysterically. Silus bent down and gently prised her away. Then he went outside, and walked to the back of the domus, where Aper lay, attempting to drag himself to some imagined safety.

'Gaius,' cried the woman when she saw him. She ran to him, held him tight, her tears flowing over him.

Aper looked at his wife, and all resistance left him.

'It's over, darling. I'm sorry.' He looked up at Silus. 'Will you spare her?'

'My orders only concern you,' said Silus. 'No one else here will be harmed. Not by me.'

Aper nodded. 'It could so easily have been the other way round. Geta on the throne, myself as Praetorian prefect. But I suppose I have you to thank for preventing that.'

'It's time. Make your peace.'

Aper nodded and closed his eyes, and as soon as he did so, Silus stepped forward and ran his sword through his chest. It burst through his back, missing the ribs, and impacted on the stone street, the tip breaking off with the force of the thrust.

Aper gripped the blade, then slid backwards and lay still. Silus pulled the sword out, and stood respectfully for a moment as Aper's newly created widow hugged him and howled.

Atius reached Silus, and stood beside him for a moment. Then he looked at Silus' sword. 'Bad luck. That was a nice blade.' Silus frowned at the comment, but couldn't deny that it was inconvenient. He didn't want to be unarmed at a time like this, especially as the number of enemies he was making seemed to be multiplying.

Across the road, one of the vigiles was watching. Covered in smoke, he looked like he was on his way home from his night shift. He seemed uncertain whether he should be intervening, but clearly realised that even if this killing before his eyes was supposed to be his problem, there wasn't much he could do against the two well-armed men that had carried it out.

Atius took Silus' sword and strode across to the night-watchman. 'Give me your axe,' he said. 'And take this sword. A good blacksmith will fix that in no time, and you can keep it or sell it for a decent amount.'

'But I...'

Atius handed over the sword, his expression brooking no argument. Reluctantly, the nightwatchman took his axe from his belt. It was short, with a wooden handle, and some nicks in the blade. It looked like it had been used that very night in helping fight a fire or rescue someone trapped. No doubt because of a blaze started by the rioting Praetorians. Atius handed it to Silus.

'Until you get a chance to pick up something better.'

Silus took the weapon and hefted it in his hand, then checked the edge. It would do for now. He looked down at the grieving woman, and over to the door of the domus, where the steward and some of the slaves looked on. He sighed. 'Let's go.'

Chapter Two

Caracalla stood before the full assembly of the Senate, dressed in a purple toga. He was outwardly calm and confident, as he should be with a double row of Praetorian guards, fully armed against the rules of tradition, arrayed around the benches of senators, thoroughly cowing them. Nevertheless, he felt comforted by the fact that hidden under the fine woollen folds of his toga he could feel the weight of the lorica he had worn as an extra safety measure.

They were gathered in the open at the top of the Capitoline hill, as when every member of the Senate gathered at the same time; the usual meeting site, the Curia Julia, was not large enough to hold them all. It was chilly, as would be expected in midwinter, even with the afternoon sun. Many of the faces he surveyed among the ranks of senators looked pale, and some were shivering. He didn't know if that was due to the cold weather or to fear.

He remembered a time when Geta, maybe only five years old, had discovered a snake beneath a rock, and had run to his older brother for safety and comfort. Caracalla had hugged him, and assured him that the terrible serpent was likely more afraid of him than Geta was of the snake. He nearly laughed at the comparison with his own feelings about the Senate at that moment – who was most afraid of whom?

But the thought of his brother, dead at Caracalla's hand, quashed any levity the way Caracalla had used a rock to crush that snake's head. A pang of anguish tightened his guts, and he forced himself to put the thoughts from his mind, in case it unmanned him.

Was he right to fear the Senate? On the surface, they looked like a body of unfit and infirm, mainly elderly men, an irrelevance to a powerful ruler who needed only to pay lip service to their opinions. But at the time of transition of power, their support could be crucial. Each man in that august body had immense wealth, powerful family and connections and a vast network of clients who owed them absolute allegiance. Many had once been military leaders themselves, for example in their times as proconsuls or governors, and as such most, though not all, were held in respect by various legions around the Empire.

Further, succession to the throne was not guaranteed purely by birth and inheritance. In the history of Rome, only three emperors had come to power by right of being the natural son of the previous Emperor – Titus, Domitian and Commodus – and the latter two had been particularly unpopular with the Senate. Caracalla had the advantage of being an incumbent Emperor, transitioning from co-Emperor to sole Emperor rather than being elevated anew. But these were still dangerous times for him, and he needed to ensure his precarious grip on power was cemented by a combination of persuasion, fear, bribery and removal of any possible threats.

It was bribery that had tipped the loyalty of the Praetorians and legions toward his favour. That morning he had travelled to Alba, to the south of the city, to gain the support of the Legio II Parthica which was stationed there. It had been a humbling and harrowing experience. At first he had been refused entry to their headquarters, the humiliation of a severity that he had not experienced since his father became Emperor nearly twenty years previously. The Legio II Parthica had been moved to Alba after serving Severus successfully in the Parthian wars, a reserve for use against rebellion and usurpation. It was the first legion stationed in Italy for centuries. It hadn't helped that due to the proximity of the legion's headquarters to Rome, Geta had come to be known to them more closely than any other legion, and many of the legionaries grumbled that they had sworn allegiance to two emperors, not just one.

It was particularly galling to Caracalla since he had led the legion into battle in Britannia. Maybe it was this that finally dragged the legion into his corner, although prolific bribery helped as well, including a fifty per cent increase in their pay, the same he had promised the Praetorians. Still, the end result was that once he had secured the allegiance of the Praetorians and the only other military force of any size stationed anywhere near Rome, his short-term position was secure. Now he could move to tactics of persuasion and fear against the Senate.

An ornate, gilded throne had been set before the senators, and Caracalla mounted the three steps leading up to the cushioned seat and settled himself. To his right was Papinianus, one of the Praetorian prefects and a relative of his stepmother Julia Domna (the other, Laetus, had sent a messenger saying he was terribly ill and could not leave his bed), and to his left was Marcellus, the recently appointed Urban prefect and commander of the Urban Cohorts. He regarded the assembly for a moment, heart racing, skin prickling, but showing his audience a furrowed brow and pursed lips. He knew his features, his thick curly beard, his broad forehead, his dark eyes, were often enough on their own to intimidate, but he needed more against these experienced men, despite their apparent submission to the display of force.

The senators murmured among themselves, and one or two of the brave ones even shouted angry questions.

'Why are the guard armed?'

'What happened to your brother?'

He waited for silence to fall, enforced here and there by the hilt of a sword or a smack around the head. Then he rose and spoke, his deep voice projecting across the peak of the hill, clearly audible to all.

'When a man kills a relative, then the deed is despised as soon as it is known, and the name of brother-killer is swiftly bestowed with harsh words on the perpetrator. The victim is pitied and the victor hated. Yet sometimes, if one were to reflect soberly upon the deed, evaluating the victor's motive and intent, one would find it both reasonable and necessary for a man who is about to suffer an injury to defend himself, rather than stand passively and submit. In that latter case, the man would be criticised for cowardice.

'My brother made many plots against me. He attempted to poison me at the Saturnalia feast. My loyal men discovered this attempt on my life, and the perpetrator confessed he was acting on Geta's orders. And yet I forgave him this foul deed, for the sake of brotherly love and unity, and at the beseeching of the Augusta, I agreed to meet him, alone and unarmed.

'But in his final act of treachery, he burst in on me while I was with Julia Domna, with swordsmen he had hired to murder me.

'I defended myself against an enemy who no longer displayed the attitude or feelings of a brother. It is proper to defend oneself against plots, just as Romulus refused to allow his brother to ridicule what he had done.

'That is not to mention Germanicus, brother of Tiberius, Britannicus, brother of Nero and Titus, brother of Domitian. Even Marcus Aurelius, who loved philosophy and excellence, would not tolerate his brother-in-law's arrogance and had him removed.'

Caracalla watched the expression of the audience. That all those emperors had murdered their brothers was no more than rumour, and particularly unlikely in the case of Marcus Aurelius, but he judged correctly that he would not be challenged on these points at this time.

'So, when poisons were prepared for me, and a sword pointed at me, I defended myself against my enemy, for I must call my brother this, in order to best describe his actions.

'So I say to you, you must thank the gods that they have preserved at least one of your emperors for you. You must lay aside your differences of opinion in thought and attitude, live your lives in security, looking to one Emperor alone to lead you, just as Jupiter is the sole ruler of the gods.'

He finished speaking, and the only sound was the shuffling of the guards and the wind whipping around the hilltop. No jeering, no boos, no applause, no cheers. He let his gaze roam over the senators, seeking out his brother's supporters. Aper was already dead and Laetus had excused himself, but there were others who had been loyal to Geta to a greater or lesser degree, and as he caught the eye of each one, they bowed their heads, or opened their eyes wide in terror.

When he was satisfied there was to be no challenge to his rule, he spoke up again.

'I hereby decree, as my first action as sole ruler of mankind, that all exiled men may return to Rome.'

This brought a gasp from the assembled senators. Men were exiled for a variety of crimes, such as treason, murder, religious reasons or merely falling out of favour of the Empire. Caracalla hoped that these forgiven noblemen would owe their loyalty to him, as a counterbalance to the African faction that had supported his brother. He hoped it wouldn't return to bite him one day.

'Now, I will take your oath of loyalty.'

He stood, straight-backed, and the senators as one chanted their allegiance to Caracalla as the sole Emperor of the Roman Empire. He clenched his jaw to keep his teeth from chattering, ashamed at the natural reaction to the extreme stress he had experienced over the last day and more. What now for Antoninus? he thought, his mind drifting. It was all about safety now. Safety for himself, and safety for Rome. There could be no return to the civil strife that led to his father ascending the throne. Rome needed a strong and permanent leader. And he would lead Rome to glory, like his hero Alexander. But first, he needed to be sure there were no more enemies within. And to be sure, he would have to be ruthless.

When the oath was finished, he simply nodded, then slowly descended the steps. As he walked away from the assembly, he felt suddenly overwhelmed with fatigue. He had not slept for a day and a half, a time period in which he had fought for his life, killed his brother, begged, cajoled and bribed two different military forces for their support and then intimidated the entire Senate into obedience. His knees gave and he stumbled. Papinianus put out an arm, and Caracalla took it. Marcellus took position on his other side. They walked together in silence, escorted by a century of Praetorians, towards the Imperial palace.

–

When Caracalla arrived back at the palace, four of his German bodyguards saluted him. He had deliberately left them behind, knowing that Romans distrusted foreigners, and correctly choosing the Praetorians as an escort more likely to win over the people and the Senate. Now that he was back in the palace, out of sight of the public, he dismissed the Praetorians. He actually trusted the Germans more than the Praetorians, since they had each individually sworn a personal oath on their gods to protect him to the death. Papinianus and Marcellus remained, waiting dutifully for his commands, but at that moment, his mind was empty.

He slumped onto a plushly-upholstered chair in his tablinum, staring into space. What should he feel at this moment? Victory? Elation? Grief? He felt only exhaustion. His eyes closed of their own accord, and he lacked the will to open them again. He sensed the presence of Somnus at his shoulder, and started to drift downwards into the realm of the god of sleep.

Geta's face appeared in front of him, real enough to smell the sweet wine on his breath. It was pale as freshly fulled wool, and held an expression of reproach and deep disappointment.

Caracalla jerked awake with a cry.

'Augustus, are you well?' asked Marcellus, leaning over him anxiously.

Caracalla looked around him wildly for a moment, then took a deep breath to calm his racing heart. A dream or a vision. It didn't matter, it wasn't real.

Suddenly he needed comfort. He was a man without a father, a mother, a brother or a wife. But he did have someone.

'I need to see the Empress. She was injured by her treacherous son. I need to make sure she is well and safe.'

He rose, and Papinianus offered his arm, but Caracalla shook it angrily away. He marched with purpose through the palace with Papinianus, Marcellus and the four German bodyguards to his stepmother's rooms. The thought of seeing Julia Domna, even in public where he could not take her in his arms, feel her warmth, kiss her hands and her lips, was buoying his spirits.

He entered her atrium and found her sitting with a group of noblewomen. To his shock, he found they were all wailing with grief. Domna was sitting on a couch with tears streaming down her face. Her hand was being held by Cornificia, the daughter of the Emperor Marcus Aurelius. Cornificia herself was weeping copiously, while offering Domna platitudes and words of wisdom.

'Terrible,' she was saying between sobs. 'A terrible, foul deed. My brother murdered my husband and son. No mother should have to watch her son die in her arms. But for Geta to be murdered by his own brother, so treacherously... the gods will punish him.'

'What is going on here?' roared Caracalla.

The cries and wails stopped instantly, and all the mourning women turned to Caracalla in shock. Fury overtook him, both at Cornificia's words, and at the sight of his lover so distraught as a consequence of his actions.

'Did I give anyone permission to grieve? Is it right and proper that a traitor against the Emperor, and the very Empire itself, should be mourned? A man who attempted to murder his brother for his own advancement. Should we bare our chests and tear our hair and cover ourselves in ashes at the passing of such a one?'

'Antoninus,' said Domna hesitantly, standing and raising a hand. Bandages were wrapped around the palm, and fresh blood had leaked through to spot the white cloth. The sight of the injury his brother had inflicted on his lover enraged him even more.

'There will be no mourning. There will be no displays of grief. A traitor is dead, and we should rejoice.'

Cornificia stood now and pointed a finger at Caracalla. Her voice was tightly controlled, but even so trembled a little in her anger. 'An Emperor is dead, the son of an Emperor, and the brother of an Emperor, if that man deserves such a title. The whole Empire should grieve the passing of one with so much promise, who could have been so much to Rome. But at the very least, his mother should be allowed to shed tears.'

'You dare speak to me that way?' Caracalla was now apoplectic with rage. 'By what right do you address your Emperor like this?'

'By right of my birth and my ancestors,' countered Cornificia. Domna put a warning hand on her arm, but she shrugged her away. 'I am the daughter of the great Marcus Aurelius. I am sister to the Emperor Commodus. My mother's great uncle was the Emperor Hadrian. I have Rome flowing through my veins. And I have watched Rome be ruled by men who deserved to become gods, like my father and yours, and I have watched it fall into the hands of tyrants, like my brother and like you!'

Caracalla was speechless for a moment. To be admonished before his bodyguard, before Marcellus and Papinianus, before all these damned squawking *women*! It was unacceptable.

'Papinianus. Arrest her. She speaks treason.'

'Antoninus, no,' pleaded Domna.

'Do as you are commanded, Papinianus.'

Papinianus shook his head sadly. 'I will not, Augustus.'

Caracalla turned to him and his jaw dropped.

'Papinianus. You disobey me?' He was genuinely stunned. Papinianus had always felt free to express his opinions, and he had not been as unequivocal in his support of Caracalla as had, say, Marcellus, for example counselling peace between the brothers when Caracalla wanted war. But never before had he directly gone against him like this.

'I'm sorry, Augustus. This is not right. Cornificia has done nothing wrong.'

'She speaks words of sedition against the Emperor.'

'Maybe she has that right. As she said, she is the daughter of an Emperor herself.'

'Papinianus. You are my friend as well as my advisor. But do not defy me, I warn you.'

'In this matter, Augustus, I must.'

The moment hung in the air. It felt like a crossroads. Which direction would he take his reign? If he was truly strong, he could forgive those who transgressed against him, just as Julius Caesar had done. He could shrug off the insults and the defiance, admonish the guilty, and continue secure in the knowledge of the unflinching support of the army, the Senate and the people.

But he was not in that position. He had bought the loyalty of the army in Italia and frightened the Senate into submission. Yet there were many discontents who supported Geta, and who would now probably oppose him, or even put forward their own candidate for the purple. Could he keep them all in check with promises of money and forgiveness of their crimes, or would they just take that as evidence of weakness, empowering them all the more to oppose him?

He had long admired Sulla, the dictator, who had secured his position by instituting proscriptions which resulted in the deaths of thousands of enemies of the state. And by state, he meant of course himself. Sulla was a brilliant general and a ruthless ruler, who nevertheless had survived his enemies so that he was able to give up his role of dictator, retire to his estates and ultimately die of natural causes. Caracalla considered him almost as great a role model as Alexander himself. And Alexander of course hadn't lived long enough to have to administer the Empire he had created. Would Alexander have been as ruthless as Sulla if he had managed to return home victorious?

Domna looked at him. Her eyes were red, her make-up blotchy. Normally he would find himself melting at the first sign of her distress. Instead, something hardened inside Caracalla.

'Guards, arrest Cornificia and Papinianus. Have them held in isolation, awaiting my judgement.'

The German bodyguards, tall, powerful, long-haired brutes, stepped forward. Two took Papinianus firmly by the arms, but he offered no resistance. Cornificia on the other hand was not so easily taken. When one of the bodyguards reached for her, she batted his hand away angrily.

'Don't you dare touch me, you dirty barbarian.'

The bodyguard turned to Caracalla with a question in his eyes. Caracalla simply nodded. The bodyguard turned back to Cornificia and attempted to take hold of her again. Her hand shot out and slapped him. The bodyguard put a hand to his cheek where a red hand print was developing. Then he smiled and backhanded her hard across the face. Her head snapped sideways and she fell to her hands and knees, gasping in pain and outrage. Giving her no time to recover, two guards grasped her under her armpits and hoisted her to her feet. In front of the disbelieving eyes of Domna and the other shocked noblewomen, Cornificia was dragged out and Papinianus was escorted away behind her, head bowed.

Domna stepped towards Caracalla, a trembling hand outstretched. He turned his back on her.

'Marcellus. I'm appointing you acting Praetorian prefect.'

'Yes, Augustus. It is my honour to serve you in any capacity I can be of help.'

'Rome is full of supporters of the traitor. We must deal with them as soon as possible. We should start with the conspirators in my brother's wing of the palace. Fetch a century of Praetorians and have them cleared out. And have those damned bricked up doors knocked down. I wish to walk wherever I want through my own palace.'

'Yes, Augustus.'

'Now walk with me. We have much to discuss, and many plans to lay.'

Caracalla and Marcellus left Domna's atrium, leaving the Empress staring at his retreating back in disbelief.

–

Dio Cassius could not seem to stop his foot from tapping. His knee jerked in time like it was a slave to some unheard rhythm. His hands grasped each other in his lap, and he leaned forward in a vain attempt to ease the tension his gut.

'You should have seen him, Festus. His brother not yet cold, and there he was, telling us we must thank the gods for his survival and put our faith and loyalty in him. Straight after attempting to justify his fratricide with a flimsy story about his brother plotting to kill him.'

Festus sipped his wine. Dio could not understand how he could appear so calm when Rome was falling into Hades as they sat there.

'It just happens that what the Emperor said was true. Geta did try to kill him. He took soldiers to the peace talks.'

Dio snorted. 'I don't believe it. Geta wouldn't do that. I believe the soldiers belonged to Antoninus, and they were there to kill his brother, right there in his mother's arms. I know that demon that sits on the throne, I know what was in his mind. And when I write my history of these times, that is what will be told.'

Festus shrugged. 'Write what you like, it is no concern of mine whether posterity hears the truth or not. But I would say this: if you want to survive long enough to complete your work, I suggest you keep your opinions on our Emperor to yourself.'

Dio raised his eyebrows. 'Of course. I am not a simpleton.'

'I'm just telling you that there is a slaughter on its way. The looting of the temples by the Praetorians was just a fore-taste. Aper is dead. Papinianus and Cornificia are imprisoned, awaiting trial. Plans are already being made to purge all of Geta's supporters.'

Dio started to tremble. 'But surely no one knows... I mean, apart from Titurius, bless his shade... no one knows that I had anything to do with Geta.'

'I know.'

'You? But you were a supporter of Geta too.'

Festus inclined his head. 'Don't worry, Dio. Your secret is safe with me. But I would have your counsel. As a learned man, and a well-respected member of the Senate.'

Dio swallowed, pushing down the nausea and panic rising from deep within.

'Go on.'

'If an alternative ruler could be found to Antoninus, would the Senate embrace him?'

'An alternative? Is there one? Geta and Caracalla have no heirs, not even by adoption.'

'You're a historian. You know there is plenty of precedent for a new Emperor coming from outside the incumbent Imperial family.'

'But there was always a candidate respected by the army and loved by the people ready to take power.'

'Really? Didius Julianus?'

'That's your best example?' Dio Cassius scoffed. 'Bought the throne at auction from the Praetorians, executed sixty-six days later.'

'Well, we are talking hypotheticals at the moment.'

'Then talk real names, or this conversation is a waste of time.'

Festus hesitated. 'There is someone who is connected to the Imperial line who could be made Emperor, if Antoninus could be done away with, and if the Senate would support him. Someone who is related to the Severans by blood. And rumour has it that he is even more closely related than official sources would have us believe.'

Dio Cassius scowled, intrigued, distracted from his anxieties by the interesting turn the conversation was taking.

'A name doesn't immediately spring to mind,' he said. 'Who?'

'Varius Avitus Bassianus.'

Dio stroked his chin. 'I don't know anyone by that... wait. Are you talking about that odd child? Marcellus' son?'

'Exactly.'

'Are you serious?'

'Deadly.'

'But... but...' Dio had so many questions and objections he couldn't work out what to say first. 'The first time I met him, he was about five years old, running around the peristylium naked with his private parts tucked between his legs, yelling, "look mother, I'm a girl."'

'Well, we've all done that.'

Dio tilted his head on one side and gave Festus a hard stare. Festus blushed. 'Well, maybe not all of us. Not exactly that. But he was just a child.'

'He is still just child!' exclaimed Dio. 'He is what, eight years old now?'

'Thereabouts.'

'And you wish to put him forward as a candidate to be Emperor? Why?'

'Because he has Imperial blood. Maybe richer blood than is officially accepted.'

'You mean the rumours about his parentage, that he is actually Antoninus' son?'

'True or not, the merest suggestion can be helpful in reinforcing a claim to the purple. And also, he is young and can be... let's say guided, by someone wiser and more experienced. And whose thinking is maybe more aligned with that of the Senate.'

'Like who?'

'That is yet to be decided. Not me, my role is behind the scenes. Not you either, I would wager. Maybe it would be more of a council. But that is getting ahead of ourselves. My question to you is, would the Senate accept him as Emperor?'

Dio considered. 'The way Antoninus has treated the Senate, before and after the death of his father, and with his blatant display of threat and intimidation yesterday, the Senate would be in a mood to support just about anyone but him. But on sober reflection, I think many would have reservations about supporting someone of such youth and such... odd behaviour. Rome has had its fill of emperors like Nero, Domitian and Commodus. For all Antoninus' faults, he has not outraged the dignity of the Roman people. Not yet, at least.'

'As far as the public know,' said Festus.

'Oh? What secrets do you know?'

'Many, but they are not for sharing, senator. I hope you understand.'

'You are asking for my advice about an act of treason, and yet you withhold information from me?'

'Come now, friend. You know I can't share everything I know. Nor, I suspect, would you want me to.' He gave Dio a pointed stare, which made the senator blanch, wondering what it was that Festus had discovered of the many aspects of his private life he would rather not become public knowledge.

'Nevertheless,' said Dio hastily, returning the conversation to its original topic. 'I think you would struggle to get the entire Senate to accept Avitus as Emperor. I suspect in fact there would be a split. The boy has Syrian heritage, and if I recall correctly, some sort of hereditary position as an eastern priest. The Senate and members of the Imperial court with eastern origins or allegiances might support him – the Syrians, Alexandrians and Greeks. But those of the West, from Gaul, Hispania, and particularly from Italia, they would not. And you could say the same for the legions. Those based in the East would likely be more supportive than those based in the West.'

'So what you are saying is that Avitus could command support from the eastern half of the Empire but not the West?'

'I believe so.'

'That's very helpful.' Festus stood. 'I thank you for your time.'

'What are you planning, Festus?'

'If I'm successful, you will be able to write all about it in your history. If not, then it is best that you know nothing.'

'Festus. Am I safe?'

The Commander of the Sacred Bedchamber shook his head. 'I fear that in Rome these days, no one is safe.'

–

It had fallen to Silus to take care of Cornificia. Of course. There would be no trial such as had been organised for Papinianus. It would do Caracalla no favours to allow this articulate noble-woman, the daughter of one of the most beloved rulers Rome had ever had, to stand in public and condemn the new Emperor. So Silus entered her cell in the basement of the palace, bearing just a simple but sharp knife.

Cornificia was in her fifties and showing signs of age, although not nearly to the same extent as someone from the poor classes of the Empire. The women in their fifties that Silus knew growing up in Britannia were toothless, shrivelled old hags, and that wasn't just the perception of a child. Poor nutrition, tough living conditions and a lifetime of manual labour took tolls on the body that the rich were never exposed to.

She stood when Silus entered, and he bowed his head.

'Lady.'

'Who are you?' Her voice was superior, her tone compelling.

'I am Silus, my lady. I am here on the business of the Emperor.'

Her eyes dropped to the knife at his belt and she paled, but gave no other outward sign of fear. If anything, her rod-like back became even straighter.

'Then state your business. You are disturbing my rest.'

The cell was cold and damp. The stone bench was covered with a straw mattress, giving some comfort beyond that of the common prisoner, but the ubiquitous bucket in the corner still spoke of the indignity inflicted on this high-born woman.

'My lady, I am sorry to say that the Emperor has decreed that your words and actions were treason. The penalty is death.'

Cornificia nodded once. 'Comforting a woman who has lost her son is treason to this madman, is that so?'

'I have no influence on the decision, my lady.'

'Of course not. Just the unthinking lackey who obeys orders without question.'

Silus knew there was no point in contradicting her. What good would it do this woman, who was bravely facing her death, to burden her with his own doubts, disappointment, distress?

'The Emperor has done you the honour of letting you choose the manner of your death.'

'Such consideration.' She pointed at the knife on his belt. 'Give that here,' she said peremptorily, hand outstretched. Silus hesitated, then passed the blade to her, hilt first. She looked along its length, checked its balance, and tested its sharpness with her thumb. Although he was now unarmed, and she held the knife, he felt no fear. He knew he could still easily overpower her, but knew too that it would not be necessary.

'This will do.' She took off her necklace and laid it on the bed, then removed her earrings, and each of four gold, jewelled rings which she wore on her smooth, fine fingers. Then she sat on the mattress, placed the knife against her wrist, and looked into Silus' eyes.

'Poor, unhappy soul of mine, imprisoned in a vile body, go forth, free now. Show them that you are Marcus' daughter, whether that suits them or not.'

She cut deep, biting her lip at the stinging pain. Blood flowed quickly, and when she swapped the hand holding the knife, the viscous liquid made it harder to grip. Silus stepped forward to help, but she shrugged him off, and sliced into her other wrist. Then she passed the knife back to Silus and lay back on the bed. One arm dangled over the edge, and blood poured from the wound, pooling on the cobbled floor, crimson rivulets streaming along the cracks.

She did not look at Silus as she died, instead staring at the ceiling as she drifted slowly away into unconsciousness. Her face remained expressionless throughout. But near the end, when her breathing was becoming shallower, her eyelids fluttering closed, a single tear formed in the corner of her eye, trickled across her cheek and dropped to the floor.

Silus waited dutifully until she was gone. He checked her pulse to ensure she was definitely dead, then whispered a prayer for the safe passage of her shade. He bowed his head and stood in respectful silence for a few moments. Then he knocked on the door for the guards to enter.

'Take care of her,' he said. 'Instructions on what to do with her body will follow. I will make sure the Emperor is informed of her death.'

He walked out of the cell without a backwards glance, moving slowly and stiffly. Two noble people, bravely dying a noble death, for no reason except the Emperor's pride and fear. And there was so much more to come.

This wasn't the work he had signed up for. He wasn't fighting Rome's barbarian enemies any more. Nor even taking one side in a civil war, joining the one most likely to keep Rome strong and safe. This was just murder. Cornificia was no threat to Caracalla.

He needed to get out.

He could run. Leave Rome, take his money, set himself up in some far-flung part of the Empire where no one would ever find him.

But what would happen to Tituria? And what about Atius? Maybe he could persuade Oclatinius to discharge him, or at least give him some time to get away. He was not needed for these executions. They required none of his skills. Let another carry out these heinous tasks.

He thought about Tituria, alone on her island. He had promised to visit her. Would Oclatinius allow it? He resolved to ask. But first, there was the trial of Papinianus to get through.

-

The Senate was gathered once more, though this time not all of them, and not enforced by the Praetorians. The smaller number of senators was able to fit in their usual meeting place, the Curia Julia. The interior of the building was quite simple, Silus reflected, compared to the lavish decorations of temples and palaces he had seen since he first arrived in Rome. The walls were fitted with plain white marble to about two-thirds of their height, and rows of wooden chairs supported the backsides of the richest men in Rome. The floor, by contrast, was striking. It was similar to a mosaic, but with larger, specially shaped pieces of materials fitted together to make specific designs, rosettes in squares and cornucopias, coloured red and green on backgrounds of yellow and purple.

At one end of the chamber was an altar and a statue of Victoria, holding a wreath and standing on a globe. Before it was a marble throne on which sat Caracalla, looking down imperiously on the gathered body. Beside him sat Domna, her face expressionless, lifeless, drawn and tired. The Emperor and Empress were flanked by four German bodyguards and before them was a row of pristinely uniformed Praetorians. Silus stood with Oclatinius at the back of the chamber, inconspicuous in the shadows. He wished he was elsewhere. He hadn't been home, hadn't changed, hadn't even had time to find a new weapon, the vigiles' axe still hanging from his belt.

Standing in the middle of the floor of the great chamber, wrists manacled, stood Papinianus. His gaze swept easily around the assembled Senate, expressing an air of respect but a complete lack of concern.

Caracalla raised a hand to speak, and the silence that fell was instantaneous.

'Papinianus,' he said. 'You have been brought here to trial to answer charges of treason. Witnesses will be brought against you. Once they have spoken, you will have a chance to answer their allegations.'

'Tribune Torquatus, tell the assembled men your grievance against Papinianus.'

A young man, nervous but looking genuinely angry, stepped forward. He straightened his tunic and his red cloak and spoke up.

'As a tribune of the Praetorians, I swear by the gods to tell the truth. When he was Praetorian prefect, I saw with my own eyes Papinianus take money that was offered to the gods in the temple at the barracks.'

This drew a gasp from the senators. Theft and sacrilege. Not a good start. It seemed unlikely to Silus though. Papinianus was very wealthy in his own right. Why steal a few coins from the gods?

'And I heard him with my very own ears denounce the Emperor Antoninus, saying it would be better for Rome if the gods took him, so there would be peace.'

Papinianus shook his head. If he had said this, Silus suspected it would have been idle talk stimulated by frustration at the impasse between the Imperial brothers. More likely, though, was that this tribune had a grudge against Papinianus; maybe he had been humiliated in some way by his commanding officer, or overlooked for some honour, or even bribed by someone for his testimony. Silus looked at Oclatinius, but could read nothing in the old man's face.

39

'Do you have anything to say to this, Papinianus?' demanded Caracalla.

'The allegations are untrue, Augustus.'

'Can you prove that?'

'Of course not. I mean, unfortunately, it is my word against his.'

'It would be if it was just one accuser. But it is not. Centurion Velius. Step forward and speak.'

Centurion Velius looked a lot more nervous than Torquatus, and a lot less like he wanted to be there. He gave Papinianus an apologetic look, then said, 'As a centurion of the Praetorians, I swear by the gods to tell the truth. I served under Papinianus, and I witnessed him uttering sacrilegious words against the divine Septimius Severus.'

'What words?' asked Caracalla.

'That your blessed father was no more divine than a cabbage, and that emperors did not become gods when they died.'

There were plenty of intellectuals in Rome who did not believe in gods or the afterlife, Silus knew, but they generally paid lip service to the apotheosis of emperors, for political expediency, if for no other reason. If Papinianus had truly said this in front of a centurion, he was being extraordinarily unguarded in his comments. Maybe the former Praetorian prefect was less popular with his men than he realised.

The third witness was a Praetorian legionary, a foot soldier of the rank and file, albeit better paid and with a shinier uniform than most legionaries. He spoke with a common accent that spoke of roots in the poorer quarters of Rome, an increasingly rare recruit to the army from the capital itself.

'As a legionary of the Praetorians, I swear to the gods to tell the truth.' He hesitated.

'Go on,' prompted Caracalla.

'Right. Sorry, Emperor, er, Augustus…'

'What do you have to say?' snapped Caracalla.

'Well, I saw the prefect here having… unnatural relations with a goat.'

The Senate erupted into laughter at that, and even Papinianus smiled at the absurdity. But Caracalla was in no mood for levity.

'Silence!' The chamber fell quiet. 'Papinianus, I have a queue of Praetorians lining up to denounce you for various crimes of treason and sacrilege. But you have served me and my father well over the years. I am not above clemency for a loyal servant. If you are prepared to swear your unequivocal and undying loyalty to me, your crimes may yet be forgiven.'

'You have always had my loyalty, Augustus,' said Papinianus.

'Your sole loyalty. No division in your allegiance. I require you to condemn my brother before this Senate.'

Papinianus shook his head sadly.

'I cannot do that, Augustus.'

Caracalla's face turned the colour of his robe.

'You... cannot? Papinianus, you stake your life.'

'I pledged allegiance to your father, and when he died to his two sons. Both of them.'

'Papinianus! You will explain to this gathered body why it was necessary that Geta should die. That I was protecting myself from his murderous intent.'

Papinianus sighed. 'Augustus, it is easier to kill a brother than to explain it away.'

It would have been possible to hear a mouse sneeze, the absence of all sound was so profound. Silus could hear his own blood pounding in his ears, and his heart started to race even as his stomach sank. Oh, Papinianus. You proud fool.

Caracalla raised his hand slowly, and pointed a trembling finger at Papinianus.

'You condemn yourself with your own words.'

Domna put a hand on Caracalla's arm.

'Augustus, consider...'

'Silus!'

Oh fuck.

'Come here.'

Silus looked at Oclatinius, who gave him a helpless shrug. Silus walked forward on legs trembling like a newborn calf. He stood beside Papinianus, facing the Emperor.

'The penalty is death. The sentence will be carried out immediately. Silus, execute the traitor.'

Silus reached down to his belt, and his hand clasped around the hilt of the vigiles' axe.

'But Augustus, I only have...'

'Do it now!' roared Caracalla.

Silus bowed his head and turned to Papinianus. 'I'm sorry,' he whispered. Then more loudly, 'On your knees.'

Papinianus did as he was told. Silus drew his axe. Papinianus' eyes widened and he looked to Caracalla. 'But...'

Silus brought the axe down hard into the side of Papinianus' neck. It bit deep.

But not deep enough.

The axe of one of the vigiles was not a weapon of battle, such as the Caledonians had used, that could cleave off limbs and heads with one mighty swing. Not even the huge axes that foresters used to fell trees. This was the tool of a fireman, used to break down flimsy wooden doors that were usually half rotted through. A hand axe, small so as to be easily portable along with the other tools that the vigiles needed to carry – ropes and buckets and hooks.

Papinianus fell to one side with a cry, clutching his neck where the axe had opened up flesh. Blood flowed, but there was no pumping, no flood. It was not a mortal wound.

Silus raised the axe again, aiming for the gash he had opened before. But Papinianus was moving now, and his hand was clamped over his neck. The axe severed three fingers and smashed into his jaw, shattering it. He fell to his hands and knees, blood leaking from his neck, gasping and howling in pain.

Silus looked around helplessly to the throne. Caracalla's face was impassive. There would be no mercy, no help from that quarter. He caught Oclatinius' eye. The spymaster looked grim, but merely gave him a nod to continue.

Silus turned back to Papinianus, lifted the axe high, and with all his strength, brought it down on the back of the former prefect's neck. It cut through spine, and Papinianus sprawled forward onto his face. He was motionless, his cries ended, but still he breathed. Silus lifted his axe and brought it down on the back of his head, again and again. Blood and brains sprayed the immaculate white togas of the nearest senators, who flinched back in horror.

When he was sure that he was dead, Silus stood up straight and faced the Emperor. Blood dripped from the blade of his axe, and his face and tunic were covered in gore.

Caracalla regarded him for a moment.

'He deserved a sword,' said the Emperor, as if he was reprimanding a wayward child.

Caracalla rose, and walked from the chamber, escorted by bodyguards, Praetorians and Marcellus. Domna remained seated, staring in horror at the bloodied and mangled remains of her Syrian relative. Oclatinius walked stiffly over to her and took her hand, then led her away. Slowly, the chamber emptied. Slaves came over, grabbed the corpse by its ankles and dragged it off, leaving a long bloody smear behind.

Silus stood alone, unmoving. He didn't know how much time passed before Atius arrived. Atius took in his friend's appearance and the evidence of the remains of the botched execution. He took Silus' arm, and slowly led him out of the building.

Chapter Three

Silus sat in a corner with Atius, as far from Caracalla's throne as possible. He still felt sick, but Oclatinius had summoned him to attend this council meeting with an invitation that strongly intimated declining was not an option. He and Atius flanked Oclatinius and Festus, who sat together, observing not only the Emperor but everyone else in the meeting.

Seated either side of Caracalla were Sextus Varius Marcellus, currently acting as both Praetorian prefect and Urban prefect, and Julius Avitus Alexianus, who was both father-in-law to Marcellus through his daughter Julia Soaemias, and brother-in-law to Caracalla through his wife Julia Maesa, Julia Domna's sister. Julia Domna, however, was nowhere to be seen, the Empress's throne awkwardly empty. Quintus Marcus Dioga, head of the treasury, and Ulpianus, the jurist, sat near two freedmen who were acting as scribes and scribbling furiously on wax tablets to take down the pronouncements and commands of the Emperor.

Caracalla talked loudly and fast, and his audience listened attentively, mouths tightly closed.

'I want work on the great bath complex that my father began accelerated. They are behind schedule. Whip slaves, dismiss overseers, spend more money, whatever is necessary. My father commanded these to be the greatest baths in the city, and when they are finished, they will shout to the city of the glory of my father's reign and of my own.'

Dioga whispered a comment to the scribes, who nodded and made a further note.

'Furthermore, I wish every citizen of the Empire to be gifted a caracallus.'

Dioga raised his eyebrows. 'A… caracallus, Augustus?'

'Am I speaking too softly for you, Dioga?'

'No, Augustus. I just wanted to clarify…'

'The common man named me Caracalla after the cloak I liked to wear in Britannia. Well, they can all wear one now, and I will own that name that they have given me.'

'Yes, Augustus.'

'And talking of the common man. I intend to issue an edict that will make all free men in the Roman Empire into Roman citizens, and to give all free women in the Empire the same rights as Roman women.'

The advisors looked at each other, genuinely surprised, the odd command about the cloak already forgotten.

'Augustus,' said Alexianus hesitantly. 'Is that even possible?'

'If I command it, it is possible,' he said.

'But… why?'

The advisors and counsellors in the room all wore expressions that made Silus suspect they all thought the Emperor had gone mad. Maybe they were starting to question their decision to back him.

Caracalla looked for a moment like he might explode at being questioned by Alexianus. But the old man had been a good advisor and friend to Severus, and strictly loyal to Caracalla since Severus died, and he bit back a retort.

'Old friend, do not look at me as if you are regarding a man possessed by demons. These ideas are not the ravings of a madman. Caracalla is a name that has been used derisively about me for some time, and it will always be with me. If I embrace the name in such an emphatic fashion, it takes all the sting out of it as an insult. Work on the baths will show the people that I care about the city and wish to improve it. And not just by building a temple that improves my own standing with the gods, but baths that are open to all.'

'But, to make all free men Roman citizens. Could that even work?'

'I expect my advisors to give me the answer to that. Ulpianus?'

The studious lawyer pinched his nose and considered. He clearly didn't want to say the wrong thing after the horrific death of his fellow jurist Papinianus, but also had his own professional pride.

'Would the Augustus allow me time to think through the legal implications and the possible consequences?'

'I can tell you one consequence,' said Marcellus, somewhat emboldened by the others who had stuck their necks out and questioned the Emperor. 'The incentive to join the legions of becoming a citizen at the end of twenty-five years' service will disappear overnight, and recruitment will plummet.'

Caracalla waved a hand dismissively. 'Nonsense. I have just increased the pay of the army. There is still every incentive for the poor of the Empire to sign up. Still, we will increase the length of service to twenty-eight years to offset this possible issue.'

'And,' said Ulpianus, putting a finger in the air, 'tax revenues will increase. Non-citizens are not liable for tax.'

'That isn't the purpose of the decree,' said Caracalla. 'Increasing tax on the poor has only a minimal effect on the treasury. But it will be a popular move with the population of the Empire.'

'Not with the Senate,' said Marcellus. 'Nor with the poor Roman citizens who will object to those they consider their inferiors being elevated to the same rank as them.'

'Nevertheless. Unless Ulpianus can find some legal or other compelling reason to make me change my mind, it will be done.'

Marcellus bowed his head.

'We will need to raise money for these measures in other ways. We can raise inheritance tax, and maybe some other taxes too. We will also debase the silver coinage. Dioga, look into these things.'

'Yes, Augustus.'

'Marcellus, I want shows in the Flavian amphitheatre, the Circus Maximus and in the theatres. Organise a lavish programme of events to entertain the populace.'

'It will be done, Augustus.'

'Next, I want my brother's name and memory damned. All signs, all paintings, all monuments throughout the Empire are to be erased. I wish none to remember that he ever existed.'

Silus was glad that Domna was not present. He couldn't imagine how she would feel, to have the memory of her son desecrated even while she still grieved.

'Now, Marcellus, Festus, Oclatinius, we turn to matters of security. There are many in the city who supported my brother, and who still oppose my rule. I am going to give you a list of men who must be disposed of. You will see to it, in conjunction with the Urban Cohorts and the Praetorian Guard under Marcellus.'

Festus and Oclatinius inclined their heads.

'I am not going to nail these names up on signs in the forum, like Sulla and Octavian did. You will deal with them privately, and with the minimum of fuss. Am I understood?'

'Yes, Augustus,' they replied in unison.

'Very well. The following lives are forfeit, and their estates are to become the property of the throne.

'Valerius Patruinus.' A former Praetorian prefect, Silus knew.

'Lucius Valerius Messalla Thrasea.' A previous consul, Silus thought. He didn't know what either of these two had done to offend.

'The son of Papinianus, who is now old enough for the quaestorship.' A threat after the death of his father. Silus felt another pang of nausea and guilt.

'Aelius Antipater.' One of the few surviving tutors of the younger Caracalla.

'Titus Claudius Pompeianus.' Grandson of Marcus Aurelius.

'Publius Helvius Pertinax.' The son of the former Emperor Pertinax.

And more. Serenus Sammonicus, an intellectual, Silus believed. The governors of Baetica and Narbonensis. The list went on and on, until Silus became almost numb to the scale of the forthcoming slaughter. Was this all necessary for the safety of the Emperor and the Empire? Or was it something more base, like petty revenge for previous slights? Or even, worst of all, was it indeed madness?

Eventually the list of condemned ended. Caracalla was breathing heavily through his nose, looking satisfied and unburdened, like he had set down a heavy load.

'I have one more duty today. I must honour three men who have stood by my side when I needed them most, who saved my life from my treacherous sibling. Step forward, Oclatinius, Silus, Atius.'

The three Arcani stepped out in front of the Emperor and bowed their heads.

'As the head of the Arcani, and two of its most skilled members, you three have done me immeasurable service in recent times. And you have served the Empire well, in Rome and abroad. Although my rewards for you cannot reflect the value of your deeds, they are a token of my esteem.

'To legionary Lucius Atius, I award the sum of eight thousand sestertii.' Atius smiled. It was a whole year's pay at the new rates for a legionary of the Urban Cohorts.

'To centurion Gaius Sergius Silus, I award the sum of twelve thousand sestertii.' A year's pay for a Praetorian. He was rich. Not senator or even equestrian rich, but set for life. He would never starve or be without food or home or a household slave. He should be rejoicing inwardly, but found it hard to summon up any enthusiasm.

'And to Oclatinius Adventus, the sum of forty thousand sestertii.' Silus was sure the old bastard didn't need the money, but his boss nodded his acceptance and replied on behalf of them all.

'We thank you for your kind gifts, Augustus, and accept them gratefully, though we were only doing our jobs, and our duty to Emperor and Empire.'

'If only all Romans were as diligent in their obligations. Now, with that final pleasant task done, this council is finished. You all have work to be doing. I look forward to reports of your success.'

He rose, and abruptly swept from the room, two German bodyguards hurrying to catch up with him.

Silus sighed. Despite the monetary reward, he felt at the edge of despair. He still wanted to serve, to be of value to the Empire, to help keep its citizens safe. But what glory was there in the role he was playing now?

He had had enough. He needed to talk to Oclatinius.

–

When Marcellus returned home from the meeting, his wife Julia Soaemias was waiting for him in the atrium. She was wearing a blue stola and a hood that covered most of her head, but still displayed the foremost part of her painstakingly coiffured hairstyle, modelled on the fashion popularised by her aunt, the Empress Julia Domna. She was thirty-two years old and had been his wife for twelve years, and if anything was more beautiful than when he had married her. At least outwardly. Beside her was the eunuch Gannys, their son's tutor, and more and more recently, his wife's advisor and confidante.

'Tell me everything, Marcellus,' she snapped. 'Leave nothing out.'

He sighed. Beautiful on the outside for sure. Increasingly domineering, though. As Marcellus' star had risen, until he was now one of the most powerful men in Rome, his wife's control over him had tightened. It embarrassed him, and he tried to assert his dominance as paterfamilias, with the power of life and death over her and their son, Avitus. But they both knew that much of his ascension was down to her. Her family connections, of course, but also her seduction of the young Caracalla.

It still humiliated him, that he had drunkenly offered his wife to the young Augustus to gain preferment, more so that his wife and Caracalla had both agreed, and even more so that Soaemias had continued to attempt to seduce him, although Caracalla after that one night had continually turned her down.

But the result of that one night of calculated, negotiated passion was uncertainty about the paternity of his son. He had been elevated to acting commander of both the Praetorian Guard and the Urban Cohorts. He stood at the Emperor's right hand. At that moment he could be considered the second most powerful man in the world.

Was it worth it? Probably, he had to concede. And maybe now he should start to behave towards his wife the way a real Roman man behaved.

'Join me in my room, my dear,' he said in an even tone.

'Tell me now,' said Soaemias.

Marcellus looked at Gannys, who was studying the wall, carefully ignoring the exchange.

'Come with me to my room, dear. Please.'

Soaemias tutted, but she followed him to a small private room near his office.

'Marcellus! What has got into you?'

'Soaemias, I am a powerful man. You should respect me as such. If you have words you wish to say, you should say them to me in private. In public, even in front of the slaves, you should behave like a dutiful wife, a good Roman matron.'

Soaemias looked at him contemptuously. 'I am the niece of the Empress! A powerful woman in my own right.'

'What you are,' said Marcellus, 'above all else, is my wife. And I wish you to start behaving like it, and not like my mother. If you have counsel for me, you should offer it in private. In public you must talk to me with respect. Or there will be consequences for you.'

Soaemias stared at him in disbelief. Marcellus felt suddenly nervous. This shouldn't be so hard. It was the normal way of things, even if that wasn't the case in his own home. But he was the Emperor's right-hand man. He had real power. Surely he could be the master of his own home. Surely now he could begin to act with the dignitas and auctoritas of a noble Roman.

'Do you understand me?'

'I do.'

'Good.'

'Now understand this. If you ever speak to me that way again, in public or in private, I will take a knife while you sleep and cut your balls off, and offer them to the mountain god.'

Marcellus gaped. He should strike her. Punish her for her words. But he quailed under her unwavering gaze. His shoulders drooped. Why could he not control her? Her domination of him unmanned him.

'Now, husband and master, will you tell me what transpired at today's meeting?' Her tone and words were sweet and correct. Maybe if she could at least pretend to respect him in public, that would be sufficient.

He paced the room. 'We are in a fortunate position, my love. To be in favour with the Emperor at such a time not just allows advancement, it preserves life itself. The list of those to die was... there were so many.'

'Who?'

Marcellus listed those he could remember off the top of his head, although he was sure there were many he had missed out.

Soaemias sat tight-lipped as she listened to the list. 'There will be many vacancies in the most important posts in the government, and in the Senate. We need to make sure our relatives, clients and supporters fill those posts as far as possible.'

Marcellus nodded his agreement. 'Power is transitory. One day Papinianus seems unassailable in his position, and the next day he is being hacked to pieces in front of the Senate.'

'And his son is now to follow him into the embrace of Elagabal.'

'Yes. We must make sure we don't place our own son in this position. We need to work together, Soaemias, to make ourselves indispensable to the Emperor, to carry out his every command to the best of our ability, and to secure my position. The lives of all of us may depend on it. Are you with me?'

Soaemias stepped forward and kissed him lightly on the side of the mouth.

'Of course, my love. Now, will you join me in the daily sacrifices? Avitus is going to lead the ceremony, and my mother will join us.'

Marcellus hesitated. He came from Apamea, a Hellenistic city in Syria, and he was brought up worshipping the Graeco-Roman pantheon. But his wife was a devotee of the god Elagabal, the supreme god of her home city of Emesa, and their son Avitus would accede to the role of Elagabal's high priest one day, the position that Julia Domna's father had occupied. Both Soaemias and Avitus undertook the worship of the Emesene gods with utmost seriousness and solemnity, and Marcellus had long since learned not to mock, demean or disrespect the Emesene pantheon in any way. And he had just lost a battle with his wife that had left him feeling unsettled. So despite his pressing list of tasks that worried at the back of his brain, he nodded.

'Let us worship.'

—

They had dedicated a small room at the back of their domus as an Elagabalium, a temple to the supreme god, Elagabal. Soaemias had told him that Elagabal was originally a god of the mountain, which was where his name came from in the ancient language of Emesa. He had been worshipped since ancient times, and was the oldest of all Emesene gods, although over time he had become associated with sun gods, particularly Sol Invictus, the unconquered sun. The walls of the

Elagabalium were frescoed with scenes of sacrifice against back-drops of Syrian countryside. The floor mosaic was a radiant sun, surrounded by minor deities, with a magnificent eagle soaring above the sun. At one end of the room was a marble altar. And in the centre was a conical black rock, a representation of the holy rock which resided in the temple in Emesa and was supposed to have fallen from the skies.

Marcellus was still unclear as to whether the Emesene rock was supposed to be the god himself, or merely a representation, or something in between. He wasn't sure the worshippers were entirely certain themselves. But in any case, the rock before them now was purely a symbol, albeit one that Soaemias had had blessed by the high priest himself.

Julia Maesa was kneeling in the centre of the room, eyes closed. She was Julia Domna's younger sister, and the family resemblance was marked, but her features were somehow more severe. Where Domna's nose looked beautifully sculpted, hers was rodent-like. Where Domna's eyes were round and open, hers were heavy-lidded. Marcellus believed that her appearance was an outward reflection of her inward ugliness. He had never liked his mother-in-law.

Maesa turned at their entrance, flicked a contemptuous look at Marcellus, and then smiled at her daughter, holding out her hand for Soaemias to join her. Marcellus' wife knelt beside her mother, and Marcellus knelt on the other side of her.

Six slaves dressed in plain robes were present in the room. Four of them were musicians, equipped with drums, cymbals, flutes and pipes. The other two were female slaves, one young and beautiful, the other much older, gap-toothed and bent-backed. They represented Elagabalus' consort, Astarte, the goddess of water and fertility, and Atargatis, the great earth mother.

Before the altar stood their eight-year-old son. He was dressed in a long-sleeved, gold-laced Syrian style robe which reached down to his feet, and on his head he wore a crown decorated with jewels of red, blue and green. He was heavily adorned with gold and silver bangles, necklaces and rings. In one hand he held a twig, a sacred fertility symbol. His face was heavily made up, pale cheeks and eyes outlined in black, the corners tilted up to give an oriental appearance. He ignored his father, mother and grandmother, fully focused on the worship of his god. Marcellus, Soaemias and Maesa bowed their heads to the stone.

'Children, it is the hour of worship of the all-powerful Elagabal, god of the mountains, god of the sun, supreme god of all gods, be they Roman, Greek or Egyptian.'

It always felt strange to Marcellus to hear his own son refer to him as child, even though he often presided over these daily episodes of worship. Avitus' voice was high, reedy, with a slight lisp which he would probably grow out of. Marcellus hoped that he would grow out of some of his other traits too. It was nice to see him in dress suited to a man, albeit in eastern style, instead of a stola, or to Marcellus' acute embarrassment, sometimes nothing at all.

A slave brought in a male calf, only a day old, still smelling of milk and afterbirth. He placed it on the altar and held it steady, stroking its head to keep it calm.

Avitus picked up a curved, wickedly sharp blade. Marcellus had long had his reservations about this, but Soaemias had insisted that Avitus fulfil all the functions of the attending priest, and to be fair to the boy, he had been doing this for a number of months now without losing any fingers.

The drummer beat a slow, soft rhythm and the cymbals laid a shimmering, quiet tone over it while the pipes and flutes played a haunting, ululating melody.

'Great god Elagabal, your all-holy wife and mother Astarte and Atargatis, accept our meagre offering, along with our bodies, our hearts and our souls.'

Avitus drew the blade in a curve around the calf's neck. It was so sharp that the young beast didn't even flinch. Blood spurted out forward and was caught in a bowl. Avitus skilfully managed to avoid getting a fleck of red on his tunic, which Marcellus was pleased with – blood was a nightmare to get out of fine clothes.

The calf's front knees buckled, then it toppled onto its side on the altar and kicked its legs, eyes flickering around the room in panic before unfocusing. It struggled for breath, then the breathing slowed and stopped.

Avitus took a jug of wine and poured it into the bowl, swirling it to mix the two liquids. He poured a libation onto the floor in front of the altar, then lifted the bowl and drank from it, blood spilling down his chin and down his robes. Marcellus cursed inwardly. He suspected he would be paying out for a new set of expensive ceremonial clothing soon.

The musicians kicked up the tempo and volume. Avitus passed the bowl to Marcellus. He took a sip of the salty, warm liquid, swallowed and passed it to Soaemias, who also drank and then passed it to Maesa. Then they rose and joined hands with each other and with Avitus and the two slaves representing the consorts. In a circle they danced around the stone, chanting and singing hymns of praise to the Emesene gods in time to the musicians.

The music built to a crescendo, and they danced faster and faster, their breathing accelerating with the effort and emotion. Marcellus' heart raced, as despite his best intentions he found himself wrapped up in the moment. Maesa and Soaemias looked solemn and devout, but his son seemed to be in some sort of ecstatic trance, rolling his head wildly, eyes narrowed to slits. There was a crash like thunder from the players and the music ended. They all fell to their knees, and closed their eyes for a moment of silent worship.

Eventually, Avitus got slowly to his feet. Maesa, Soaemias and Marcellus did the same. He held out his arms.

'My children, go with the peace of Elagabalus, god of gods.'

'Yes, father,' said Maesa, Soaemias and Marcellus.

Then Soaemias added, 'Now go and study your Greek grammar. If you get behind, Gannys has permission to thrash you.'

Avitus flushed, turned and fled from the room.

'You could have let him get out of his robes before you reminded him he is a little child,' said Marcellus.

'He will be a child for precious little time. Less than most, I fear.'

Marcellus wondered what made her feel like that, but he had other matters on his mind.

'Slave, get me a cup of wine. I will be in the tablinum.' He kissed Soaemias on the cheek, nodded to Maesa and headed for his study, mind full of games, plays, races and executions that he had to organise.

—

'I've had enough,' said Silus. 'I want out.'

'You can't just walk away from the Arcani,' said Oclatinius simply, as if it was a truism.

'You think you can stop me?'

'Of course I can.'

Silus glowered at Oclatinius, whose face remained serene. The spymaster had a temper, but he only let it show for a reason. His ability to control his emotions and fail to rise to the bait could be infuriating for anyone trying to argue with him.

'This is not what you promised when you recruited me.'

'Is that so? Tell me what I promised you. Tell me what I swore to the gods would be yours.'

Silus thought back to that time in Britannia, soon after the death of his family, at his lowest ebb, when Oclatinius had taken him under his wing and trained him. He had nearly walked away, but Oclatinius had offered him the chance to avenge his wife and daughter, and he had pledged himself to the Arcani and their head. But had he actually ever promised him anything?

Searching his memories, he couldn't think of a single vow that had come from Oclatinius' lips.

'Promises are chains that restrict us,' said Oclatinius. 'I make it a habit to refrain from making them wherever possible. But when I do make them, I keep them. Such as my vow to serve the Emperor Antoninus.'

'Emperor Caracalla, you mean?' said Atius.

Silus and Oclatinius both gave him a dagger stare, and he shut his mouth, abashed.

'Well, maybe it wasn't a promise. But I did not think this was what being an Arcanus was about. I'm not working as a spy. Not even an assassin. Just a common executioner.'

'We all serve at the Emperor's pleasure. Do you think I enjoy commanding the death of men who have served Rome with honour and dignity?'

'Then why do it?'

'I just told you. My oath is a chain. I swore to serve the Emperor, and I will until I die. And you swore the same.'

Silus looked down. His word was important to him too, although he knew it was not unbreakable. Some things were even more important than a vow. Nevertheless, he did not break his word easily. For example, he had promised to visit Tituria in her island exile, and he intended to see that through. It gave him an idea.

'Maybe I could have some leave?'

Oclatinius stared at him.

'Some what?'

'A break. From all this. Oclatinius, I'm so sick of it. So tired.'

Oclatinius spoke slowly, his words measured.

'Within the last nundinum, one Emperor has murdered another, the Praetorians have sacked their own city, the Senate has been cowed into submission by the Praetorians, the former Praetorian prefect has been hacked to death in front of the Senate, by you, I don't need to add, and there is now a long list of prominent Romans who are to be executed, while the army are kept in check only by bribery and the general population don't know whether to rejoice, riot, or hide away in terror. And you want a holiday?'

'He's got a point,' said Atius.

Silus wondered why he was friends with the big idiot. But it was true, he did have a point.

'Don't you have a mission for me outside of Rome, at least? So I can get away from all this madness.'

'Silus, much as it pains me to say it, you are my best man. The two of you are my best team. I don't want to lose you at this crucial time. But I don't want to have you so disillusioned you don't do your job properly. Or even decide to desert. I do appreciate I am asking a lot of you at the moment, but the Emperor is asking a lot of us all. From many people, he is taking everything. Be grateful you are not one of those.'

'Sir, has the Emperor gone mad?' asked Atius, bluntly as always.

'Honestly, Atius, I don't know. I don't think so. His actions are affected by grief, anger and fear. But they are rational. He is making his position safe. And he is doing what many rulers and emperors have done in Rome's history, without them being called mad.'

Atius nodded, and Silus had to agree with the assessment. Not that it made the things he was being asked to do any easier.

'Listen, Silus, I don't need you for anything right now. Most of the executions are being performed by the Praetorians and the Urban Cohorts. The Emperor largely wants them to be public, not hidden from view and performed by the more secret elements of his forces. And Festus and his men can take up some of the slack for a change.'

'Sir, do you trust Festus?' asked Silus.

'What makes you ask, Silus?'

'Just a feeling, sir. I don't have any evidence, but my gut says maybe he was behind some of the things that have been going on.'

'Festus is none of your concern, and you will not be repeating what you just said to anyone outside this room, do you understand?'

Oclatinius' tone was uncharacteristically shaky and high-pitched.

'Yes, sir. I'm sorry.'

Oclatinius shook his head. 'It is I who should apologise. But please, leave Festus to me. He and I have a long history. Professional and... non-professional.'

Silus waited, but nothing else was forthcoming.

'Silus, I don't want to lose you from the Arcani. I can attempt to force you to stay and do your duty, but after your development over the last year and more, I would not be confident of success. I will think about your request. But for now, I have a surprise for you.'

He went to the door of his office and spoke to the slave waiting there. The slave hurried away, leaving Silus in suspense.

'What is it, sir?'

'You do know the meaning of "surprise", don't you, Silus?'

Moments later the door opened, and in walked a plumpish woman in her early middle-age, looking confused.

'Apicula!' cried Silus.

'Master!' She looked genuinely pleased to see him. She put the dog down and ran forward, hugging him tight. 'Oh master, I'm so glad you are well.' Silus hugged her back, pleased but a little awkward in her embrace. She stepped back, looking embarrassed, flushed but grinning broadly.

A shrill yapping came from Silus' feet. The little dog was jumping up and down, desperate to be noticed.

'Issa!' Silus reached down and scooped the little dog into his arms. She immediately started to lick his face, her stump of a tail wagging furiously. Her breath stank, a combination of bad teeth and her habit of eating faeces she came across in the street, animal or human, but Silus couldn't push the little bitch away. She was all he had left of his family and remained dear to him.

He looked at Oclatinius, who was smiling indulgently.

'Where did you find them?'

'Silus, I knew where they were the moment they fled.'

Silus, Atius and Apicula all looked at him in shock.

'You sent me to kill her!' said Atius, tone accusatory.

'Only after my spy had told me that she had already fled. And to where.'

'But I made sure no one was following me,' said Apicula. 'I hid with an old customer in a village outside Rome, a farmer who only visited the city on market days.'

Oclatinius simply looked smug.

'And the tablet, it's safe?' asked Silus, enquiring after the letter written by Titurius revealing that his daughter Tituria had seen Caracalla in bed with his stepmother Julia Domna.

Apicula looked stricken. 'Master, I'm sorry, I failed you. I kept it with me until I reached my friend's farm. I buried it beneath the floor of my room. But when I came to look for it, when Oclatinius' messenger came for me, it was gone. I don't know what happened. The floor didn't even look disturbed. But the box I put it in was empty.'

Silus put a hand to his mouth. If that tablet, with its evidence of the Emperor's transgressions with his stepmother, became public, it would be disastrous for the Emperor. And fatal for Silus and for Tituria, seeing as he had pledged to keep the tablet safe, and used it as insurance to keep the little girl alive.

'Apicula,' he whispered. 'Oh, no.'

Oclatinius reached into his desk and drew out a wax tablet. It was closed, its outer leaves covered in dirt and dust. He brushed some off, blew away the rest. Then he passed it to Silus.

'You had it all along?' gasped Silus.

'It's not the sort of thing you leave lying around. Even buried under the floor of a country farm. I thought it would be safer in my hands.'

'But, why didn't you give it to the Emperor?'

'And lose my best man? Give me some credit for sense.'

Silus shook his head. 'And why give it to me now?'

'Because that was the bargain. You keep the tablet in exchange for Tituria remaining alive. The tablet is less of a threat to the Emperor now it can't be used by his brother, but it could still be very damaging at a vulnerable time in his reign. You have your leverage back to protect Tituria. I trust you to be mindful of its safekeeping.'

Silus turned it over in his hands.

'You can trust me,' said Silus.

'Can I?'

Silus looked him in the eye. 'Yes. You can.'

Oclatinius nodded, looking satisfied.

'Now, take your slave, and your dog, who incidentally smells like she drinks from the Cloaca Maxima...'

'She does,' muttered Atius.

'And get some rest,' continued Oclatinius, ignoring the interruption.

'Yes, sir.' Silus ushered Apicula and Atius out, holding Issa under one arm. He considered how best to conceal the tablet now. Depositing wealth and important goods at temples was a common way of ensuring security, but they didn't seem particularly safe after they had been pillaged by the Praetorians. He resolved to find a small-time private banker and deposit it in his safe for the time being, although at a later time he thought he would take it out into the countryside and bury it.

He closed the door behind him and wondered how soon it would be before he was summoned to this office again for another distressing duty.

–

Soaemias felt the man behind her quickening his pace. His hands were on her hips, gripping her as he thrust into her. His balls slapped against her with a soft damp noise with each thrust, and she moaned aloud every time he pushed inside her. He was getting closer, but so was she. It was going to be a race

– would she get there before him? She reached between her legs to stimulate herself and then she was arching her back, eyes rolling as the climax washed over her.

She recovered herself just in time to pull away. He groaned, and his seed spurted over her back rather than inside her. She turned over and looked up at him with a satisfied grin.

'That was close,' he said.

'Risky,' she agreed. 'But doesn't that make it more exciting?'

'I'm not sure,' he said.

She reached out and cupped his balls, two soft fruits in his sack, and squeezed gently. He winced as she increased the pressure.

'You think this painful. Imagine what it would have been like if you had genuinely been castrated, as everyone believes.'

Gannys raised an eyebrow. 'I prefer not to think about that. Besides, how would you feel if I had been castrated? Not as good as you feel right now.'

'Maybe. I've never had a eunuch, but I've heard that if they were castrated as adults, they can still perform adequately, and with no chance of an unwanted pregnancy.'

Gannys carefully eased himself free from her grip and lay on his back on the bed.

'We have my mother to thank for this, of course,' said Gannys.

'Your mother?'

'You never met her, of course. But she wanted a daughter, not a son. When I was young, she tried to dress me as a girl, but I always resisted, much to her resentment.'

Soaemias sighed. 'Avitus likes to dress as girls without any prompting from me.'

'And you indulge him.'

'I find him hard to say no to. I want wonderful things for him, Gannys, the very best. He is such a wonderful child – intelligent, thoughtful, utterly devoted to our god.'

'Blessed be the name of Elagabal. Anyway, whether out of spite or some unhinged desire to believe it true, she put it about that I was a natural-born eunuch, that I had been born without balls.'

Soaemias giggled. 'Surely your encounters with women quickly disproved that?'

Gannys shook his head. 'Mother was very controlling. She considered herself paterfamilias since father died before I was born. When I was young, Mother would not allow slaves to care for me. Only she bathed me or dressed me. When I was older, she did not allow me to mix with girls. By the time she died, the lie was so much part of me, I didn't know how to let it be known that I had been whole all along. So I was only ever intimate with slaves who were sworn to silence, or with whores who did not know I was supposed to be a eunuch born to a minor equestrian family. You are the first free woman I have been intimate with.'

'You honour me,' said Soaemias. 'And I must admit it is a wonderful pleasure. Marcellus is old and boring and was never interested in my satisfaction in bed. But it is so hard for a noblewoman in Rome to seek comforts outside her marriage without causing scandal. To have a real man who everyone believes a eunuch living in my house, able to spend time with him alone without tongues wagging – it's a precious gift from your mother.'

'Not one she would have been happy to bestow, I feel, the mad old cow,' said Gannys sourly, and Soaemias laughed.

'Regardless, you are here in my bed, while my husband waits on our insane Emperor.'

Gannys looked around nervously, though it was obvious they were alone in her bedchamber. Cuckolding the commander of the Praetorian Guard was dangerous enough, but it was nothing compared to uttering words of sedition against Caracalla.

'Please, Gannys, stop looking like a scared hen. Caracalla is unstable, a murderer, a tyrant, and unfit to rule.'

'He will not rule forever.'

Soaemias regarded him steadily. 'This is true. Now, you may think you are a true Roman man. But you work for me, and it is your job to keep me content. Do your job.'

She grabbed him by the hair, and forced his head down, across her body, between her legs. As she felt his tongue go to work, in an act no dominant Roman man would consider, she closed her eyes and gave herself to the sensations.

Chapter Four

'Numidia is on the verge of open rebellion,' said Oclatinius. Giving bad news to an Emperor, especially one currently as unstable as Caracalla, was always a risk, but Oclatinius had lived long enough and seen enough to feel little anxiety, and to show none. 'I have had a report from an informer in Cirta. The city is split between Geta's supporters and your own, Augustus. The province itself is split along the same lines.'

'And where stands the governor?' asked Caracalla.

'Publicly, Quintus Cornelius Valens has sworn an oath to you. Privately, my informer tells me he is intriguing against you. Gauging the level of support he has in Numidia, and even sounding out powerful men in Rome.'

'Like who?' asked Caracalla in a dangerously low voice.

'My informer didn't say.'

Caracalla looked at Marcellus. 'What are your thoughts?'

'Rome is yours, Augustus. If there is going to be a threat to your rule, it is going to come from the provinces.'

Caracalla gave a thin smile. 'I admire your confidence. There is much work to be done before my position in Rome is secure, but I think we are making progress. I think you are right about the provinces, though. Which legions are based in Africa now?'

'In Numidia, just the III Augusta, plus a few detachments from other legions. The II Traiana in Alexandria is a long way from Numidia but easily reached along the coast by boat or foot. The VII Gemina in Hispania is closer, but the governors in the peninsula are solid. I think.'

'But I don't have to tell you how close Numidia is to Sicily,' said Oclatinius, 'and from there, it is a short distance to Rome. You may command the loyalty of the legions in Britannia, Germania and Syria, but if Valens brings his legion to Rome, gathering troops on the way, you would have only the Praetorians and the II Parthica to oppose them. Probably enough, but not by a comfortable margin. More worrying would be if he marched east to Egypt or persuaded the Egyptian prefect to join him with the II Traiana. He could then cut off the grain supply to Rome, and the city would starve. Your rule depends on providing bread to the mob.'

'I'm well aware of that,' said Caracalla sourly. He sighed. 'I need to send someone loyal to take control, someone with authority.'

'Dioga?' suggested Oclatinius.

'No, not enough military experience.'

'What about Oclatinius here?' suggested Marcellus.

'I'm sorry to say this, Oclatinius, but you don't carry the authority. Fear and respect, yes, but you are not in a position to command legions or take over governorships. And I need you here in Rome now more than ever.'

'Then it has to be Marcellus,' said Oclatinius.

Marcellus spread his hands. 'Augustus, my place is at your side.'

'Is there no one else?' asked Caracalla, somewhat plaintively. 'I am loath to lose Marcellus at this difficult time.'

'As Marcellus said, Rome is all but secure. The risk is from the provinces. Marcellus is your closest ally, and he has the intelligence and sense to squash this threat.'

Marcellus glowered, clearly reluctant to take this posting far away from the centre of power, but unwilling to contradict Oclatinius' positive assessment of his capabilities.

'You are right, Oclatinius. I'm sorry, Marcellus. It has to be you. You will go to Numidia and you will relieve the governor there.'

Marcellus nodded, resigned. 'Thank you for the honour, Augustus.'

And in truth, it was an honour. Marcellus' rise to a high position from relatively humble beginnings had been rapid, particularly since the death of Plautianus, the confidant-turned-traitor of Septimius Severus a few years before, who had hated Marcellus. Since then he had held the prestigious role of procurator of the aqueducts, and later procurator of Britannia. In all that time, though, he never been promoted to senator.

'Augustus, I agree with your decision. But may I suggest that you take action to increase Marcellus' authority even further. He is currently Praetorian prefect and Urban prefect, but he is still an equestrian. His task would be much easier if he was senatorial rank.'

'You are right, Oclatinius. What do you suggest?'

'Admit him to the Senate with the rank of propraetor. That should make it obvious to all that he is a man who commands respect and who wields the authority of the Emperor and the Senate.'

'It shall be done.'

Marcellus gave Oclatinius a genuine smile of thanks, but Oclatinius merely shrugged it away.

'There are precious few military resources I can spare to assist you with this, Marcellus,' said Caracalla. 'With only one legion and the Praetorians in Italy, if another governor decides to march on Rome, I will need every man. I'll give you a small detachment of legionaries from the II Parthica. You will have to win the loyalty of the III Augusta for yourself.'

Marcellus looked uncertain, and understandably so. Marching into a province on the verge of revolt with little more than his personality as sword and shield was a challenge.

'If I might suggest,' said Oclatinius. 'I could spare my men Silus and Atius to accompany Marcellus. Their skills may prove invaluable in assisting Marcellus with his task.'

'But what if they are needed in Rome?' asked Caracalla.

'I believe we have sufficient resources here for what we need to do between the Praetorians, the Urban Cohorts, the speculatores, the frumentarii, Festus' staff of the sacred bedchamber, Festus' and my network of priests, seers and astrologers who act as informers. Besides, given what they have done for you lately, their lives may be in danger from Geta supporters wanting revenge. A posting outside Rome might be prudent...'

'Yes, yes,' said Caracalla. 'You have made your point. Send them with Marcellus.'

Marcellus shot Oclatinius a grateful look.

'We will need to discuss replacements for your two positions, Marcellus,' said Caracalla.

'Well, you have Quintus Maecius Laetus,' said Marcellus. 'He could continue in his current role as co-Praetorian prefect and do the job on his own.'

'There is recent precedent for a position once shared to be continued by just one man,' said Caracalla wryly.

Oclatinius and Marcellus looked at each other, uncertain whether a laugh was expected. Fortunately, Caracalla continued before they had to decide.

'Laetus is hopeless. I have never fully trusted him, and when word got out that he might be part of my proscriptions, he feigned illness so he didn't have to present himself at the palace. I was never going to have that coward executed anyway. He is too ineffective for there to be any point. So no, he cannot do it alone.'

'How about Gnaeus Marcius Rustius Rufinus?' said Oclatinius. 'He is a man with a good reputation and has served Rome and its emperors well for many years.'

'Agreed,' said Caracalla. 'And the Urban prefect.'

'How about Gaius Julius Asper?' said Marcellus. 'He and his son are consuls for the year, he has a lot of experience, and his loyalty to your father and yourself has never been in question.'

'Oclatinius?'

Oclatinius looked thoughtful. 'I have some concerns about his... competence. But Marcellus is right, his loyalty is impeccable. And at this moment, that counts for more.'

'Good. It is decided. Now, I believe there are some senators waiting to see me. You will both attend me while I hear them.'

'Before you do, Augustus, there is one matter I would like to bring to your attention,' said Oclatinius. This was going to be even more delicate than the problem with Numidia, he knew.

'Go on.'

'The vestals.'

'What about them?'

'Are you aware of their importance to us?'

'Talk to me as if I'm not.'

'Well, obviously, their main duty is to keep the sacred fire burning in the Temple of Vesta, and all the sacred duties which go with their office. The mob think very highly of the importance of this role in keeping the city and the Empire safe. Famine and floods have been blamed on the vestals failing to perform their duties diligently, or being let down by those responsible for the vestals' well-being.'

Caracalla nodded non-committally. Oclatinius realised he was likely telling the Emperor things he was very familiar with, but for what was to come, he needed to be clear as to what was at stake. He continued.

'The people also believe the vestals capable of various magics through their prayers – capturing runaway slaves, finding lost children, healing disease. If the vestals are impious, the people get very angry at the thought of the danger that can put them in personally. We also need to consider that the loyalty of the vestals to the Emperor is of paramount importance. The vestals are too highly regarded to allow any doubts about their allegiance.'

'Get to the point, Oclatinius.'

'Augustus, there is a rumour going around the population regarding the chastity of four of the vestals.'

'Four?' exclaimed Marcellus.

'Four.'

'There are always rumours about the chastity of the vestals,' said Caracalla. 'It was once even said that I had deflowered one myself.'

'This rumour does not concern you, Augustus, but your brother.'

Caracalla became suddenly very still. Oclatinius swallowed.

'Augustus, it is being said that after your father's death, Geta visited the temple secretly on a regular basis. That he regularly debauched four. Only the very youngest, and the Virgo Vestalis Maxima, were untouched, and they were only left alone because of the extremities of their age.'

'Six years old and sixty years old,' put in Marcellus.

Oclatinius watched mixed emotions play across Caracalla's face as the implications sunk in. On the one hand, this showed his brother in a terrible light, and the more Geta's character could be tarnished, the easier it was to justify Caracalla's actions. On the other hand, Caracalla was the Pontifex Maximus, and thus in charge of the vestals. The people would not allow him to let this sacrilege and treason against the city itself go unpunished.

'Is it true?' he asked.

Oclatinius spread his hands in apologetic uncertainty.

'I have not been able to confirm it at this stage. My spies have observed Geta entering the temple on multiple occasions, but that could be for political reasons, attempting to gain support, finding out secrets confided to them by those consulting them as seers and sages, or even attempting to find out the contents of the wills they keep.'

'The visits themselves will be enough proof in the minds of many.'

'I could torture some of the slaves that attend the vestals to find out more. With your permission.'

Caracalla shook his head. 'It would add nothing. The belief of the people is all that matters here. Anyway, we both know that slaves under torture will just say whatever it is they think we want to hear, so are likely to condemn the vestals, whatever the truth, to save their own skins.'

Oclatinius inclined his head in agreement. He had no compunction about using torture where it was necessary or deserved, but he agreed that it usually served little purpose, and just ended up with broken or dead slaves, with the rest of the servants of the household or institution scared and resentful rather than productive. And Oclatinius took no pleasure in inflicting suffering for its own sake. He caused enough death and misery as part of his job that he had no need or desire to take it up as a pastime.

'What is your command, Augustus?'

Caracalla sighed. 'They must be tried, found guilty and executed. Marcellus, attend to it before you depart.' He rubbed his face wearily. 'Now, send in the senators.'

–

'We are going where?' Soaemias' voice was like the screech of a vixen.

Marcellus shook his head. His wife was still adjusting to the new reality or their household, but at least her anger was directed at him in private, so he was prepared to tolerate it.

'It is a great honour, my dear,' he said. 'I am made a senator at last. With the rank of an ex-praetor. And I am going to become a governor.'

'You are currently both Urban and Praetorian prefect. That is where the real power lies. If you doubt it, just read your Suetonius. Find out about who made Claudius emperor. And Galba. Look at the power Sejanus wielded. The Praetorians even sold the throne to Didius Julianus!'

'Calm yourself. The Praetorian prefectship is a poisoned chalice. You want examples from history, look no further than Plautianus and Papinianus.'

'But... Numidia? There is no glory to be had there.'

'There is honour. And a valuable service to the Empire. And also, as I believe this interests you, there are riches to be had there. Being a governor of a settled province, which it will be once I have put down the brewing revolt, is very lucrative.'

Soaemias paced up and down, searching for words, barely able to speak in her anger.

'What about our son? He is to be high priest of Elagabal one day. At least if we have to leave Rome, can't we go east, to be near our home, near the birthplace of the Lord Elagabal?'

'I go where the Emperor commands, my dear,' said Marcellus, still managing to maintain his equanimity. His wife seemed to be struggling with something, and he wasn't entirely sure what it was. He understood she might be reluctant to leave Rome, the centre of power, but it wasn't for long, and in these turbulent times, having some distance between themselves and the capital may not be entirely a bad idea.

'Refuse,' she said abruptly. 'Tell him he still needs you as Praetorian prefect.'

'He has replaced me already.'

Soaemias gripped her hair in her fists and let out a screech of frustration.

'Marcellus. You are hopeless.'

'Hopefully you have got this out of your system while we are in private. I am sure I don't need to remind you there will be consequences if you put on this sort of display in public. Oh, and I hear Avitus was wearing a dress made entirely of silk yesterday.'

'What of it?'

'You indulge him, and his peculiarities. He is old enough for this nonsense to stop. Men's clothes only, from now on. Now excuse me, I have four sorry vestals to execute. I will see you at dinner.'

–

Silus attended the execution at the forum, like many others. Apicula and Atius stood with him. The crowd looked on expectantly with a mix of horror and excitement. Four vestals stood together in a huddle, looked down on by Caracalla, who was seated on a high throne which was placed on a dais. They were dressed in the formal attire of their office, a long white woollen stola, a palla pulled over the head and pinned at the shoulder and a white woollen veil lifted back over their heads. Red and white woollen ribbons were tied in their elaborately braided hair to symbolise both their commitment to keeping the fire of Vesta burning, and their purity and chastity. Two other similarly dressed vestals stood nearby, one elderly and one a young child, holding hands and weeping loudly.

'Clodia Laeta, Aurelia Severa, Pomponia Rufina, Cannutia Crescentina,' proclaimed Marcellus from the dais at the foot of the throne. 'You have been found guilty by the college of pontifices of breaking your vow of chastity. This treason, this sacrilege, endangers everyone in Rome. Worse, your crime was committed with the traitor Geta, compounding your treason. The sentence is that set down since the time of the kings of Rome, burial alive.'

Marcellus stepped forward, and one by one, removed the veils and ripped the symbolic ribbons from their hair, as they shook and tears streamed down their face. The two uncondemned vestals then stepped forward and wrapped each of the condemned in a grey shroud such as would be worn by a corpse for burial. The young girl tried to cling onto Clodia Laeta, but an Urban Cohort legionary pulled her away roughly, which drew some shouts of disapproval from the crowd.

Clodia Laeta turned towards the throne, and said in a loud voice, 'The Emperor knows that I am a virgin, I am pure.'

Caracalla remained expressionless and nodded to the guards. The vestals were led each into one of four waiting litters, and once they were seated, the curtains were drawn to hide them from view. They were then borne in a procession through the streets, followed by sombre priests, wailing relatives of the condemned and the ambivalent crowd, torn between horror at the treatment of these beautiful young women, anger at their crimes, and a prurient thrill.

They arrived at the Campus Sceleratus, the evil field, just within the city walls by the Colline Gate. Here there was a raised mound under which a small underground vault had been prepared. It was forbidden to shed the blood of a vestal, but it was also forbidden to bury anyone within the city walls, alive or dead. To bypass these two laws, the chamber contained enough food and water to survive a few days, together with a lamp, a table, and four couches, so they were not technically being buried, but placed in a habitable room.

When the litters came to a halt, Caracalla lifted his hands skywards and uttered a prayer to the Olympians. Then he stepped forward and pulled the curtain aside. He offered his hand to help Clodia Laeta down, and then repeated this with the other three litters. The vestals stood before the hole in the side of the mound, staring in horror at the ladder leading down into the darkness.

Two speculatores from the Praetorians stepped forward. Fortunately, Oclatinius had not suggested Silus for the role of executioner. He didn't know what he would have done if he had been given that order.

One by one, the young women were taken to the ladder and led down, each taking a last look around at the light, catching the eyes of relatives, before descending into the dark.

The last to go was Cannutia Crescentina, a tall, willowy woman who was trembling like a leaf in a storm. At the top of the ladder, she suddenly stopped. The speculator with her urged her forward, but abruptly she ripped her arm from his light grasp and ran.

The crowd gasped as she fled, her shroud flowing behind her, bare feet slapping on the cobbled streets.

Marcellus saw Silus in the crowd, and caught his eye as the terrified vestal ran past him.

'Silus,' he yelled. 'Get her.'

Though his heart ached for the poor girl, the instinct to obey was deeply ingrained, and he raced after her. The crowd cheered and jeered as he followed her down a narrow street, gaining on her quickly as she shoved a bemused street seller aside, then nearly tripped over a snuffling pig. Looking back and seeing Silus right behind her, she turned to the steps at the side of an insula leading to the upper floors and raced up them.

Silus took the steps two at a time, but the girl was young and light, and she remained just out of his reach until she got to the top and ran out onto the roof. When Silus made the top of the stairs, she was standing on the edge, a crowd gathered below, in full view of the ceremony at the Campus Sceleratus. From five storeys up, he could just make out the throne from where Caracalla was looking on, Marcellus by his side.

He reached out a hand tentatively.

'Cannutia. Come down. You don't have to do this.'

She backed away, shaking her head.

'Please, this is not the way it is supposed to be. The gods will not be pleased.'

The words sounded hollow, even to him.

'I don't want to die,' she said, her voice little more than a whisper. 'But I am not stupid. I know what suffering there is in starving to death. Better to end it quickly.'

'Please, take my hand. Come back down. You will be with your sister priestesses.'

'I'm innocent,' she said. 'I have never been touched by a man.' She looked him straight in the eyes as tears flooded down her cheeks. 'Do you believe me?'

'I do believe you,' he said, and he meant it. She held his gaze for a moment, then nodded.

'Thank you,' she said, and stepped off the edge.

She made no noise as she fell, but a collective cry came from the crowd as she hit the crowd with a solid, final thump. Silus didn't look over the edge. He walked slowly back down the stairs, and back to the Campus Sceleratus without even a glance at where the body lay in a spreading pool of blood.

When he reached the burial chamber, the executioners had already pulled up the ladder and were blocking up the entrance. The spectacle over, the crowd began to disperse, feeling strangely unfulfilled as they realised they were not actually witnessing the death of these women. Atius clapped Silus on the shoulders. 'Drink?' Silus shook his head slowly.

Marcellus came over to speak to Silus. 'You were too slow. I hope the gods aren't angry with you.'

'I doubt it,' said Silus. 'I don't believe it is me that has sinned here. Nor that poor girl.'

Marcellus' eyes narrowed, but he didn't respond to the implied rebuke to the Emperor.

'Well, I hope not. We are going to be seeing a lot more of each other for the foreseeable future.'

Silus frowned in confusion. 'What do you mean, sir?'

But Marcellus had turned away, seeing a senator that he needed to talk to. He shouted and waved, walking over to him and putting an arm around the man's shoulder as they disappeared into the crowd. Silus looked at the mound that concealed the terror and suffering of three petrified young women. He felt suddenly nauseous.

–

'How is your hand?' asked Caracalla.

'It heals, slowly,' said Domna. She was seated on a carved ebony chair with a flowing ivory inlay, a high back, and a silk cushion. It was a seat emphatically for one. Her hands were clasped demurely in her lap, and her gaze was downcast. Caracalla sat on a wooden bench, a seemly distance away from her. Several slaves stood nearby in attendance, ready to serve water, wine or delicacies at the snap of a finger.

'You didn't attend the execution.'

'No.'

'It was necessary.'

'So you say.'

'They were guilty, Domna.'

'If that is what you believe, then who am I to disagree, Augustus?'

Caracalla let out an exasperated sigh.

'What do you want from me, Domna?' he exclaimed.

'What could you possibly give me? Can you return what I have lost?'

Caracalla gave a scowl, his broad forehead deeply furrowed.

'I have told you – you are not to mourn.'

'No, Augustus. I have stoppered up the amphora containing my tears. I shall ensure it does not leak. I would not wish to suffer Cornificia's fate at your hands.'

'Cornificia took her own life.'

Domna merely regarded him steadily, an unfathomable sadness in her eyes.

'Domna, I need you.'

She looked pointedly at the slaves within earshot, but he ignored them. He leaned forward and took her uninjured hand in his. She passively let him take it, limp in his grasp.

'I need your counsel. I need your advice. I need your love. I need...' Now he did look round at the slaves. 'I need it all.'

'I am yours to command, Augustus. Your loyal servant.'

He let the hand drop and sat back.

'How long are you going to keep this up?'

'How long will Geta remain dead?' she snapped.

Caracalla jumped to his feet so suddenly the heavy bench tipped over backwards with a crash, startling the slaves.

'Get out!' he yelled at them. The slaves scurried away like kittens frightened by an exuberant hound.

'Domna, I want things to be the way they were.'

Domna looked him straight in the eyes. He could see moisture welling in her bottom lids, close to overflowing, but remaining contained. 'So do I, Antoninus. With all my being. But time does not run backwards.'

He got down on his knees before her. 'What can I do?'

Domna let out a breath like a whisper of wind. She reached out and touched his cheek, stroked the curled beard. 'I honestly don't know.'

Caracalla's head dropped. After a moment he stood, and turned his back on her.

'There is still much blood to be shed. And when it is done, I will leave Rome to campaign against the Germans. I hope...' he trailed off, his voice thickening. Then he simply said, 'I'm sorry, Domna.' And without turning back to see the tears finally overflow, he left her chamber.

—

'He leaves Rome soon.'

'For where?'

'Numidia.'

Festus watched a drunkard totter past, lean against the wall to vomit copiously, then stagger on. The moon was gibbous, nearly full, so the arch they sat beneath cast an eerie shadow against a silvery background.

'To deal with the unrest, I suppose.'

'You are well informed.' It wasn't a question.

Festus turned to look into the eyes of the hooded figure by his side.

'This changes things,' he said.

'Only in terms of timings. Will you be ready?'

'Of course.'

'You understand that for me, the stakes could not be higher?'

'That goes without saying.'

A nod of the head beneath the hood. 'I'll be in touch.'

Festus watched the figure depart down the dark street and felt a frisson of excitement. Oh Oclatinius. The game is on.

'You're going to Numidia,' Oclatinius said.

'Where's Numidia?' asked Atius.

'Africa,' said Oclatinius. Atius still looked blank.

'Keep going south until you hit the sea,' said Silus. 'Then keep going some more.'

'Well why didn't you say that?'

Silus wouldn't confess that he was a little hazy about Numidia's exact location himself, but he knew it was a long way from Rome, and as far as he was concerned, the further the better.

'Why are we being sent there, sir?' he asked.

'You are to accompany Marcellus and his family. He is going to take over as governor.'

'We are going to be bodyguards?' asked Atius.

'More like dogsbodies,' said Oclatinius. 'You will be under his command, though of course you will continue to report back to me. But I will still be in Rome, so you will also have to act with some autonomy, as you see fit. I'm putting faith in you both – I hope you understand that.'

'Yes, sir. But you haven't really explained why we are being sent.'

'There is unrest in the province, and the current governor, Quintus Cornelius Valens, is planning a revolt. If that happens, he could threaten Rome directly, or take Egypt and starve it. Marcellus is to replace him and restore order. Your job is to support him in any way necessary. Up to and including assassinating the current governor.'

Silus nodded. 'More of the same, then,' he said sourly.

'No, Silus. Very different. This man is a threat to the security and safety of Rome, and a traitor. He must be dealt with. And Marcellus is a good man. You are to protect him. He will be travelling with his family, too, so their safety will also be your responsibility.'

'Yes, sir. But why us?'

'Firstly, because you are good, and I trust you both for this vital mission. Secondly, you expressed a desire to get away from Rome. And thirdly, because your lives may be in danger if you stay.'

'Festus?' asked Silus.

Oclatinius frowned. 'I have no evidence of that. But you have angered and disappointed a lot of people in a short space of time. Let's call it a precaution, while things settle down.'

'There is one other thing. You will sail first to Syracuse. There, Marcellus intends to spend a few days meeting with the Governor of Sicily and other officials. That will give you time for a side trip.'

'A side trip where?' asked Silus, genuinely confused.

Oclatinius looked exasperated. 'Lipari! Tituria!'

A broad smile broke across Silus' face, and he felt a sudden lightness like he had not felt for months, or longer.

'Thank you, sir.' He grabbed Oclatinius' hand and shook it firmly. 'Thank you very much.'

'You depart in two days. Take this Imperial signet ring, in case you need some authority.'

He handed Silus a gold ring with an engraving of Caracalla in profile. Silus placed it on his finger, deciding it was the safest place for something of such high value.

'Get yourselves ready,' continued Oclatinius. 'Silus, make sure Apicula has enough money to keep herself and your apartment. Atius, say your goodbyes to whichever barmen and whores are going to miss you. Good luck. Now get out.'

Chapter Five

The experience of days on a boat, rolling, yawing and pitching, was no more pleasant for Silus than his last time travelling in this way. If he wasn't actually vomiting, then he was feeling nauseous and inappetent. Most of the legionaries that accompanied them seemed to be in a similar situation. Atius by contrast was quite happy, drinking with the sailors and sharing their biscuit and salted fish while exchanging tall stories.

Marcellus had a set expression on his face which suggested he felt no better than Silus, but was damned if he was going to show it. Soaemias, on the other hand, if she had any symptoms of seasickness, went about her day as if she was strolling through the Forum Romanum. Waves breaking over the side of the boat showering her in spray, sudden lurches of the deck to one side or another, a downpour of freezing rain – these she treated as minor inconveniences.

Silus had been invited to worship with Marcellus' family, and having no particularly strong allegiance to any god, he was happy to attend the ceremony. Atius, on the other hand, politely declined. Although he was not the most obedient of followers, his faith in the Christos forbade him from worshipping other gods. So Silus had sat respectfully and watched and listened to the ceremony that revolved around the strangely shaped black stone the slaves had lugged aboard with much grumbling. He had witnessed the singing and dancing and sacrifice of a young lamb, and the young boy Avitus dressed in his fine priest's robes, acting like the role of Elagabal's representative on earth was his by right.

After the ceremony, he leaned against the rail on the port side of the ship, cuddling Issa and watching the Italian coast in the distance slowly slide by. Soaemias joined him and stood beside him in silence for a few moments. A fishing vessel sailed past going the opposite direction, and the captain waved as he past. Silus waved back, then felt foolish when Soaemias gave him an amused look.

'Do you know what that mountain is over there?' she asked him, pointing to a peak just visible through the spray and haze.

'I've been this way before,' said Silus. 'That is Mons Vesuvius.'

Soaemias nodded. 'And you know its history?'

'Everyone knows. Even when I was a child in Britannia, my father told me of the death of Pompeii and Herculaneum.'

'Mountains hold power. They keep it chained within themselves, and men walk over them, farm and build on them, not respecting what these ancient beings can do to them. Until something angers them, and they destroy the mortals that have offended them.'

Silus didn't want to picture the panic and suffering of those buried by the volcano's eruption. He had had enough of misery, and hoped that this trip would be an escape from all of that, even if it proved to be a temporary respite. He smoothed his little dog's head, taking comfort from the repetitive motion, and her affectionate response.

'The name Elagabal means god of the mountains in the Aramaic language. My god was worshipped as a mountain god long before he was linked to the sun.'

Silus nodded, not sure what she expected from him.

'Elagabal is a mighty god, Silus. And my son will become his high priest.'

'I'm sure he will be a very good at it,' he said, hoping that was the right thing to say.

'He will have power. Supreme power.'

'As a high priest?'

She gave him a sideways glance, then turned her back to the rail, and looked at the deck. Avitus was sitting cross-legged, eyes closed and humming to himself, drawing odd looks from the sailors, some of whom made signs to ward off evil. Gannys kept a watchful eye on him from a short distance away.

'Tell me, Silus, who does he remind you of?'

Silus looked at the boy, with his smooth skin, pre-pubescent and not yet roughened by acne or the first whiskers. His first thought was of Julia Domna, which was not surprising, since she was his great aunt. Then he looked again. His nose was delicate, not broad and flat. His eyes were gentle, not angry. His mouth was soft.

But then a stray wave sprayed him, and his broad, prominent brow furrowed in a frown, and Silus' mouth opened in surprise.

'Are you saying that he is… that his father is…?' He couldn't bring himself to say the words.

Soaemias smiled conspiratorially. 'You are here to serve Marcellus. But one day, my son may have need of your help. Will you give it?'

Silus remembered Oclatinius' words about promises being chains. But the beautiful Syrian mother, looking into his eyes with a commanding, penetrating stare, bewitched him.

'Yes, mistress. I will offer him whatever help is in my power, should he one day need it.'

Soaemias gave a self-satisfied nod.

–

'We are going too slowly,' said Aziz to the captain, Tamas, for at least the tenth time.

'As I keep telling you,' said Tamas, not bothering to conceal his irritation 'we are making full use of the wind, and the rowers are pulling at maximum cruising speed. Yes, we can go faster, but only for a short distance before they begin to fatigue, and we will end up losing time overall.'

Aziz ground his teeth. He had been given so little time to prepare. Festus had come to him and told him that he had just a day to find a fast ship that could take him south, together with a crew of armed criminals dangerous enough to take on a detachment of legionaries. He had scurried around the docks and warehouses, pulling in favours, bribing gladiators, homeless veterans and burly criminals to make a small crew of pirate marines. He had found the Cilician captain of a fast merchant vessel that was used for transporting the more perishable of trade goods, and paid him handsomely for his time. Tamas had almost backed out when he saw the motley crew of beggars and criminals that he would be required to transport, but when Aziz increased the reward, greed won out over caution. Festus had said money was no object on this mission, and Aziz had taken him at his word.

Cilicians had a fine history of piracy, Aziz had reflected, so this job should be second nature to the captain, though he had refrained from telling him the truth of his orders. But the tide and wind had not been in their favour, and they had set sail half a day later than he had hoped. So now he clenched his fists and paced the deck and prayed for an optimum wind.

'Mons Vesuvius,' said Tamas, pointing to a peak in the distance.

Aziz reached inside his cloak and fingered the small, conical black stone that always he wore on a leather necklace, close to his chest.

God of the mountains, help me now.

–

Silus managed to keep down some bread and stew, then went to the back rail to keep his eyes on the horizon. One of the sailors had taught him this trick to reduce nausea, and it seemed to work. He wasn't sure why. Somehow it seemed to fool his body into thinking he wasn't actually being thrown all over the place by the vicissitudes of the sea. They were around half a day's sail from the straits of Messana now, and once they had passed through that it wasn't far to Syracuse. Then he could leave Marcellus to his Sicilian business, and fulfil his promise to visit Tituria. Issa sat at his feet, licking her arse with avid strokes of her tongue. The presence of the little dog, the last remnant of his murdered family, gave him great comfort, and he was glad he was on the sort of mission where he could bring her with him.

A ship in the middle distance caught his eye. His gaze had drifted over it before, when it had been on the horizon, but now it seemed to be gaining on them fast. Obviously in a hurry to be somewhere. Maybe an Imperial messenger, heading around the toe of the Italian peninsula to take orders to some provincial governor in the east or the south? But as he watched, it seemed to bear directly towards them, and a sense of unease grew in the pit of his stomach.

He found the captain and pointed the vessel out.

'What sort of ship is that?'

The captain used his hand to shield his eyes from the midday sun, which was still fairly low on the horizon given the time of year. He squinted and frowned.

'It looks like a fast merchant ship. But it has a fair turn of speed. Their captain is really pushing the oarsmen.'

'Why would he be doing that?'

'Beats me. At that speed they will tire soon, and he will have gained nothing.'

'So maybe his destination is nearby?'

'There are no major trading ports near enough to be worth that speed.'

'What else is around here then?'

The captain shrugged. 'Just us.'

Silus watched the ship for a moment longer. He understood enough about sailing to know that the fastest route between two ports was not a straight line, as the ship tacked with the wind. But it seemed to him that all the ship's manoeuvres brought it closer and closer to them.

'Do me a favour,' he said to a nearby sailor. 'Can you shut my dog below decks? I need to talk to Marcellus.' The sailor grumbled as he took her, holding the smelly dog at arm's length as she tried to lick his face.

When Silus explained his concern, Marcellus joined him and the captain at the stern to look at the ship for himself.

'Are they chasing us?' asked Marcellus.

'It's possible,' conceded the captain.

'How far to the nearest safe port?'

'Far enough that they will catch us before we reach it. If that is their intention.'

'Captain, do me a favour,' said Marcellus. 'Get my wife and son below decks and shut them safely away. Gannys too, I suppose.'

The captain rolled his eyes, and walked off to do Marcellus' bidding, muttering that he was no one's slave.

'Pirates?' Silus asked Marcellus.

'It's possible. Strange though, so near to Rome. Bold pirates.'

'Something else then. Someone coming for you?'

'That seems more likely. I'll tell the legionaries to ready themselves for a fight.'

'I'll go and sober up Atius.'

Silus was being a little unfair on his friend given the time of day, and in fact, Atius had just had one well-watered cup of wine, which meant he had his wits fully about him. When Silus told him of the possible threat, he was instantly alert, and strapped on a breastplate and short sword. Silus armed and armoured himself similarly, and they went to the back of the ship to monitor the progress of the pursuing vessel while the legionaries rushed around readying themselves for battle.

When the ship came within hailing range, a short number of yards behind them and to their port side, the captain called to them across the water.

'You have chased us hard. What is your business with us?'

The captain of the other ship, standing in the prow, called back, 'Drop your sails. We are just here for your cargo. No one needs to get hurt.'

'You have made a mistake. This ship is on the business of the Emperor. We carry only messages, no cargo of value to pirates.'

'I'm sure you won't mind if we don't take your word for it, and check for ourselves?'

'That won't be possible. We are carrying documents relating to the security of the Empire, and they cannot fall into the hands of anyone else. You may trade them to the Emperor's enemies.'

'I wasn't asking. Drop your sails or we will board you.'

Marcellus spoke up now.

'Hear me,' he yelled across the rapidly closing gap between the ships. 'I am Sextus Varius Marcellus, propraetor, new Governor of Numidia. If you cease your pursuit of us now, this matter will be closed. But if you continue, we are well able to defend ourselves and I will ensure every man of you is crucified. Just think about hanging on the cross with no water while the rats chew your toes and the crows peck out your eyes!'

The captain of the other ship laughed, and pulled level so that for the first time they got a clear view of the men lined up along the side, ready to board. Although they were not equipped to the standards of the legionaries, they greatly outnumbered them, around thirty tough-looking men to the ten legionaries of the Second Parthica, together with Marcellus, Silus and Atius.

Silus and Atius exchanged looks. This was going to be a real fight.

The other ship abruptly swung in towards them, and their captain reacted too slowly to avoid it. The legionaries let out a hail of javelins, two of which hit home, one grizzled pirate tumbling backwards, the other falling between the ships just as they crashed together with a huge spout of water and the crack and groan of stressed, fracturing timbers.

A dozen pirates leapt across with a roar before the ships parted and the gap became temporarily too wide to cross. Immediately a flurry of desperate hand-to-hand fighting broke out. The legionaries locked shields and stabbed out with swords, and two more pirates fell back with a cry. But there were too few legionaries to block the entire length of the deck, and pirates rounded the sides of their shield wall and began to hack at the unfortunate legionaries at either end. As those men turned to face the threats on their flanks, the cohesion of the wall began to break apart.

Marcellus stood with Silus and Atius behind the legionaries, biting his lip. He saw a gap in the line appear as a legionary's helmet was caved in by an axe, and drew his sword, preparing to step into the breach. Silus put a hand out to prevent him, and Atius moved forward, quickly grabbing the fallen legionary's shield and furiously shoving and hacking the pirate who had felled him.

The numbers of combatants were roughly equal at that moment, but the pirates had a gang of reinforcements itching to get into the fray once the ships moved close enough again. The captain of Marcellus' ship was trying to keep them apart, but the pirate ship was faster, and they began to close again.

'Sir,' said Silus urgently. 'We need to get rid of this lot before more of the buggers arrive.'

'I know that, but what do you suggest?'

Silus had been on the front lines, had been eye to eye with barbarians trying to kill him. He suspected that for all Marcellus' experience in government and in the field over the years, this was the first time he had been so close to the bloody violence of battle.

'Advance,' said Silus.

Marcellus frowned for a moment, then understood. The line of locked shields still held, just, and the pirates were fighting on the edge of the deck. If they were forced two paces backwards, they would be overboard. Rather than holding position, as was the textbook tactic for defence against superior numbers, they needed to push.

'Legionaries, on the count of three, one step at a time, you will advance,' yelled Marcellus.

The desperately fighting legionaries managed to let out a chorus of grunts in acknowledgement.

'One. Two. Three. Advance!'

Silus threw his weight into Atius' back, and Marcellus pushed another legionary near the middle. The pirates slid backwards, slipping on wooden planks that were becoming slick with blood.

'Again, advance!' yelled Marcellus, and with a cry the legionaries pushed forward. Now the pirates teetered on the edge of the deck, the churning foam behind them. Suddenly their focus shifted from fighting to keeping their balance. One of the legionaries thrust his gladius into an off-balance pirate who tumbled backwards with a scream and then a splash.

'Again, advance!' And with this next step, half a dozen pirates disappeared over the side, just as the ships came level again. If any of the pirates could swim, it was of no help to them as the sides of the ships crashed together again, crushing heads and bodies like a boot squashes an ant.

Now it was the legionaries who were off balance, the weight they were pushing against suddenly gone, and they were near the treacherous edge of the deck.

'Legionaries, two steps back on my command,' yelled Marcellus without prompting, to Silus' approval. 'One. Two.'

The legionaries retreated to a more secure and stable position and prepared to meet the next wave. Two pirates who had not been directly in front of the legionaries in the last attack still fought, but as Silus watched, a legionary thrust his gladius through the throat of one. The other, though, skirted the end of the line and charged at Marcellus, sword raised high. Marcellus was watching a dozen more pirates leap across from the pirate ship and did not notice as the sword descended towards his head.

Silus' blade deflected the blow to one side, so it crashed into a mast behind them. Marcellus flinched and looked around in alarm, but Silus had already advanced, taking the attacker away from the governor, as it was his job to protect.

The pirate had a long scar from brow to cheek, one eye grey and watery. His rough beard was flecked with grey, and his breath smelt of strong wine and fish sauce. He fought like a gladiator, cautious now his surprise attack on Marcellus had failed, holding his sword before him, ready to thrust if the opportunity arose.

Silus would rather have faced a veteran. They were trained to fight in groups and generally had no experience with single combat. For gladiators, one-on-one fights were the be-all and end-all of their training and their experience, and their very lives depended on learning all the tricks, honourable or otherwise, that would keep them alive in the arena.

Silus circled the gladiator in a clear space on the deck behind the line of legionaries, who were now bracing as another wave of pirates leapt across from their ship. He watched his opponent's eyes carefully, looking for any signs of a move. The sword was in his peripheral vision, but it was the eyes that moved before the weapon, even if it was just a little tightening around the corners, a widening of the pupil.

But of course the gladiator knew the same, and when Silus feinted, the gladiator fended it away easily, then followed up with a thrust of his own. Silus parried, realising that they were evenly matched.

Abruptly the gladiator lunged at Silus with a flurry of slashes from left to right and back again. Silus retreated, one step, another, towards the rail on the far side of the ship behind him. Across the deck he could see the legionaries being pushed backwards by the new wave. Marcellus had now joined the line, and was fighting hard alongside Atius, who was doing his best to keep him safe while fending off the pirate who opposed him. Almost all the armed pirates had now crossed onto their ship. The sailors remained on board the pirate ship, most unarmed, some carrying knives, hammers or other tools, but looking like they had no intention of joining the fight unless they were personally threatened. Similarly, the sailors on Silus' ship hung back, looking anxious but not prepared to commit to combat.

He stepped forward, sending his own flurry of cuts and thrusts at his enemy. The gladiator grunted, retreated a short way then stood fast. They traded blows and Silus felt his arms become heavier. He wondered how his endurance would compare to a man who spent all day every day training.

To his right, near the prow, something caught Silus' attention. He glanced across and nearly missed a thrust aimed at his midriff. He jumped back just in time, pressed forward, then took a step back to give himself breathing space.

Young Avitus had emerged from below decks. Under one arm he carried a small black stone, and in his hand he held a short knife. Under the other arm was Issa, tongue lolling, tail wagging as she looked around at the chaos with interest.

What in the name of all the gods of the underworld was he doing?

As Silus watched in horror, the boy knelt before the stone, praying loudly in a foreign, eastern language, the knife held to the trusting little dog's throat.

Silus let out a roar of anger and charged forward. The gladiator was taken aback by the sudden onslaught, and finally Silus managed to find a chink in his defences, a thrust slicing through the vessels and nerves in the pirate's armpit, making him drop his sword. He grimaced, clutched the wound, held up his other hand in an attempt to surrender, but Silus had not time to accept as he saw the boy lift his knife.

He thrust his sword deep into the gladiator's chest, letting out a guttural cry.

'Avitus! No!'

He did not arrive in time.

But another did.

A hooded figure leapt from the prow of the pirate boat and landed lightly with bent knees on the pitching deck. Taking barely a heartbeat to regain his balance, he ran at Avitus, and just as the blade began its descent towards the little dog, he grabbed the boy around the waist and swept him away.

Issa dropped to the deck with a disgruntled yelp, then, deciding that maybe it was time to make herself scarce, she trotted off to hide behind a group of barrels.

The hooded figure dragged Avitus towards the rail, but the boy was not a limp weight in his arms, but a wriggling, biting, scratching wild cat. His resistance gave Silus time to reach the hooded man. He grasped his arm and wrenched. The assailant grappled for Avitus, but the boy twisted away, then kicked him hard in the shin. The hooded man cried out, and Silus followed up Avitus' attack with a punch of his own aimed at the man's throat.

But he was quick. He ducked, twisted away and came back into a fighter's stance with a knife held in his hand.

Silus thrust the boy behind him and held out his sword. His new opponent was slight and short but well-toned. His features were hidden by the hood, but Silus could still make out intently burning eyes within. He saw anger, but also calculation. The eyes flicked right to where the battle raging was starting to swing in favour of the defending legionaries. The soldiers were using the same tactic, again advancing on the pirates, forcing them backwards. Some, who had seen their comrades fall in the previous wave, broke off and leapt back onto their own ship. Once that happened, the fight was over. The attack disintegrated, some skewered by thrusting gladiators, some tipped over into the sea, a few making it back across the gap, though more than one of these missed their targets and fell screaming into the surf.

The hooded figure hissed his frustration. Then he took two quick steps back to open a safe gap between himself and Silus, turned and leapt from off the prow, back to his own ship. Silus pursued him to the deck rail, but made no move to chase him onto his own territory. The figure shouted at his captain to break contact.

Oars dipped into the waters, pulled hard, and within moments the two ships had parted. The pirate ship turned hard to port, and rowed fast away in a direction perpendicular to Silus' ship's vector.

Silus stared after it for a moment, then turned angrily on Avitus.

'What the fuck were you doing with my dog?'

Avitus returned his look with equanimity.

'The battle looked to be going badly. I decided to invoke the help of the great Elagabal. And I needed a sacrifice.'

'You were going to kill my dog for your weird eastern god?' His voice rose, and without conscious thought, he raised his arm, ready to strike the precocious little bastard.

A firm hand caught his wrist, and he whirled in fury to find himself looking into Marcellus' face, exhausted, drenched in splashes and spurts of blood, but calm and resolute.

'Silus. What are you doing?'

Before Silus could reply, a woman's voice screeched at him, 'Get away from my son, you thug.'

Soaemias stepped between them and gave Silus a hard shove backwards, then knelt and threw her arms around Avitus, who accepted the hug with a bemused expression.

Silus shook his hand free from Marcellus, then flicked his fingers. Issa came running over and jumped into his arms, licked his face, little tail wagging frantically. He fussed her behind the ears, but his cuddle was broken short by Soaemias stepping up to him, her face inches from his.

'How dare you? You, who should be protecting my husband, and my son. Yet you threaten to strike him. Marcellus, this brute should be executed.'

'Quite so,' said Gannys, who had emerged from below decks with Soaemias once the fighting was done. 'Completely unacceptable. Have him crucified.'

The last resistance of the pirates had been mopped up, all dead or fled except for two prisoners, one of whom was so mortally injured he didn't look like he would live more than a few minutes. The legionaries began to attend to their own wounds, and those of their comrades, but some noticed the commotion near the prow and gathered around to spectate.

Silus took a step forward. Gannys backed away but Soaemias stood her ground, and he put his face so close to hers that their noses almost touched.

'Understand this,' he said. 'This dog is my family, as much as your son is to you. He attempted to kill her. I will not allow that.'

'Silus,' snapped Marcellus. 'Step away.'

'Come on,' said Atius. 'The little one is fine. No harm done.'

Silus turned on Marcellus.

'I am sworn to protect you, Marcellus, and your son too. But I warn you: if any of you threaten my dog again, I consider my oath void, and I will not be responsible for the consequences. Do you understand?'

Without waiting for an answer, he stalked off to the stern of the boat, where he stood, hugging Issa close, and wondered how he would cope if the little old girl, the last remnant of his old life, was gone.

—

Silus kept himself to himself for the rest of the day. He was uninjured but his muscles ached from the exertions of battle. He spent hours with Issa in his arms, staring out over the prow, eyes unfocused, memories good and bad sliding across his mind's eye.

He discussed the attack with Marcellus and Atius that evening. They all had their own pet theories as to the motivation. Atius thought there was no need to look beyond simple, opportunist piracy, and to attribute it to anything more was paranoia. Silus and Marcellus had seen too much politicking in the last year or two to believe the attack could be coincidence. But the motivation was obscure. Marcellus thought it was an assassination attempt on him, either in revenge for his role in the downfall of Geta, or an attempt to weaken Caracalla by someone thinking about positioning themself for power. Silus supposed that this theory was most likely, but something about the hooded figure, his actions and manner, hadn't sat right. Why abduct the boy? To extort co-operation from Marcellus? For money?

And he was no ordinary pirate. Silus could tell from watching him, with every movement a lesson in economy of motion, smooth, agile, that this man had some skill. Not like the gladiator, trained to fight and nothing more. This was more like an assassin. Like an Arcanus.

Silus knew that Atius and he were not the only Arcani, that Oclatinius had a network of spies and informers as well as a handful of fully trained and inducted assassins like the two of them. But he also knew that they were rare, and distributed throughout the Empire. So did this mystery man belong to Oclatinius? That made no sense; he must be a freelancer, a rogue, or else he served someone or something else. Silus had no answers, and their discussions led nowhere. Marcellus apologised for the actions of his wife and son, and Silus grudgingly shook his hand and retired for the night.

The day after the attack, Avitus approached him. He held a small piece of hard biscuit. His manner was not nervous or diffident, and he had not seemed particularly shaken by the attempted abduction.

'I would like to give this to Issa,' he said.

Silus looked at the tack. 'She won't be able to chew it. She is old and has bad teeth.'

Avitus nodded and walked away without a word. A few moments later he returned with a bowl of chicken stew, gently steaming.

'She will be able to eat this.'

Issa smelt the food and started to wriggle in Silus' arms. Silus nodded and put her down on the deck, and Avitus placed the bowl in front of her. It was not too hot, and the little dog lapped at it greedily, grabbing out soft pieces of meat and chewing them before returning to the tasty broth.

Silus smiled down indulgently, then looked quizzically at the boy. He returned the stare steadily.

'It seemed the right thing to do,' said Avitus. 'The battle looked to be going badly. I wanted to sacrifice something to Elagabal. Something valued, something loved, to stop us all being killed. In fact, what we needed was you. You saved both my father and myself yesterday.'

Silus opened his mouth and closed it again. It was hard to argue with the logic, and he also appreciated that Issa had not been simply a convenient life to end, but one carefully chosen because Avitus had observed how much she meant to him.

Avitus knelt beside her and fussed her behind the ears. She looked at him suspiciously for a moment, clearly worried he was about to take the food away, then, deciding him well intentioned, went back to eating.

'I will not attempt to sacrifice her again.'

'That is good of you.' Silus couldn't help the sarcastic response, but he also knew the boy was attempting a reconciliation, and he appreciated it. 'Thank you for bringing her the food. You can see she loves it.'

'Avitus! What are you doing? Get away from that brute. You, Silus, stand away from my son.'

Silus looked up to see a red-faced Soaemias bearing down on them both. He was about to make an angry retort when Avitus stood and said smoothly, 'Calm yourself, Mother. This is unseemly.'

Both Silus and Soaemias looked at the young boy in surprise at his adult admonition.

'Avitus...'

'No, Mother. Silus saved Father's life yesterday, and prevented my abduction by those criminals. Without him, you would have lost us both.'

Soaemias looked from Silus to Avitus and back again. Silus shrugged. Issa was licking the bowl clean, so he bent down and picked her up.

'Avitus, it's time for worship. Come and lead us in prayer.'

Soaemias held out her hand and the young boy took it. Silus watched them walk away, swaying with the motion of the boat, looking for all the world like a mother and child. Yet he couldn't help but feel that the dynamic between them was far from the usual maternal-filial bond. He shook his hand and looked back out to sea. In the distance, the coast of Sicily swam hazily into view.

—

Syracuse had once been the most powerful Greek city in the Mediterranean, with a might sufficient in its time to defeat the rival cities of Carthage and Athens. That had been before the ravages of the Punic War, and defeat by the Romans, and the city had declined greatly since its heyday. Although now just a regional capital, rather than a great power in its own right, its importance as a port for trade from east and west, as well as for the export of agricultural produce from the island of Sicily itself, meant that it was still a bustling metropolis.

When they disembarked at the docks, the legionaries had to clear a path for the Numidian governor-to-be and his family and entourage through workers and slaves bent over with sacks of grain on their shoulders, donkey carts laden with exotic spices, and perfumes and ox carts hauling amphorae of olive oil and wine.

The legionaries led the way to the governor's palace where Marcellus and his family would stay while Marcellus conducted his business on the island. The two Arcani accompanied them through the city, and said their goodbyes at the Imperial gates. Marcellus did not enquire where Silus was going, just asked that he return within the week so they could continue their journey on to Numidia. Silus assured him that he would be back well before that, and shook his hand, not without warmth. Marcellus had done nothing wrong, and even his son had tried to make amends in his own way. His wife had stayed frosty towards him, but Silus paid that little regard – her opinion meant little to him.

Back at the docks Silus asked around for a ship to take him to Lipari. Although the moorings were rammed with vessels of all sizes jostling for space, it took some time before they finally found a captain going in roughly the right direction. They did not have the resources to commission a ship to make a dedicated trip just for them. Fortunately, this cheerful seaman was due to leave in the morning with a cargo of marble bound for Neapolis and it only required a small diversion to take them to Lipari. Even then, the trip did not come cheap, and the sum the captain first demanded nearly made Silus choke. Eventually they agreed on a price, and the captain told them he would be casting off at first light, with or without them.

They secured some cheap lodgings near the docks, then Atius persuaded Silus that they should find out what nocturnal pleasures the old city could offer them. After an evening of drinking, gambling on cock fights and wrestling matches, some dicing, and Atius' inevitable acceptance of an offer from a local beauty of a turn with her for half an hour at a reasonable price, they sat at a table outside a tavern, sipping wine that they had no need or real desire for.

They were near a wharf and could watch the slaves still busy at their work at this late hour, loading and unloading various cargoes. Silus reflected that for all his misfortunes in life, all his losses and regrets, he was in a good place right then. Out of Rome, in a vibrant city, about to fulfil a promise to a child he was fond of. He stroked Issa's head, who had been a mostly well-behaved companion to them that night, except for the time she had urinated on an off-duty legionary's sandals. The offer of a drink had defused that situation and Silus realised that they had made it through the whole night without a fight.

The smell of cooking meat drifted towards them, and his stomach rumbled. Full as it was of liquid, he still thought there was room for a sausage or a pie. But he felt too lazy to stand.

Instead he took another sip of wine, and took advantage of the relative quiet, compared to the interior of the drinking den, to chat to Atius.

'Sorry if I was an arse on the trip.'

'I didn't notice,' said Atius. 'You are always an arse. How would I tell the difference?'

'You know what I mean.'

'Look, I know what that dog means to you, and why. But what are you going to do with her? You are hardly living a settled life, and it isn't always easy to find somewhere safe to stow her while you are off killing people who need to be dead.'

It was true. He should really have left her behind with Apicula, but he had been feeling down, and wanted the company of someone who loved him unconditionally. Well, almost unconditionally, as long as she got hugs and food. Now he wondered if he was being selfish. And an idea occurred to him. One that was a little hard to consider, but which at the same time was very right. He decided he was too drunk to think about it then, so he changed the subject.

'What do you make of this religion that Marcellus' family follow? This Elagabal god.'

Atius spat. 'There is only one god.'

'Sure, sure.' Silus didn't really know what to believe when it came to religion. He had an inclination to Mithras, a respect for the old Olympian pantheon, a scepticism for newer eastern gods like Serapis and Christos, and an absolute belief in ghosts and magic. 'Well, I guess worshipping a black rock is no stranger than worshipping a man who was crucified like a common criminal.'

'Careful,' warned Atius in a growl.

Silus held up his hands. 'I'm not trying to start an argument. No offence intended. I know you hold your faith close to your heart. But you don't always seem to believe in the way the priests of Christos say you should.'

'What do you mean?' asked Atius, looking genuinely confused.

99

Silus looked at the wine stains down his tunic, the lipstick smeared across his cheeks, the bruises, cuts and scars on his bare arms that were evidence of his violent profession and violent tendencies.

'It doesn't matter. Shall we turn in for the night?'

Atius drained his cup and stood, reaching a hand out to the table to steady himself. Silus picked up Issa, whose eyes kept involuntarily closing. He would miss her badly.

Chapter Six

Two Praetorians waited for them as they rowed ashore. The captain of the marble cargo ship had promised to return in three days, and they had better be ready and waiting or he would sail straight on. Time was money, after all.

They jumped out into the surf, pulled their boat up onto the beach and lifted out their packs. Once Issa was sure she was well clear of the sea, she leapt over the side, ran in excited circles for a minute, then stopped abruptly to defecate.

'I am centurion Tuccius. This island is restricted,' said one of the Praetorians abruptly. 'State your names and business.'

'Welcome to Lipari,' commented Atius. 'May I recommend the food in our fine taverns, and the views from walks along the cliffs are spectacular.'

Silus discreetly kicked his friend in the shin.

'Gaius Sergius Silus. Centurion of the Arcani. This is Lucius Atius, also of the Arcani.'

'And this is Issa,' said Atius. 'She is a war dog on detachment from the front lines.'

Silus sighed. 'Centurion Tuccius, we are here with the knowledge and permission of Oclatinius Adventus, head of the Arcani. I bear the seal of the Emperor.' He showed the centurion the signet ring which displayed Caracalla's likeness that Oclatinius had given him.

'Very well,' said Tuccius grudgingly. 'But you still haven't stated your purpose here.'

'We are here to see the prisoner.'

The Praetorians exchanged meaningful looks.

'What prisoner?'

Silus let out a humourless bark of laughter. 'Really, centurion. Even if we didn't know about her existence, might we not get suspicious about the presence of a detachment of Praetorians on this tiny, insignificant island? We are here to see Tituria. Take us to her.'

'Why do you need to see her?'

'Your rank is way too low to need to know that, soldier.'

The Praetorian bristled, but Silus' face stayed neutral, matter-of-fact.

'Fine,' growled Tuccius. 'I'll take you to her. She is being tutored by her guardian, Myrtis. But I suppose she can be disturbed.'

The Praetorians took their weapons from them, searched their packs, then escorted them up a long stone staircase to the villa at the top of the cliffs. The building showed clear signs of neglect, with overgrown gardens, bushes once finely topiaried run wild and stone paths with weeds sprouting through cracks. The entablature on the columns facing them was discoloured with lichen, and there was moss on the roof.

Silus had been here before of course, with Daya. The thought of the late Arcana, and the mission they had carried out here, caused a sudden painful cramp in his guts. He clenched his teeth and put the memories to the back of his mind.

They were led through an atrium, whose impluvium was green with algae and pondweed, and into an open room. Seated cross-legged on the floor, looking up at a round-bodied, middle-aged woman, her back towards him, was Tituria. He watched teacher and pupil for a moment, heart jumping at the thought of seeing her, stomach clenching with anxiety at her reaction to seeing him. He felt paralysed, desperate to call to her, give her a hug, terrified of her response.

Issa took the matter out of his hands and went scampering across the floor to jump into Tituria's lap. The tutor screamed and jumped backwards.

'It's a rat!' she screeched.

Issa put her paws on Tituria's shoulders and started licking her face furiously.

'Eww, stop, stop,' giggled Tituria. 'I know where you put that tongue, Issa.' She picked the dog up, her arms around her chest, twirled her around, then saw Silus standing in the doorway and stopped dead.

They looked at each other for a long moment, and Silus thought his heart would jump out of his chest, it was racing so hard. Hesitantly, he held out his arms. She left him like that, feeling increasingly foolish, increasingly hopeless. Then she ran forward and threw her arms around him. Her cheek pressed against his chest, and his strong arms hugged her tight, and suddenly they were both crying uncontrollably. Silus was aware that Atius was a short distance behind him, and didn't know whether he was shuffling uncomfortably, grinning stupidly or laughing at him. And he didn't care.

Eventually they parted, and Silus wiped his eyes and his runny nose. Tituria did the same and smiled up at him.

'You came to visit.'

Silus nodded. 'I said I would.'

The lady who had been tutoring Tituria finally regained enough composure to approach.

'I am Myrtis, Tituria's guardian. Who might you be?'

'I am Gaius Sergius Silus. This is Lucius Atius.' He gestured vaguely behind him.

'And what business do you have here?' Her tone was brusque, nervous, but she was trying to assert her authority.

'That is none of your concern. Now, Tituria and I are going for a walk. Atius will want wine and food, and I will also want some sustenance when we return. See to it.'

He put an arm around Tituria's shoulders and guided her away. Issa followed at their ankles.

Once they were out of earshot, Tituria said, 'Thank you for putting her in her place, Silus. She isn't a nice tutor.'

'Does she treat you badly? I can put a stop to that easily enough...'

'No, no. She just clearly doesn't want to be here. Any more than I do. So she is grumpy most of the time, and it makes me miserable.'

They walked out of the villa and along a clifftop path. Tituria pointed south.

'That island is called Vulcano. The god Vulcan visits sometimes and stirs up the fires beneath the earth. That northernmost tip is called Vulcanello. It came up out of the seas only three hundred years ago.'

'Your tutor is doing some good then.'

'She prefers to teach me sewing, weaving and cooking. I have to beg her to teach me the things that interest me. Rhetoric, Greek, philosophy, history.'

'You have an active mind, little one.' It was her curiosity that had led her and her family into disaster, ending in their deaths and her exile. But as he was responsible for their deaths, he was not about to remind her of that, even if he could be so cruel as to point out the consequences of her actions.

'I'm so bored, Silus. And lonely. Myrtis hates me because I am the reason she is stuck here. The guards hate me for the same reason. I am allowed no other visitors – even when I see ships dock or boats come ashore, the guards keep them away. Will I be here forever?'

'I don't know,' said Silus truthfully. 'I hope not.' He wondered if there was something he could do to shorten her exile. The recall of the exiles that Caracalla announced had not been extended to Tituria. The Emperor was clearly prepared to forgive those who had sinned against his father, but still considered Tituria a threat. Maybe if he was of sufficient value to the Emperor, he could make some bargain with him. Or one day, when Tituria had been long forgotten, he could just spirit her away. For now, though, he would not give her false hope. What he would give her was the only thing he could.

He sat down on a rock and patted his knees so that Issa jumped onto him, overjoyed to be given attention as always. He hugged the little bitch, inhaling her doggy smell, feeling the texture of her fur on his cheek. Memories flooded over him, of his home in the vicus in Britannia, arguments with his wife about the dog, his daughter playing obsessively with her to the delight of them both. Then he sighed and passed her to Tituria.

'She is yours.'

Issa cuddled up to Tituria, who looked at Silus with wide eyes. It had been to Issa that Tituria had first responded after the loss of her family. The dog was obviously still dear to her.

'Do you mean it?'

'She is an old lady. Too old to be accompanying me on adventures across the Empire. She needs someone to look after her in her retirement.'

'Me? You trust me with her?'

'I can think of no one I trust more to take care of her.'

Tears filled Tituria's eyes as she pulled Issa to her face and cuddled her like a doll.

They sat together and watched the sea in companionable silence until the breeze started to chill them, and their bellies began to rumble.

When they returned to the villa, Myrtis had prepared a simple meal of bread, cheese, olives and dates. Silus wondered if she was being deliberately insolent in offering them such poor fare, but she had forgotten that she was feeding soldiers, and as long as it was not rotten and it was of sufficient volume to fill an empty stomach, they were unlikely to complain.

They sat together, Atius, Silus and Tituria, and talked about trivia – weather, clothes, what Issa liked to eat and how much exercise she needed. In the afternoon they played games – ludus latrunculorum, knucklebones, fetch with Issa. A game of hide and seek became uncomfortable for Silus when he found himself alone in the room in which he and Daya had assassinated Caracalla's wife Plautilla and Plautilla's young daughter.

He looked around the small bedroom and felt a chill. Had the bodies been properly put to rest? Or were their shades still there, standing behind him, breathing cold wind down his back?

When Tituria found him and let out a shriek of joy, he physically jumped, then put his hand to his suddenly racing heart. He took a few deep breaths to calm himself, then gave her a weak smile and tousled her hair.

'My turn to hide,' she cried, and raced off.

That night Atius and Silus shared a bedroom that Myrtis had begrudgingly prepared for them. Atius was soon asleep, snoring loudly. Silus lay on his back, eyes shut but sleep evading him. Pale images of Plautilla and her daughter floated just behind his eyelids, and merged with the dead, bloodied visages of his own wife and daughter.

He gave up on sleep, walked out of the villa, past Myrtis' room, from which sounds of creaking bed furniture and guttural groans were emerging, out through the atrium and along the cliffs. He sat on the edge, legs dangling into open air. Beneath him waves whipped up by winter winds crashed against the rocks, throwing spray up to the height of several men standing on each other's shoulders. He marvelled at the power of the sea, so far beyond the might of man. Even the Emperor with all his legions was as nothing if the sea decided to turn on him, sink a fleet, flood a city. It could take the life of a man without the slightest interruption to its ebb and flow. A wave would not pause if a human body was thrown in its path. The tide would not alter its rhythm. He could cast himself off this cliff now and it would inconvenience no one, nothing. He stared into the darkness and a tear welled up in his eye, fell, joined its kin. One drop in an ocean.

He shook himself. Maybe the world didn't need him. Maybe he didn't need the world. But he wasn't ready to leave it yet. Certainly not of his own accord. And if anyone else wanted to try to make him go, they would be in for a fuck of a fight.

He might not be happy now. He might not be quite sure what he was fighting for.

But one day, things might be different. And until then, he would carry on.

–

The god of the mountain and the sun, the great god Elagabal, had blessed him, he was sure. He had prayed and sacrificed that morning to the success of his mission, and the sun had broken through an overcast sky, shining down on him and suffusing him in warmth. Aziz was a man of few doubts, but whatever misgivings he ever had about a mission were always dispelled after worship, giving him a certainty that was almost ecstatic.

That Elagabal was with him was confirmed when he spied his target walking with his family out of the governor's residence and into the city. The great god had guided him here. Together with a little inside information, of course.

Four legionaries escorted them. Marcellus was not completely stupid or reckless, and the failed attack on his ship had obviously made him more cautious than usual. Aziz knew he had generally walked Rome with only a solitary slave as a bodyguard.

It would make no difference. Aziz was well prepared. Some of his pirate crew, the ones who had survived, had quit when they reached Syracuse, but half a dozen remained, and he had hired half a dozen more thugs from a Syrian gang leader who ruled a run-down district near the docks.

He had waited patiently for the moment, but knew it would come. He had been informed that Soaemias would tell her husband she was not prepared to stay cooped up in the governor's palace for the entire length of their stay in Syracuse without at least a trip to the market and to see the sights, and Marcellus was too much under his wife's thumb to refuse her.

He trailed them at a discreet distance through the ancient streets of this Greek-founded city, almost as old as Rome itself. Although it was nowhere near as crowded, noisy or overwhelming as the capital city, it still buzzed, and anyone navigating its cobweb of alleys and thoroughfares had to jostle past a bustling throng of citizens and visitors, as well as the carts and wagons that were banned in Rome during daylight hours.

Aziz followed near enough that he could hear them arguing. Marcellus was uneasy, and was begging his wife that they return to the safety of the governor's residence. She dismissed his concerns with an imperious wave of her hands as she made a beeline for a stall in the market square selling fine silk dresses, imported at great expense from the East. The young boy and his tutor, Gannys, joined her, stroking the material and praising its quality.

It was time. They were sufficiently far from the residence, sufficiently distracted. He nudged the lad he had hired as a runner and sent him scurrying to where his men waited nearby. Now he had to rely on the obedience and competence of others, something he was never comfortable with. His breathing tightened as he waited.

There was a crash at the far end of the square and raised voices. He looked over to where a wooden trestle table had been upturned by an angry customer, spilling bronze and silver jewellery over the street. The stallholder screamed at the man while passers-by scrabbled around to pocket expensive rings and necklaces that had rolled into gutters and the cracks between cobblestones.

The legionaries accompanying Marcellus and his family looked nervously towards the disturbance, which was rapidly dissolving into a mini-riot. Two of them advanced forward to attempt to assert some control over the situation, while the other two fingered the hilts of their weapons and scanned the crowd for threats.

The two advancing legionaries were quickly swallowed up by the jostling crowd, which included several of Aziz's men, making sure they got behind the soldiers and cut off their retreat. At the same time, behind the Marcellus party, the rest of his men advanced from several directions.

They weren't actors or spies, and although some of the thugs tried to disguise their direction of travel and target, the legionaries quickly picked up on at least two of the men advancing towards them. They shouted a warning to Marcellus and drew their weapons.

All of Aziz's men rushed forward at once. Innocent bystanders attempted to scatter, but some got pushed to the ground or clubbed with the hilts of swords and axes if they were too slow to move.

The two sides clashed with a roar that reverberated around the square. Eight of Aziz's men, who had not been involved with creating the disturbance to lure away half of Marcellus' guards, fought against just three – Marcellus and the remaining two guards. Aziz hung back and watched.

The square was still crowded as people screamed and attempted to flee, or to get to loved ones or prized possessions. This worked in favour of the defenders, who didn't have to face all of their attackers at once, and were able to use bystanders as distractions and human shields. The quality of the replacements that Aziz had recruited in Syracuse was not up to the standard of the gladiators and veterans from Rome. They were untrained, unfit, and overconfident. So despite their numbers, they made little initial impression against Marcellus and his men.

Furthermore, the two legionaries at the far end of the square had seen the attack and were forcing their way back through the crowd to lend their assistance. They were slowed by the fleeing shoppers and merchants, but made steady progress towards their commander and his family.

Still Aziz hung back and watched. Waiting for the moment.

Marcellus and his two legionaries had formed a protective semi-circle around Ganny and his wife and child, who hugged each other, wide-eyed and terrified at the battle raging scant feet away. Aziz watched them intently as he began to slip through the crowd, edging a respectful distance to the right of the battle.

One of his men fell to a sword thrust through the side of his neck and he dropped to the ground, hand clamped in vain to the rent gushing blood. A legionary took a wound to his upper sword arm. He swapped the sword to his other hand and continued to defend, but less effectively. The two distant legionaries approaching suddenly found themselves beset from behind, as those of Aziz's men who had started the disturbance caught up with them. But they had made sufficient ground to join up with their comrades, so Marcellus now had four legionaries by his side, albeit against a swollen number of foes.

Training and stamina began to tell. Aziz's men started to flag, breathing heavily. When another of their number was taken down by a slice to his head, a double-handed blow from a furious Marcellus that cleaved open the bone, their morale wavered.

Marcellus saw the turning point in the battle, and urged his men to advance, to break the attackers' hearts and rout them. The legionaries stepped forward, one step, another, thrusting and slashing hard. Aziz's men dropped back.

It was time.

Unheard above the screams of the crowd, the clash of the weapons, the roars and cries of the combatants, Aziz sneaked in behind Marcellus and his men.

Gannys saw him first, from the corner of his eye. He turned, opened his mouth.

Aziz elbowed him in the side of the head and he crumpled to the floor without a sound.

Soaemias stared at the attacker, and he gave the woman a hefty shove, sending her stumbling backwards, tripping over the hem of her stola and landing on her backside.

The boy looked up at him now, penetrating blue eyes fixed on his, and for the briefest of moments, he felt paralysed, bewitched by the simple power.

'Elagabal strengthen me now,' he whispered. And he dropped a large sack over the boy's head. He pulled it all the way down to his feet in one smooth motion, then hoisted him onto his shoulder, turned and ran.

This time, the sack precluded biting or scratching. And there was no chance of rescue. No Arcani lurking nearby, ready to play saviours. He knew they were away.

He glanced over his shoulder. Marcellus and their men hadn't even noticed what had happened just at their backs, so transported by battle rage were they. Soaemias stared, slack-jawed, seemingly paralysed for precious moments, before she began to scream and shout for help. Her cries were lost in the din of the melee in any case.

Aziz reached an alley at the edge of the square and gave one last look behind him. His men were turning to flee, some dead, some wounded, most insufficiently committed to the fight and the cause to have taken significant damage. It didn't matter. Killing Marcellus would have been a bonus. But his mission was accomplished.

He tarried just long enough to see Marcellus step back from the fight, turn to see his wife in a heap on the floor, his son gone, to look frantically look around him, shouting his son's name. Then Aziz hurried away down the alleyway, clutching his prize tight, and headed in the direction of the docks.

—

'Silus, you piece of shit! Where have you been? You were supposed to be protecting me!'

Silus stopped in his tracks. After he had disembarked at the Syracuse docks, he had gone straight to the governor's residence to report to Marcellus.

Saying goodbye on Lipari had been hard. He had promised to return, and to do all he could to secure her release. He had tried to navigate a path between the Scylla of false hope and the Charybdis of despair, but had not managed to take away the look of overwhelming sadness in Tituria's eyes that must have channelled what was in her heart. It had been hard to get her to break the final hug before he got into his boat to row out to rendezvous with the cargo ship.

He took comfort, difficult as it was for him personally, in seeing her hugging Issa tight as they rowed away. The little dog watched her master leave in some confusion, but he had left her many times before, and she did not appreciate that this time was different. She wagged her tail, and intermittently sneaked a lick of the tears running down Tituria's face.

So his emotions were dark and fragile and he bridled at Marcellus' tone.

'You knew I would be gone for a few days. Oclatinius approved it.'

'I don't give a fuck if the Emperor himself gave you permission! You weren't here when I needed you!'

Silus now took in the frantic look in Marcellus' eyes, the bruises, grazes and cuts on his face and forearms. He looked to Soaemias, who was sitting uncharacteristically quiet, and Gannys, who was nursing a hen's egg-sized lump that protruded from his temple.

'What happened, sir?' he asked, damping down his own raw feelings.

Marcellus slumped down in his chair now, his hand on his forehead.

'They took my boy, Silus. They took my son.'

Silus stared in shock. Atius had grown very still beside him. No quips or attempts at humour from him this time.

'When?'

'Yesterday.'

'Sir, tell me everything.'

Marcellus hid his face in his hands and his shoulders heaved once, twice. Then he rubbed his face roughly with his palms, and looked up at Silus with glistening eyes. His voice catching, he outlined the ambush, how they had fought off the attackers, but that when the battle was won, he had found his Gannys stuporous, his wife hysterical and his son vanished.

When he had finished talking, there were a few heartbeats of silence.

Then Soaemias spoke in an eerily flat voice.

'Have him executed.'

They all looked at her in confusion.

'What?' asked Marcellus. 'Who?'

'Silus. Have him executed. He failed you, and now our son is gone, maybe dead. He must die.'

Silus gaped.

'Sir, this is not my fault. You know that.'

'I do not know that, Silus!' shouted Marcellus abruptly. 'All I know is my little boy is gone, and you weren't here to do your job!'

Silus took a step back, wondering if he should be considering flight. Behind him, at the door of the chamber, two legionaries stepped closer together, blocking the exit.

Marcellus shook his head. 'Bring him back to me, Silus, or I will have your head.'

Fear and anger warred inside Silus, and Marcellus' unjust words felt like salt rubbed into the raw wound of his heartache. He took a step forward and grabbed Marcellus by the collar of his tunic with both hands.

The legionaries took a step forward, but Atius barred their way, his sword half drawn.

'I will find your son, sir,' Silus hissed into Marcellus' face, specks of spittle hitting the governor's cheeks. 'It is not my fault you lost him. But it is my duty to return him to you. And I will do that in spite of, not because of, your threats. And you,' he said, pushing Marcellus back into his seat, and whirling on Soaemias. 'You had better think very carefully before you threaten violence against an Arcanus in the future.'

Soaemias shrank back from his vehement words.

'Marcellus,' she whispered in a shocked voice. 'Are you going to allow this outrage?'

But Marcellus looked like a man already defeated.

'Silus. Forgive me. He is all I have. I know that you understand what it is like to lose a child. Don't let me go through the same. Please, find my boy.'

Silus took four long deep breaths though his nose, letting his temper recede like an ebbing tide with each wave of breath. When he felt he was sufficiently in control, he spoke.

'I will do everything I can, sir. Atius, with me.'

Not trusting himself to say more, he turned and walked to the exit.

The two legionaries barred his way uncertainly, looking to Marcellus for orders. But Marcellus once more had his face in his hands, and was now weeping openly.

'Get. The fuck. Out of my way.' Silus pronounced each word carefully. His hand was off his sword, but the threat in his voice could not be mistaken.

The legionaries exchanged glances and stepped back. As he passed them, one of them whispered to him, 'Bring him back. He's not a bad kid.'

Silus paused and nodded, then strode out.

—

The obvious first step was talking to the survivors of the fight. The legionaries could tell them nothing of use about their attackers, except that they were mainly amateurs, but they had managed to capture one. He was a Syracusan native, and he had taken a lacerated hamstring from a legionary gladius as he had turned to flee.

He spoke Greek, a language that fortunately Silus had had some exposure to. Although far from fluent, his father had ensured that he knew the basics, since a large part of the Roman Empire including the elites spoke Greek instead of Latin, and during his time in Rome, he had encountered many Greek speakers. Although he preferred to talk in Latin, it was sometimes easier to chat in the native language of another. Atius too knew some Greek from his religious instruction with his mother as a child – the tales and words of the Christos were written in Greek, as was the Septuaguint, the Jewish holy writings that followers of the Christos also read.

So they were able to converse without too much difficulty with the Syracusan thug, and even interject some curses.

'Who hired you, you cocksucker?' asked Silus without preamble.

The Syracusan looked up at him from the reed mattress he was lying on with a resentful expression. 'Go fuck yourself.'

Silus knelt beside him and inspected the deep slash on the back of his calf.

'Looks a bit tender,' he commented, then thrust his finger into the wound. The Syracusan screamed and convulsed, but Atius held him down. Silus twisted his finger, then took it out and inspected it. It was covered in sticky clots, scabs, and bits of flesh. He wiped it on the Syracusan's tunic, then tried again.

'Who hired you?'

The Syracusan breathed heavily through clenched teeth, then muttered. 'I don't know his name. Hurt me if you like, but…'

Silus took him at his word and shoved his finger once more into the hole in his leg. The Syracusan screamed and cursed.

'Wait, wait…' he groaned. 'I'll tell you what I can. I don't know his name. But he spoke Greek with an eastern accent. Sounded like the Syrians who work in the warehouses.'

'What did he look like?'

'He always wore a hood. He was a small fellow, but he looked tough despite that.'

'What did he tell you?'

'That we were going to kill an important Roman and kidnap his son.'

Silus raised his eyebrows and looked at Atius. So it wasn't just an assassination attempt. Avitus had been a target all along. And the kidnapper sounded like the man Silus had fought on the ship. So that was no opportunistic piracy either.

'We've got enough from this one,' said Silus to the legionary guarding the Syracusan, in Latin. 'Do you have any others?'

'Only corpses.'

'What are you going to do with this one?'

'I can't imagine it will be less a punishment than crucifixion.'

The Syracusan looked at them, uncomprehending.

Poor bastard, thought Silus. But there could be no other realistic outcome after the crime he had committed.

They went next to the market where the fight and abduction had taken place. There was no sign that there had ever been a disturbance. It was once more thronged with people, and the stallholders were advertising their wares in loud voices, while shoppers milled about, looking for a bargain, or haggling to create one.

They talked to several artisans and merchants before they found one that had any useful knowledge that he was prepared to share. His stall was at the far end of the square from where the fighting had taken place, but he had seen the boy being grabbed and carried away in a sack by a small, hooded man. For the price of a copper coin, he showed them the alley that the abductor had taken, and Silus and Atius explored it.

The alley was narrow and dirty, mainly residential but with a few shop fronts on the ground floor of blocks of apartments. They knocked on several doors and interrogated several shop owners before they got lucky. A cobbler had seen the man with his struggling load run past, and out of curiosity he had sent his apprentice to follow at a safe distance. He summoned his apprentice, who told them nervously that he had tailed the man as far as the docks, where he had lost sight of him.

The docks were busy as always, gangs of slave labourers sweating over their tasks, despite the mildness of the winter weather. The dock workers and sailors were a reticent group, and none were prepared to talk until Silus became more free with his bribery. Even then, it took them some hours before they finally tracked down someone prepared to speak who also had anything useful to say.

The help came from a Cretan ship captain called Iason, who had been supervising the loading of his ship when he had seen the hooded man with his wriggling sack embark on the boat next to him and disappear below decks. The captain of that boat was an acquaintance of Iason, familiar enough to greet each other and discuss the weather and any new shipping hazards they had heard of. Sometimes they would talk about their cargoes, their jobs and their lives in general; Iason was not on good enough terms to quiz him on the unusual cargo he had just taken on board, but he knew the man's itinerary well enough.

'He trades incense and spices between Alexandria and Syracuse,' said Iason. 'It's his regular run, and he finds it very profitable.'

'You sail the same route?' asked Silus.

'Not me. I take wine from Crete to Ostia, stopping at Syracuse for provisions.'

'Could he have been sailing to a different destination this time?'

'I doubt it. He seems to be a man very set in his ways. Only ever travels to and from Alexandria. If you wanted a different destination, you would choose a different ship.'

'When did they set sail?'

'With the tide this morning.'

Silus cursed. If Marcellus had been a bit more proactive the previous day, before Silus' return, rather than wallowing in misery, he might have managed to catch up with his son before they left Sicily. But it was no use regretting what might have been.

'When is the next ship to Alexandria?'

'I don't know any that are docked here now that are going in that direction. There will probably be one coming in tomorrow or the day after that will stay a few days then head that way.'

Silus shook his head. They had to get moving before the trail went too cold.

'Will you take us there?'

'Me?' asked Iason in surprise. 'I'm not going to Alexandria. I have a hold full of the finest Cretan wine bound for Ostia.'

'Will it spoil?'

'Well... no, it improves with age, but that's not the point.'

'We will pay you handsomely. It will more than make up for any losses.'

'But I have a woman in Ostia, waiting for me.'

'Aren't there women in Alexandria?' asked Atius.

'Of course.'

Silus named the sum they were prepared to offer.

'That would pay for a lot of women,' commented Atius.

Iason swallowed, then stuck out his hand. Silus shook it.

'When do we leave?'

'If we wait until tomorrow...'

'I want to leave now.'

Iason thought for a moment, the large payment clearly running through his mind, and the risk that he could lose it to another captain if he delayed.

'Give me two hours to re-provision.'

'Perfect. We'll return then.'

When he reported back to Marcellus, the governor-to-be gave a small smile.

'Thank you, Silus. I knew you wouldn't let me down.'

'I haven't found him yet. May I ask why you didn't start looking for your son yesterday?'

Marcellus frowned. 'Soaemias was so distraught, I couldn't leave her. And I did ask the Sicilian governor to start a search for the thugs who escaped, but they had vanished completely.'

Silus didn't pursue it any further. He felt Marcellus should have done more, but for all the man's braveness, and his abilities in some areas, Silus wasn't sure he always had much common sense or initiative. He suspected that Marcellus had actually been waiting for his return, hoping the Arcanus would make everything right.

'Atius and I are travelling to Alexandria shortly.'

'We will accompany you,' said Soaemias abruptly. She had been sitting quietly by Marcellus' side, head bowed, showing no signs or paying any attention to the conversation.

'My love…' began Marcellus.

'Mistress,' said Silus. 'I hear Alexandra is a dangerous city. Let Atius and me handle this.'

'No. He is my son. I will go there. For him.'

'We leave in two hours…'

'We will be ready.'

Silus looked at Marcellus, who looked back at him in resignation with a small shrug. Silus sighed and nodded.

'Very well, two hours at the docks. Don't be late.'

–

They were of course late, and by the time Soaemias' slaves had loaded up her possessions, her trunks of clothes, jewellery and make-up, as well as the black stone and other religious paraphernalia, plus the legionaries, Gannys and the household slaves, they were four hours behind schedule.

Iason protested about the weight of all the extra passengers and their luggage, but the ship seemed to Silus' inexpert eye to still be riding high enough in the water, and with some extra payment, Iason was content to set sail, albeit with some extra prayers and sacrifices to Poseidon.

Soaemias settled herself near the prow, cross-legged, closed her eyes and chanted prayers to Elagabal. The sailors eyed her with suspicion, making signs to ward off evil when they thought that neither she nor her husband were looking.

They cast off and sailed south, skirting along the eastern Sicilian coast until they reached the open waters of the Mare Nostrum. From there, they turned east towards the Greek coast, from where they would turn south-east. The sails were set full, the oarsmen settled into their cruising stroke rate, and they headed towards Egypt and Alexandria.

A fast ship could make the journey in ten days in the best conditions, but winter winds and unfavourable currents had to be navigated, and twice they had to take shelter in safe harbours and sit out violent storms.

There were no safe harbours once they began to traverse the Mare Nostrum from its north to its south boundaries, leaving the Greek peninsula behind. Silus experienced severe and relentless seasickness from the incessant undulations and oscillations of the ship's motion, and ate little on the journey, even less of which he actually kept down.

Once, he thought that the ship would sink, and that all would be lost. A huge storm whipped up waves as high as a house, and the winds cracked a mast, the sail swept to sea along with a screaming sailor. A legionary was washed overboard by a surge of brine from the side, and he vanished instantly from view beneath the dark water.

Iason screamed at his oarsmen to pull harder, and at the sailors to trim the sails. Beneath the decks, Soaemias, Marcellus and Gannys prayed for salvation to Elagabalus, Atius prayed for forgiveness of his sins to Christos and Maria, and Silus prayed for help to Jupiter, Mithras, Poseidon, Brigantia, the household lares, the names of his ancestors and anyone else he could think of.

Whichever deity it was that was listening, the storm eventually abated, and the crew were able to make enough repairs to keep the ship afloat and moving onwards on its journey. A few muttered that they should toss the Syrian witch overboard, and Silus was inclined to agree with them. But the voyage continued, and Soaemias regularly took her place at the prow of the boat to pray to Elagabalus, and for the rest of the time studiously ignored Silus, for which he was grateful.

It took around three weeks until the lookout spotted their destination. And what a sight it was. Although the sun had not yet breached the horizon and the skies were still a dark black-grey, the location of the harbour of Alexandria was clearly visible because of the light shining out into the pre-dawn from the lighthouse.

Silus had no idea how they accomplished it, but the light from a huge fire was projected out across the sea to guide ships into the twin harbours. It could be seen from an enormous distance. The ship navigated unerringly towards the beacon, and as they neared, the waves became less violent. The sun peaked over the horizon, throwing its beams through a gap in the clouds onto the underside of the overcast sky, turning the east into a fiery orange.

As they neared shore and the sky lightened, Silus saw the vast tower that supported the fire and the mirror that projected the light, and knew he was looking at the famous Pharos of Alexandria, one of the six remaining of the Seven Wonders of the World. Their horrendous journey was at an end. Now the real work would begin.

Chapter Seven

As soon as the ship entered the Great Harbour, the easternmost of the two harbours that were split by the heptastadion, the motion of the waves ceased almost completely. So sheltered was the inlet, part natural, part man-made, that despite the raging wind on the open ocean, the last short part of the voyage to the docks was so smooth it was like sailing on a barge down a canal.

Silus thought it felt almost unnatural, after three weeks of being in constant motion, to have a steady horizon to observe. Iason came and stood beside him as the pilot guided them in towards their berth.

'You've never been here before then?' said the captain.

'I'm from Britannia,' said Silus. 'I thought Rome was a long way from home. I feel like I have travelled to the ends of the earth.'

'The world is a lot bigger than you realise, my friend.'

'So you know the place?'

'A little. It's old, but not as old as many cities. Founded by Alexander the Great himself, hence the name.'

'I know that much.'

'They say when he first decided to build a vast city on this part, they marked out the streets and regions with flour as they had no chalk. But as fast as they laid it down, the birds came to eat it. Some people thought it was a bad omen. But the soothsayer told Alexander that it showed that the city would go on to become the food-giver of the world. And he was right.

Alexandria, and below it Egypt, feeds Rome. Without it, the capital of the Empire would starve.'

Silus whistled appreciatively. Although the seaborne traffic was much reduced in the winter season, there were still plenty of vessels in the docks, and many entering and leaving the harbour.

But it was the city beyond the docks that caught his attention. He knew that it was past its prime, that its zenith was before the Romans had occupied it, but it still looked magnificent.

Rome too had overawed him when he had first arrived there from the remote province of Britannia at the northern edge of the Empire. But it had been dirty, irregular, a city built hotchpotch over the centuries as the needs of an ever-changing population and an ever-expanding Empire had dictated.

This was different. It had been planned, and it had been designed by the conqueror of the whole world, the greatest general who had ever lived, and it had been built by his successors and turned into a seat of learning and culture that still beamed out across the Empire like its most famous structure, shining light into the fog and darkness of ignorance. Its vast structures of limestone and marble, obelisks and palaces and gardens and buildings whose purpose he could only guess at, overwhelmed the senses, and humbled Silus completely.

Atius summed up his feelings succinctly.

'Fuck me, Silus,' he said. 'Fuck me.'

—

Silus couldn't help staring around him, aware that he was marking himself out as a naive newcomer, but not caring. It was so beautiful. So magnificent. Behind him on the island of Pharos, the lighthouse was illuminated by the early morning sun, collecting its rays and hurling them out to sea from atop its 400-foot tower. In front of him, situated on a projection into the harbour, the waterfront was dominated by the Caesarion, the massive temple of the Imperial cult. It was piled high with dedicated offerings against its sides, and it was girdled with religious pictures and statues wrought in gold and silver. Within the structure he could glimpse porticoes, chambers, gardens, groves and wide-open courtyards. Further away, on a hill to the south-west, looking down over the city and the harbour, was the Serapeum, a vast complex of buildings surrounding the marble, colonnaded Temple of Serapis. And at every point along the skyline, temples of various sizes, shapes and designs jutted towards the heavens, imploring whichever god they were dedicated to to pay attention to them, to find them worthy.

Atius and Silus walked together down the gangway and onto the docks, ignoring the dock workers, paying no attention to Marcellus calling after them, or Soaemias screeching out, 'Silus, Atius, where are you going?' It was just all too fantastic, and at that moment, Silus could not bring his thoughts to bear on anything other than how small and humble he was, and how magnificent was this city he was so fortunate to find himself in.

That all changed when Atius kicked the cat.

It was a complete accident. Like Silus, Atius had been gazing at the rooftops, the buildings and temples, his mouth hanging open. Looking upwards, he had failed to spot the black cat basking on the walkway, soaking up some early morning rays. The cat, of course, was used to complete respect, and though it had seen Atius bearing down on it, until this moment in its life, it had always been revered so thoroughly that even laden carts and wagons had altered their courses around it, rather than have the temerity to ask it to move.

Atius would have had no such compunction, and would have gently but firmly nudged it away if he had seen it. But he hadn't. So his large, booted foot, swinging through the air ready to take a next step, had connected heavily with the cat's torso, and pitched it through the air. It let out a piercing shriek as it flew, legs spread wide in an attempt to slow its speed. Then its head knocked the edge of the walkway, and it tumbled into the sea with a splash and disappeared.

Atius looked around bemused, letting out a half grin.

'Stupid creature,' he muttered. 'Hope it's OK.'

But the surrounding dock workers weren't smiling. Almost to a man, they had stopped their work and were pointing and muttering ominously. Those who did not look angry, such as a pair of long-haired, pale-skinned, Gallic-looking slaves, or a dark-skinned Aethiopian overseer, were backing away slowly.

From the corner of his eye, Silus saw a small figure sprint along the causeway and dive into the water with barely a ripple. He nudged Atius, who now noticed the stir he had caused. More workers came over to join their colleagues, who told them what had happened and indicated Atius.

Marcellus, Soaemias, Gannys and four legionaries caught up with Silus and Atius.

'What's happening?' asked Marcellus.

'Atius killed a cat. I don't think the locals like it.'

'He did what?' gasped Gannys.

'What's the problem?' asked Atius, an uncharacteristic edge of agitation in his tone.

'You cursed fool,' hissed Soaemias. 'Don't you know the cat is sacred to Egyptians?'

Silus did have some memory that they revered the little balls of fur, teeth and claws, which in Britannia were tolerated and vaguely encouraged for pest control purposes. Maybe this cat was a prized rat catcher.

'We apologise for the accident with the cat,' Silus called out to the men who were now forming a circle around them in large numbers. 'We can pay the owner for its value.'

'Silus, no,' warned Soaemias, but it was too late. Muttering turned into shouts of anger.

'Cat-murderer!'

'Sacrilege!'

'Death to the killer!'

The first missile thrown was a piece of soft fruit, which hit Silus on the upper arm, but it was soon followed by pieces of wood and pottery as the crowd smashed up cargo to use as weapons. The small party that had just disembarked crowded together, arms up to fend off the attack, and retreated slowly down the gangway back towards the boat as the dock workers advanced.

'Stop! I have the cat!'

A slight woman, drenched from head to toe, water streaming from her long hair, was standing on the dock side. The cat was lying on its side, fur bedraggled, not moving and not breathing. The angry dock workers turned and stared, momentarily shocked into quiescence by the sight of their sacred animal dead. Then they turned back towards Silus' party with hatred burning in their eyes.

'Wait, wait!' cried Silus, clinging to a desperate hope. He had seen his father drag a half-drowned Maeatae child from a river when he was just a young boy himself. To the amazement of all who had thought the little girl dead, his father had brought her back from Hades by pumping on her chest and blowing into her mouth. He didn't know if it would work for an animal, but he had nothing to lose.

He knelt down by the limp body and touched his fingers behind its elbows. There was a heartbeat, faltering, but present. He pressed down with his palm on the chest, and was rewarded by a little spurt of frothy water coming from the mouth and nose. Inwardly reflecting on the things he had to do to get Atius out of trouble, he leant down and blew firmly into the cat's nose and saw the chest inflate. He pressed again on the chest, rhythmically, with no idea how fast or how hard he should push, but acutely aware how much depended on saving this little animal. The mission. Finding Avitus. Atius' life!

The cat gasped, its back arching upwards, limbs extended. The watching crowd, who had been holding a collective breath, let out a long sigh of wonder. Silus wasn't confident yet. He had seen soldiers die who had made that same convulsive movement as they breathed their last. But the cat gasped again, coughed and spluttered, and began to breathe more regularly. Its eyes remained tightly closed, but its paw came up to bat at its nose, as if to remove a fly.

Silus sat back, and the woman who had dived into the water after the drowning animal held the creature aloft.

'She lives! The stranger has saved the sacred cat. I will cherish her and ensure she returns to full health. The stranger's friend will not be punished for this. I, Tekosis, priestess of Isis, so declare. Now disperse and return to your work, and the blessing of Isis, wife-sister of Osiris, mother of Horus, creator, protector of the seas and harbours and harvests and this great country of Egypt, who guarantees her worshippers comfort and luxury in the life to come, go with you.'

The crowd reluctantly dispersed, grumbling and throwing dagger glances towards Atius, while showing a more ambivalent reaction to Silus, a mix of fear and respect.

Silus turned to the priestess.

'Thank you,' he said. 'You saved us.'

Tekosis cradled the cat in her arms like a baby. 'I saved Bastet, you fool,' she said, matter-of-factly. She spoke Greek, but her accent was strong native Egyptian, a type of intonation that he had encountered among the Egyptians that lived in Rome. He looked at her properly for the first time, her long, white robe clinging to her slender body, long, black hair cascading down her back, still dripping. Her nose was pointed, her eyes large, but the dark kohl that would normally accentuate them into an almond shape had smudged and was now smeared across her fine cheekbones.

Silus felt his breath had been taken away as thoroughly as the drowned cat's, then realised he had been staring for way too long. She cocked her head on one side, and gave him a quizzical half-smile.

'Um... who is Bastet?' was all he could think of to say.

'This is Bastet. The goddess in cat form. As all cats are. And Bastet is the soul of Isis.'

'And you... you are a priestess of Isis?'

'I am Tekosis, as I said. Maybe you should introduce yourself.'

'I am Silus. From Britannia.'

'Just another Roman, no matter where you say you come from.'

'Aren't you?'

'I am Egyptian,' she said, an angry flash in her eyes.

Silus was contemplating what to say next when Atius appeared at his side.

'That was amazing, Silus. I thought I was dead meat for sure. Was that some sort of magic?'

Tekosis also waited for his reply with interest.

'Of course not,' scoffed Silus. 'When have you ever known me to do any magic? I learned it from my father. The poor little beast had lost the air from its lungs, and I put some back.'

Tekosis nodded at this, seemingly satisfied.

'Silus, Atius. Leave this native be and attend me.' Soaemias' voice cut into their conversation like a rusty knife.

Silus gave Tekosis an apologetic shrug. 'I would like to thank you more properly for your help today. Where can I find you?'

'I am the priestess of the Temple of Isis Lochias. I am easy to find.'

Silus nodded, mumbled his thanks again, and turned back to Marcellus and Soaemias.

Marcellus fanned his face with his hand, blowing air between pursed lips.

'That was quite a welcome,' he said. 'I had heard the Alexandrians were excitable, but that was something else.'

'He disrespected their sacred animal. He should be executed, as a sign of our good faith.'

Silus gaped. This was the third time Soaemias had called for the execution of one of the Arcani. He was starting to get the impression that she really didn't like them. 'It was an accident. And the cat survived.'

'I was talking to my husband, not asking your opinion, Arcanus.'

Silus opened his mouth to retort, but Marcellus held up a placating hand. 'The first and only order of business, darling wife, is to find our son. It is Silus and Atius who tracked him here, and it is their job to bring him back to us. If they fail, then maybe we can revisit this matter.'

Soaemias looked distinctly unsatisfied, but did not reply. Silus didn't feel particularly mollified by those words either.

'Now Silus, Atius,' said Marcellus. 'Perhaps you could escort us to the prefect's palace. And maybe we will reach it without an assassination attempt, a kidnapping or inciting a riot.'

–

The prefect of Egypt was a position of such potential power that it was not entrusted to anyone of senatorial rank. As the breadbasket that fed Rome, anyone taking control of Egypt could hold Rome hostage, and so its administration was given to a prefect of equestrian rank. Although this lower station did not necessarily reflect on the prefect's ability, it made it less likely that he would be able to command sufficient support to lead a rebellion or usurp the throne.

Unfortunately, the prefect received no special training in how to run the unique province, with its arcane laws and customs, its complicated pantheon and its volatile population. Lucius Baebius Aurelius Juncinus had only been in the job for a few months, and he already looked worn out.

Silus sat on a comfortable wooden chair in a meeting room decorated lavishly with gold and silver fittings and adornments. Marcellus and Silus sat with the prefect, sipping wine and eating grapes. Juncinus was an affable man in his forties with a neatly trimmed beard and a toned figure suggestive of one who continued to exercise regularly and eat frugally. Beside him sat a tall man with eastern features. Juncinus had introduced him as Gratidius, the legate of the Legio II Traiana stationed in Alexandria.

Atius had been sent off to secure accommodation within the palace for the two Arcani, and Soaemias was ordering around both her own entourage and the palace slaves to unload their luggage, make a liveable space for her and her husband, and attend her as she bathed.

The prefect noticed Silus examining the decor. 'This was one of the Ptolemies' palaces. I forget which one. There were so many, and they all married their sisters. But they certainly knew how to decorate in style.'

Silus nodded in non-committal appreciation. He had never been one for opulent living. His tiny, run-down lodgings in the Subura suited him fine, although he would have been even happier in a small hut in a vicus in northern Britannia, or even a tent in the forest.

'What sort of country is this?' asked Marcellus. 'We had barely stepped off the boat when the crowd erupted. I get that the cat is sacred to them and everything, but still...'

'You got off lightly,' said Gratidius. 'You are lucky the cat survived. A Roman soldier was executed once for accidentally killing a cat. If the creature hadn't made it, we might have had no choice but to put your fellow up on a cross, or the city might go up in flames.'

'Is it really that unstable?'

'Juno's tits, Marcellus, this place is crazy,' said Juncinus. 'I've been here a little while, but I haven't got close to scratching the surface of how it all works. No one prepared me for any of this. I'm a good soldier, and I know Roman law, so they sent me to replace Aquila. They didn't tell me the people who lived here are all insane.'

'Baebius Juncinus,' said Marcellus. 'We need your help.'

'Of course. How could I refuse a propraetor, former Urban and Praetorian prefect and favourite of the Emperor?'

Silus wasn't sure if there was any irony in Juncinus' tone, but Marcellus either didn't think there was or chose to ignore it.

'You may have heard I am to take up the role of Governor of Numidia?'

'I have. Even in winter, news still travels fast from Rome. We heard of the death of Geta only two weeks after it occurred.'

Silus noted the neutral terms he used for the death of the co-Augustus, avoiding terms such as 'murder' and 'committed'.

'We have been attacked twice on the way. Once near Neapolis by what we originally thought were pirates.'

'Pirates? That's unusual these days. Especially that close to Rome.'

'Quite. But we were then attacked again in Syracuse. And this time my...' His voice caught in his throat and he took a sip of wine.

Silus finished his words for him. 'They took the governor's son.'

'Took?' Juncinus sounded confused. 'Took where?'

'If we knew that, we would have him back by now.'

Juncinus whistled. 'I thought when you first mentioned pirates, it was someone trying to stop you taking up the governorship in Numidia. Someone who wants the rebellion there to succeed.'

'That would be the obvious conclusion,' said Marcellus. 'But why would they abduct my son? How does that advance their cause?'

'Well,' said Juncinus. 'You're here, aren't you? Numidia is a long way from Egypt.'

'Simpler to kill me.'

'It sounds like they tried,' said Gratidius. 'Isn't that so... Silus, was it?'

'Yes, legate. And yes. The pirates would have killed him, if I hadn't intervened. And the legionaries tell me the attackers in Syracuse pressed him pretty hard too.'

'So they took his son when they failed to kill him, as a second best alternative.'

'Maybe,' said Silus.

'You seem doubtful,' said Marcellus.

'It's just… it sounds like it was the same man who tried to take Avitus on the ship, as the one who actually succeeded in Syracuse. And in each case, he hung back until the defenders were fully occupied, then chose his moment to make his attempt on your son.'

Marcellus frowned. 'What are you saying?'

'I may be wrong. It just feels like you either weren't the real target, or that killing you was of secondary importance. That taking your son was their aim all along.'

'That doesn't make any sense,' said Marcellus. 'Why would an eight-year-old boy be of value to anyone? Except as a hostage for a ransom. And then surely there are easier ways to make money.'

'Maybe for leverage against you, to make you do something as Governor of Numidia that is against the interests of the Emperor.'

Marcellus shook his head. 'Caracalla would have me replaced and executed instantly if I tried to go against his wishes. Surely that would be obvious to all.'

They all sat in contemplative silence for a moment. Then Juncinus spoke up again.

'I still don't know why you came to Alexandria.'

Marcellus nodded to Silus to explain, and Silus outlined the investigations that had set them on this course. Juncinus listened politely.

'I understand, but how can I help?'

'We were rather hoping you could tell us that,' said Marcellus. 'You know how the city works.'

'I think we have already established that I don't.'

'But do we have your permission to search for the boy with a free hand?' asked Silus.

'Of course. But you had better do it without breaking any laws, Roman or Egyptian. Or religious. Or Greek, or Alexandrian, or Jewish, or… or… gods, I wish I was back in Rome.'

'You don't have any advice for us about how to go about our search?' asked Marcellus.

'No. I'm sorry.'

Marcellus' shoulders slumped.

'But,' continued Juncinus, 'I can introduce you to someone who may be of more use.'

'Oh?'

'His name is Canopion. He is my hypomnematographus.'

Silus glanced at Marcellus to check if he was being stupid. But Marcellus looked equally confused.

'The hypomnematographus is an Alexandrian citizen, and a member of the Boule. He is the chief of my chancery.'

'Boule?' asked Marcellus.

Juncinus threw his hands in the air. 'I did tell you it's complicated. Go and see Canopion. He can explain the intricacies of Alexandrian society better than I will ever be able to. But I suggest you take a number of wax tablets with you so you can make notes.'

–

Canopion the hypomnematographus had offices in the prefect's palace, and after Juncinus had introduced them and retreated, he cleared his schedule for them. Silus would have preferred to talk to him on his own. Marcellus was too emotionally involved. But Marcellus insisted, and in any case, Juncinus told them that as a local aristocrat, there was no way that Canopion would see someone of Silus' sort without someone senior present. Silus tried not to take offence at the prefect's words – he was used to being looked down on by the higher ranks of Roman society. But it was clear that the hypomnematographus also considered himself vastly superior to a mere foot soldier from the remote north, no matter how skilled or respected others thought him.

Canopion had typically Greek features – a long straight nose lacking the Roman bump, wavy dark hair, liberally salted with grey in his case, and large brown eyes with a full mouth. He used that nose to full effect, looking down it from his elevated chair at the two men before him, not even attempting to keep the sneer from his lip whenever he regarded Silus.

Silus decided he would take the initiative.

'What exactly does a hypopneumoniagrapus do?' he asked, taking pleasure in deliberately mispronouncing the title.

'A *hypomnematographus*,' said Canopion, emphasising the correct form, 'is a senior magistrate and advisor to the prefect, assisting with judiciary matters. He is selected from the senior ranks of the Boule. The council,' he added when Silus continued to look blank.

'Sounds important. But you have no authority of Roman citizens, is that correct?'

'I... no, that is not my jurisdiction. But there are others who...'

'Thank you. We would like to ask you some questions. The prefect said you wouldn't mind assisting the governor here.'

Canopion's eyes flicked between the two, clearly wondering about the dynamics at play. Which one actually spoke with authority?

'Of course. However I can be of assistance.'

'The governor's son has gone missing, and we believe he was brought here to Alexandria. With the bad weather, he cannot have arrived long before us. How would you advise we go about enquiring about the arrival of his ship, and tracking him down in Alexandria?'

Canopion sat back and spread his hands.

'The first part is easy. The second, I really couldn't say.'

'Tell us the first part first, then.'

'You need to go to see the procurator Phari.'

Marcellus sighed. Silus knew why – the administration in Alexandria seemed to be completely different to any other part of the Empire and Marcellus, who was from Syria, had fought in Britannia, who had followed Severus in Africa province and had held high office in Rome, felt totally out of his depth here.

'Who is the procurator Phari?'

'He is the official who collects the harbour dues at the ports. He is also responsible for protecting the shipping lanes against piracy and attack from foreign threats. And importantly for you, he strictly regulates the flow of persons and goods into and out of the port.'

'We didn't report to him when we arrived,' said Marcellus, confused.

'A man of your rank would not have been detained, but you can be sure your captain will have given a full inventory of crew, passengers and goods to the office of the procurator Phari as soon as you arrived.'

'So we can find out when this ship docked, and who was on board?' asked Silus, interest now piqued.

'If you have enough detail, the procurator's civil servants will be able to look up its arrival. As for who was on board, that will depend on what name they used, of course. But it may be that you will be able to find the official from the procurator's office that inspected the boat, and he may recall some detail of use.'

'Thank you,' said Marcellus, and Silus also nodded his thanks. The pompous aristocratic official was being of more use than anticipated.

'And the second part?' asked Silus. 'How might we find a missing boy in this city?'

Canopion steepled his fingers and pressed them to his lips.

'I presume you intend to go and talk to people and see if you can find him with a combination of bribes, threats and appeals to good nature.'

Silus shrugged. Put like that, it didn't seem the most solid of plans, but he didn't have anything better at this stage.

'Then I think you need to understand how Alexandria works a little better.'

Marcellus inclined his head, indicating for the hypomnematographus to continue.

'Alexandria was founded over five hundred years ago by Alexander the Great when he...'

Marcellus held up his hand. 'Is a history lesson really necessary?'

Canopion looked put out. 'It certainly helps to understand the interplay of races here. But if you want the short version...'

'It would be a help. Time is pressing.'

'Alexandria has a diverse population made up predominantly of Greeks and native Egyptians, plus Romans – mainly in government in the army – and Jews. The number of Jews is relatively small, although once more growing. They revolted a hundred years ago, and at the time many were killed or forced into exile.

'The Greeks are descendants of the men who came with Ptolemy when he took Egypt as his prize when Alexander's empire fell apart. The Egyptians have been here since before time began.

'In terms of social ranking, ignoring the Romans who govern by right of conquest, the upper echelons such as myself are Greek. We have our own council, the Boule. We administer our own taxes, and our families are part of the Bouletic class – the aristocrats. All others in Alexandria are just part of the ochlos – the mob – be they Greek, Alexandrian, Jewish or anything else.'

Silus was beginning to understand where Canopion saw his position in society. Just like the Greeks in their home country, he paid lip service to his Roman overlords while not so secretly considering himself and his friends and family vastly superior to them, and indeed to everyone.

'What about the Christians?' asked Silus. 'I heard there are a lot of them here.'

Canopion considered the question. 'It's hard to tell. The Emperor's father, blessed be his name, ordered the Alexandrian Christians purged about ten years ago. Many were killed. Those who didn't flee or hide were beheaded or burnt. It was a difficult time, even for those of us who stick to the faith of the old gods. But slowly they returned, and even though the divine Septimius

Severus decreed a ban on conversion to Christianity, they now preach openly in the city. And it is not like with the Greeks and the Jews and the Egyptians – you can't tell a Christian from the colour of his skin or the shape of his nose, even though some think of them as a separate race.'

'So the city is volatile because there are so many factions?' asked Silus.

'Maybe. Pagans hate Christians, Christians hate Jews. Native Egyptians hate the Greeks. The Greeks look down on the native Egyptians. Everyone hates the Romans. Well, not everyone,' he said hastily, as Marcellus' eyes narrowed. 'Of course I have the utmost respect for the culture and power of Rome.'

'You said maybe,' said Silus. 'Why else is there so much trouble here?'

'The native Egyptians trace their history back longer than anyone, and feel they are owed more respect than they get. Then there is the unique nature of Alexandria, which they think is part of Egypt but also somehow separate from and above it.

'But I think really it is just in their nature, the mob. They are volatile from birth, and take offence at anything and everything. A missed greeting. Being turned away from the baths. A lack of a certain type of vegetable at the market.'

'This is all fascinating, but how is this going to help me find my son?' asked Marcellus.

Silus put a hand on his arm. 'Sir, we are both foreigners here. We need to know how to talk to the locals without causing offence to get them to help us.'

'Good luck with that,' said Canopion. 'They wouldn't spit on a Roman to put him out if he was on fire. Not unless they owed you.'

Owed me? thought Silus. Did the priestess owe him for saving the sacred cat? He suspected it was more the other way round. She had saved Atius and himself by her quick thinking and her calming of the mob. But she was the only native he had met so far, and he doubted it would be easy to get other introductions. Besides, though he only half admitted it to himself, he had another reason to see her again. Her face and her body in its damp tunic had remained in his mind's eye since he had first seen her. He should pay her a visit, he thought, with Atius. On second thought, no, he couldn't trust Atius not to say the wrong thing, especially as she was a priestess of Isis and Atius was a follower of Christos. He would see the priestess on his own.

–

As Silus approached the Temple of Isis on the Lochias promontory, his heart was beating faster than it should be from the short walk from the Imperial palace. The temple was near the water's edge, built on top of a small mound of earth to raise it above the other buildings nearby. An open outer space was surrounded by columns, with the temple itself entered through an ornate doorway. He walked into a brightly lit room painted with colourful frescoes of scenes from the stories of the Egyptian gods, with a red and white background colour scheme throughout. A few worshippers sat in quiet contemplation, and a temple servant swept the corners of sand and dust. His footsteps echoed in the calmness.

One picture caught his attention – a painting of a goddess he presumed to be Isis, with a serpent wrapped around her wrists and some sort of mythological creature at her feet. It was a long green animal with scales and a lengthy tail, and a strange mouth like a huge beak full of teeth. His head was tilted to one side as he tried to work out what it could be when a voice made him jump, and his heart, which had calmed, began to race again.

'Silus, wasn't it?'

He whirled to find himself face to face with Tekosis, and his heart missed a beat. She was wearing a long robe that led down to her feet, and a scarf was pulled over her hair. Only her forearms and her face were visible, but her beauty was enough to render him speechless. Strands of dark hair escaped the scarf to hang over her forehead. Intricately applied kohl accentuated her already large eyes, no longer smeared from her dip in the harbour.

She smiled gently, and the breath caught in his throat.

'Have you forgotten your name?'

'Yes. No. Yes, it was Silus. It still is.'

She let out a little laugh that was like a sweet melody plucked on the high notes of a lyre.

Pan's balls, Silus. Get a grip. You're on a mission, stop behaving like a love-struck boy who has only just cast aside his bulla and donned his toga virilis.

'Well, I'm glad we have established that. Are you here to worship Isis, or for some other reason?'

'I'm here to see you, actually.'

'Well, isn't that sweet.'

Silus bit the inside of his cheek hard to restore his concentration and studiously kept his gaze locked on her face so his eyes didn't inadvertently roam her body.

'It's not a social visit. Is there somewhere we can talk?'

Tekosis did not seem disappointed at this news, and although the upward tilt at the corners of her mouth straightened, the smile remained in her eyes.

'We can talk in my chambers.'

Tekosis led the way and Silus found himself captivated by the sway of her hips as she walked. Damnit!

Her chambers turned out to be a small suite of rooms, including a bedroom and a reception-cum-living room. She gestured to him to sit on a wooden chair with a cloth seat, and she sat opposite him. The bedroom was visible through a drawn curtain, with a luxuriously upholstered bed, nightstand and a basin and chamber pot in the corner. She caught the direction of his gaze.

'Is this uncomfortable for you?'

'I just worry about... propriety. Not for my sake, of course, but as a priestess, are you allowed to receive a man alone in your private quarters?'

She let out that melodic laugh again. 'As a priestess of Isis, I can do what I like. This is Egypt, not Rome. I'm not a Vestal Virgin.'

At the mention of the priestesses of Vesta, Silus grew sombre. He had tried not to think about that horrific incident, but suddenly he was transported there again, watching the terrified expression on the young girls as they were taken down to be buried alive, hearing once more the terminal thud of the falling vestal who had tried so desperately to escape.

He was brought back to the present by a touch on his knee. Tekosis leaned forward, concern on her face.

'I'm sorry. We heard of what happened to those poor girls. Were you there?'

Silus nodded, and this time it was not the priestess' beauty that choked his voice.

Tekosis stood, walked to a side table and poured two glasses of wine from a jug. She handed one to Silus and sat back down. He looked down into the liquid and swirled it around. It was blood red, much darker than he was used to. Tekosis saw him looking at it suspiciously.

'When the great sun god Ra became old, men made fun of him. So he summoned his daughter, the goddess Hathor, mistress of the stars, mistress of love, protector of the sun god, and ordered her to punish the blasphemers. But once she had a taste for killing, she would not stop, and continued to slaughter mankind indiscriminately, taking the form of the lioness Sekhmet and drinking the blood of men. Ra, realising mankind was about to be totally destroyed, began to feel sorry for the humans, but even the gods could not stop her blood lust. So while she slept, the gods mixed wine with red pigment and poured it over the land. When she woke, she thought the wine was blood and drank it all. She then became so drunk she forgot about killing, and became calm and merry.

'We drink blood red wine to this day. And in some places, they still celebrate the festival of drunkenness in her honour.'

'Well, that sounds like it could be fun,' said Silus, and took a deep draught. It was very sweet, flavoured with herbs and spices he couldn't identify. It was a far cry from British beer, but he decided he could get used to it.

'Are you ready to tell me why you are here?' asked Tekosis. 'It isn't to worship Isis, and it isn't to visit me. And I'm sure you didn't come here just to sample my wine.'

Silus took another drink. 'I didn't intend to come to Alexandria. Before I arrived, I knew hardly anything about the city, and knew nobody here. But I am on a mission, a search for... something. And I will need the help of someone who knows the city well. So far, I have been introduced to the prefect, who knows nothing, and the hypomnema... hypoenema...'

'The hypomnematographus,' supplied Tekosis helpfully. 'There is a man who believes he knows his worth.'

'He did seem rather full of himself.' Tekosis was good at putting him at his ease, just like she had calmed the rioting mob. Was it a professional skill, or was she just a natural? he wondered.

'So tell me about your search.'

'I am looking for a boy.'

Tekosis raised her eyebrows.

'No, not like that. I mean, a specific boy. One who has gone missing.'

'I see. And you think he is in Alexandria?'

'I do. We know the ship he was taken on set sail for Alexandria. We have checked with the procurator Phari and it arrived here three days ago. The boy was not declared as part of the ship's manifest, but we are sure he must have been on board. The ship has now departed, but before it went, it was thoroughly searched by the procurator's officials, and he is certain the boy was not on board. So he must be hidden in Alexandria somewhere.'

'I'm sorry to hear of these troubles. But I don't see how I can help.'

'If this was Britannia, or even Rome, I would talk to witnesses, follow leads, sneak into houses, kick down doors, maybe bribe, maybe threaten. But I have a feeling, after our welcome yesterday, that that approach may not be successful here. Alexandria seems to be a uniquely dangerous city, and to be honest I'm at a loss how to proceed.'

Tekosis nodded. 'I can see your problem. How well do you understand the politics here?'

'The hypomnemomomo... Canopion... tried to explain it to us. But he seemed to have his own perspective on things. To him, if you weren't part of the aristocracy, you didn't seem to be worth notice. I doubt it is among the upper echelons of society that I am going to need to look for the kidnapper.'

'As you said, he is full of himself. He belongs to a race and a class who believe in their innate superiority over all other men. But he forgets he is a newcomer to our land. Our civilisation is vastly older than his.'

'So you are a native Egyptian?'

'To my shame, I am half-Greek. My father's side. But I was raised by my mother, and I am Egyptian and Alexandrian before all else. And my greatest hope is that one day Egypt will be free of the Romans and the Greeks who stand on the bent backs of my people.'

'You are a revolutionary?'

Tekosis smiled. 'Of course not. That would be treason. Anyway, Romans and Greeks are not the only threats to the Egyptian way of life.'

'Really? Who else?'

'The Christians.' Her pretty faced twisted into an ugly snarl.

'How do they threaten you? Don't they preach peace and love?' He had learned a little from Silus, and if his friend was typical of a follower of Christos, he didn't have a problem with the strange cult.

'They want peace and love only for their own kind. If you aren't Christian, they want you to become one, or they believe

142

you are damned. And they believe there is only one God, like the Jews. The Christians want to destroy the old gods and supplant them with their own triple deity.

'And then there are the Jews themselves. They were largely killed or chased out of Alexandria after their great revolt a hundred years ago, when they tried to tear down and desecrate temples of the old gods, like this one. But they are creeping back into the city, and who knows when they will turn against the gods of Egypt and Rome again.'

'The Romans are very tolerant of other religions,' said Silus. 'They welcome them and adopt them. Worship of Mithras and Isis and Serapis is common in Rome. But the Christians and Jews accept no other gods, not even the divine emperors, and the Romans don't like that.'

'I know there are many Isis worshippers in Rome. Tell me, Silus, which god do you follow?'

'I don't really…' Again he found himself struggling for words. How did she do that to him? 'I mean, all of them I suppose. Any.'

'Who is the first on your lips when you are in danger?'

'I guess that would be Mithras. But it's a long time since I was in a Mithraeum, and I'm not an initiate or anything like that. Not even a raven.' The raven was the lowest rank of the seven grades of initiation in Mithraism.

Tekosis stood abruptly. 'Come. Follow me.'

She led him out of the chamber, through a large meeting room, to a hefty wooden door at the back of the sanctuary. She took out a large bronze key, turned it in the lock and pushed the door wide. She walked through, beckoning Silus, who entered behind her.

The room was well lit by high-up barred windows through which streamed shafts of sunlight. As elsewhere in the temple, the walls were painted in beautiful frescoes, images in which the goddess featured heavily, with a supporting cast of other gods – bearded Serapis, the Ibis-headed Thoth, beetle-headed Ra.

Various strange beasts decorated the margins of the frescoes, including a fat animal that looked like an aquatic pig, and another of those long lizards with the scary teeth.

But more impressive and eye-catching were the contents of the room. A tall marble statue of Isis and Serapis holding hands. Silver and gold cups, plates, bowls, decorated with religious symbols. And in pride of place, on a marble altar inlaid with gold at the far end of the room, was a foot-high golden statue of Isis. The goddess held a sceptre topped with an ankh symbol in one hand, and there was an empty throne on her head. One breast was exposed, and she was nursing the baby Horus. It was beautiful, and clearly sacred, as well as highly valuable.

'This is the sacrarium. It holds the most precious and sacred objects of the temple.'

'It's beautiful,' sighed Silus, and he meant it. The scent of incense filled the air, and the sounds of harmonious chanting drifted out of the main temple area. He was in an exquisitely decorated room, before these magnificent artefacts, in the presence of a stunning woman. He felt a little light-headed, and took two deep breaths to calm himself.

'I can see it is affecting you,' said Tekosis. 'Isis is here with us.'

At that moment, in that place, with that woman, he could believe it.

'Do you want to know about her?'

He nodded, eyes fixed on the figurine.

'Isis is the wife-sister of Osiris and the mother of Horus. She is a kindly goddess, maternal, caring, and she helps us on the way to the afterlife. Her magic powers are great, and she protects the earth, the skies and the sea. She is the cleverest of all the gods, and she has power over fate itself.'

'You sound very proud of your god.'

Tekosis looked at him in surprise. 'Who wouldn't be proud of their god?'

'Well, some of them are not so special. I mean look at the behaviour of Jupiter, the serial adulterer and rapist. Or Mars, who supervises destruction and death. Or Pan, who killed a nymph when she refused his advances.'

Tekosis looked thoughtful. 'The gods of Greece and Rome are very different in character from the gods of Egypt.'

Silus turned towards her. 'Why did you bring me here?'

'You seem like you are seeking a deeper truth.'

He shook his head. 'Really, I'm a shallow man. What you see is all there is of me.'

She looked into his eyes, and he suddenly felt like her gaze was penetrating into his soul.

'I see very well, Silus.'

Silus swallowed, then shook his head to clear it of sweet fumes and seductive thoughts.

'Will you help me?' he asked.

'In your quest? No.'

He stared at her. 'But...'

'Haven't you been listening to me, Silus? I am Alexandrian and Egyptian. I do as I am required by the Imperial authorities and the local Boule. But I belong to Isis. And the goddess has no interest in a Roman boy.'

'But think of his mother and father. Think how scared the boy must be.'

Tekosis reached out to touch his cheek. 'You are a good man, Silus. I will pray to Isis that you find the boy. Now, it is my time for private worship. Please excuse me.'

'That's it?' Silus felt as deflated as a burst bladder.

'I hope you will visit me again.'

'Will you at least let me know if you hear anything, from your worshippers, or other natives?'

She considered. 'Yes, I will. Goodbye, Silus.'

Silus looked at her for a long moment, expecting something else, though not really sure what. Then he turned and walked disconsolately away, aware that he was disappointed on both a personal and a professional level. He trundled slowly out of the temple and walked back to the prefect's palace.

Chapter Eight

Atius joined in with the prayers and hymns in the little church, but his mind was elsewhere. He was disgruntled that Silus hadn't taken him along to see the priestess, partly because it felt like his friend didn't trust him, and partly because he would have liked to see the pretty young woman again himself. And though he was tempted to explore Alexandria, the chaos on the docks and the worry that someone who might still be bearing a grudge on behalf of the cat might recognise him made him more cautious. The overt religiousness of every aspect of the city, with its temples and sacred symbols and animals, made him realise it had been a long time since he had shown any proper devotion to his own god. So he had spied a palace slave with a necklace in the shape of a fish, and asked where he might find a place to worship the Christos.

The church was sparsely decorated, little more than a room for worshippers to gather. It was not purpose-built, just a private dwelling that had in the past opened its doors to become a meeting place for Christians, and eventually had become purely a place of worship, a so-called domus ecclesia. At one end was an altar with a marble cross. The walls were painted in a rather amateurish way with scenes from the life of Jesus – the feeding of the 5,000, the sermon on the mount, the birth and the crucifixion.

He wasn't sure why he had gone to worship. He had been a follower of the Christos all his life, had been taught the tales and the instructions of the Messiah and his followers by his mother since he was in the crib. He had always taken his beliefs for granted, never questioned them, but equally never taken them particularly seriously. He broke some of the ten commandments on a regular basis, particularly the ones about lying, killing and adultery. He even recalled once when he had coveted a female servant that his neighbour had purchased, before he remembered that too was forbidden.

The room was half full of worshippers on their knees. They seemed to come from the whole spectrum of races and classes in Alexandria – Greeks, Romans, native Egyptians, those from the eastern Empire such as Syrians and Jews. Some wore expensive clothing and jewellery, while others wore little more than rags. Atius suspected that the wealthy worshippers wouldn't even acknowledge the poor ones if they met on the street, but in this service, they shook hands, sang, prayed and venerated the Christos together.

The priest who led the ceremony had red-grey hair, a high forehead and a long, pointed nose. He had been looking nervous and unsettled throughout. Atius assumed it was either his usual manner, or that he was in constant fear of the authorities in a city that had experienced a massacre of Christians just a decade before.

But after another prayer, the priest cleared his throat and announced in a wavery voice, 'Brothers and sisters in the Christos. We are hugely honoured today by the presence of one of the greatest among our number. Origen, son of Leonides the martyr, will lead us in the Eucharist.'

A gasp went out among the worshippers as a figure at the front, who until now had been hooded, stood and threw his hood back to reveal a man in his late twenties with Greek features, jet black hair and a round, slightly effeminate face. Atius looked at him with mild curiosity. His name obviously meant something to the worshippers, but Atius had never heard of him.

He clasped the priest's hand firmly. 'Thank you, Brother John.'

He remained respectful as he took the loaf of bread that was offered to him by the priest, and broke it in half. He spoke in a clear, unwavering voice.

'Our Christos broke the bread at his last Passover meal, saying this is my body, given for you. Do this in remembrance of me.'

He passed the halves to the congregation, who each took a piece and swallowed with heads bowed and eyes closed. When all had eaten, the bread was passed back to the priest, who consumed the remainder. The priest then blessed a silver goblet of wine and passed it to Origen. Origen spoke again. 'He took a cup and after giving thanks he gave it to them and they all drank of it, and He said, "This is my blood of the covenant, which is poured out for many."'

He passed the wine around, and everyone took a respectful sip before passing it on. The wine was sweet to Atius' taste, and strong, so he could feel it slide down his throat and settle in his stomach. He had taken the holy Eucharist before, although it had been admittedly some time. But it felt somehow different this time. He wasn't sure why. Was it the foreign setting? Origen's sincere tone? Or was there something more? Was the Christos really with them?

When the ceremony was over, and the priest, John, had drunk the last of the wine, they all sat in perfect silence, heads bowed, eyes closed. It had been a long while since Atius had spent any time in quiet contemplation. Usually the strong wine or beer, and the perfume of the women in his company, overpowered his thoughts. But now he found himself alone, in the dark behind his closed lids, in near silence, broken only by the breathing sounds of the other worshippers.

His thoughts drifted over his recent past. There was a lot of violence. Battles, fights, murders. What would his mother make of what he did now? What would the Christos say, if he returned in all his glory, this very day? They were uncomfortable thoughts.

'Brothers and sisters, followers of the Christos.' Origen's words cut through his reverie. 'Our world is a wonderful place.

God's creation includes the delicacy of a sparrow, the beauty of a rose, the might of the mountains and the river. But the devil also works on this earth, and he tempts us perpetually to turn away from God and his teachings. Some say that the outward world is so constituted that it is impossible to resist it. But he who says that, look inward, and see whether there is not some other motive that would account for his approval or assent to the misdeed.

'For example, should a man have decided he will refrain from sexual intercourse with a woman, and then a woman comes to him and solicits intercourse from him, she alone is not sufficient to make him break his resolution. He does so because he likes the pleasure and does not want to resist it. But a man of greater discipline and knowledge will suffer those same incitements, and his reason and virtuous convictions will stop the excitement and weaken the lust.

'So it is with all our temptations, whether it is to neglect the poor and needy, to indulge in sins of the body, to fail to show proper adoration and worship to our Lord, or even to deny our faith in times of trial, it lies within each of us to resist those temptations, and to take the righteous path. Each and every one of us can be everything the Lord wants us to be.'

There was a moment of silent contemplation of the words. Then the priest read a passage from the Septuaguint, finishing with, 'This is the word of the Lord. Amen.'

'Amen,' replied the congregation.

The priest said, 'The Lord's blessings be upon you. Go in love and peace, in the name of our Lord. Amen.'

'Amen,' chorused the congregation again. They rose, briskly or slowly and stiffly depending on their age, health or weight, and clasped each other's hands, offering each other the peace of the Lord.

One pretty young girl, long dark hair concealing half her face, with piercing blue eyes and full red lips, clasped Atius' hand for longer than was necessary and held his gaze with a coquettish half-smile.

He let her hand drop and turned away. At the front of the room, Origen was shaking hands with members of the congregation, who were treating him with the respect and awe of royalty. Atius walked to the front, leaving the rejected girl behind him. He waited his turn as the congregation queued up to show their respect to the revered Christian.

When he came face to face with the kind-looking, sombre man, all the words he had been rehearsing in his mind disappeared, and he stood before him, opening and closing his mouth like a beached fish. Origen smiled at him, and his anxiety eased, although he still couldn't remember what it was he wanted to say.

'What's your name, brother?'

'Atius,' he managed.

'A Celt?'

Atius nodded. 'Celtiberian, sir.'

'You need not address me as sir. We are all equal under the eyes of God.'

'Yes, s… brother.'

'When did you begin to follow the Christos?'

'All my life. I learned the stories of the Lord at my mother's knee.'

'And yet you seem uncomfortable here.'

He was perceptive, thought Atius.

'I am not as devout a follower as I should be,' he said, dropping his head and feeling himself flush in a most uncharacteristic way.

'None of us is as devout as we should be. Only the Lord himself is perfect.'

'But I have committed many sins.'

'None of us are free from sin. But brother, you seem troubled.'

Atius had to admit to himself that he was. It had been so long since he had really stopped to just think, and now his thoughts were threatening to overwhelm him. To his acute shame, he felt tears welling up in his eyes, and to his horror they began to fall to the floor.

Origen put a finger under his chin, raised his face so he could look into his eyes.

'Brother, you are new here, so you may not know that I am in hiding. The authorities have taken issue with my preaching. But I reside with a wealthy widow who is a fellow follower of the Christos. She lives in a villa near the Park of Pan, next to the cisterns that supply the baths. Her name is Phryne. She would be very happy to receive you in the fellowship of the Christos, and I can talk to you more there.'

'I would like that.'

Origen nodded, the matter settled. 'Go in peace, Atius.' He clasped Atius' hand.

'Go in peace, sir... brother.'

Atius stumbled out into the bright light outside the domus ecclesia and blinked. Then, mind whirring, he walked slowly back to his quarters.

—

'What's wrong?' asked Silus. Atius was staring down into a cup of grape juice, swirling it absently.

'Nothing,' said Atius defensively. 'What's wrong with you?'

'Nothing either,' said Silus, who had until that moment had his head in his hands, face like a professional mourner at a funeral.

They were quiet for a moment longer. They sat at a table outside a tavern near the prefect's palace. Silus had yet to explore the city, only seeing the sights on the short walk from the palace to the Temple of Isis Lochias. But the city was parading past him, and he was able to observe the sheer variety of peoples present. Rome of course had a diverse population, but was predominantly Italian in ethnic origin, whereas Alexandria had Jewish, native Egyptian and Greek ethnicities from its very founding. Beside this was the immigrant population, made up of the various peoples of the Empire, mainly Asian and African – Syrians, Mauretanians, Galatians, Aethiopians – as well as traders from even further east such as Parthians and Indians.

'I met someone,' began Atius, just as Silus said, 'I like the priestess.'

They looked at each other for a moment in surprise.

'You met someone?' asked Silus.

'You like the priestess?' asked Atius.

'No, no. You first. Tell me everything.' Atius hadn't had a serious relationship since Menenia, their old commanding officer's daughter who he had rescued from the barbarians in Britannia, and even that probably didn't count as serious. Atius had never shown any intention of making things more permanent with her. So for Atius to have met someone, enough to make him look morose and thoughtful, was interesting news.

But he wasn't forthcoming.

'Tell me about the priestess.' Silus realised that, equally, he had had no relationship of any sort since his wife had died. He hadn't even indulged in prostitutes, not for moral reasons particularly but for lack of desire. The closest he had come to love was his fellow Arcanus Daya. And he had killed her.

'I... it's nothing. She wouldn't help.'

'But?'

Silus clamped his mouth shut, then decided there was nothing wrong with opening up to his best friend.

'There is something about her. Something... captivating.'

He waited for Atius to laugh or make some sarcastic comment. But his friend just listened patiently.

'It doesn't matter, I suppose. Of all the ridiculous fantasies, a beautiful young Egyptian priestess.'

'Stranger things have happened. There is no harm in seeing her again anyway, is there? Maybe she will have heard something.'

'Maybe. I might visit again tomorrow. Purely for the mission, of course.'

'Of course.'

'Your turn then. Who is she?'

'It's not a she.'

'Oh?' Silus was surprised. He didn't care whether someone was into same gender relationships, though he shared the Roman prejudice against a male taking the submissive role, whether that involved being dominated by a woman or a man. He couldn't imagine Atius playing the submissive, but it was strange that he had never noticed him show any interest in men before. Maybe he hadn't met the right one.

'Do you want to tell me about him? What caught your eye?'

'It's not my eye, Silus. It's my heart.'

Silus blinked. 'Your heart? Already? It must be someone special.'

'It is, but not in the way you think.'

'I'm listening.'

Atius ran a hand over his face.

'Why is this so difficult to talk about?' he wondered out loud. Silus correctly figured that was a rhetorical question and kept quiet.

'Well,' continued Atius. 'You know I am a follower of the Christos.'

'I knew from when we first met in the prison cell of the Caledonian fort. You were singing hymns of praise to your God.'

'Yes. I was raised to believe that way by my mother. But I have never really thought about it before. Believing in Christos was just a part of me. An important part, but something like supporting a faction at the races. Christos and his father were my team, and for someone else it may be Mithras, or Isis, or Minerva.'

'Most worshippers of other gods don't see it like that. They may have a favourite, but they don't care who other people follow, as long as it doesn't inconvenience them. And they will often worship multiple gods themselves, depending on what they are praying for, or which deity the festival is in honour of.'

'I know. But we are commanded to worship only God and no other.'

'It's what has been getting your lot in trouble since the time of Nero. And the Jews before that, of course.'

'What I'm trying to say is that my faith was a part of me, but not a major part. Just something that was often at the back of my mind, unless I was actually in an act of worship or prayer, which honestly wasn't that often.'

It was true, Silus was much more likely to disturb Atius in the company of a woman than his god.

'So what has changed?'

'This man. Origen his name is. He spoke, and his words meant something. I don't know. It sounds stupid to say it out loud.'

'Go on,' encouraged Silus.

'It wasn't what he said, although his words were deep and important. It was how he said them. Like... like God was speaking to me directly.'

He flushed and stopped talking, looking down into his cup again.

Silus reached out and put a hand on his shoulder. 'Thanks for sharing with me, friend. It's hard to open up those inner feelings sometimes, isn't it? Whether it is about love, or loss, or something else.'

Atius looked up and smiled gratefully.

'You could do something to help me.'

'Name it.'

'Come with me to see him.'

Silus was taken aback. 'Atius, you know that I am no Christian. Why would you want me there? Are you trying to get him to convert me?'

'No, no, it's not that. It's just... I'm nervous.'

Silus let out a laugh, then choked it off when he saw how embarrassed his friend was.

'I know, mock me. I've faced down hordes of barbarians, been tortured, helped assassinate dangerous men. And I am scared of seeing a preacher.'

'Don't worry,' said Silus. 'Some men have a power that far exceeds their physical size or apparent position in life. If you want me to come with you, I will. Just don't expect me to leave singing hymns of praise to the Christos and all his angels.'

–

'We are here to see Phryne,' said Atius.

The porter, a bulky native Egyptian, looked them up and down disdainfully.

'The mistress is busy.'

'We came at the invite of... one who is a guest here.'

The porter looked half-interested, but said nothing. Atius wet his finger and drew the sign of the fish on the wall of the vestibule. The porter looked at the sign for a moment, drying and leaving a mark in the sheen of dust. He rubbed it away with the sleeve of his tunic hastily, then scowled at them.

'Wait here.'

'Is the worship of Christos so dangerous?' asked Silus.

'I have never really thought about it too much. There have been edicts and persecutions, but I have always kept my head down, and it never seemed to be relevant to me personally. But in Alexandria they had a big massacre of Christians not so long ago, so they are understandably still cautious.'

They waited at the entrance to the impressive villa in this beautiful area. They had walked past a theatre, baths and beautiful, well-maintained gardens that citizens could relax in. All the houses around the Park of Pan were large, ornate, and decorated with statues and friezes. This was definitely a well-to-do area, not quite on the same scale as the Palatine in Rome, but maybe one of the other more expensive areas, like parts of the Esquiline.

After a few moments, the porter returned and beckoned them through. They were shown into a room filled with plushly-upholstered furniture, and settled into softly cushioned chairs. Silus looked around at the wall paintings. The subjects were peaceful and neutral – the Nile and the sea, trees and birds. No religious symbols at all, be they Christian or any other god. Presumably another sign of caution – people of all religions, including Roman and Greek officials, would be received here, and they might object to overt signs of Christianity.

A slave girl, a dark-skinned Aethopian, came in and offered them water and some dates. Silus took them, but Atius waved them away. Silus realised his friend was too nervous to eat anything. They waited in silence, until eventually an elderly lady entered. Both of them stood straight way, inclining their heads in respectful greeting. The lady took each of their hands lightly, before indicating they should sit. She took a seat opposite them and accepted a cup of water from her slave.

'I am Phryne.' Her voice creaked with age, but was clear and firm. 'My porter said you wished to see me.'

'Yes,' said Atius. 'Well no. Not you exactly. Which isn't to say... I mean, I'm sure you are...'

'My friend was told by a man called Origen that he may find him here.'

'Is that so?' She tutted and shook her head. 'That young man is altogether too trusting. After what happened to his father, too.'

'I'm sorry,' said Atius. 'Silus, we should go, we are being a bother.'

Silus marvelled at this new, diffident Atius, and wondered if it was an improvement over the previous brash, sarcastic model. If it was a permanent change, he would miss his old friend.

'Nonsense,' said Phryne. 'I am just being a fussy old woman. Nyx, summon the house guest. I believe he is at prayer currently; make sure you wait until he has finished.'

'Yes, mistress,' said the slave, and left.

'So you two are fellow travellers on our path?' asked Phryne.

Silus waited for Atius to reply, but when he said nothing, Silus filled in. 'My friend Atius here is a follower of the Christos. I am here merely to keep him company.'

Phryne smiled, and her expression was kindly.

'Well, maybe you will see or hear something today that will affect your journey.'

'Maybe,' said Silus, unable to help himself smiling back.

Presently, Origen entered the room, with Brother John from the church service at his side. Silus rose to shake his hand, but Origen gestured to him to sit. Then, most bizarrely, Origen took a bowl of water from the slave, and knelt at Silus' feet. He unlaced his sandals and removed them one at a time. Silus looked across to Atius in bewilderment. His friend just shrugged.

Origen took a cloth and bathed the dust and sand off his feet. Profoundly weird as the situation was, Silus had to admit that having his feet cleansed was a pleasant sensation. When Origen had finished, he patted Silus' feet dry with a towel, then moved over to Atius and repeated the process. Atius stared down at the holy man in awe throughout.

When it was finished, Origen sat down and smiled at them both. Phryne bowed respectfully to Origen, ordered her slave to remove the bowl and said, 'I will leave you brothers to your discussions.' She shuffled out, her slave taking her arm to aid her.

'Iesous the Christos said, "Now that I, your Lord and Teacher, have washed your feet, you also should wash one another's feet. I have set you an example that you should do as I have done for you."'

Silus looked confused, but Atius and Brother John nodded their agreement.

'What is your name, brother?' Origen asked Silus.

'I am Silus.'

'A friend to Atius, our brother in Christos, am I right?'

'Yes, sir.'

'Please, do not call me sir. I am a servant of the Lord and of all who follow him or seek to know his word.'

'I'm here just to keep Atius company... brother.'

'I see.' Origen turned to Atius.

'And you, brother, what brings you to the home of our friend in Christos, the Lady Phryne?'

'You said I could visit, sir, brother. And I wanted to hear more of your words.'

'I am not going to preach to you. But I can listen. And we can converse about life and the ways of the Lord.'

'I would like that.'

Silus sighed inwardly. This was clearly going to be a fascinating morning.

'Before we begin to discuss religion and philosophy, may I ask a favour?' he asked Origen.

'If it's in my power.'

'I'm not sure if Atius has told you why we are in Alexandria.'

'He has not.'

'We are on a mission on behalf of Sextus Varius Marcellus, the new Governor of Numidia.'

Origen stiffened. 'You work for Rome?'

'We do.'

'I see. Brothers, I think maybe I am prevailing too much on the Lady Phryne's hospitality. She is a poor and simple old lady, and it is unfair of me to invite guests that become a burden to her. I think I should ask you to retire. Maybe we will meet another day...'

Silus thought that Phryne looked anything but poor and simple, and was sure she would resent the description. Still, he was pleased that they would now be able to leave without him having to find some other excuse.

But Atius spoke.

'A centurion came to the Lord and said, "Lord my servant is lying at home, and is paralysed and suffering."'

Origen looked at Atius through narrowed eyes, but said nothing. Atius looked upwards, seeming to search his memory. 'The Lord said he would go to the centurion's house to heal the servant, but the centurion said, "I am not worthy to have You under my roof. But say the word and I know my servant will be healed. For... for..."' Atius stumbled.

"'For I too am a man with authority,"' supplied Origen. "'With soldiers under me. I say to one go, and he goes, and to another come, and he comes, and to my servant do this, and he does it." And Iesous said, "I tell you in truth that I have met no one in Israel with this man's faith." And he said to the centurion, "Let it be done as you say." And the servant was healed.'

Atius nodded in thanks for the help with the story.

'Tell me why you mention this tale of the Lord.'

'My mother told me that story. She said it didn't matter if you were Jewish or Roman, or Celtiberian. All you needed was faith in the Lord.'

Origen pursed his lips, then bowed his head. 'You shame me.' He looked at Silus. 'Ask your favour.'

'We seek a missing child. The son of Marcellus. He was abducted and brought to Alexandria, and we followed the kidnapper here. But now we are at a loss. Alexandria is a big city. And a confusing one.'

Origen nodded. 'It's a noble mission. From the look of you both I expected that maybe... well, no matter. But how can I help you?'

Silus wasn't sure whether or not to be offended by the comment about their appearance. He ran a hand over his unruly beard, noted a few shallow scars under his fingertips, and thought that maybe he did have the countenance of a man of violence.

'I think you know many people in Alexandria. And people trust you. Or at least your people do. Have you heard anything about a missing child? An important one.'

'I'm sorry no, I haven't. But you are right, people do talk to me. How old is the child?'

'Around eight or nine years.'

'His name?'

'Varius Avitus Bassianus.'

'And is there anything else I should know about him?'

Silus hesitated. Avitus' religious beliefs wouldn't endear him to Origen, but it would be useful information for him nevertheless.

'He is a follower of an eastern god, called Elagabal. He is meant to be high priest one day.'

Origen frowned. Then he said, 'Well, there are a lot of false religions in Alexandria. And if he is just a boy, it is not his fault how he was raised. He has plenty of time to see the light and be brought to the true path.'

'So you will help us?'

'My power to assist you in this is very limited, but yes, I will find out what I can. There is a poor innocent child separated from his parents. And the Lord said that the Kingdom of Heaven belonged to such as these.'

'Thank you.'

'And now, to heavenly matters. Tell me, Atius. How good is God?'

'God is... great?'

'Of course. But how great?'

'I don't know.'

'That is the correct answer. I think deeply about these things and pray on them for guidance. I have proved on first principles that God is not corporeal. Therefore, God is incomprehensible, and incapable of being measured. So if we were to obtain any knowledge of God, from our own thoughts or reflections, God must by necessity, by necessity mark you, be many degrees greater than we could possibly imagine.'

Atius opened his mouth and closed it again, eyes narrowed as his brain tried to follow the argument. Silus didn't even attempt it.

'This type of argument is fascinating for philosophers and followers of your faith,' he said. 'But I think it is maybe too theoretical for a simple soldier like me. And I do have a mission – a boy to find. Atius, please, stay here and talk to the wise man. I will take my leave.'

'As you wish,' said Origen. 'It was a pleasure to meet you.'

Silus rose, bowed respectfully to Origen and patted Atius on the shoulder. His friend acknowledged him vaguely, then returned his attention to the holy man. Silus left the sounds of theological conversation behind him.

–

Silus found himself wandering through the streets of Alexandria on his own. He didn't know how he felt about his friend's newfound fascination with Christianity. He hoped it wouldn't interfere with either their friendship or their work. But Atius was his own man, and Silus had never tried to stop him doing anything before. Well, not unless it was really stupid.

The Park of Pan was a short distance from the Via Canopica, the huge tree-lined boulevard that bisected the city from east to west. It was impressive, on a level with the Via Sacra that ran through Rome. And as busy, with a constant heavy flow of traffic, as well as professionals and artisans of all types crying out for business. To the west he could see the huge marketplace, the agora, which was a rough equivalent to the Roman forum. He was tempted to go and lose himself among its attractions, and forget the rest of the world – his mission, his job, the alluring priestess.

But the job needed to be done, and he was making scant progress on tracking the boy down. For all he knew, he had already been smuggled out of the city, and was on his way to another place in the vast Roman Empire.

But he didn't think so. Why go to the trouble of making the long and hazardous journey from Syracuse to Alexandria when other cities were nearer? They had come to Alexandria for a reason.

Should he go and see Tekosis again? Maybe she would have some information for him. Or maybe he just wanted to see her, ridiculous as that was. He sighed, and set off east down the Via Canopica, admiring the awe-inspiring temples, monuments and other buildings. He would have to find someone who could tell him what they all were when he had time.

He passed the royal quarter, where the prefect's palace was, and turned north towards the Temple of Isis Lochias. His heart started to beat a little faster in his chest. He wasn't sure if it was from nervousness or excitement. He swallowed the fluttering sensation in his stomach down as he approached the temple.

A woman ran out of the temple, screaming, the hem of her tunic flapping around her knees in the breeze she made from her flight. Silus stopped in surprise as she fled in his direction. She saw him, screamed again, and veered off.

What was going on?

Now a man ran out, a temple servant with a shaven head and a long tunic.

'Help!' he cried. 'Thieves.'

Silus caught him by the arm as he passed by, pulled him up short.

'What is happening?'

'Men in the temple. Thieves, murderers. I must get help.' He ripped himself free and hurried off.

Silus drew his sword and ran.

The temple was dark inside, and it took a moment for his vision to adjust. Then he saw two burly men. One grabbed a marble statue of a cat and dashed it to the ground. It was solid, so it didn't shatter, but the head broke off and rolled away. He laughed.

The other had a priest by throat, pressed up against a wall, and was pounding his fist into his face. Blood spurted from the bald man's nose, and he struggled feebly against his attacker.

Then, before Silus could react, he drew a blade from his belt and thrust it up under the priest's ribs.

Silus flew into motion. With the priest still sliding slowly down the wall, clutching at his killer, Silus hit the attacker in the back with his shoulder, smashing his face into the wall. The man crumpled to the floor, stuporous.

The other attacker recovered after a moment's shocked immobility. He took the cat's head and hurled it at Silus. Silus ducked to his left, and the head smashed against the brickwork. The attacker drew an axe and said something that sounded like an Egyptian curse. He charged at Silus, and Silus raised his sword to block the attempt to hack at his head. He turned the blow away and downwards, then raised his sword to counterattack.

The man was not a skilled fighter, but he was big and aggressive. He waved his axe left and right at waist height, making Silus jump backwards, once, twice.

It was nicely predictable. On the third swing, Silus stepped outside the arc and thrust his sword into the man's guts. He twisted and pulled his weapon free. The Egyptian grabbed at the hole in his abdomen, which was leaking large quantities of blood and foetid-smelling brown liquid. Then he toppled forward.

Now the noise of combat had died down, he heard more commotion from further inside the temple. A man yelled, another laughed, and then a woman screamed, high-pitched and despairing. Silus ran into the large meeting room that was adjacent to Tekosis' chambers.

The noise was not coming from the chambers, but from the sanctuary. The great wooden door was hanging wide open. Silus sprinted through.

Three men were inside. One held the golden statue of Isis aloft in both hands, a look of wonder on his face. The other two held Tekosis down on the altar. Her robe had been torn apart, and her lip was cut and bleeding. She struggled and wept as one of her attackers positioned himself between her legs, leaning forward to pin her down with one hand on an exposed breast.

With a cry of rage, Silus gripped his sword with two hands and swung with all his strength. The carefully maintained edge cleaved straight through the neck of Tekosis' attacker. His head parted from his body, and tumbled sideways through the air, rotating as it went, to land on the floor with a heavy thump. The decapitated corpse toppled forward onto Tekosis, pumping blood from the meaty wound over her face and body.

Tekosis screamed hysterically, and the man on the far side of the altar who had been holding her shoulders stared in disbelief. His paralysis was fatal. Silus leapt onto the altar, stood towering above the man, sword still in a double-handed grip. The man let go of Tekosis and raised his hands in defence.

He might as well have been holding his hands up against a collapsing tower. Silus thrust down with all his strength and all his weight. The sword entered behind the man's collarbone, and went deep down into his chest, lacerating heart and lungs. The killing blow of a gladiator. He fell backwards with barely a sound, dragging the sword out of Silus' hands.

Silus whirled, aware that there was a third attacker, and he was suddenly unarmed. But the third man was gone, and he had taken the gold statue with him.

Silus briefly considered giving pursuit. But Tekosis was still struggling to push the dead body off her chest, sobbing uncontrollably. Silus jumped down from the altar, grabbed the body by the collar of its tunic and hurled it to one side. Tekosis threw herself off the altar, landing on her backside on the floor, and scuffled backwards away from Silus until her back hit the wall.

She sat there, gasping and choking on her sobs, one hand extended palm out to Silus, fending him away, the other hand clutching her torn robe closed. Silus squatted down on his haunches a respectful, safe distance away.

'Tekosis,' he said quietly. 'It's me. Silus. Do you remember me?'

She stared at him for a moment, then put her hand to her mouth. Unable to stop the reflex, she leaned to one side and vomited, her body convulsing heave after heave as she emptied her stomach contents. When she was done, she looked up at Silus in misery. Strands of saliva and vomit hung from her mouth. Her white robe had turned as red as a butcher's apron. Tear tracks stained her cheeks.

Silus looked around him, found a relatively unbloodied part of one of the attacker's tunics, and ripped free a cloth. He moved towards Tekosis and she shrank back further against the wall. He made a soothing noise, as if he was talking calmly to a frightened animal. He spat on the cloth, then reached out and wiped her face in long slow strokes, cleaning away the blood spatters and tears and vomitus.

When she was a little cleaner, he held a hand out to her. She hesitated, then took it, and he helped her to her feet. She tried to push him away, then her knees gave way, and he caught her, supporting her weight until she found her strength again. Slowly he helped her out of the sacrarium. As she walked through to her chambers, she took in the destruction and the dead bodies of the priest and his killers. Once she was inside, he stepped out, shut the door, and went to inspect the surviving assailant. He was breathing noisily through his smashed nose, conscious but only just. Silus tore his tunic into strips and twisted them together to form two ropes with which he bound him hand and foot. Then he went to retrieve his sword. He heaved it out of the chest of the dead man and cleaned it thoroughly on the man's clothing. When he was satisfied it was spotless, he sheathed it and stood outside the closed chamber door, his arms crossed.

From inside came little sounds, splashing water, scrubbing, soft crying. After a long while, Silus knocked tentatively on the door. He was rewarded by a scream.

'I'm sorry. I didn't mean to scare you. I just wanted to check all is well.'

For a moment there was silence – no movement, no words. Then the door swung open.

Silus looked inside. Tekosis was standing in the middle of the room. Her long hair was wet. Her face was clean. She wore a clean robe, pristine white. She looked incredibly vulnerable, and incredibly beautiful, and Silus' heart caught in his throat in wonder and pity.

She remained still for an extended moment. Then she took two rapid steps forward and clutched him, crying into his shoulder. He hesitated, then wrapped his arms around her and held her close until her sobs subsided.

When she was cried empty, he carefully released her. She stepped back and wiped her tears and nose.

'Thank you, Silus. You saved me from…' She couldn't finish the sentence. Silus just nodded.

'Who were they?' he asked.

'Native Egyptians. Hired thugs who live in the countryside. Someone paid them to come here and do this.'

'Who would do that?'

'The Jews.' She spat on the floor. 'They hate other religions. They have their one god, and no one but Jews are allowed to worship him, but neither should they worship anyone else because in their eyes all other gods are false.'

'Are there many Jews in the city?'

'Fewer than there once were, praise be to Isis. Many were killed when they rebelled a hundred years ago. They destroyed and desecrated many temples, the Serapeum, the Nemeseion, temples to Greek and Roman and Egyptian gods. They damaged my own temple, this Temple of Isis Lochias. And for it, they were punished. The Greeks and Alexandrians slaughtered them, once the Romans had regained control. But they have crept back into the city and grown in number since then. Even though they keep their heads down and don't take an active part in city life now, it is still rumoured that they murder non-Jews, desecrate our temples, and steal our babies for their rituals. They should all be thrown to the beasts.'

Silus listened to this diatribe in shocked silence. He was aware that Jews were not well-liked throughout the Empire, but there had been none where he grew up, and he wasn't sure if he had ever met one. Some of the foreign soldiers in the auxiliaries in Britannia may have been Jewish, but they were all easterners to him and he hadn't enquired that closely.

The Romans were intrinsically xenophobic, with no respect for other cultures or peoples. But he hadn't come across such naked hatred for other inhabitants of the Empire before. External enemies, yes, but not fellow citizens and residents. He wondered why the Jews were tolerated at all if they were so evil.

'I think you should drink some wine.'

Silus went to the side table from where Tekosis had poured him wine before. There was still some in a jug, and he poured a generous quantity into a cup and handed it to her. She drank, and he watched her trembling hands as she tried not to spill any.

There was a knock on the door.

'Priestess? Priestess!'

Silus opened the door to come face to face with a Roman legionary, sword drawn. Behind him, three others were looking around at the death and destruction within the temple.

'Who are you?' barked the legionary, pointing his sword towards Silus' throat. 'What are you doing here?'

'I am Centurion Silus,' said Silus calmly. 'Of the Arcani. Working for Governor Sextus Varius Marcellus.'

'Oh,' said the legionary. He dropped his sword and saluted. 'Sorry, sir. What happened?'

'I'm trying to find that out myself. The priestess has been assaulted and a priest has been killed. There has been a theft, too.'

'Theft?' asked Tekosis, confused. Silus realised that in her fear and distress, she hadn't noticed that the statue of Isis had been taken.

'The big gold figurine of your goddess,' said Silus. 'The last surviving attacker took it and fled.'

'Oh no.' Tekosis held her hand to her chest and paled even more than Silus thought was possible.

'Was it very valuable?' he asked.

'Its value doesn't matter,' she snapped. 'It is my goddess, the personification of her here on earth. It is blessed and sacred. And now the Jews have it, and they will do unholy things to it.'

She put her face in her hands and began to sob again.

'The Jews?' asked the legionary, confused.

'She believes the Jews are behind the attack.'

'Probably right,' commented the legionary. 'Nasty, untrustworthy bunch.'

'There is no evidence it was them.'

The legionary shrugged non-committally.

Tekosis clutched Silus' tunic. 'Silus. Will you find it for me? Please? Bring back our sacred statue. Or the temple will be desecrated.'

Silus hesitated. 'Legionary, can you give us some privacy for a moment? And can a couple of your men take the man I tied up to a cell at the royal palace so I can question him later?'

'Of course, sir.' The legionary left the room and closed the door behind him. Tekosis looked at Silus questioningly. Silus thought for a moment, unsure how to put into words his thoughts, or whether he even should. Tekosis filled the silence.

'You saved my life.'

'Maybe. They may not have killed you.'

'Why not? If they were prepared to desecrate a priestess, why would they stop at killing her? They killed my fellow priest.'

Silus acknowledged her point with an inclination of his head.

'What did you want to say to me, Silus? Will you help me?'

Silus' mouth worked as he formulated the words.

'Yesterday, I asked you for help.'

Tekosis looked at him steadily, face expressionless. Silus continued.

'You said it was none of your business and you weren't interested.'

'I didn't use those words.'

Silus searched his memory. 'You said you belong to Isis, and the goddess has no interest in the fate of a Roman boy.'

'Yes. Something like that.'

'So tell me, why should I, and the all-powerful Emperor of Rome whom I serve, have any interest in the fate of the religious symbols of your goddess?'

Fury flashed in Tekosis' eyes. But it didn't last. Too much fear and emotion had gone through her in the last hour to sustain anything as powerful as anger. Her shoulders slumped.

'Won't you do it for me?'

'Why do you need me? I'm not a native, I don't know my way around Alexandria.'

'I know of the Arcani. I know your reputation. I know what you do. I don't have men working for me who could do this on my behalf. And as you have said, of what interest would it be to the Roman authorities?'

Silus cocked his head on one side. 'And what will be in it for me?'

Tekosis flushed and pulled her robe tighter around her.

'Of what help will this be to my mission?' he clarified.

'Oh.' She thought for a moment. 'Listen. I have no men, no network of spies gathering intelligence on my behalf, no assassins who work for me. But I do know people in this city. People who respect me. I can ask questions on your behalf. Words in the right ears. I can't guarantee anything. But I can do what I can.'

'A trade then. My help for yours.'

'If that's what it takes to get your help, then yes.'

Silus nodded and extended his hand. 'We have a deal. I will look for your goddess. You will look for my missing boy.'

Tekosis shook his hand, and he noticed it had regained some strength.

Silus looked around. Tekosis' private chambers had not been damaged, but he knew the rest of the temple had taken a beating. 'Do you live here all the time?'

'Yes.'

'Would you like me to arrange somewhere else for you to stay? Until the place is repaired?'

Tekosis smiled. 'I will not be driven out of my home and my holy temple. I will stay here.'

'Very well. I will go and talk to the attacker who survived. And I'll make sure the legionaries guard the temple, at least for now. I'll come back when I have more to tell.'

'Thank you. And I hope I have something for you then as well. And Silus. Keep the theft secret. If it gets out that someone has stolen the sacred statue, the city will explode. That will help no one. I will keep the sacrarium locked, and say I am rededicating it.'

Silus nodded. 'I'll tell the legionaries to keep it to themselves too. They won't want to see a riot either, as it would be them that would have to deal with it.'

Tekosis gave a half-smile. 'Thank you, Silus. For all of it.' She took his hand and squeezed it gently, and all the images of snot and tears and vomit and blood and angry words vanished from his mind.

Chapter Nine

The basement of the royal palace had a suitably dingy and smelly cell. The Egyptian prisoner was chained by manacles to the wall, and was now fully conscious, though his face was a mess where it had impacted the masonry in the temple. The legionary closed the door behind them, muttering that he didn't know why they were bothering to interrogate the man when everyone knew it was the Jews. Silus and Atius were left alone with the prisoner. Silus stood a foot in front of the man, who let out a long stream of Egyptian which Silus presumed was not complimentary. With index finger extended, he poked the Egyptian hard in the eye.

He screamed, rattled his manacles, tried to put his hand to his eye in vain, and then let out another stream of curses. Silus held up his finger again, and he twisted his head away. Atius took hold of his chin in a firm grip and turned his face back towards Silus.

'I presume you speak Greek.'

Another stream of Egyptian expletives. Silus jabbed him hard in the eye again, evoking another scream.

'Yes, yes, I speak Greek,' said the Egyptian.

'Progress,' commented Atius.

'What's your name?' asked Silus.

'Ankhtakelot.'

'You were hired, weren't you, Ankhtakelot?' asked Silus. 'You didn't raid the sacred Temple of Isis just for fun, or for a valuable statue that you would never be able to sell.'

The man grunted and Silus wiggled his finger.

'Yes, we were hired.'

'Good. By whom?'

The Egyptian clamped his mouth shut.

'There are worse torture instruments than a finger, you know,' said Silus.

'What will happen to me?'

Silus exchanged glances with Atius. 'You killed a priest. What do you think should happen to you?'

'If you want to find out where the stolen statue is, or who was behind it, then you should let me go.'

'We could just torture it out of you. You would tell us eventually, in return for a quick death.'

Ankhtakelot started to shake, his bravado evaporating.

'I will tell you everything. Just let me go.'

Silus turned to Atius, and covered his mouth with one hand to whisper in Latin, 'How fanatical do you think these guys are?'

'I have no idea,' Atius whispered back. 'We don't know why he has done this. You are thinking he might give us false information under torture, and then by the time we find out we have already killed him?'

'Maybe.'

Silus turned back to the Egyptian. 'Fine, here's the deal. Tell us all you know. We will check it out. If you are telling the truth, we will see what we can do about getting you a lenient sentence.'

The Egyptian considered, but he knew this was a generous offer.

'A man came to our village. We work in the fields on the banks of the Nile, near the city of Dmi-n-Hr. The Greeks call it Hermopolis Mikra. He said he would pay us well if we raided a temple and stole an artefact for him. The inundation was below expectations last year; times are hard.'

'Inundation?'

The man looked at Silus and Atius in confusion. 'The inundation of the Nile? You don't know about it?'

Silus shrugged.

'It's the most important thing that happens in Egypt every year. If the Nile floods too much we drown, too little and we starve. Just right, and everything is good. Why are we talking about this?'

'You brought it up.'

'Look, we were hired to steal a statue, and do some damage while we were there. That money will allow our village to feed itself for a year.'

'Your village survives, though a priest dies and a priestess gets raped.'

'Raped? I didn't...'

'One of your friends did. Or tried. But he is dead now.'

The prisoner looked down, at least a little shamefaced.

'Now, tell us who it was that hired you.'

'I don't know him.'

'Was he Jewish?' asked Atius.

'I couldn't tell.'

'His accent, his appearance? Did he look or sound Jewish?'

'I didn't speak to him!'

'Then who did?'

'Menkheperresenb!'

'What? Is that a curse?'

'Menkheperresenb is my brother!'

Shit. This one knew nothing.

'Where is your brother?' asked Silus tentatively, fearing that he had put his blade through the one who could help them get to the bottom of the raid.

'He fled. With the statue. He must have thought I was dead, or he would never have left me.'

Silus grunted. Greed and fear were powerful enough emotions on their own. Together, he was sure they could lead a man to abandon his own brother, regardless of whether he thought he was alive or dead.

'So he will have returned to your village?'

'Yes, that was the plan. Then the man who hired us was going to come to the village five days after the raid, to collect the statue and pay us.'

Now they were making progress. They just had to get to the village, beat up this man's brother, this Menkhythingy — he would have to write that down — and then wait for the man who had hired them to turn up. He might need some extra help if they were going to subdue a whole village though. It was time to report to Marcellus in any case.

'Tell us how to reach your village.'

—

'What's going on, Silus?' asked Marcellus. His voice was strained and there were dark rings around his eyes. His beard was unkempt, his hair messy and he didn't look like he had had much sleep.

'Sir, we need some legionaries.'

'You've found him?'

The hope in Marcellus' voice was heartbreaking, and it was worse when Silus had to disabuse him.

'No, sir.'

'But you have a lead?'

'Not exactly, sir.'

'Damnit, Silus, have you made any progress at all?'

'I don't know why you put any faith in these thugs,' said Soaemias, seated in a plush chair and being attended by her ornatrix, who was making adjustments to her hairstyle. 'Send them back to Rome. They are doing more harm than good here.'

Marcellus threw her an annoyed glance, but didn't contradict her. At least she wasn't calling for Silus' execution this time.

'Explain yourself, Silus.'

'Sir, Alexandria is a nightmare. All these factions that hate each other. It's like the houses in the poorest parts of Rome, ready to go up in a fire that would consume the city if someone applies a spark.'

'It's not like you to offer an excuse for failure, Silus,' said Marcellus.

'It's not an excuse, sir. I am telling you the reality. And I haven't failed.' At least not yet, Silus thought.

'Fine. Tell me everything.'

Silus took a deep breath and let it out slowly.

'I met a woman.'

Marcellus rolled his eyes, but didn't interrupt.

'The priestess of Isis. The one who helped us when Atius had his little... mishap.'

'What about her?'

'I went to see her, to see if she would help us.'

'How could she do that?'

'The priests and priestesses hear everything, eventually. She could find out a lot for us, if she was so minded.'

'And is she so minded?'

'Not at first. But then I came to her aid when her temple was attacked. And she has agreed to help me now. But only if I do something for her in return.'

'Go on.'

'I am to recover a stolen religious artefact, and find out who was behind the attack.'

'It was probably the Jews,' said Marcellus. 'But how are you going to find the artefact?'

'I have tracked it down to a village south of Alexandria, on the banks of the Nile. If I travel there in time, with a small force of men, we can capture the one who ordered the attack.'

'This just seems like an unnecessary delay.'

'Sir, if the mob find out this statue is missing, there will be a riot.'

'I don't care if Alexandria falls into the sea! I just want my son back!' Marcellus' voice was rising, and Silus tried to keep his tone calm.

'And what if your son is caught up in a riot? Trapped in a burning building, or trampled by an angry mob?'

Marcellus subsided.

'Besides, this is how we find your son. It enables us to get assistance from someone much better connected than the prefect, or the Greek elites who run this place without any idea what is actually happening in their own city.'

'This is ridiculous,' said Soaemias. 'Marcellus, I can't believe you are even listening to this nonsense. Have these idiots thrown out.'

'And what is your plan to find our son, dear?'

'We round up some Jews and some followers of Christos and execute them, then threaten to kill more until our son is produced.'

Silus clenched his jaw but said nothing. He could feel Atius tensing beside him, and he reached out and lightly touched his arm, mentally urging restraint.

'I have to say, Silus, your way seems a bit of a long shot.'

'At the moment, sir, I believe it is our best chance. And it has the double benefit of keeping the city pacified. Whereas the mistress's plan here would achieve the exact opposite.'

Marcellus hesitated, but before could speak, Silus said urgently, 'Give us the legionaries, sir. We will sail down the Nile tomorrow, sort this matter out, then come back and find your boy. And if we don't, your wife's plan is still an option.'

'Very well. But if my son is not found soon, then people will start to die, and to Hades with the consequences.'

'Yes, sir.'

—

The day after she was assaulted, it was as if the event had never occurred, thought Silus. At least outwardly. Tekosis was immaculately dressed and adorned, make-up covered her bruises, and her demeanour was serene. If he looked closely, he could see the swelling around her cut lip, but a casual observer wouldn't be able to tell.

He watched her for a moment. She knelt on a cushion in the main hall before a small altar. A white dove sat patiently in a gold cage, cocking its head curiously. She lifted her arms to the heavens and intoned a prayer. A number of worshippers, also kneeling, gave the required response. She opened the cage, reached in and took out the bird. She soothed it gently with strokes of her fingertips, and it remained calm, not attempting to flap.

With one smooth action she picked up a sharp curved knife from the altar and slit the bird's throat, then held it over a silver bowl. Now it struggled and jerked, but she continued to soothe it until it was still, head flopped over to one side. She laid it respectfully on the altar and then picked up the bowl with both hands. She lifted it to her lips, tilted her head back, and took a deep sip, then replaced it.

'We give thanks to you, great goddess. Accept this humble sacrifice as a sign of our devotion.'

She turned to the congregation.

'The blessings of the goddess be with you all.'

The worshippers murmured their response. 'Blessings of the goddess.' Then they slowly rose to their feet and filed out. Now Tekosis noticed Silus, standing at the back, and she smiled and beckoned him over.

He approached her, still a little nervous in her presence. She held out both hands and he took them, and impulsively placed a kiss on one hand. She giggled, a tinkling little laugh, and then pulled her hands back.

'How are you?' he asked with genuine concern.

'The goddess heals, Silus. I am as new.'

He knew that was not true – the slight swelling on her lip gave that away. But he was pleased she seemed in good spirits after the traumatic event. He knew how badly that sort of violation, or attempted violation, could affect a woman. He also knew that those hurts were not always visible on the surface, and he wondered how she really was. But he didn't know her well enough to question further.

'I have some news for you. The men who attacked you were from a village near Hermopolis Mikra.'

'We call it Dmi-n-Hr,' corrected Tekosis.

'Yes. There. They were paid by someone to steal the statue and desecrate the temple.'

Her face twisted in anger. 'The Jews,' she said. 'I knew it.'

'The man who hired them is going to collect the statue from their village in a couple of days. The governor has given me some men, and we are going to travel there, recover the statue and apprehend whoever was behind all this. Then we will find out for sure.'

Tekosis smiled, stepped forward and threw her arms around him. She planted a soft kiss on his cheek, then stepped back.

'Thank you, Silus,' she said. 'You don't know how important this is for me. And for the city.'

'It's a bargain, remember,' said Silus, his face tingling from where her lips touched. 'While I am gone, you will do your best to find the boy.'

'Yes, yes,' she said. 'I will try. It's all I can promise.'

Silus nodded.

'When do you depart?'

'We don't want to arrive too early, or we will have to keep the villagers subdued for a long time. We will sail tomorrow morning.'

'And until then?'

Silus shrugged.

'Then why don't you have a proper look around our beautiful city?'

'It sounds like a good idea, but I wouldn't know where to start.'

'Would you like a guide?'

'Well, I suppose. Do you know where I could find one?'

She laughed again.

'I'm offering my services, silly.'

'Oh. Well. That is very kind. If you don't have duties here?'

'My work is done for the day. Let's go.'

—

Silus' legs ached. Alexandria was a big city, and he felt like he had walked every inch of it, although he knew in reality he had barely scratched the surface. She had taken him to the Mouseion and Great Library, and they had walked through the vast campus with its gardens with colonnaded walkways, and sat on one of the exedra, the semi-circular seats that broke the line of columns intermittently. From there they watched the earnest, serious scholars wander past, deep in conversation with each other, or musing alone, silently, or often in loud voices. Tekosis had commented how self-absorbed they were, how detached from the real world, and Silus was inclined to agree.

She had shown him around the library, with its huge numbers of scrolls of almost all the books that had ever been written. She had told him how the original rulers of Alexandria, the Ptolemies, had ordered all ships that came to the busy harbour searched for books, which were confiscated and copied before being returned. Although there had been a fire in Caesar's time, most of the library had survived, and the vast amount of information contained here was unimaginable to Silus.

Now they were at a lecture, sitting at the back, listening to a long-haired philosopher declaiming loudly to the audience of rapt students. The subject was Aristotelian metaphysics, something about existence, and how things can continue to exist when they change. It reminded Silus of something his father had told him. He had broken an axe head chopping wood and had to buy a new one; the next week he had broken the shaft, and had to carve himself a new one. His father had asked Silus whether it was still the same axe, a question which had kept his boyhood self up late at night trying to work it out.

Thinking about an axe brought back another memory, sudden and unwelcome. The weight of the tool in his hands, covered in blood, Papinianus groaning at his feet.

Tekosis noticed the sudden change in his demeanour, took him by the hand and led him out of the lecture.

'Are you well? I know it was a little boring.'

He smiled weakly. 'Philosophy makes my head ache.'

'You aren't religious, and you aren't philosophical. What are you, Silus?'

'I like to think I'm practical.'

Tekosis nodded. 'I believe you are. Would you like to see something else?'

The next stop was the tomb of Alexander the Great. Silus couldn't help but be impressed at the thought that the greatest general the world had ever known was buried in a crystal tomb beneath this little pyramid. But the throng crowded around the mausoleum, showing respect, worshipping or just gawking, and they couldn't get near.

So Tekosis took him to the Serapeum in the south-west. This enormous structure, situated on a ridge that ran along the south of the city, was visible from most places in Alexandria. When they got close, Silus realised that like the Mouseion, this was also a complex of buildings – a library, lecture halls and shrines to various gods. The complex consisted of large arches, with huge windows situated above each arch. Inside were various chambers, courtyards and chapels. Tekosis took him first to the subsidiary shrine of Isis, where she paid her respects to the high priest of that temple.

The Temple of Serapis itself was enormous, surrounded by gigantic marble columns. When they walked inside, the first thing that demanded attention was a titanic statue of Serapis.

The god's arms were outstretched, and they were so long they touched the walls of the temple to Silus' left and right.

Tekosis took Silus by the hand and led him to a corner.

'Look at this.'

Silus frowned, his eyes adjusting to the gloomy light inside the temple. There was an odd-looking contraption, with a reservoir, and some strange mechanical collection of gears and levers.

'Do you have an obol?'

Silus searched through his purse and pulled out one of the small silver coins they used for currency in the Greek-speaking half of the Empire. He handed it to her, and she inserted it into the machine. She held out a clay vessel beneath a spout. There was a metallic whir, and water poured out into the vessel, continuing until it was three-quarters full. Then the flow stopped with an abrupt click.

'What just happened?' asked Silus, confused.

'Well, some see it as a miracle. The reality is that this machine was invented by a great inventor called Hero. It dispenses a measured amount of holy water when you insert a coin. It saves the priests from the boring job.'

She splashed the water over her face and neck, then did the same for Silus.

'The blessings of Isis and Serapis be upon you. Now you are purified, let me show you some more wonders.'

She showed him a metallic, moving piece of work that she said represented the position of the earth at the centre of the universe, a fountain which flowed continually, powered, so she said, by the light of the sun, a tableau of Hercules and a dragon which, when a stone was lifted, caused Hercules to shoot the dragon with an arrow, the dragon emitting a hissing noise. There was even a model of a person who, when a lever was pulled, blew air through a trumpet to make a noise.

Tekosis laughed at Silus' amazed reaction. He had never seen anything like it.

'How is all this possible?'

'Silus, Alexandria is the seat of learning. More than Athens or Rome. We have had the greatest philosophers and the greatest inventors, all drawn here by the library and the Mouseion. The city may not be in its golden age any more, but I believe that time will come again.'

'How?'

She reached out and touched his face. 'All things are possible to the gods of the city. Isis and Serapis will protect and nurture us, as they always have.'

The touch of her fingers was gentle, and he let out an involuntary sigh.

'Will you take me back to my temple?' she asked.

'Of course.'

He held out his arm, and she took it, and they walked together, making light conversation, Tekosis pointing out land-marks and sights, Silus asking interested questions.

Night was falling as they reached the Temple of Isis Lochias. The main room was quiet, just two or three devoted worshippers. Silus eyed them suspiciously, but decided the two old women and the small child were no threat. He accompanied Tekosis to her chamber doors.

'Good night, then.'

She stepped forward and kissed him lightly on the lips. He looked at her in confusion. She stroked his beard with her fingertips, then circled her arms around his neck and kissed him again, more deeply this time. He leaned into the kiss. She tasted of spice, and smelt of strong but not overpowering perfume. Her body was warm, and felt slight, fragile in his arms. He worried he would crush her if he squeezed too tight.

When the kiss broke, he looked deeply into her eyes.

'I don't understand. You're a priestess.'

That tinkling laugh again. 'Silus, you are funny. I'm not a Vestal Virgin. Isis, the Queen of Heaven, the Maker of Sunrise, is the goddess of love and fertility. She is the wife of Osiris and the mother of Horus. Can such a one be chaste?'

'Well, no...'

'And the goddess lives through me. She is inside me. Should I insult her by behaving in a way alien to her nature?'

'Definitely not,' said Silus, warming to the line of reasoning.

She took his hand and drew him into her chambers. It was dim, an oil lamp burning scented oil on a table. She reached up and undid a brooch, and with a shrug of her shoulders, her dress fell to the floor. He gasped as he saw her naked body in silhouette, slim and petite. She pulled him to her, stepping slowly backwards until her calves were against her bed. She lay back on the bed and looked up at him. He hesitated. Swallowed. Then he fell into her, and let her envelope him.

Chapter Ten

Silus was glad when the river journey ended. Not because he had been on a boat, although that was usually unpleasant for him. But sailing the Nile and sailing the Mare Nostrum in midwinter were as far apart as cuddling and gladiatorial combat. In fact, the trip down the river had been interesting. Their captain had been a good guide, explaining to them the cycles of the Nile. In Egypt, three seasons mattered, and they weren't the ones that the rest of the world used. The inundation of the Nile, when the great river flooded its banks and irrigated the lands with water and rich soil, occurred from July to November. When the waters receded, the sowing began, which lasted until April or May. Then it was time to harvest before the next inundation, as well as to repair the dykes and clear the irrigation canals of debris. On this cycle depended not only the prosperity of Egypt, but the ability to feed Rome itself. The population gave many offerings to the Nile god Hapi, so that the inundation would be sufficient to properly irrigate the lands, while not being so extreme as to destroy the dykes and the homes of the populace.

The boat captain was also careful to pay appropriate respect to Hapi, on whom his life and livelihood depended. He pointed out the hippopotami to Silus and Atius, strange animals like enormous pigs that looked peaceable as they munched on river plants. The captain informed them that they killed more people in Egypt than any other animal, would happily overturn a boat, and despite their rotund appearance, could outrun a human on land.

They also saw some real examples of those strange creatures that they had seen pictured on wall paintings in Alexandria – long, green, scaly, long-mouthed creatures called crocodiles, which were also deadly. But both creatures were holy and were treated with reverence by the captain and his crew.

Silus had quite enjoyed the gentle rocking of the boat as it sailed upstream southwards, watching the farm workers on the shores, feeling the gentle breeze on his skin, mild despite the time of year. He had thought of the temperature in northern Britannia and Caledonia at this time of year and smiled that he was avoiding it.

So no, it was not the experience of being on the boat that had so relieved him when they docked at their destination just north of Hermopolis Mikra and disembarked. It was the fact that he would no longer be cooped up on the ship with Atius, and his smug, knowing smile.

When they had embarked in Alexandria, Atius had casually asked Silus where he had stayed the previous night, as he hadn't returned to the palace. When Silus had reddened, he had pushed harder, until Silus had confessed he had spent the night with the priestess.

'I'm so proud of you. My mate has finally got his end away. And not just with anyone. With a priestess, no less.'

Comments of this sort had continued for the entire trip, to the amusement of the legionaries that had been assigned to them, and to Silus' rising irritation.

When they were ashore, Atius said, 'Are you sure you don't want to return to Alexandria with the boat? We can handle things here. I don't want you to pine for your new love.'

'Jupiter's cock, Atius, won't you give it a rest? She is not my new love. It was a one-off. I'm sure she won't be interested in doing it again.'

'Were you a bit crap? Out of practice?'

'Actually I was fucking good, not that it's any of your business. Now can we drop this?'

In fact, Tekosis had hardly been off Silus' mind from the moment he had left her the morning after their night of passion. His thoughts were full of memories of the smell of her perfume on her skin, the sounds of her moans, the feel of her smooth body...

Damnit, he needed to concentrate now.

The captain gave them directions to the village, a half hour's march away. He had suggested they could get there quicker if they rode camels, but Silus had taken one look at the unreliable-looking, oddly-shaped animals and decided they would be better on foot. So they set off along a dusty road, marching past workers who put down their shovels and hoes to watch the soldiers.

The directions were accurate and they reached the collection of small houses uneventfully. The first thing that Silus noticed was that the roofs were all flat. He supposed that was because there was no rain, and a sloped roof was unnecessary, but it gave the place a strange, exotic appearance. The walls of the buildings were made with mud brick and the roofs were palm logs layered with reeds and topped with hardened mud.

Although too small to call itself a town, the village was not tiny, and a sizeable group of people had gathered by the time they marched into the central square. Silus indicated for the four legionaries accompanying them to halt, which they did in good discipline, remaining in formation and at attention. Silus waited, and after a few moments, an old man stepped forward.

He had long white hair, a receding forehead, and a long beard hanging down from his chin while his cheeks were clean shaven.

'I am Amenisenb, elder of this village.' He spoke heavily accented Greek. 'May I know your name?'

'I am Centurion Gaius Sergius Silus, working for the new Governor of Numidia, Sextus Varius Marcellus.'

Amenisenb looked him up and down. Silus wondered what impression he gave, armed but unarmoured and not wearing any uniform. But with four legionaries in full battle dress behind him, he figured it didn't really matter.

'And what brings you to our village, Centurion Silus? We have paid our taxes.'

Silus scanned the faces of the villagers. The sun was behind the soldiers, so the locals, men, women and a good number of children, squinted at them. He read some concern there, but it was only the normal level of anxiety that a group of armed men, official or not, would instil. Largely they seemed relaxed, not worried that they were about to be arrested or attacked. So it seemed that the village as a whole was not complicit in the raid. That was good. He didn't want to think about what would happen if retribution for the desecration was brought down upon these simple families.

'We are here to find a man named Menkheperresenb.' He had practised the name, repeating it aloud a number of times while on the trip down, and he could see from the face of the elder that he pronounced it correctly.

'He is not here,' said Amenisenb.

'But this is his home?'

Amenisenb hesitated, glanced at the soldiers, then nodded.

'When did you see him last?'

'Not for some time.'

'Hours? Years?'

'Many weeks,' said Amenisenb.

Silus nodded to Atius. Atius drew his sword in a smooth motion and pointed it at the elder's throat, so the tip pushed his chin up, indenting the skin.

'It's not a good idea to lie to me,' said Silus. 'I see a lot of families here. Women and children. Don't endanger them by harbouring one criminal.'

Amenisenb pressed his lips together.

Silus shook his head and sighed.

'Kill him,' he said. Atius drew his sword back. Amenisenb closed his eyes, but did not shy away.

'Wait!' A woman's voice. An elderly woman pushed her way through the crowd. 'Please, don't kill my husband. I will tell you what you need to know.'

'Mukarramma, no,' said Amenisenb.

'I won't let them hurt you, husband,' said Mukarrama. She spoke to Silus directly. 'Ask your questions.'

Silus put out a hand to restrain Atius. 'Tell me, lady, when was Menkheperresenb last in this village?'

'He was here today. He went to the city to buy some new clothes. He said he had money coming to him soon.'

'Yes, he would think that. He returned recently from a journey to Alexandria?'

'He did.'

'Mukarramma, stop!' cried another woman from the crowd, this one much younger, and heavily pregnant.

Mukarramma looked round at the woman who had spoken, and her face creased in anguish. 'I'm sorry, Anuketmnata. I can't lose my husband. He is all I have since Aakheperka died.'

'Who are you?' asked Silus of the woman who had just spoken.

'I am Anuketmnata, the sister of Menkheperresenb.'

These names were getting confusing, Silus thought. He concentrated on trying to remember the important ones.

'So if you are sister to Menkheperresenb, you must also be sister to Ankhtakelot?'

She looked at him in surprise. 'How do you know that name?'

'What did Menkheperresenb say happened to the men who went to Alexandria with him?'

She looked doubtful. She brushed her long, dark hair from her eyes. 'He said that they had stayed in Alexandria.'

'And did he say why they had all gone there?'

'He said it was on business. A man hired them to do some work. Centurion, what do you know of my brothers?'

Silus spoke loudly so that everyone gathered could hear.

'Menkheperresenb, Ankhtakelot, and the other men from this village were hired by someone to go to Alexandria, desecrate the Temple of Isis Lochias, and steal the statue of Isis.'

A collective gasp went through the crowd.

'Every one of those men who did this crime are dead, except Menkheperresenb and Ankhtakelot.'

Several women in the crowd cried aloud and began to wail. One young woman dropped to her knees, tearing her hair. Another, older, sagged against her husband, and a third simply fainted. Silus spoke over the sounds of grief.

'Ankhtakelot is a prisoner in Alexandria. He may be executed. There may be retribution on this village. Executions. Your homes burnt. Your crops. It depends what happens here, in this village. Whether we recover the statue. Whether you all co-operate. His brother Menkheperresenb is the one who agreed to this. Who met the man who hired them. I want him, I want to recover the statue, and I want the man who hired him.'

He looked around the crowd, who were silent apart from some soft sobs.

'You,' he pointed at the sister whose name he had already forgotten. 'When is Menkheperresenb returning?'

'This afternoon,' she said quietly.

'No one is to warn him we are here. You will find us a house that we can stay in and bring us food and water. When he returns to the village, you,' he pointed to the elder, 'will personally come and fetch me. We will remain here until our business is done. Then we will leave. We will pay for our board and lodgings. No one will be harmed. Unless you defy me. And then the consequences will be upon your own heads. Is there anyone here who does not understand what I have said?'

Silence, not even sobs now.

'Good. Anhkisenb, was it?'

'Amenisenb,' said the elder glumly.

'Arrange a place for us to stay with a view of this square.'

Amenisenb looked helplessly at his wife, who nodded firmly. 'It shall be done.'

–

Mukarramma had brought them bread, goat's cheese and beer. It was better fare than he had expected, having stormed into the village and threatened them with violence. He suspected they were trying to mollify them in the hope of getting better treatment. Mukarramma herself appeared calm when she handed over the baskets of food and the jugs of drink, but he could see the surface of the liquid rippling, giving away the fine tremor in her hands.

The beer was strange, thick and sweet, but not particularly strong, so it was more refreshing and nourishing than the sort of beer he was used to from Britannia. The legionaries, who were more used to wine, were less impressed, and drank sparingly. Atius, too, drank little.

'Not to your palate, my friend?' asked Silus.

Atius shook his head. 'It's not that. It tastes fine. I've just been thinking maybe I should cut back a little.'

Silus' eyes widened in surprise, but he decided now was not the time to follow up this interesting statement. He cut a wedge of cheese, broke it in half, and gave one half to Atius. He ate the other half slowly and waited. One of the legionaries broke out his knucklebones, and Atius joined in the game, while Silus looked out of the window surreptitiously, hidden in the shadow cast by the sun against the walls.

Children played in the street. Two girls were dancing, an odd rhythm that looked like they were pressing grapes with their feet. Three boys played with a leather ball, the two larger ones tossing the ball over the head of the smaller, who leapt to try to catch it with consistent lack of success. The older boys laughed when the younger started crying and stomped away.

Such a normal scene. The skin colour, the clothing, the buildings were different, but the child's play was just the same as he used to see on the streets of the vicus in Britannia. Yet his vicus had been destroyed in a violent raid. Egypt was in no real danger of enemy raids, but a village like this could be razed to the ground and its inhabitants crucified if the ruling power, be it Romans, or before them Greeks, or even the Pharaohs before them, willed it. He hoped the children here would avoid any retribution that their stupid elders might have brought down upon them.

Amenisenb opened the door and closed it quietly behind him, peering through the crack before he pressed it shut.

'He's here,' he said in a loud whisper. Atius rolled his eyes at the theatrics. The village elder had obviously missed his calling as an actor.

'Point him out to me,' said Silus. There was no way he would distinguish his target from the other male villagers, he thought, given he had previously only glimpsed him briefly in the dark. He was wrong.

Menkheperresenb came swaggering down the street like he was royalty. He had a gold chain around his neck and silver and gold rings. He had a purse of coins that he was tossing out to the children who were following him like he was a gift giver on the Saturnalia. Over his shoulder he carried a bag with a heavy object in it. Silus realised he must have gone to the city and got a loan using the expensive statue as collateral. Menkheperresenb was clearly not a man to wait until money was in his possession before he spent it.

Once Menkheperresenb passed the door, Silus eased it open, gesturing to Atius and the soldiers to stay put, and approached him from behind. He put one hand on his sword, creeping up on him quietly. But then a dog barked loudly at Silus, and Menkheperresenb turned and saw Silus.

Silus called out, 'Menkheperresenb! Stop there, in the name of the Emperor Antoninus.'

Menkheperresenb's mouth dropped open. 'You!'

He seemed to recognise Silus better than Silus recognised him, but maybe that wasn't surprising – the Egyptian had been in the temple for longer, so his eyes had been better adjusted to the dark, and there was only one of Silus for him to remember. Regardless of whether he knew Silus was Tekosis' saviour in the Temple of Isis, he obviously knew he was in trouble if an agent of Rome was confronting him in his home village. Without a word he turned, put his head down and sprinted away.

Silus cursed and set off in pursuit, at the same time calling for Atius and the legionaries. His drawn sword encumbered him, but Menkheperresenb was also slowed by the heavy sack, which bounced around, slamming painfully into his back with each step.

A toddler tottered out from a house straight into Silus' path. Cursing, he swerved, just avoiding stepping on the tiny child. The toddler swayed in surprise, fell onto its backside and started to howl with fists clenched and eyes tightly closed. At the end of the street was a modest temple, and Silus thought Menkheperresenb might be heading there for sanctuary. But he turned a corner and disappeared, and Silus chased after him. He grabbed at some crates stacked at the end of the street to help him take the corner faster, and as he swung round, the top two crates toppled over, spilling duck eggs over the street in a mess of shell and omelette. An enraged woman yelled at him, but he ran on.

Menkheperresenb was only around thirty yards ahead, and he was doing his best to lose Silus by using his local knowledge of the village. The trouble was the village was too small for that to work. This was no Subura. And when Menkheperresenb took a sudden right turn down an alley, Silus saw that the little street would lead round the back of one of the houses that flanked it.

He ran at the front door, shoulder first, and the flimsy wood splintered. An old man sitting on a chamber pot yelped and covered himself with his hands, but Silus was through the room before he could stand. Silus continued through a back room, and seeing Menkheperresenb running past, leapt head first through the back window, whose shutters were fortunately wide open.

He grabbed Menkheperresenb with both arms, and the Egyptian's sack went flying through the air, Silus' sword spinning off in the opposite direction. The two men rolled through the dust, and Silus immediately began to wrestle to get on top and pin him down. They were of similar size, but Silus' training and skills showed quickly, and to add to that, Menkheperresenb kept trying to reach the sack instead of concentrating on fighting off Silus. Within moments, Silus had Menkheperresenb pinned down, and all resistance had left the Egyptian.

Atius and the legionaries reached them a few moments later.

'Looks like you have everything under control here, Silus. I'll be off.'

'Legionaries, hold this man.' Two of the soldiers grabbed him under the shoulders, and Silus carefully got to his feet, breathing heavily from the unexpected exertion. He put his hands on his knees, took three deep breaths, then walked over to retrieve his sword from the dirt.

'Atius, get the sack. Let's see what's in it, as if we can't guess.'

Atius picked up the sack and pulled out the contents: the heavy, foot-high state of Isis in finest gold. The legionaries stared in outright greed at the valuable object. Silus walked over to Atius and inspected it. It was largely unharmed, except the sceptre with the ankh symbol that she carried was a little bent. A good goldsmith would fix that easily.

'Please,' said Menkheperresenb. 'Give it to me. I need it.'

Atius looked at Silus in bemusement. 'Is he serious?'

'You stole this. Why would we give it back to you?'

'Because he will kill me!'

'Don't worry about the man who hired you. He will be captured...'

'Not him. Jabari. From the city of Dmi-n-Hr.'

Silus looked at Atius, who shrugged.

'Who is Jabari, and why does he want to kill you?'

'He lent me money. On good terms. There is no problem, as long as I pay him back.'

'How much?'

'One thousand drachma.'

Atius whistled. 'He doesn't do things by halves, does he?'

'And you were going to pay him back when you sold the statue?'

Menkheperresenb nodded.

'Why not just wait until the statue was sold?'

Menkheperresenb shrugged helplessly. Silus couldn't understand the stupidity, but then he caught sight of Atius nodding sympathetically, and realised that not everyone was able to delay gratification.

'What will happen if you don't pay him?'

'He will kill me.'

Silus tutted. 'Actions have consequences.'

'He will kill my sister, Anuketmnata.'

A crowd of villagers had caught up with them now. At the front was Anuketmnata, one hand cradling her swollen belly. Silus gritted his teeth.

'Not my problem. I have to return this statue to where you stole it from. I suggest you find another way to pay your debts.'

Menkheperresenb fell to his knees and grabbed the hem of Silus' tunic.

'Please, I beg you. I have nothing. The crops were poor, and Roman tax farmers took what little we have. I cannot repay him.'

Silus pulled his tunic free and turned away.

'Wait, wait. You say you want to catch the man who hired me. I can help you. Let you know when he is going to arrive.'

Silus thought for a moment. It would certainly make it easier if they had this man's co-operation. It might avoid a chase like he had just gone through to capture this one, which might even end in the man's escape. But what could he do to help? He didn't have a thousand drachma and didn't think his help was really worth that much anyway.

'Your assistance would be useful, although not essential. But what can I do to help you?'

'You are soldiers. You could arrest Jabari!'

'On what charge?'

'I don't know. You are Romans, you always make the charges up anyway!'

'Arresting people isn't really my style. Look, I'm sorry for your problems, but you have really brought them upon yourself. You are going to be taken to Alexandria to be turned over to the Boule, or whichever local authority will deal with you. Your sister's husband can protect her.'

'She has no husband. He died of fever. Please. The last man who wronged Jabari, he had his men rape the debtor's wife, and then had her impaled alive on a stake, right in front of him. He didn't kill him until she was dead.'

Silus looked at Menkheperresenb's sister. She said nothing, looking back with a mixture of defiance and fear. He was finding it increasingly difficult to harden his heart. He turned to Atius.

'What do you think?'

'I think it's a while since I killed someone who deserved to be killed.'

Silus nodded.

'Right. We really have better things to do than this, but it shouldn't be too time consuming, and we still have two days before the man who hired you arrives, yes?'

Menkheperresenb nodded.

'Fine. Tell us where to find this Jabari, and we will take care of him.'

'Take care of him?' Menkheperresenb looked confused. 'How will you do that?'

'Leave it to us. We are experts. In return, you will meet the man who hired you, and we will arrest him once he is distracted with you.'

'Yes, I will do as you say. And what will you do about his men?'

'His men?'

'Yes, of course. He says he doesn't trust native Egyptians. He travels with ten bodyguards.'

Fuck.

–

Jabari was a big man and a happy one. He was rich, above the law, and had everything he desired in life – four wives, the oldest of which kept the rest in line, as well as a small harem of slaves. The finest wines and foods from around the Empire. A magnificent house, filled with fine tapestries, ornate furniture and fine Greek and Egyptian statues. Bribes to the local authorities kept them from his door, allowing him to pursue his business interests unhindered. And he was at peace with his rivals in the city, who knew him to be so powerful and ruthless that existing in harmony with him was the best option for all.

Jabari traded in stolen goods, loaned money at crippling interest rates, put pressure on local businesses to pay him money in return for his protection, and occasionally had his men take part in a robbery themselves, if anything valuable enough to interest him came to his attention. He spent a small portion of the day overseeing his empire, threatening debtors, intimidating anyone who did not conform to his wishes, and giving instructions to his deputies.

But for the most part, he spent his time enjoying the pleasures he had worked so hard for. Sumptuous meals, heady drinks and lots and lots of sex.

At that moment, he was thinking about his new slave, a very young girl from Aethiopia. He had sated himself with two Roman slave girls earlier – he loved the feeling of power that came from having representatives of the world's ruling Empire bent over for him. But he thought he would be ready to break in the young, dark girl later on.

First he had some business to attend to, which shouldn't take long. One of his guards announced that there were two foreigners who had come to ask for a loan. The sum made him interested. Ten thousand drachma. That could lead to a good profit, provided that he was comfortable the men could repay it or had sufficient collateral. He took a long swig from his coloured glass, reached across to squeeze the thigh of the Roman slave girl sitting to his left, and gestured to the guard to show the applicants in.

The men were bearded, rough-looking. Their faces were red, suggesting pale skins from northern climates, unused to the sun in Egypt, even in the winter. Their clothes were functional, in good repair, but not expensive. They held themselves with confidence.

Jabari looked over to the two guards by the doorway. They were reassuringly solid, armed with long curved swords. He nodded to the two men to approach him.

'Your names?'

'Silus and Atius.'

'What is your business?'

'Loans.'

'I see. How much are you seeking?'

'No, I think there has been a misunderstanding. We are not here to borrow money.'

Jabari's eyes narrowed. 'Is this a joke? Why are you wasting my time? Do you not know my reputation?'

'We know it well. That is why we were forced to come here, out of our way. It is most inconvenient.'

Jabari felt the conversation getting out of his control, a situation he was completely unused to.

'If you don't want to borrow money, why are you here?'

'To repay a debt.'

'You didn't need to see me for that. My bookkeeper could have taken your money.'

197

'We aren't going to repay you in coins.'

Now Jabari felt really confused. He looked again at his guards, warning them with his eyes to be ready for trouble, though of what kind, he wasn't sure. The men had been thoroughly searched, and there was nowhere for either of them to carry concealed weaponry. The guards tensed, putting their hands near the hilts of their swords.

'You are testing my patience. I am this close to having you killed on the spot.' Jabari held his thumb and first finger a short distance apart. 'Pay your debt or get out and stop wasting my time.'

He wasn't sure why he didn't order his guards to strike them down. Something in their eyes stopped him. He would be happy at that moment if they just left.

The larger one of the two turned and walked to the back of his reception room to the oaken double doors. But instead of walking through them, he pulled them fully closed, and slipped the wooden bar into place across them.

The guards stared for just long enough to let him complete the action, then drew their swords simultaneously and charged, one from either side. The large foreigner moved faster than Jabari would have believed possible. He stepped rapidly to the left. The left-hand guard swung his sword, but the foreigner was inside the arc of the swing, blocking the sword arm with his forearm, following up with a headbutt with his forehead to the bridge of the guard's nose. He gripped the sword arm, pirouetted on the spot to present the back of the first guard to the other, and shoved him hard.

The other guard was bringing his sword down in a double-handed blow at the space where the foreigner had been standing moments before. It struck the top of the first guard's skull, biting deep, and getting stuck in the bone. He sank to the floor, knees giving way like an ox felled at sacrifice. The sword jammed in the split bone, and the second guard wrenched at it desperately. It came free with a sudden force that made the guard stagger back, the sword barely remaining in his grip as it flew upwards over his head.

It was all Atius needed to finish him. He stepped forward and punched the guard hard in the throat with his fingers extended, a much sharper impact than a fist, and one that collapsed the guard's windpipe. Cartilage rings, supposed to keep the airway open, folded inwards, permanently cutting off the air supply to the lungs. The guard dropped his sword and clutched at his throat, his face turning red, then blue, as he gurgled, trying to force wind through the blockage. In moments he was face down on the floor, chest still heaving for a short while, before the efforts became weaker, and stopped.

Silus had kept Jabari in view for the whole time, while watching his friend do his work, ready to intervene if it was necessary. As expected, it wasn't necessary. Jabari watched the fight in stunned amazement, his mouth hanging open, so a trace of drool slid down the corner of his mouth unnoticed. His slave girl let out tiny whimpers, eyes wide, both hands pressed to her mouth.

Atius picked up the sword of the choked guard, and weighed it in his hand.

'Useless piece of shit for this sort of work, don't you think, Silus?'

'Showy and pointless,' said Silus. 'Give me a knife any day over that for bodyguard work.'

'Who are you people?' Jabari managed to say, in a hoarse whisper.

'We're Arcani. You probably haven't heard of us out here. It doesn't really matter.'

'What do you want with me?'

'Well, as I said, we are here to pay off a debt. Someone owes you money, and we need a favour from him, so we said we would take care of his problem. The trouble is, we don't have the cash. And we heard that you aren't the sort of person to be lenient when it comes to repayment terms.'

'I'm a businessman. If people don't pay, they...'

'They watch their wives get raped and impaled.'

Jabari went white.

'There has to be respect.' His voice was barely audible. Silus looked him up and down. Corpulent, sweaty, wide-eyed and terrified. He imagined that once, in his prime, he had been a man to fear in his own right, but that nowadays his power came from his employees, his paid muscle, who carried out his ruthless instructions. At that moment, Silus could see little to respect.

Atius handed the sword to Silus. Silus gave it one or two experimental swings.

'Please,' said Jabari. 'It was just business. I will forgive your friend his debt. I will pay him. I will pay you.'

'I don't think he would believe it. What's to stop you reneging as soon as we are gone?'

'I give you my word as a...' He trailed off. Silus gave a half-smile.

'You don't have anything to swear on, do you? Nothing that you actually give a shit about.'

'I...'

Silus swung the sword, two-handed, horizontal, neck high. The stroke was perfectly placed, slicing through the throat all the way to the bones, but without touching them. Blood bubbled out of the laceration like a spring bursting forth from the ground and flooded down his rounded chest. Jabari reached up with both hands, trying to stem the flow, then toppled forward off his chair to lie face down on the floor, a crimson pool spreading around him.

Now the slave girl drew a deep breath, and before Silus could stop her, screamed at the top of her lungs. Moments later, there was a hammering at the door. The shouts that followed were in Egyptian, but they were obviously asking if something was wrong. The slave's continued screams told them that clearly something was very wrong.

'What now?' asked Atius.

Silus took Jabari's hand, which had a distinctive-looking signet ring. He gave it a tug, but rolls of fat prevented it moving. He used the sword to hack the finger off, and stuffed it into his belt, hidden by a fold of his tunic.

Silus looked around. The room had a high, barred window.

'How many guards did you count?'

'Six, plus whatever reinforcements they can call on. It's a big house, there may be others.'

'The window, then?'

'Sometimes it's best to keep it simple.'

They pushed a wooden chest over to the wall beneath the window and stood on it together. It creaked under their weight but held. They grabbed hold of the iron bars.

'On three. One, two, three!'

They both heaved. The walls cracked where the bars were buried into them, but stayed firm.

The hammering at the doors changed in tone. Something heavy was being rammed against it now, and the bar holding the doors shut was giving a little more with each thump.

'Again, on three. One, two three!'

They pulled, and pulled again, and finally were rewarded with a crack as one bar came loose from the top part of the window. Once that was free, they were able to use their weight and the leverage of the loose bar to work on the others. Just as the whole grill came free, the wooden bar on the doors splintered. A gap appeared in the door, and they caught a glimpse of furious faces.

Silus boosted Atius up and out through the window, then Atius reached down for his friend.

With a huge crash, the doors flew open and smashed back against the walls that held them. Guards poured into the room, then hesitated as they saw the carnage for the first time. Silus grabbed Atius' hand and leapt.

One of the guards sprinted across the room and jumped to grab Silus by the ankle. Silus kicked down hard with his other foot, and was rewarded by a crunch and a yelp. Atius pulled hard, and Silus felt his shoulder almost wrench out of his socket. He grabbed the window frame and scrambled out before anyone else could take hold of him.

They tumbled down onto the street together and looked up and down. They had surveyed the area before and had a rough idea which way to head.

'Come on.' Silus raced off through the residential area. There were few shops or stalls here. Jabari's house had been impressive, but it was built in a poor part of town, all the better to do business away from the authorities. There were a few pigs and chickens scratching in the dirt, some children playing, old men sitting on benches watching and commenting and cats sitting in the shade studiously ignoring everything. A dog joined in the chase, a medium-sized smooth-coated tan mutt, which snapped at their heels and barked for a hundred yards until it got bored.

Yells of pursuit followed them, but some distance back. It had obviously taken a little while for the guards to get through the window in enough numbers to feel brave enough to start the pursuit. They must have been intimidated by the sight that had confronted them when they burst into the room.

It was enough of a head start for Silus and Atius to get clear. They zigged and zagged, taking random turns, until the noise of their pursuers faded away. Then they slowed to a walk, discarded the curved swords, and emerged from a narrow passageway on a main street. A small collection of stalls was situated about a hundred yards away, and they wandered over nonchalantly, letting their breathing slow, and paused to check out some pottery. Silus looked around surreptitiously, while Atius picked up a jug with a spout and handle and turned it over in his hands speculatively.

'All clear,' whispered Silus.

'Let's find some transport and get out of here.'

The potter gave the men speaking the strange language an odd look, and watched them with vague interest as they went off in search of a mount.

Silus quickly realised that he had found a mode of transport that he hated even more than a horse or a boat. The camel driver who had led them in a train of three had laughed when Silus had mounted the kneeling beast and then let out a distinctly unmanly yelp as it had got to its feet. He had seen a camel fight a lion in the arena from a distance, and had seen them illustrated in mosaics, but he had not appreciated how big they were until he was up close. And how tall. If he tried to jump down from its back, he was pretty sure he would twist an ankle, if not break it. On top of this he had to endure not so subtle comments from Atius, usually a variation of, 'Is this the best ride you've had recently?'

Not only this, but the motion as it walked had made him as nauseous as a boat trip. Ship of the desert, indeed. And in a final indignity, his thoughts kept drifting to Tekosis, to the night he had spent with her, her smooth body, her curves, her touch, her cries — which inevitably led to a swelling between his legs that was excruciating as the camel he was astride bumped up and down.

But the beasts had returned them to Menkheperresenb's village in good time, faster than the donkeys they had used on their outward journey, and the legionaries looked relieved to see them. Menkheperresenb too seemed glad of their arrival and came hurrying over to greet them.

To dismount, the camel driver had his beast fold its legs underneath it, so he could slide easily from the saddle. Silus waited impatiently for the driver to instruct his own mount to do the same, but the driver walked up to him, gave him a gap-toothed smile and held his hand out. Silus sighed and tossed down the agreed fare, a few copper coins. The driver put the coins in his purse and then held his hand out again.

'What do you want?' asked Silus in Greek, but the driver shook his head, his smile still plastered in place. 'I've paid you the agreed sum.'

Silus looked down and wondered whether he could try jumping off the camel. But he risked injuring himself and endangering the mission needlessly. And he could imagine Oclatinius' reaction as he explained his reason for failure. 'I was jumping off a camel, sir.'

The driver said something in the native Egyptian language. Silus looked helplessly at Menkheperresenb, who translated for him.

'He says the price has gone up. It is double now.'

Silus pulled his knife from his belt – he had recovered it from where he had hidden it before visiting Jabari. He reached forward and touched it lightly against the side of his camel's neck.

'Tell him that if he doesn't make this beast kneel down right now, I will cut its throat and it will fall down.'

Menkheperresenb translated and the driver's face filled with alarm. He spoke a command word to the camel, and held its reins as it sank down, forelegs first, nearly pitching Silus over its head, before its back legs went down and Silus was able to dismount with relief. The camel driver grabbed Silus' mount around the neck and showered it with kisses, whispering affectionate words in its ear. The camel ruminated impassively.

Silus looked away in disgust.

'Sir,' said Menkheperresenb earnestly. 'Were you successful? Is he dead?'

Silus tossed him the severed finger with the signet ring. Menkheperresenb caught it and looked at it in shock that turned to delight.

'Thank you, sir, thank you.'

'Your debt is cleared. Now it's your turn to hold up your end of the bargain.'

'I will, sir. And then I am free to go?'

Silus hesitated. It rankled to give him a pardon after what he had done. On the other hand, it was not his job to police this country or administer justice. He had one mission, and everything else was just a means to completing it.

'Yes, you are free to go, as long as you stay out of Alexandria. If I hear you have returned there, for any reason at all, I will kill you. Do you understand?'

'Yes, sir, thank you, sir.'

'Fine, make sure you are prepared. The man who hired you arrives tomorrow?'

Menkheperresenb nodded.

'And he will have ten men accompanying him?'

'Last time he did.'

'How were they armed?'

'Four with clubs, four with swords.'

This would be a problem, Silus thought. This would take a little planning.

'Get someone to fetch us some food and drink. We are thirsty and hungry. I need to talk to my men.'

–

Silus watched from a ground floor window in a house that faced the main street through the village. Menkheperresenb stood in the middle of the thoroughfare, shifting nervously from foot to foot. He held the gold statue in both hands. Silus had had his doubts about entrusting the murderer and thief with the valuable item, but decided that he was well enough guarded and well enough frightened that the risk of him trying to abscond was low.

The group of men walked slowly and confidently into the village. The sun was behind them, and although Silus squinted, it was hard to make out their features. The leader looked vaguely familiar, although Silus couldn't quite place him. He looked over to the roof of the house opposite, where Atius waited. Atius was watching him, waiting for his signal, unable to see the intruders from his position. Silus held a hand up. Not yet.

The men came closer. Silus ground his teeth, hoping that Menkheperresenb's nerve would hold. He needed him to draw the men in further.

They lacked all caution. After all, what did ten armed men have to fear from a small Egyptian village? The leader stopped in front of Menkheperresenb and said something. Menkheperresenb looked around him nervously.

Silus slammed his fists together, the sign for Atius to attack. Atius repeated the motion to the legionaries who had been watching him. There was a whistling noise, and three stones flew down from the roofs into the men, who had been packed together. One who had been holding a club loosely in his hand crumpled instantly, forehead caved in. Another dropped his sword, yelling loudly, as the impact broke the upper bone of his right arm. The other stone did not find its mark, but it was a good start.

The legionaries had not come in full battle array. They wore breastplates and had gladii, but no spears and no shields. But an ambush worked best when it started with a missile attack. So Silus had had to improvise. Using strips of cloth provided, with some grumbling, by the villagers, Silus had fashioned three slings. Atius was familiar with their use, having had training in a large variety of weapons, and one of the legionaries had also learned to use a sling as a child before joining up. Silus had demonstrated the technique to two other legionaries, but he had little confidence they would make a significant impact. He of course was skilled in the sling, having been taught by his father, but he had another role for himself.

Next, the other two legionaries stood and hurled spears. Wood was scarce in Egypt, and Silus had had to break down a door and fashion a pilum from the planks with his knife. They were poor weapons, unbalanced, not really heavy enough. But with gravity assisting, they flew down from the rooftops with some force. One took one of the men in the chest and he flew backwards, arms spread, to lie flat on his back in the dirt. The second looked like it would find its mark, but the target ducked when the stones flew past him, and the spear went over his head.

All this had happened in just a few heartbeats. And in that space of time, three of the ten guards who had accompanied the man behind the attack on the Temple of Isis were dead or disabled. It still wasn't an even fight, but the numbers were closer than they had been.

The intruders in the village were in complete disarray now. Having been assaulted by missiles from roofs on both sides of the street, they didn't know whether to take shelter, charge the roof, or run, and if so in which direction. Three more slingshots whistled down, but this time with the men more alert, only one hit home, and that a glancing blow to the left shoulder of one of the guards.

The leader of the group was turning this way and that frantically, completely at a loss what to do. He gave no clear instructions to his guards, just yelled at them incoherently. They did nothing to protect him either, not gathering around him to shield him with their bodies, or hustling him away to shelter. They were clearly just mercenaries doing a simple bodyguarding job for the lowest rate of pay and had no loyalty to the man who led them.

Silus gave another signal, and Atius and the legionaries charged down from the rooftops, down the external staircases, swords drawn, roaring a savage battle cry. Now the intruders clustered together, backs against each other, as if they faced superior numbers. In fact, there were still seven of the armed men against Atius and the four legionaries.

It was not standard military doctrine for legionaries to rush singly into attack. They were trained to fight behind shields, protected by their neighbours to the left and right, and if they charged, they charged in line. But these legionaries did not have shields, and Silus had gambled that the men they faced were not trained soldiers. Their response proved him right. Two men peeled away from the back of the group, throwing their weapons away and running at full tilt away from the fight, out of the village and into the desert. The remaining five lifted their swords and clubs to meet the attack.

They traded blows and it was immediately clear that the paid mercenaries were inferior to the highly trained legionaries in every way – strength, stamina, weapon skill, tactical cohesion. The legionaries protected each other, turned aside blows meant for their comrades, while the mercenaries fought as individuals. Some of them had ferocity, some had street cunning, but it counted for little against the united professionals. The mercenaries began to give ground.

It was time for Silus to strike. He slipped out of the window of the house he was still concealed in and walked slowly up behind the leader. The red-haired man was facing away from Silus, one hand on his mouth, staring in horror at the battle in front of him. He remained completely unaware of Silus until he grabbed his arm and forced it up behind him, while simultaneously putting his arm around his neck. The man who was supposed to be leading the guards let out a cry, which was choked off by pressure from Silus' forearm.

'Drop your weapons,' yelled Silus in loud, clear Greek. 'I have your master.'

Atius and the legionaries took a step back, to allow their opponents the time and space to assess their situation and surrender. The men looked around at their captured leader, then exchanged disgusted glances and tossed their weapons onto the ground. One of them spoke up. 'He is nothing to us. He just hired us to escort him on this journey. Let us go, and we will leave here straight away.'

Silus nodded to the legionaries. There was no point spilling the blood of these men, and they didn't deserve it – they had done nothing wrong that he knew of. The legionaries stood back, making a corridor, swords still drawn. The mercenaries hesitated, fearing a trick.

'Go. You have my word you will not be harmed if you leave now and don't come back.'

The mercenaries shuffled away, the legionaries laughing and hurling insults at them as they went.

'Leave fighting to the real soldiers.'

'Run home to mummy, little girls.'

Atius watched them go, then turned to where Silus was holding the men's leader. He stared, frowned, then gasped.

'Brother John?'

—

Brother John stared up into the bright sunlight. He was seated on a stool, a legionary sword prodding him painfully in the back. Silus stood before him, the sun behind him, looking down at the priest. Atius stood to Silus' right, hands clasped together, face taut with distress.

'I will ask you again. Tell me what you are doing here.'

'My answer is the same. I was visiting this village to bring the word of the true God to the pagans.'

'Why this village? Why so far from Alexandria? Haven't you got enough holy work to do in the city?'

'The Lord commands us to take his word to the whole world. Not just the Jews, not just the Romans, not just the Greeks, but everyone.'

'So it is a coincidence that you are here, in the place where the men who attacked the Temple of Isis Lochias come from. Where the statue of Isis has ended up?' He gestured to the gold statue, guarded by one of the legionaries.

'I know nothing about any of that. I am here doing God's work.'

Silus hit him hard across the jaw with a closed fist that rocked the priest backwards and forced the sword tip deeper into his back. He cried out, then released a low groan. From the corner of his eye, Silus noticed Atius was tight-lipped. This clearly wasn't easy for him.

'Tell me, Brother John. Was it about the money? The gold statue? Even melted down, it would be worth a fortune.'

Brother John glared at him.

'Talk to me. You must understand how much trouble you are in. Not only for yourself, but for your cult.' He glanced across at Atius. 'Your faith, I mean. When word of this gets out, there will be riots in Alexandria. And your fellow Christians will be targets. They will be slaughtered.'

The priest looked troubled but said defiantly, 'I am doing God's work.'

Atius suddenly grabbed the priest by the collar, heaved him off the stool and threw him to the ground. Sand and dust flew up in a puff around him as he landed on his back. Instantly, Atius was on top of him, hands at his throat. He squeezed, choking the priest, who grabbed Atius' wrists and tried in vain to prise them apart.

'This is not God's work!' cried Atius. 'Killing. Raping. Stealing. This is the work of the devil. I should know!'

Brother John's eyes rolled up into his head, his hands went slack and fell away.

'Enough, Atius,' said Silus. Atius continued to strangle the unconscious priest until Silus gave him a hard shove, sending him toppling sideways. Atius rolled over onto his back and thumped the ground with both fists, letting out a roar of frustration. He pushed himself upright, got to his feet, then walked over to the nearest house and kicked the wall hard.

Silus bent over Brother John. His breathing was raspy but regular. As he watched, his eyelids fluttered, then opened. He took some deep breaths, tried to sit up, then flopped back. Silus indicated to two of the legionaries to help him up, and they lifted him under the arms and put him back on his stool.

Silus slapped him lightly around the face. 'Are you with us, Brother John?'

The priest groaned, but he was able to give Silus an ice-cold glare.

'You pagans will all be sent to hell when the Lord returns on the day of judgement.' His voice was hoarse but chilling. 'And you, Atius, professing the faith and assisting these worshippers of devils and false gods. These are the same people who murdered Origen's father. Who murdered my mother and sister for the simple crime of worshipping the true God. I curse you all.' He spat on the ground, a gob of saliva quickly absorbed into the parched earth.

'Sir,' said one of the legionaries nervously. 'These Christians know powerful magic. They sacrifice babies and drink their blood so their god gives them power over other men.'

'That's not fucking true!' yelled Atius, striding over to the legionary and pushing him in the chest. The legionary took a step backwards, then squared up to him.

'Stand down, both of you.' Silus' voice brooked no dissension. He wondered for a moment when command had become second nature to him. It had certainly seemed an alien thing when he had first found himself in charge of other men in Britannia. Now, with all he had done and seen, he had the confidence to feel that he knew best. Not necessarily that he was right, just that he was more likely to be right than those who surrounded him.

Atius growled at the legionary, then turned away.

'You really won't tell us anything?' Silus asked. 'Tell us who ordered you to do this?'

'I take orders only from my God.'

'Fine. We will take you back to Alexandria. We can hand you over to the authorities there for torture, to find out everything you know. Origen too.'

'Silus...' Atius began.

'Silence!' Silus snapped at his friend. 'This has gone far enough. Christians, Jews, followers of Isis and Serapis and whoever else. Fuck the lot of them. We need to find a lost boy, and we are going back to Alexandria to do just that.'

Chapter Eleven

Varius Avitus Bassianus sat cross-legged on the floor before the conical black stone, but his mind and soul were somewhere else. The scent of incense filled the room. His eyes were closed, and he whispered words in a foreign, exotic tongue, musical and fast, one word running into the next. Behind his closed lids, he could see himself soaring over Emesa like an eagle, a place his mother had described to him in detail, with its eastern style of temples, its thronged markets, the mausoleum in honour of Soaemias – the former King of Emesa and high priest of Elagabal, after whom his mother had been named. And in the centre of all, the vast Temple of Elagabal, ornamented with gold and silver and precious jewels, marble steps leading to its six-columned façade, beyond which the huge black conical stone was visible. His spirit circled the city, his soul filled with joy at visiting the home of his ancestors, even while his body mourned its separation from that holy place, and the great stone of Elagabal, where he longed to worship.

Aziz watched in fascination and reverence, on his knees and prostrated with arms before him stretched towards the boy priest.

Avitus' body jerked, his breathing came faster, he tilted his head back and with eyes tight shut, let out a cry of ecstasy and release. Then he opened his eyes, took six deep breaths, and sang a prayer.

'Lord of the mountain, lord of the sun. Bring your light to shine upon us. Beseech the great mother Atargatis to bestow on us her protection and warmth, and beseech Astarte to give us her love, and the water of life.' The complex words and phrases sounded strange coming from the mouth of such a young boy, but his mother and his tutor Gannys had taught him from a very early age the rituals and prayers of their god.

'Lord Elagabal, let it be as your priest prays,' said Aziz fervently.

Avitus opened his eyes and looked around him. The room was dimly lit with flickering candlelight, which illuminated basic but comfortable furniture. There was a bed against one wall with a feather mattress, a table with a jug of water and a plate of fruits, and in the corner a chamber pot, freshly emptied and cleaned. Was it a bedroom, a temple, or a goal cell? Avitus wondered. He felt a sense of disappointment at not finding himself in Emesa, but was otherwise unperturbed.

He rose and poured himself some water, and drank deeply, then ate some figs. The ritual ecstasies always made him hungry and thirsty. He turned to Aziz.

'I have been here some time, Aziz. You kidnapped me, and now keep me in comfort and worship with me. You honour me, but you will not let me leave. You say all is as the Lord Elagabal wills it, but I still don't really understand.'

'I know, Your Blessedness. But today someone who has come to see you will explain it all.'

'Who?'

'He should have arrived by now. I will bring him to you.'

Aziz left the room and closed the door behind him. Avitus heard the door locking, and then a bar falling into place. He sighed, sat on the bed, and picked up his favourite doll. It was wooden, with a long wool dress, and its painted face had black outlined eyes and full red lips. He hugged it, then lay down on the bed and closed his eyes.

A few moments later, the door opened, and Aziz came in again. This time he had someone with him. Avitus sat up.

'Gannys!'

Avitus jumped out of bed and ran to him to give him a big hug around the chest.

'It's good to see you, Avitus.'

The big Syrian tousled Avitus' hair affectionately.

'What's happening, Gannys? Are you here to rescue me?'

Gannys exchanged a look with Aziz that Avitus couldn't read.

'You don't need rescuing, Avitus,' he said. 'You aren't in danger.'

'Then why can't I leave? Why can't I see Mother?'

'Sit down, Avitus, please.'

Avitus sat on the edge of his bed, picked up his doll and cradled it in his arms. Gannys knelt before the stone and closed his eyes, moving his lips in silent prayer. Then he sat in a chair opposite Avitus.

'You know well your heritage, Avitus, but let me remind you. You are descended through your mother, and your mother's mother, from the line of the priest-kings of Emesa. Although Emesa is now ruled by the Romans, the great Lord Elagabal is still supreme there, and one day you will take your rightful place as his high priest.

'But there are some of us that believe you have a dual destiny. A destiny to rule the world, as well as the heavens. Aziz has been working with me, and with some powerful friends in Rome and Syria, to make something momentous happen.'

Avitus regarded Gannys with curiosity and trust. Gannys stood and walked over to the table, poured himself some water and took a sip.

'What I am about to tell you is very secret, Avitus, and you will not repeat it to anyone outside this room. At least, not until everything that we hope will come to pass, has come to pass. Do you swear?'

'On the Lord Elagabal, Atargatis and Astarte.'

'There are powerful people who believe that the current Emperor in Rome is the wrong one. They supported his brother Geta. Now they fear Antoninus, and they are right to. He is massacring his enemies in Rome even as we speak.'

'I am not his enemy,' said Avitus. 'My mother is the Empress's niece. My father is beloved of him.'

'This may be difficult for you to hear, Avitus. But there are some who believe that Antoninus is your father.'

Avitus stiffened. 'He is not.'

'I am sure they are just rumours,' said Gannys quickly. 'But they may be useful rumours.'

'Useful for what?'

'To justify your claim.'

'Gannys, you are confusing me.'

'Avitus, we want you to become Emperor.'

Avitus gasped. 'The Emperor of the whole Roman Empire?'

'No,' said Gannys. 'Antoninus has too firm a stranglehold on Rome, and the West. But we have support in the East. Not long ago Geta and Antoninus discussed splitting the Empire in two. There are good reasons for doing it – it has become large and unwieldy. But that doesn't really matter now. If we split the Empire in two, the peoples of the East, especially Syria, can be free from the terrible reign of Antoninus. We can be free to rule ourselves in the way we wish. And that means we can bring the worship of Elagabal to all our lands, so the great god of the mountain and the sun can be put in his rightful place at the top of the pantheon!'

Avitus' eyes lit up.

'It's possible?'

'More than possible. We are going to make it happen.'

A dreamy look passed over Avitus' face. Then he frowned.

'Why did you have to kidnap me?'

'Don't think of it as a kidnap. I just arranged with my friend Aziz here to bring you somewhere safe, away from the Emperor, and away from your... father. Marcellus knows nothing about any of this, and I doubt he would approve.'

'And why am I here in Alexandria?'

'Because this will be the new capital of the eastern Roman Empire.'

'But why Alexandria? Why not Syria?'

'I regret that you have not had the opportunity to see this marvellous city. But it is the second biggest city in the Empire, founded by Alexander, the greatest general in history. It has a culture and an intellectual heritage that exceeds Rome and Athens in reputation. And it is a city of religion, where followers of Yahweh, Christos, Isis, Serapis and Jupiter rub shoulders.'

Avitus found himself struggling to keep up, and his eyes wandered, drifting over towards the black stone. If he was Emperor, he could bring the original stone, that was said to have descended from heaven, from Emesa to Alexandria. And he could require everyone to bow down before it, whatever god they followed.

'Avitus. Do you understand what I am telling you?'

'You are saying I am going to be the Emperor, here in Alexandria, and the great god is going to rule everyone.'

Gannys smiled. 'Yes, that's about the size of it.'

'Excellent, when does it happen?'

Gannys hesitated. 'You know in the Circus, the race can't start until all the chariots are at the start line? We are waiting for our chariots to get in a row.'

'We are going to fight in chariots?'

'No, I was talking figuratively. We need to ensure that our allies in Numidia, Judea and Syria are ready to strike when we say. We will co-ordinate so that on the day you are declared Emperor of the new eastern Empire, the governors and military commanders and their legions are able to swear allegiance to you.'

'I am going to be Emperor,' said Avitus in a dreamy voice. 'People will bow down to me, and everyone will worship the mountain god.'

'Yes,' said Gannys. 'I swear it. My lord.'

Avitus smiled, then the smile faded. He cuddled the effeminate doll, a traditional girl's toy, tight, and stroked its woollen hair gently. At that moment, he looked much more like an eight-year-old boy than an Emperor and priest-king.

'I miss mother,' he said.

—

Origen spoke to the crowd gathered in the agora in his clear voice, loud without shouting or raising his pitch. He was a skilled orator, and the audience was rapt. Silus and Atius stood at the back. They had legionaries to hand, but doubted they would need them. They were not rash enough to attempt to confront the preacher in front of a large group of his followers. So they listened and waited.

'Being a follower of the Messiah is not the safe option. When I was just a boy, my blessed father Leonides was beheaded under the persecution of our faith by the Emperor Septimius Severus, a pagan surely inspired by the devil. I travelled to Rome last year, and I saw that his son is no better. Like most in Rome, he worships the pagan gods, both of Rome and of the East, and he is said to whore and drink, just as he murders his opponents.'

No wonder he was in hiding, thought Silus. Those words alone were enough to have him executed on the spot. But there would be a riot if they tried right now.

'I should have joined my father in his martyrdom, and I would have, though I was but seventeen years old. But my mother hid my clothes, so I could not go with him, and I live with that shame today. I have lived my life trying to make up for my failure that day. I have made many sacrifices. I have done harm to my own body, maybe rashly in my youth, an act that in some respects I regret, but in other ways I am proud of this demonstration of my devotion. I have lived many years in hiding, and I have devoted my life to studying the scriptures and teaching their word. I say this not to flatter myself, but to show you my sincerity.

'But my time to talk to you is short. It is illegal under the Severans to change religion, or to attempt to convert any of you. So you can hear my words, and choose your own path. Therefore, I say to you all, be happy with your lives, and find contentment with communion with God, not in pleasures of the flesh or possession. The philosopher Socrates said, "He who is not contented with what he has, would not be contented with what he would like to have."

'You say to me, "Why do you tell us the words of a pagan Greek?" And I say to you that the Israelites made their temples out of gold they had brought with them from Egypt. How useful to the children of Israel were the things brought from Egypt, which the Egyptians had not put to a proper use, but which the Hebrews, guided by the wisdom of God, used for God's service.

'So we can listen to the words of the great thinkers, and with open minds and hearts, consider what they can teach us. I urge you, then, to read the works of Socrates, Plato, and Aristotle, as well as the scriptures and the words of the Messiah. In them, learn how to be one with God, to reject the temptations of this world, and to love your neighbour. Follow these simple instructions, and when the Christos returns, you will surely be among the saved.

'Now, join me in prayer.'

Origen held up his hands and closed his eyes, and the entire crowd dropped to their knees before him. Silus marvelled at the control the charismatic preacher had over his congregation. He got to his knees to avoid literally standing out, and Atius did the same. They bowed their heads and listened to three long prayers of intercession, thanksgiving and praise, murmuring Amen in the appropriate places. When the prayers were over, Silus glanced over at Atius. His friend was openly crying, tears streaming down his face.

Silus didn't understand. He squeezed Atius' shoulder. 'What's wrong?' he whispered.

'His words are so right,' said Atius 'And yet he has commanded such evil.'

'We don't know the extent of his involvement,' said Silus. 'We haven't put Brother John to torture yet.'

'How can he not know?' said Atius miserably. 'You see in how much respect he is held here. Brother John would not dare to do what he did without approval from Origen.'

Origen said words of blessing to the crowd. 'Go with God, and the face of the Lord be always turned to you.'

'And to you,' chorused the crowd, and got to their feet, clasping hands with each other, some smiling, some serious, some looking like they were experiencing a moment of pure joy. Then they began to disperse. Silus looked over at the legionaries, who appeared relieved that the meeting was over, without any need to intervene, and no attempt at disruption from others in the city. He had been told that on other occasions, worshippers of Isis and Serapis had come to jeer and catcall, sparking scuffles that had meant the legionaries had had to wade in with clubs and swords, and there had been serious injuries and fatalities on all sides.

Origen shook hands of some of his most ardent admirers, but seemed to be looking around for someone else. When he didn't see the one he was looking for, he frowned, and made his way slowly out of the agora, with a few of his followers escorting him.

'Let's follow,' said Silus. 'Make sure he is going back to Phryne's house. Then when his disciples – is that what you call them? – have left, we will pay him a visit.'

–

When the porter opened the door of Phryne's elegant house, they did not wait to be announced. Silus pushed past him, and when the porter tried to reach out to stop him, Atius grabbed him by the throat and pushed him hard against the wall.

'Don't test me today,' said Atius, and the porter held up his hands in meek surrender.

They walked into the atrium and found a slave there throwing scraps of food to the fish in the impluvium. The big carp swam lazily near the surface, opening their mouths wide to gulp down the morsels.

'You, slave,' snapped Silus. 'Fetch Origen.'

'Master, I don't know...'

Atius half drew his sword and took a threatening step forward. 'Do it now.'

The slave let out a little yelp and ran through the archway leading deeper into the house.

It was Phryne who appeared first.

'How dare you barge into my house?' she said, wagging a finger in Silus' face. 'I treated you like a guest, showed you my trust and you abuse my hospitality in this way? You should be ashamed.'

Silus stood straight, not retreating an inch in the face of the aggression from the old woman, and she seemed taken aback, clearly not used to failing to intimidate someone.

'If Origen doesn't appear right now, I am having you arrested for harbouring a criminal, and I will have your slaves tortured to find out what they know.'

She gaped at him, her face whitening. But before she could speak, Origen stepped through the atrium entrance.

'There is no need for this unpleasantness,' he said gently. 'My lady, I am sorry for this intrusion into your house, and that apparently I am the cause of it.'

Phryne gathered herself. 'It's not your fault, brother. I can summon all my slaves, and they can hold these men while you leave, if that is your wish.'

'You can try,' growled Atius.

'That won't be necessary. Would you allow me to take these men somewhere quiet so I can talk to them about whatever concerns they have?'

'If that is your wish, brother, then of course.'

Origen inclined his head, and then indicated to Silus and Atius to follow him. He led them through the villa to a smaller room than the previous one they had been entertained in, further into the depths of the house, where they were less likely to be observed or overheard. He gestured to wooden chairs with linen seats, and when they sat, he settled himself opposite. He fidgeted for a few moments, trying to get comfortable, a pained expression on his face. Eventually he seemed satisfied. He noticed them looking at him oddly.

'You were at my meeting today? I think I saw you at the back.'

Silus nodded.

'You recall I mentioned the bodily harm I inflicted upon myself? It still troubles me.'

Silus frowned in confusion. He had been about to embark on an angry diatribe, but curiosity got the better of him.

'What harm are you referring to?'

Origen sighed. 'Since I first started teaching, I have preached to both men and women. And in the first flush of youth, with temptation all around, I wanted to ensure that there was never any doubt as to my motives, or any opportunity for slander about my actions to circulate. It says in the Book of Matthew, "There are those who have made themselves eunuchs for the Kingdom of Heaven's sake," and I took this as a literal commandment.'

Silus and Atius stared in shock.

'You... you actually...'

'I castrated myself. Yes. Nowadays, I believe that not everything in the scriptures is literal, but that every word carries a lesson for us. Unfortunately, my younger, more foolish self had not come to that understanding. It pains me to this day.'

Silus whistled. Atius looked even more confused and conflicted than before.

'I don't understand,' said Atius helplessly. 'You do something that shows such devotion to the Lord. And then you are involved in such wrong.'

Now it was Origen's turn to frown.

'What are you talking about?'

'Come on,' said Silus. 'We know all about it. Don't hide behind your piety and sanctimony. You are as bad as the rest of us.'

'I do not deny that I am a sinner. That is why the Saviour had to die. To take away the sins of people such as me. And of you, regardless of whether you appreciate his sacrifice. But I don't know what you are specifically referring to.'

'You were looking for someone after your preaching today,' said Silus. 'You seemed to be expecting someone. Who?'

'Brother John,' said Origen, matter-of-factly. 'I was surprised he did not attend. He is usually diligent in coming to my prayer meetings.'

'He is in our custody. Awaiting torture and trial.'

'What?' Origen looked genuinely shocked. 'Why?'

'Are you still going to pretend you don't know?' asked Silus.

Origen sat back, winced, adjusted his position, then looked Silus in the eyes.

'Tell me why you have him.'

'I know your answer to this already, but I presume you heard about the attack on the Temple of Isis Lochias?'

'I did. A most unfortunate event. But if they worship false idols, then they do not have the protection of the almighty God, and evil can befall them.'

Silus refrained from asking whether Origen's father had had the protection of the almighty God when he had his head cut off.

'So you approve?'

'I don't condone violence. But the Lord works in his own ways, and maybe it will show the people of this wicked city the way of the pagan is the way to damnation.'

'So you deny instructing Brother John to carry out the attack?'

Origen shook his head. 'Brother John? I heard it was the Jews.'

'That's what everyone said,' said Silus. 'Though with not a shred of evidence, I might say. In fact, it was your own disciple who hired native Egyptian thugs to murder, destroy, steal and rape.'

'How many commandments do you think Brother John broke there?' asked Atius, his voice like vinegar. 'I'm not a scholar like you. But I think there was one about not killing. One about not stealing.'

'And Atius tells me that you are not supposed to bear false witness,' said Silus. 'So let me ask you again. Did you instruct Brother John to desecrate the Temple of Isis Lochias?'

'I did not!' said Origen angrily. Then his shoulders slumped. 'Brother John is a zealot, his zeal fuelled by the violence his family had experienced, but different from the way tragedy inspired me. He shows no understanding of tolerance of another's point of view. I wish that all would convert to the true path, and I fear for the souls of those who worship false idols. And I have likely expressed to Brother John my contempt for those who tempt their fellow men away from the true path, towards the jaws of hell. But I have never instructed him to violence.'

'Well, that is how he interpreted it. He hired thugs to attack the temple and steal the gold statue of Isis. Why would he do that? Greed?'

Origen shook his head. 'He won't have taken the statue to sell it. Despite my words today, where I compared the use of Greek scholarship to the use of Egyptian gold by the Jews, Brother John would not sully himself with pagan gold. He would have intended to destroy it. Probably in a public ritual, so that all would see the power of God over Isis.'

'I'm not a native Alexandrian, but even I know that would have caused a riot.'

'It would. But he wouldn't have cared about that. Zealots don't give any thought to the consequences if they believe what they are doing is right.' Origen looked at Silus. 'What will happen now?'

'The authorities will not want to make this public, for fear of the unrest. Just a quiet word with the right people to let them know that the crime has been solved, the perpetrators punished. Hopefully no retribution against the Jews, despite what everyone in this city seems to want. And the statue returned.'

'And Brother John?'

'It will go hard for him. Torture to find out the extent of his crimes, and then a quiet execution.'

'I would plead for clemency.'

'I think you are in no position to plead for anything. Even if you didn't directly order the attack on the temple, your inflammatory words incited it. And your speech in the agora today was treasonous enough to have you executed without trial.'

Origen's mouth tightened, but he did not blanch or tremble.

'Your threats mean nothing to me. My body is the Lord's, and if he chooses to take it, so be it. But I would like that no harm come to Brother John.'

Silus found the anger welling up in him again. 'That man hired thugs to kill, steal and rape. The poor innocent priestess Tekosis would have been violated if I had not arrived in time to save her.'

'Poor innocent priestess.' Origen let out a mirthless laugh.

'What's so funny?'

'Do you think you know Tekosis?'

Silus had thought he had been getting to know her pretty well, but something in Origen's tone suddenly made him doubt this. Origen went on.

'She drinks strong wine. She fornicates. She worships a false god.'

All things that Silus himself did, at least in Origen's eyes. Though he didn't like to think of what he had done with Tekosis as fornication. It had been freer than he was used to, wilder, but it had felt like an act of love nevertheless.

'There are many in Alexandria who are guilty of the same,' said Silus. 'Why pick on her?'

'You asked me to listen to my followers, to find out where the missing boy is, and who took him.'

'Yes.' Silus suddenly felt nauseous as his anxiety about Origen's next words arose.

'I want leniency for Brother John.'

'He deserves none.'

'Nevertheless. You want to know what I know. Release Brother John without charge.'

Silus ground his teeth. He had already made a deal with the leader of the Egyptian village thugs which had gone against the grain, and now to let the man who hired them go free rankled sourly. But the same principle applied. His job was to find the boy. He looked at Atius, who nodded agreement.

'It shall be done, if you tell me what you know.'

'Tekosis did not meet you on the docks when you arrived by accident. Her temple was nearby, and she was watching and waiting for you. She knew you were coming.'

'How?'

'Because she had been told so by the ones who took the boy.'

'But... she saved us.'

'I do not know all of her motivations or instructions. You can ask her those, if she is prepared to share them with you.'

'How do you know all this?'

'I have a follower. He has converted from following Isis to the true Saviour. But I have had him remain close to the followers of Isis, so that he can inform me of their evil plans, whatever they may be. He works in the temple, and though he has to feign continued obeisance to the false goddess, he knows that ultimately it is for the glory of Christos that he does this.'

Silus shook his head. 'None of this makes sense. How do I know that you aren't just implicating an enemy?'

'I have no enemies,' said Origen. 'Just those who oppose the will of God, who know no better, or who are unwitting agents of the devil.'

'If you thought it would be to the benefit of your cult, you wouldn't hesitate to frame someone else.'

'"You shall not bear false witness." One of the commandments. Brother John may have broken commandments with his zealotry, but I do not.'

'What else do you know?'

'All I know is that Tekosis watched for your arrival at the docks and she reported it to her co-conspirators. And that she is somehow involved in the whole conspiracy to kidnap the boy.'

'Why was he kidnapped? Why is she involved? Who are the other conspirators?'

'I know none of these things,' said Origen.

Silus looked away, biting his lip, trying to quell the feeling of anger and betrayal welling up inside. Atius put a hand on his shoulder, but he shrugged it off.

'You will release Brother John?' asked Origen.

'I said I would,' said Silus.

'And I suppose you will go to see Tekosis next. I would be grateful if you made no mention of my follower who supplied the information. I would not like to see him endangered.'

'I will keep him out of it,' said Silus, rising. He pointed a finger at Origen. 'You are not blameless here. For all your moralising, your preaching about what is right, it is your hatred of other religions that led John to commit this crime, and because of it, people are dead.'

Origen bowed his head. 'If there is wrongdoing on my part, I will ask my Lord for forgiveness. But I have co-operated with you, told you what I know. What happens next is up to you. But be careful. If you take a wrong step, the consequences could be severe. For you, for the boy, and for Alexandria.'

Silus opened his mouth to retort, but he knew the preacher was right. He would have to tread very carefully indeed from here.

In the street outside Phryne's house, Silus and Atius looked at each other sombrely.

'Fuck,' said Atius.

'Fuck,' agreed Silus.

'We both thought we had met someone special. Turns out my guy is a bit of an asshole, and your girl is in with the kidnappers and has been lying out of her backside to you all along.'

'It's funny really, isn't it,' said Silus. Neither of them laughed.

'Do you want me to come with you to see Tekosis?'

'I'd rather do it on my own. If you don't mind.'

'Of course. Will you arrest her?'

'Marcellus is going to want to see some concrete evidence of progress. Especially if we are releasing Brother John.'

'She will be put to torture.'

Silus' face wrinkled in distaste. 'Unless I can get her to tell us everything.'

'Even then she might not be spared.'

'I know. But if she is part of a conspiracy to kidnap the child of a Roman governor, then her fate may well be out of our hands.'

Chapter Twelve

She had her back turned to him, standing before the altar in silent contemplation. He watched her, picturing the curves beneath her robe, remembering her scent, her soft skin, the gentle moans in his ear, the expression of ecstasy on her face. He wondered now if any of it was real. He wanted to cry. He wanted to hurl the heavy gold statue that he held in his arms against the temple walls.

He wanted her.

She turned as if sensing a presence, and when she saw him, she smiled broadly. Then she noticed what he was carrying, and her face lit up in delight. Her hand went to her mouth, and she ran forward and threw her arms around him. He tensed, did not return the kiss.

She took the statue off him, lifted it reverently into the air with outstretched arms.

'Thank you, Silus. Thank you so much, in the name of Isis.'

She walked straight to the sacrarium, unlocked it and entered. Silus followed as far as the doorway, and watched her kneel before the empty table where the statue had sat, and put it back in its rightful place. She bowed her head and intoned a lyrical and melodic prayer of thanksgiving. Then she sprang lightly to her feet and grabbed Silus around the waist, leaning forward to kiss him full on the lips. Her small wet tongue slid into his mouth, and for a moment he found he was losing himself in her once more.

He took hold of both her arms and moved her a step back. She didn't object, just continued to smile happily.

'How did you find it, Silus? Where was it? Who is responsible? Was it the Jews?'

'No, priestess. It wasn't the Jews.'

She frowned, and he noticed her face was less attractive with that expression. 'Who then?'

'I'm afraid I can't tell you. But be assured that the criminals have been dealt with and will not bother you again.'

Now she noticed the coldness of his words, his demeanour. 'Silus, what is it? What's wrong?'

Silus swallowed, and his mouth worked as he searched for the right words.

'Is there anything you want to tell me?'

She cocked her head on one side, gave a confused half-smile. 'About what?'

'Please, Tekosis. Tell me what's going on.'

'Silus, you aren't making sense.'

Silus sighed deeply. 'Tekosis, I know that you are involved with the kidnapping of Avitus. I ask you again. Please, tell me everything you know. It will go much easier for you, if you do.'

Now her face twisted in anger. 'I will tell you nothing, Roman. Isis curse you.' She spat on the floor.

'Then you will come with me to the prefect's palace. I will hand you over to Governor Marcellus, and you will be put to torture.'

'Silus,' she gasped. 'You wouldn't.'

'Come with me.'

Her hand struck out at him, bent, claws out like a lashing cat, aiming for his face, his eyes.

But he was quicker. He grabbed her wrist, twisted. She let out a small cry, and he felt a lurch in his stomach at the sound, so like her recent cries of passion. He put her arm up behind her back, and marched her from the temple, past stunned worshippers who interrupted their prayers to stare.

Outside, Atius was waiting with four legionaries. They put her wrists in manacles, and led her away.

Though he tried to hold them back, tears rolled down Silus' cheeks. Unashamed, not caring who was watching, Atius stepped up to him and took him into a strong, brotherly embrace.

—

'Torture her,' said Marcellus angrily. 'Whip her back off her. Or put her on the rack. I don't care. Just find out where my son is, then execute her, publicly and slowly.'

The words chilled Silus. It was bad enough to hear them spoken about anyone, worse about a woman, but terrible when it was a woman that he had recently slept with and had maybe started to care for. But what could he say? And how would he feel in Marcellus' position?

Of all those gathered in this small council of advisors to Marcellus, it was Soaemias that spoke up first.

'You cannot torture and execute a priestess of Isis. Not in Alexandria. Certainly not in public.'

'I can do as I please!' declared Marcellus. 'And I will. Silus, see to it at once.'

'Governor,' said Baebius Juncinus. 'While your concern is understandable, as is your wish to find the truth as quickly as possible, may I respectfully remind you that though you are a most powerful and influential person, and beloved of the Emperor, Egypt is mine to govern, unless the Emperor himself decrees otherwise.'

'I know that, prefect. But we are talking about my son!'

'Yes, but if we do as you say, it will spark civil disturbance such as has not been seen in this city for years. And you will travel on to Numidia, hopefully with your son, while I am left with legionaries to try to restore peace to a city tearing itself apart.'

'Fine, then we do it in secret.'

'No, beloved,' said Soaemias. 'You cannot keep a thing like that secret. If you torture her and release her, it will become known. If you kill her and dispose of her body discretely, she will be missed soon. In either case, the end result would be as if you stripped her naked and flogged her in the agora.'

'I have to agree with the Lady Soaemias,' said Gannys deferentially. 'Much as I want to be reunited with the young master as soon as possible.'

Marcellus leapt to his feet. 'Then tell me, all of you who say what cannot be done. Tell me what we should do.'

'You should consider releasing her, before it is noticed that she is gone,' said Gannys.

'Are you mad?' shouted Marcellus.

'I could talk to her,' said Silus quietly.

'I mean, as insane as a dog with the rage?' ranted Marcellus at Gannys. 'Why would I allow the only person we have yet found who might lead us to my son to go free?'

'She might listen to me,' said Silus.

'Why don't we just stop punishing criminals altogether? All the murderers and traitors, all those awaiting execution in the arena. Let's just open the gaol and let them wander the streets.'

'Sir,' said Silus.

Marcellus whirled on Silus, panting hard. 'What is it?'

'Let me talk to her.'

Marcellus looked at him, red-faced, chest and shoulders heaving.

'What good will that do?'

'I have come to know her. A little. Maybe I can persuade her to tell me what she knows. By a combination of threats and bribery.'

'Do you think you can do it?'

'There is nothing lost by me trying.'

'Nothing but time.' He considered. 'Very well.'

'I should do it,' interjected Soaemias.

'What?' asked Marcellus, confused.

'It should be me that talks to her. Woman to woman. A mother's appeal, for the sake of my suffering child.'

Marcellus hesitated. Silus frowned. He wanted to be the one to talk to Tekosis. He couldn't help but look forward to spending time with her, even under these circumstances.

'The Lady Soaemias makes a good point, but I don't believe Tekosis would respond to it. She is not a mother, and she is quite dedicated to her cause. If she is genuinely involved in the disappearance of Avitus, then she has obviously already hardened her heart to your son's distress.'

Marcellus thought for a moment, then nodded. 'Go to her, Silus. Talk to her. But don't take long. If you have not come back to me with information before the day is out, then I will take a whip to her myself, and I will not let anyone stop me. And if that doesn't work, I will summon the legion and tear this city apart!'

Silus bowed, ignoring the glare from Soaemias, and hurried away.

–

The guard stood to attention when Silus approached the cell, and unlocked it, removing the hefty bar so it swung open. He stepped inside and Tekosis turned abruptly, a simple pottery cup of wine in her hand. She looked guilty, like she had been caught doing something she shouldn't, but Silus couldn't see anything in the cell that was forbidden. And when he looked closer, she had tears in the corner of her eyes, and her face was pale. She looked much smaller than he remembered, and her self-assurance had vanished. She looked more defeated than after the villagers had assaulted her in the temple.

She carefully laid the cup down on a table, making sure she spilled none of it, then turned to face Silus.

Instead of speaking, he looked around the cell. Besides the table with some basic food and drink on it, there was a low bed with a reed mattress, a bucket in a corner, and a three-legged stool. By the standards of other cells he had seen, it was distinctly luxurious. Despite his anger at her, he was glad she wasn't being mistreated.

Yet her next words made his bowels clench.

'The gaoler says they are going to torture me.'

He wanted to take her in his arms, to reassure her that everything would be fine, that she was in no danger. Yet paradoxically, that might endanger her more. If he could not persuade her to open up to him, then she might indeed be put to torture, regardless of the pleadings of Soaemias and Gannys. The hardening in Marcellus' demeanour since Avitus' disappearance, both towards Soaemias and generally, had been very noticeable to Silus.

'What did he say?'

'He seemed to enjoy it, telling me what they would do. He said they would strip me, and whip my body raw. And that if I did not tell them what they wanted to know then, that they would put me on a rack and rip my limbs from their sockets.'

Silus swallowed down the bile rising in his throat.

'Then talk to me. Tell me who has Avitus. Tell me where to find him.'

She pressed her lips together and shook her head, keeping her eyes fixed on him.

'Come on, Tekosis. Make me understand. Why are you involved? Why won't you tell me what you know?'

'Do you really not know me, after everything I've told you?'

'Clearly not.'

'Then you haven't been listening. I told you, Isis and Egypt come before everything for me.'

'I gathered that. But that doesn't explain why you are involved in the abduction of the boy.'

'I haven't admitted that I am.'

Silus cocked his head on one side and raised his eyebrows.

'Egypt and Isis,' she said.

'He is some sort of priest, of this god Elagabal. You fear his god as a threat to Isis?'

'No, Silus. We have discussed this. Like Rome, Egypt does not fear to have another god join her pantheon. Look at Serapis, a Graeco-Egyptian god, taking on aspects of Osiris, Apis and Greek deities, who has in many eyes taken the place of Osiris as the consort of Isis. When you come to Alexandria for the first time, the most imposing building you will encounter is the Serapeum. Built by the Greek newcomers to help spread their culture and cement their power here.'

Silus shrugged, not seeing where this was going.

'We all know that there is power in gods, but it goes way beyond their immortal and divine abilities. Their mere names inspire men to the heights.'

'Which heights? What are you talking about?'

'Why couldn't his god Elagabal become the new husband of Isis? Imagine what message that would send to the world. A union of Syria and Egypt. It would be glorious. It would renew the pantheon, give it new life and energy, and help to fight off the threat from the Christians.'

'So you are telling me all this – the kidnapping, the piracy, the attempted murder of Marcellus – it is just to install Avitus as a new priest? In Alexandria? Presumably as some sort of puppet. And you would of course be glorified as the priestess of Isis, his bride.'

'I never got involved for my own glorification, Silus. I would like you to believe that.'

He shook his head. 'It's not enough. Why Avitus? There must be others in Syria that worship Elagabal that you could have brought to Alexandria to introduce the cult, and with much less risk than kidnapping the son of one of the most powerful people in the Empire.'

He turned to the table and picked up the cup of wine.

'Silus,' said Tekosis sharply. Her eyes were fixed on his hands.

'Talk to me, Tekosis. Spare yourself the torture.'

Tekosis looked anguished. 'Let me drink. I need to settle my nerves. Then I will talk.'

Silus gave a half-smile. 'Is this wine really such a panacea?' He passed her the cup. She took it gratefully in both hands then stared down into it. She was still for a moment.

'I did like you, Silus. I didn't take you to my bed for the glory of Isis or Egypt, or for the conspiracy. I did it because I wanted to.'

Silus didn't know whether that mattered any more.

'Don't think less of me. I did what I thought was right.'

She put the wine to her lips and drank deeply, almost draining the cup. Then she replaced it on the table and said, 'Isis, intercede for me with the Lord Osiris and guide me to the afterlife.'

A sudden sense of alarm flooded over Silus.

'Tekosis. What have you done?'

'I'm beyond your justice now, Silus. Beyond the reach of your torturers.'

He picked up the cup of wine and saw some crushed leaves in the bottom. He picked them out and sniffed. They smelt musty, like rat urine.

'Hemlock,' said Tekosis. 'It won't be long now.'

Silus threw the cup against the wall, where it shattered into shards.

'Who gave you the poison?'

'You think I would give up their name now? When I have just chosen death over betrayal of the cause?'

Silus grabbed her by both wrists, staring into her eyes.

'Tekosis, listen to me. I know you are doing what you believe is right. But the consequences will be terrible. Marcellus will set the legions loose in the streets if he doesn't find his son soon, and I have seen what happens when the soldiers are given their head in a city. The suffering will be incalculable. Fire, rape, robbery, murder. So many innocents dead.'

Doubt crept into Tekosis' eyes.

'He wouldn't. Soaemias wouldn't let him.'

'Soaemias has some control over him, true, but I know Marcellus better than you. He has become the Emperor's right-hand man by doing anything he needs to do to get what he wants.'

Tekosis' pupils were wide, making it seem like her eyes had turned black, and she had a tremor in her hand. Was it doubt and fear, or the poison working already?

'Tell me where the boy is. Do the right thing. Egypt can still be great. The boy could still bring Elagabal to Egypt and introduce his worship here. But he must be returned to his father, safe, soon.'

Tekosis sat down on the bed heavily.

'I don't know where they are keeping him,' she said, and her voice carried the first traces of a slur.

'Who else is involved?' said Silus urgently.

Tekosis leaned forward, gripping her stomach, and let out a groan.

'Oh. It burns. I didn't expect... the pain.'

Silus knelt down in front of her and grasped her hands.

'Tekosis. Trust me. I recovered your idol. I respect her, but I fear for her, and for this city. Tell me something, anything, so I can reunite the boy with his father and stop him bringing down the wrath of the legions on the people.'

'The legions,' said Tekosis, and her voice was becoming a whisper.

'The legions,' said Silus. 'What about them?'

'The legate. He is part of it.'

'Gratidius? Why? In what way?'

'Don't know. Silus, I'm scared. I don't know what is right.' She gasped. 'My heart. It races. Hold me, Silus.'

Silus put his arms around her, held her close. She whispered in his ear. 'Did I do the right thing for Isis, for Egypt, by being a part of all this? Or am I doing the right thing by telling you about it now?'

'You are doing the right thing now,' he said with as much conviction as he could muster. From his point of view, it was right, saving a boy, preventing severe retribution on the city. From her point of view, with her different loyalty and perspective, maybe not. He had no idea. But he was going to give her as much reassurance as he could in her last moments. 'The information you just gave me will save many lives. And will prevent a backlash that could threaten your city and the worship of your goddess.'

She looked up into his eyes, and tears rolled out of the corners. She tried to say something, but instead of words, a trickle of clear drool emerged and ran down her chin. Then her head went back in a vicious spasm. The veins and tendons in her rigid neck stood out like little serpents.

And the convulsions began. She collapsed onto her side on the bed, and her whole body shook violently. Her mouth foamed, and she let out guttural gasps and groans. He struggled to keep hold of her as she writhed and twitched. The seizure became more and more violent, until abruptly it stopped. She remained rigid in his arms for a long moment and Silus searched her eyes desperately for any sign of consciousness. For what seemed an eternity, her gaze appeared to lock on his.

Then she went limp, and the room filled with the acrid smell of faeces as her bowels voided.

Chapter Thirteen

Silus strode into Marcellus' tablinum, shoving the guard at the door out of the way before he could react. The guard ran in after him, drawing his sword.

'Sir,' gasped Silus. 'I have information.'

'I'm sorry, sir,' said the guard. 'I couldn't stop him.' He looked at the Arcanus suspiciously, knowing he was outmatched even though Silus was unarmed. 'Shall I summon help?'

'No,' said Marcellus. 'Get out and close the door.'

When the guard had done so, he snapped, 'Come on then, Silus, out with it.'

'Tekosis is dead.'

Marcellus jumped to his feet and slammed the desk with both hands.

'Jupiter's cock, Silus, you incompetent fool! What did you do to her? I thought you were just supposed to be talking to her!'

'Someone supplied her with poison, sir.'

'What?' He sat back down. 'How did they get to her?'

'It must have been someone trusted by both her and by the guard.'

'You questioned the guard?'

'Of course. The shift had just changed before I got there. It would have been the previous guard that would have seen who visited her. Unfortunately, he has vanished. He is not in the barracks, nor in any of the places his comrades thought he might be. I fear he is likely to be dead.'

'So we have nothing?'

'On the contrary, sir. Before she died, she gave me a name.'

'Tell me.'

'Gratidius.'

'What? Explain.'

'She said she didn't know. I think I believe her. They were more or less her dying words.'

'What else did she say?'

'It was mainly self-justification, talking about how great Isis and Egypt were. But she also said some things about your son I didn't really understand. How they have brought him here because of his role as a priest of Elagabal.'

'What does that have to do with anything?'

'She said there was a plan to bring the worship of Elagabal to Alexandria, to unite him with Isis, in order to unite Egypt and the provinces of the East.'

Marcellus considered. 'So they plan to inspire some sort of religious revolt? Like the Jews did?'

'I think so, but not one restricted to one particular race. It's more to do with geography.'

'But there are other priests of Elagabal. Yes, Avitus is destined to be high priest, but surely they could have found someone else – there would be many priests of Elagabal, adults, who would love an opportunity to spread the worship of their god, and would not need to be coerced. Why my son?'

Silus spread his hands helplessly.

Marcellus bit his lip. 'So where does Gratidius fit into this?'

'I don't know, sir. But he is Syrian, isn't he?'

'His family is from Emesa I believe.'

'I think I should speak to him.'

'Do so, straight away. With my full authority to do whatever is necessary to find out where my son is.'

'Where may I find him, sir? Is he at the barracks?'

'He was visiting the prefect this afternoon. You may find him still there if you hurry.'

Unfortunately, Silus was just too late to intercept Gratidius at the prefect's office.

The prefect's secretary informed Silus that he had left just moments before, and had seemed to be in a hurry when he left. Silus insisted on seeing the prefect, pushing his way into his office when the secretary stalled him.

'Silus? How dare you barge in here?'

'I apologise, prefect, but time is of the essence. What did you say to Gratidius?'

Juncinus made a sour face, but obviously read Silus' expression of urgency.

'He came to ask me what progress had been made in the search for Avitus.'

'Did he tell you why he was interested?'

'Well, no. I just presumed he thought it of importance to him, in his role as commander of the Roman forces here.'

'And what did you say?'

'That there was no news, except that we had taken the priestess of Isis Lochias into custody.'

'What was his reply?'

Juncinus frowned. 'I don't recall. He just said he should return to his duties in the barracks and left. Quite hurriedly, now I think about it.'

'Thank you for your help, prefect. I am sorry for the inconvenience, but I must go and find Gratidius straight away.'

'I understand, Silus, and your disrespect is forgiven. This time.'

Silus rushed out of the office, making his way towards the main palace entrance. When he emerged from the palace, the sky above him had turned a dark purple, and in the west, the orange sun illuminated the underside of the clouds with a glow like the hot embers of a bonfire. The barracks were to the east, outside the city walls, beyond the tombs and sepulchres of the Jews. He oriented himself, intending to proceed towards the barracks, the site of Gratidius' power and authority, where he would surely be heading.

But as he passed through the gates, he grabbed one of the duty guards by the shoulder.

'Gratidius. Did you see him? Which way did he go?'

The soldier looked confused. 'The legate? Yes, I saw him running west.'

West? That was the opposite direction to the barracks. What was that way?

The docks!

Shit. Gratidius was fleeing. He believed that Tekosis would have given his name up, and obviously wasn't as certain of the loyalty of the troops as he would like. Silus put his head down and ran.

Like the colonies that Rome built from scratch, but unlike the ancient cities such as Rome or Athens, Alexandria was built on a grid pattern of streets. So as he ran westwards, he realised that he could be on a parallel route to Gratidius. He had to hope that he had guessed his destination correctly, and could intercept him there.

Although nighttime was approaching, the streets were still busy, and he had to weave through the people of all classes, races and religions, and the animals, sacred, domestic and incidental. He took great care not to step on a cat or kick a wandering ibis, though he was much less considerate to the people that slowed him down, who received a hard push out of the way with shoulder or forearm.

He ran past the great, ancient obelisks, the tomb of Alexander – still crowded with the curious and the devout – past the library and Mouseion, then turned north, with the Caesarion to his right and the harbour straight ahead.

Of course the docks were huge and thronged, and the failing light did not help him. He hurried along the wharves, straining his neck to see over and around the dockers and sailors and travellers in an attempt to spot his quarry. If he was right, Gratidius would be by one of these boats or ships, negotiating desperately with a captain to buy urgent passage. If he was wrong, the chance to find Avitus would have slipped through his fingers.

He grabbed a sailor who was leaning against a post, eating a pie.

'Have you seen a Roman looking for passage? Tall man, Syrian, in uniform.'

The sailor's reply was muffled by meat and pastry. 'Not feen a fing. Fuck off.'

Silus ran to another. 'A Roman. Tall, dark-skinned. Have you seen him? I have money.'

'How much?'

'Tell me if you've seen him, and I'll tell you how much.'

'No, you tell me how much and I'll tell you if I've seen him.'

But at that moment, there was a fortuitous parting of the crowds, like a cloudy sky parting briefly to reveal a glimpse of the sun. And through the gap, Silus saw Gratidius, fifty yards away, shaking his finger in the face of a mariner, holding up a bag of coins in the other. Silus pushed the sailor he was talking to aside, and ran towards Gratidius.

The crowd closed up again, and he momentarily lost sight of the legate. He jostled and shoved, and one slave with a sack of wheat over his shoulder lost his balance and tumbled over backwards. The sack landed on the foot of a sailor who shouted in pain and pushed the slave hard. The slave, knowing better than to raise his hands to a free man, cowered down, holding his hands up in defence as the sailor laid about his head with closed fists.

The commotion caused Gratidius to turn. His eyes fixed first on the fight, then drifted sideways to see Silus struggling through the crowd towards him. His mouth dropped, and he turned and fled.

Silus cursed and redoubled his efforts to close on the fleeing commander. It was like swimming through honey, men impeding his every step. But Gratidius was struggling too, grabbing slaves and merchants alike and thrusting them out of his way with curses. He threw frequent glances over his shoulder towards Silus to see if the Arcanus was gaining. In fact, Silus was getting no nearer, but neither was he falling behind, and he was managing to keep Gratidius in sight the whole time.

Suddenly the dock ran out as Gratidius reached the heptastadion, the long, narrow causeway that led out to the island of Pharsos. Deriving its name from its length – the equivalent of seven stadia, or roughly three-quarters of a mile – the causeway had been built at the founding of the city to link Pharos to the mainland and to create two safe harbours, the Great Harbour to the east and the Eunostos Harbour to the west.

Silus saw Gratidius hesitate. The docks to the west of the heptastadion were just as crowded as those to the east that they had just come through, as were the roads leading south into the city. To the north, the traffic travelling on the causeway, mainly donkey carts transporting various loads, was more ordered. And although it was in some ways a dead end, the island of Pharos was a good size, with a town and a small port of its own on its northern shore.

Gratidius made a hasty decision and ran onto the causeway. He intercepted a cart hauling wood as fuel for the lighthouse, grabbed the driver and threw him to the ground. He leapt onto the cart and flapped the reins hard. The donkey trotted forward, surprised at the sudden command to accelerate. It was no great speed, and Silus found that by sprinting towards it, he was gaining, little by little.

But he could not maintain that speed for long, and quickly found his breath was coming in deep heaving gasps. Still, he found himself mere feet behind the donkey cart, almost near enough to leap onto its back. Gratidius turned and saw how close his pursuer was. He reached to the back of the cart and grabbed a bolt that held the back gate of the cart closed. He struggled with it, wiggling it frantically to loosen it. Then with a yank, the bolt came loose, the gate flapped open, and a dozen large logs rolled out into Silus' path.

He had no time to run around them, so he tried to hurdle them. But his fatiguing legs did not do as they were told. He stumbled as he leapt, didn't get as much height or distance as he had aimed for. For a moment it seemed nevertheless that he would clear all the logs as they rolled down the causeway towards him. But they were not rolling in an ordered way, and the second to last was angled differently from the final log, and so moving at a different speed. The last log bumped into it, slowed, and Silus landed on top of it, his leading foot disappearing backwards beneath him, pitching him forward onto his face.

He landed heavily, breaking the fall with outstretched hands, palms grazed by gravel and sand. He pushed himself painfully to his feet, cursing as the cart put distance between them. He gingerly tested his weight, making sure nothing was broken or sprained, then set off at a slower trot, watching the cart gradually increase its distance from him.

Another donkey cart appeared behind him, this one carrying kindling. Silus stepped out in front of it, his hand up. The driver reined the donkey in, coming to a stop just before him.

'Get out of the way, you idiot,' the driver shouted at him.

'I'm taking this cart, in the name of the Emperor of Rome.'

The driver looked back at his rickety old cart, then at his ageing donkey, and then back at Silus, wearing an expression of confusion.

'You want this cart?'

'Move aside,' snapped Silus.

'But my master...'

Silus showed the blade at his belt, and the driver blanched and jumped down.

'All yours, sir, but I warn you, this one is a real bastard.'

Silus leapt up into the seat, grabbed the reins, and flapped them up and down vigorously.

The donkey stood still, chewing at some leftover hay stuck between its teeth.

'Move, you bastard.' The donkey turned its head slowly, gave Silus a contemptuous glance, then continued to chew impassively. The driver looked on with a look of self-satisfied, told-you-so amusement.

Silus drew his knife and stabbed the donkey in its backside.

It wasn't a deep stab, the tip of the blade penetrating the tough hide maybe a quarter of an inch. It must have felt like a particularly vicious horse fly bite. The donkey let out an outraged bray, and set off in a panicked gallop.

The change into motion was so abrupt it caught Silus by surprise, and he fell over backwards, into the cart, dry twigs parting so he hit his head on the wooden base as his feet flew comically up into the air. He ignored the mocking laughter from the driver that echoed after him down the heptastadion, and he struggled back into his seat, and fumbled for the reins.

He had no control over the charging equid, and the reins in his hands were little more use to him than a child's comfort toy. But he had no real need to give instruction. The road was straight, with no option to veer off on the wrong course, just dark sea to left and right. And the donkey was galloping at full pace.

He looked ahead and saw that he was once more gaining on Gratidius, who looked behind him frequently while urging his own beast on to greater speed. The other traffic on the road gave the two racers a wide berth, seeing them coming from far off. All of them gawped at the sight of the remarkable race.

Silus was only a hundred feet behind when they reached the end of the heptastadion. The road branched at this point, heading to different destinations on the island – the docks, the lighthouse, the temple, the town. And now they encountered heavier traffic, as roads converged onto the narrow causeway, and there was no room for the other road users to get out of the way. Gratidius' donkey found its passage blocked, and stopped suddenly rather than plough into a slow moving ox-wagon.

Gratidius' curse was loud enough for Silus to hear, despite the distance, although this was now rapidly closing as his own panicking donkey charged on. He saw Gratidius dismount, and run on foot.

The two oxen pulling the wagon which had stopped Gratidius had plodded their way around the obstruction, and were heading slowly but inexorably towards Silus. He pulled on the reins hard, but the donkey was having none of it, still in total blind panic as he attempted to flee whatever outsized insect had attacked his rear end.

Just as the donkey ran head first into the oxen, Silus let out a loud cry and jumped sideways, clear of the impending crash. He rolled several times, hearing the noise of the collision as the world tumbled around him. He came to rest on his front, and lay for a moment, taking a breath. He looked up to see a cart wheel trundling straight for his head, and heard at the same moment the carter yelling at him to get out of the way. He rolled to his right, and the heavy wheel rolled over the spot his head had occupied the briefest heartbeat before.

Painfully he stood. The donkey looked dazed but unharmed. The oxen had stopped but appeared to have taken no injury whatsoever. The cart that Silus had been riding had overturned and thrown a wheel. He supposed that the top speed of a donkey was much lower than that of a horse. If that had been a horse-drawn chariot, the horse would have been a broken mess and the chariot would have been firewood.

Up ahead, he saw Gratidius threading his way through the traffic, heading north. Silus pictured the topography, remembering the lighthouse and the harbour when they had first sailed into Alexandria. A promontory on the north coast of the island of Pharos ran to the east, forming the northern part of the Great Harbour. Boats regularly docked there, beneath the soaring height of the lighthouse at the tip of the promontory. Gratidius must be hoping for one last chance to find a berth on a vessel out of Alexandria. And only Silus could stop him.

It was a gruelling chase of endurance. Both men were fit, relatively young, and bulky enough to be able to push through the crowds. As they moved north, the traffic and density of the crowds thinned and they both increased their speed. They passed residential houses, administrative buildings, shops and the ornate Temple of Isis Pharia. But always the view ahead was dominated by the lighthouse.

Though his breath was short, his chest heaving with the effort of trying to close the gap on his quarry, Silus could not help but look up at the wondrous structure. Three hundred feet tall, built from large blocks of limestone, with granite reinforcing the angles for strength, the lighthouse was made up of three tapering tiers, the lowest square, the middle octagonal and the top circular. Four statues of the god Triton blowing horns to guard against shipwrecks stood guard at each corner of the lowest floor, while at the top was a statue of Triton's father Poseidon, keeping watch over the harbour and the seas.

But the most wonderful part of the construction was the mirror at the highest point, which reflected the sun's rays out to sea during the day, and the light of an enormous fire at night. Night was indeed falling, and as Silus watched, a small glow at the top of the tower grew and burst forth into a bright flame.

The failing daylight made it harder for Silus to keep Gratidius in view, but in fact he was gaining on the legate. Being a soldier meant that Gratidius had to maintain some degree of fitness to keep the respect of his men, but he didn't train nearly as hard as a legionary. Silus, on the other hand, kept himself as fit as his work allowed, and the difference began to tell. By the time they reached the narrow strip of land leading out to the lighthouse, Silus was only a score of feet behind. Although they had passed a handful of docked boats, there was no way Gratidius would have been able to board one and escape before Silus was on him, let alone negotiate the terms of passage.

Though Silus' lungs and legs were screaming in pain, he was spurred on by the knowledge that he would soon overtake his quarry. Gratidius knew it too. And he was running out of land. Beyond the lighthouse was only sea.

Gratidius stopped at the ramp leading up to the lowest level of the lighthouse and looked back. Silus could see the desperation on his face. The legate began to run up the steps on the ramp. Silus groaned. He had a bad feeling about where this was leading.

Silus only appreciated how enormous the lighthouse was when he was right up next to it. The ramp leading to the door on the lowest floor was mounted on sixteen magnificent arches. The lowest level of the lighthouse was vast, housing the horde of workers required to keep the lighthouse fuelled and operating. Silus followed Gratidius inside, and found himself in a hollow structure with dozens of rooms for living quarters or storage. Another internal ramp led up to the second floor, wide enough for two oxen to be pulling a cartload of wood slowly up towards the pinnacle.

Gratidius pushed past surprised lighthouse workers, slaves and overseers, and mounted the ramp, with Silus hard on his heels. If Silus had thought the chase had been challenging up to this point, it required a whole new level of endurance and willpower now. The gradient of the ramp was steep, and he had to force his legs beneath him to keep moving ever upwards. When they reached the second floor, Silus had to stop and lean against a wall, gasping hard, fearing he might pass out with the exertion. Gratidius looked back, and seeing his pursuer had stopped, did likewise. They stared at each other, chests heaving, unable to speak, separated by mere feet, too exhausted to move.

Silus gulped down some deep lungfuls of air, and forced himself into motion once more. Gratidius' shoulders slumped momentarily, then he too started to move.

There was no ramp up from the second floor, just an internal staircase, so all the fuel had to be moved upwards by hand from this stage. Slaves with sacks of wood on bent backs made their way slowly up the staircase, while others with empty sacks came down, moving not much faster.

Their gait could not really be called running now as they ascended the staircase. Silus' calves were on fire, the muscles of his ribs groaned with each inhalation, and still they went on. This floor was half the height of the lower floor, but was still about a hundred feet high, and when they finally reached the upper floor, they were both spent.

Silus stumbled up the last step, rounded a corner and was hit by an immediate blast of heat and light. The fire was huge, roaring and spitting as it worked its way through forests of logs that succumbed to its vast appetite. Although most of the smoke was billowing upwards into the sky, there was enough swirling around in the wind that when Silus took a gasping breath, he immediately bent over and coughed uncontrollably.

Gratidius likewise had stopped to cough spasmodically. Silus straightened, taking control of his breathing, and made his way towards Gratidius. Gratidius gathered himself and stumbled away.

'Gratidius,' cried out Silus, his voice cracked and hoarse. 'What's the point? There is nowhere to go.'

Gratidius waved to the workers, a group of slaves stripped to the waist, blackened with soot, who had stopped to stare at the unexpected interlopers. 'I am legate Gratidius,' he said and pointed at Silus. 'That man is an assassin. Seize him.'

The slaves stared in incomprehension. Some of it was due to a genuine inability to understand the Greek that Gratidius spoke, but others could not comprehend why a Roman soldier would expect them to aid him in a matter that was clearly none of their business.

Gratidius waited a moment for them to react, and when he realised they were going to do nothing, he cursed and pushed himself back into motion. His path took him around behind the enormous mirror that was reflecting the fire's light miles out to sea. Silus followed, and the slight excess in his energy reserves compared to his quarry's gave him just enough edge to catch up. As Gratidius staggered away, breathing hoarsely, gripping the rail that surrounded the summit of the lighthouse, Silus finally reached him, grabbed him by the collar, and hauled him backwards.

Gratidius yelped and fell clumsily. For a moment he lay still, breathing deeply, and Silus wondered if he had injured him. He hadn't thought that he had knocked his head, but just as he was about to step forward to check, Gratidius levered himself onto his hands and knees and looked up at Silus.

'You killed Tekosis,' said Silus, and his voice, though cracked from the heat and smoke, was as cold as ice.

Tekosis was the first woman Silus had slept with since the death of his wife. He wasn't sure what that meant, but he was sure that he had wanted to find out. And he was sure too that this man kneeling before him had provided the poison that had allowed her to take her life.

'Why?' asked Silus, trying to keep a pleading tone out of his voice.

Gratidius coughed and spat a glob of phlegm.

'To avoid this,' he said with a sardonic half-smile.

'Good plan,' said Silus bitterly.

They were both silent for a moment, ignoring the onlooking slaves as they slowly recovered their wind.

'Why get involved at all?' Silus said eventually, when talking had become easier.

'Why does anyone do anything in this Empire? Power, advancement, money.'

'Not everyone is motivated by those things.'

'True,' said Gratidius. 'There are also the fanatics.'

'And it's fanatics you got into bed with?'

Gratidius nodded. 'I thought they would be a useful means to an end.'

'They probably thought the same of you.'

'I do support their cause. I just thought there would be something in it for me.'

'And their cause is what?'

'You don't know?'

'I want to hear it from you.'

Gratidius sighed. 'They kidnapped Avitus so they could make him ruler of the eastern Roman Empire, and make his god Elagabal the pinnacle of the pantheon.'

'And where does Isis come into it?'

'She would be his consort.'

'But she isn't the consort of Elagabal. How can humans decree it to be so?'

'You are so naive, Silus. Look at Serapis, worshipped here at the moment before all others, revered throughout the Empire, including by the current Emperor and his father. And yet he was invented just a few centuries ago by the Ptolemies, a synthesis of Apis the bull and Osiris, lord of the underworld.'

'You can invent a god? Why would you do that?'

'To give the new half-Greek, half-Egyptian city of Alexandria a god that could be worshipped by all, that would unite everyone in the city and the country.'

'Alexandria hardly seems to be united.'

'Well, Jews, Christians and Romans did spoil things somewhat.'

'Where is Avitus?' said Silus.

'Why would I tell you that?'

Silus pulled his knife from his belt. 'You think you have choices right now?'

Gratidius seemed to shrink. He was unarmed, exhausted and on his knees.

'It's probably too late now.'

'What do you mean?' asked Silus, a cold feeling coming over him.

'Why do you think I decided to run, instead of stick it out? Once Tekosis was captured, Aziz would know that the plan would likely be discovered. He will probably take matters into his own hands, against the will of the leaders of the plot.'

'What are you talking about?'

'Aziz is a true fanatic. If he thinks he has lost the chance to elevate Avitus here on earth, I think he will take them both to the next world, and hope the sacrifice will inspire the revolution he craves.'

'Shit. Shit, shit, shit.' He took a step forward and pressed the knife to Gratidius' throat. 'Tell me now. Where is Avitus being held?'

'In a room below the Serapeum,' said Gratidius.

Silus' eyes flicked out over the city, the huge Temple of Serapis far away, barely visible despite its bulk in the dim dusk light.

Gratidius grabbed the knife, wrenched it aside and threw himself at Silus. The knife clattered to the floor. Reactions dulled by fatigue and the noise and smoke, Silus was a fraction too slow. Gratidius forced him backwards, against the rail that separated them from a 400-foot drop onto the rocks below. The wood creaked, and Silus heard a crack that sent his heart racing. He grabbed Gratidius around the throat and squeezed with all his strength, but behind him, he felt the railing, never designed to be tested like this, begin to give.

Against all common sense, he turned his head and saw, way down below, waves crashing against jagged rocks on the seaward side of the promontory. Panic overtook him, and he twisted his body, hurling Gratidius sideways. The legate hit the railing hard, and with a crash and a howl of despair, he disappeared over the edge.

And pulled Silus with him.

Silus flailed, grabbed out with one hand, latched onto one of the wooden posts supporting the rail. His body felt immensely heavy, and he looked down to find Gratidius gripping his legs in a tight hug. The legate whimpered as he slid down Silus' shins, then came to a halt at his ankles.

Silus grasped the post with his other hand, managed to hook the crook of his elbow around it.

'Help me,' gasped Gratidius.

The post began to creak as its middle bent alarmingly. It wasn't meant to bear more weight than a light strip of wood.

'Climb up me,' said Silus, cursing himself for stupidity as he said it.

Gratidius hauled himself upwards, his feet skittering against the wall to try to gain extra purchase. But this pushed them both outwards, which changed the angle of the weight on the post, making it bow even more. Gratidius inched himself upwards, painfully gripping Silus' legs in his terror.

The post cracked, a split running diagonally along its length, which continued to enlarge. In moments it would give way.

Silus closed his eyes, wrenched one foot away from Gratidius' grip.

'Silus, what are you doing? Please…'

Silus smashed his heel down into Gratidius' face.

The grip eased, but one kick wasn't enough.

The second was.

The impact on the legate's face shuddered up his leg. With a scream that diminished with distance, Gratidius fell into the darkness.

Silus didn't have time to look down. He swung himself sideways and grasped the next post along with his left hand, just as the post in his right hand came free, and flew over his shoulder.

He gripped the undamaged post tightly and screamed at the slaves to come and help him.

No longer in personal danger, and no longer worried about picking the losing side, they hurried over to haul Silus back up onto the platform at the summit of the lighthouse. He lay there like a fish chucked into the bottom of a boat, gasping for air.

Chapter Fourteen

'It's over,' said Gannys.

'It is *not* over!' said Aziz.

Avitus looked from one to the other, confused, and becoming a little frightened.

'What's happened?' he asked, his voice quiet in the small chamber.

The two men ignored him, focusing on each other, their faces inches apart.

'Tekosis knows too much,' said Gannys. He broke contact with Aziz and paced the room, hands clasped together before him. 'We don't know how much she will have told Marcellus' men. If the reputation of those Arcani is half true, they will have extracted every ounce of information she possessed, and she will have begged to tell them more.'

'She's dead,' said Aziz. 'I got the poison to her.'

'Not quickly enough. And now you say Gratidius has fled. It's falling apart.'

'Am I not going to be Emperor any more?' asked Avitus.

Aziz turned to the boy at last.

'We are going to glorify Elagabal, my lord.'

'So everything is going to plan?'

'Plans change, my lord. But all is well.'

'What change?' asked Gannys. 'What are you going to do?'

'I am going to fulfil my vow. The people of Alexandria will know the power of Elagabal, and will bow down and worship him.'

'You will do nothing without orders,' said Gannys firmly. 'Do you understand me?'

'I know to whom my loyalty lies,' said Aziz.

Even the young Avitus could tell that was no answer. Gannys clenched his fists and ground his teeth. 'Just wait for my return. I need to get back to Marcellus and Soaemias. They will be wondering where I am. And pray to Elagabal for me that Tekosis has not mentioned my name.'

'Go,' said Aziz. 'I will look after the precious lord. Return at dawn.'

Gannys eyed him suspiciously.

'Why dawn?'

'Because it will be the beginning of a new day.'

Gannys opened his mouth to reply, but clearly could not think of a retort.

'Do *nothing*.' He swept out of the chamber.

–

Silus stood as still as possible before Marcellus, and not just from respect to authority. Every muscle in his body screamed at the slightest movement. He made a mental note to add distance running to his training regime. If Gratidius had been slightly fitter, he would have escaped, and Avitus might have been lost beyond recovery.

'Sir, Gratidius implied there was some urgency.'

He had relayed what Gratidius had confessed, which was frustratingly less than he could have found out if he hadn't let the soldier fall to his death. But he had told Silus that the threat to Avitus may have become more acute since Tekosis' capture, and he was trying to impress this on Marcellus.

Marcellus, though, was hesitant, listening to advice from Gannys and Soaemias as well as Silus.

'Gannys, explain again why I can't just send a cohort of legionaries into the Serapeum and search it from cellar to summit until they find my son.'

'Because,' said Gannys, 'I fear that would alert the abductors to their discovery. Legionaries marching through the Serapeum entering every room cannot be disguised, especially at night when there is little other activity. The kidnappers might decide to do away with Avitus and themselves rather than be caught. They will know that the punishment that awaits them will be far worse than a simple, self-inflicted death. And if they commit suicide, why wouldn't they take Avitus with them?'

'Marcellus,' said Soaemias earnestly. 'Don't take any action that would endanger our boy.'

Marcellus threw his hands up. 'But what do I do?'

'Sir, as I already said, send Atius and myself. We will find him for you.'

Silus wished he was as confident as he felt. The chances of successfully finding the boy in that vast complex, without alerting the kidnappers, and then rescuing him alive, seemed slim. But he was confident that it was Avitus' best chance of survival.

'How will you do that?' asked Marcellus uncertainly.

'We are Arcani. Trained in infiltration, in secrecy. I don't know exactly how we will find him and rescue him, but I know that we can. Sir, we are the best.'

Atius stood stiffly beside him. Silus knew he was unused to hearing his friend boast, and it was true that arrogance was not really part of his make-up. But this was a means to an end. He needed to be chosen to rescue Avitus. Not only did he believe he had the best chance, he genuinely cared about the boy's fate, and the welfare of his parents.

'Very well,' said Marcellus with obvious reluctance. 'You have proven yourself many times, Silus, to me, and to the Emperor. I will put my trust in you. Find my son. Rescue him, please.'

'Sir, if I may,' said Gannys.

'What is it?'

'Might I suggest they delay their mission until daylight?'

'What? Why?' Silus asked, surprised.

'I gave my reasoning already. The Serapeum is a quiet place at night. If you start sneaking around, searching rooms and asking questions, you might alert the kidnappers.'

'That's ridiculous. It's easier to remain undetected at night.'

'If you are infiltrating an enemy camp, maybe. But during the day, you can blend in as if you are one of the visitors or worshippers. It will be much less risky.'

'Sir, I was told time is of the essence.'

Marcellus put his finger and thumb together and picked his lower teeth with his fingernails.

'I don't want to take any unnecessary chances.'

'There will be risks either way,' said Silus.

'I'm aware of that,' said Marcellus. 'Soaemias, dear, what do you think?'

Soaemias toyed with the material of her dress, looking down into her lap. Then she looked up and spoke decisively.

'We should wait for the morning. The legionaries can be stationed nearby for backup. Silus and Atius can find him then.'

'Yes,' said Marcellus. 'I agree. Silus, those are your orders. You will wait for sunrise before you begin the rescue.'

Silus sighed and his shoulders slumped.

'Yes, sir.'

He hoped they wouldn't be too late.

–

'Where are we going?' asked Avitus.

'To immortality,' replied Aziz.

Avitus still wasn't sure whether he was a captive or an honoured guest, and being led quietly with a firm hand on his shoulder through the Serapeum complex in the last hour before sunrise did nothing to reassure him.

'Am I still going to be Emperor?' he asked.

'More than that,' said Aziz. 'You are going to become a god. You are going to reign at the right hand of our Lord Elagabal.'

That sounded good, thought Avitus, and yet he couldn't suppress a shudder down his spine.

The slaves and priests of the temple were beginning their daily tasks, cleaning, sweeping, some early prayers of worship to Serapis, Isis and Anubis. None paid attention to the slight man and the young boy walking briskly through the gardens.

Avitus looked around him as Aziz marched him on. The faintest glow in the sky to the east was allowing him to see a little of his environs. Mainly shadows, but even so, he could appreciate the magnificence of the buildings and grounds. His attention was caught by a shrine to Anubis, a small fire burning before a statue of the jackal-headed god, who was carrying the scales he used to weigh the hearts of the dead. He dawdled for a moment to look up at the canine features, but Aziz grabbed his wrist and tugged.

'Hurry, my lord. We must be in place in time.'

'What place? In time for what?'

'The Lord Elagabal will reveal all,' was the only answer. Avitus began to wonder whether he should continue to follow this man. But Gannys had said he should. And he trusted Gannys.

They entered the main temple of the Serapeum as a pale orange glow illuminated the horizon, where it could be glimpsed between the buildings. The enormous statue of Serapis immediately grabbed Avitus' gaze and held it firm. They walked slowly, reverently, towards it. At the periphery of his vision, Silus saw other grand statues – Isis, Apis the bull, as well as strange mechanical contraptions and tapestries and murals in gold, red and blue.

Aziz led Avitus to the altar before the statue.

'It's so big,' said Avitus in awe.

'And yet dwarfed by the power of the Lord Elagabal.'

Then two cloaked, hooded figures stepped out from behind the statue. It took Avitus a moment to recognise them in the gloom. First the man, maybe identified before the female form because his presence was expected.

'Gannys? What are you doing here?'

And then his eyes focused on the woman beside him.

'Mother?'

—

'Technically it's still not sunrise,' said Atius as they hurried along the Via Canopica.

Technically he was right, as the sun's presence was no more than a glow in the east at this stage.

'Technically, I don't give a fuck,' said Silus. He paused at a crossroads, saw the bulk of the Serapeum on its hill to the left, and turned in its direction down the Via Serapea.

'Marcellus thinks you are delaying a further hour. The legionaries won't be in place until then.'

'Something smells wrong,' said Silus. 'It doesn't make sense. Why did Gannys insist we wait until dawn? We are trained and experienced in working undercover at night.'

'Maybe he is one of those people who just have to be right.'

Silus shook his head. He had been awake most of the night, playing the conversation with Marcellus and Gannys over in his mind, but unable to stop his thoughts drifting away to his terrifying experience at the top of the lighthouse. When he had managed to doze for some short moments, he had dreamed of dangling over the edge of a cliff, with a monstrous Scylla, multiple heads on sinuous necks full of sharp teeth, rearing out of the water and snapping at his heels. He had jerked awake and been unable to fall asleep again, and instead had gone over his plan for the day.

Which was... fluid. In fact, it only went as far as: get to the Serapeum and start looking. He hoped inspiration would strike him when he got there.

'Come on, let's speed it up.' He broke into a loping run, which a grumbling Atius matched. His legs felt like they had been beaten with sticks; the abused muscles felt more like they were bruised than fatigued. He put his hand on his short sword, reassured by the cold metal. If things went badly wrong, there was always a sharp edge to fall back on. But he feared that if it came to that, Avitus would be lost.

They ascended the steep hill atop which sat the vast Serapeum complex and its grounds and subsidiary buildings, the incline making them breathe a bit harder. The sun was peeping between the buildings, a shaft of light turning the peak of the temple orange-pink. When they entered the complex, they stopped, catching their breath, and looked around.

'It's quiet,' said Silus.

'It's still more or less nighttime,' said Atius, a little grumpily. 'Where shall we start?'

Atius nodded at the enormous temple that dominated their eyeline.

'Seems to be as good a place as any.'

–

Soaemias kept her features impassive, though when her son ran to her and threw his arms around her waist, she placed a gentle hand on the top of his head. Avitus snuggled into the warmth, reassurance flooding through him.

'Mistress,' said Aziz, bowing low.

'My servant.'

'I'm sorry, mistress. This wasn't the way it was supposed to be.'

'Fear not,' said Soaemias. 'All will be as the lord of the mountain and the sun wills it.'

Aziz kept his head bowed.

'Julia,' said Gannys. 'What are we doing here?'

Soaemias threw him an annoyed glance. 'Quiet Gannys. Your role is simply to be a witness to the glory that is about to come, the descent of the lord to this world.'

'What are you talking about? What are you going to do?'

Soaemias ignored him and knelt before Avitus. She took his face in both her hands and looked into him deeply. Avitus noticed that her eyes were full of tears.

'What's wrong, Mother?'

'I love you, my son. You don't know how very proud I am of you. You have been so brave.'

'Gannys told me the plan. I wasn't sure whether you knew about it or not, and I wanted to tell you, but I couldn't, because you weren't here. It sounds amazing. I'm going to be Emperor!'

A tear overflowed, trickled down her cheek.

'You are going to be more than an Emperor,' she whispered. 'You are going to be a god.'

She stood up straight, gripped his shoulders for a moment, then stepped back. Avitus felt Aziz step up close behind him.

'Soon the sun will come up above the horizon,' said Soaemias, 'and its rays will shine through that high window, to light up the statue, and us. The lord of light, Elagabal himself, shows us the time and the place.'

'And then what?'

'Then the Lord Elagabal will come for you.'

Avitus looked from his mother to Gannys to Aziz in puzzlement. Soaemias had closed her eyes, and she looked to be open to no further discussion. Aziz's face was blank, emotionless. Gannys, by contrast, was open-mouthed, staring at Soaemias.

'Julia. You surely don't mean to…'

'Silence,' said Soaemias.

Avitus looked around the temple. One or two priests threw them curious glances, but such was Soaemias' air of confidence that they asked no questions, and simply went about their duties. The sunlight peeked through the high window, illuminating the wall behind them, and as it rose, the shaft of light slowly descended towards the statue, as if being guided there by Elagabal himself.

'The time is nearly upon us,' said Soaemias, her voice tight, strained. 'We shall pray.'

'O Lord Elagabal, god of the mountain and sun, supreme ruler over the skies and the earth, hear me. Descend on us from your heights, in all your power and glory, and begin your rule among us. Accept the blood of your servant, the innocent child destined to be your high priest, as a sign of our devotion to you. O lord, find us worthy of your coming.'

Blood? Avitus stared at his mother in shock. His young, naive mind was struggling to make sense of the words he had just heard. Whose blood? His? Maybe they were going to prick his finger.

'Julia, no,' said Gannys, his voice high-pitched and strained.

Aziz stepped behind Avitus and put an arm around him, across the top of his chest. The gesture, if it had come from his father, would have seemed protective. Now, coming from Aziz, it chilled the boy. He twisted, wriggled, but the grip tightened, and he felt a sharp point prick his neck.

'Hush, my lord,' whispered Aziz. Avitus went deathly still, suddenly feeling unable to move, even if he had dared.

'Do not be afraid, my darling son,' said Soaemias. 'This is just the beginning. You are about to transform into a god, to serve at the right hand of the almighty Lord Elagabal. There will be no pain, only rapture.'

Avitus wasn't sure what rapture was, and the blade sticking into his neck was already causing pain, but this was his mother speaking, and he desperately wanted to believe her.

'Soaemias, this isn't what we planned,' said Gannys, a pleading tone in his voice.

'It is what we must do now that the original course of action is impossible.'

'This will achieve nothing. A worthless sacrifice that will lead to your husband and the Emperor cracking down on the worship of Elagabal, so all who believe in the god of the mountain will fear for their lives.'

Aziz sneered. 'You have so little faith. A true believer would not doubt as you do. Maybe that is why the Lord Elagabal saw fit to stop the original plan, because of your weakness. This is the way it must be. The only way.'

'Madness has taken you,' gasped Gannys. He tried to take a step forward, but Aziz tilted the knife into a more acute angle, ready to plunge. From the corner of his eye, Avitus watched the line of illumination from the rising sun descend down the wall behind him. If the time until that line hit the statue measured the heartbeats of his life, it was terrifyingly short. Or else his glory was wondrously near.

The sunlight touched the top of the statue of Serapis' head, and slid down his face.

'It is time,' said Soaemias. 'Glory be to our lord.' She nodded to Aziz.

Avitus took a breath and knew at that moment that he trusted his mother more than life itself. He looked her straight in the eyes and said in a clear, small voice, 'I love you, Mother.'

Soaemias' face fell instantly, all colour draining from it. Her mouth dropped open and she stared at him, then at Aziz, who was raising his knife. She lifted her hand hesitantly. Aziz gripped the knife tightly, preparing to strike.

Avitus waited. If his mother wanted to stop this, then that was because it was the right thing to do. If she wanted it to go ahead, that was right too.

Soaemias looked at Aziz, at the knife tip, trembling as it was held tight. She looked up at the face of Serapis, shining bright in the morning sun. Then she bowed her head. Avitus closed his eyes, tensed, guts clenching, unable to hold back the fear despite his faith. Aziz raised the knife higher.

And then a loud voice, coming from the entrance to the temple, echoed around the huge chamber.

'Stop!'

Chapter Fifteen

Avitus opened his eyes and stared. Two men with drawn swords rushed through the door at the far end of the temple and charged towards the altar. They halted a few feet away, their gladii pointing forward, one towards Aziz, one towards Gannys. Aziz hesitated and looked to Soaemias.

'Silus, Atius. Come to worship?'

'I knew it,' said Silus, breathing hard. 'I knew you, Gannys, must be involved. But you, Julia Soaemias. I really, really hoped not. How could you do this to your own son?'

The fanaticism that would compel you to endanger or even take the life of your own child was surely alien to most, but to Silus, who had had his daughter ripped away from him by violence, something he would give his own life in an instant to change, it was incomprehensible.

'You cannot understand, Silus. You who believes in nothing. For us, who worship the Lord Elagabal, our faith is everything.'

'I have faith,' said Atius. 'My God, the same God the Jews worship, rejected the sacrifice of Abraham's son.'

'Ah yes, you are a follower of the Christos, aren't you, Atius? And did not your God sacrifice his own son for the sins of others?'

'Yes, but…' Atius paused, confused. Silus wondered if he was wishing Origen was there to help him out, but this was not a time for a philosophical debate.

'It doesn't matter whether I understand,' said Silus. 'All that matters is the boy. Tell your man to let him go.'

A small crowd had gathered now, priests, slaves, worshippers, some scholars who had been drawn into the temple by the commotion. They looked on with fascination, unsure of what they were witnessing, but knowing that violence was imminent, and unwilling to miss out.

Aziz looked to Soaemias for instruction. But her indecision of a moment ago seemed to have vanished, her faith hardened by these non-believers who threatened her in this holy sanctuary, and by the audience who would bear witness to this ultimate act of faith. She raised her voice.

'All you gathered here, you will carry word of what you have seen to the city, to the Empire. You are witness to the rise of the Lord Elagabal, who from this day forward will rule the heavens and the earth, supreme over all men and all gods.'

There was a gasp from the onlookers. Religious tolerance was weaker in Alexandria than most parts of the Empire, and for someone to claim their god was superior so publicly, in a sacred place, was provocative in the extreme. Angry mutterings rose from the ranks of those gathered.

Silus took a step forward. 'Soaemias, release Avitus. You can still worship your god and have your son.'

'No!' said Soaemias. Sharp, trying to remain firm, to suppress any doubt.

Silus took another step forward. Almost within reach of the boy.

'No!' she cried again. 'My son will become a god. Aziz. Make the sacrifice!'

Silus threw himself at the descending knife. The point rushed down towards the boy's exposed neck, the fragile skin covering vessels pulsing with life-giving blood. Silus was too far away to grab Aziz's knife hand.

But he was near enough to reach the knife.

In the auxiliaries, in the long nights in the tents with his contubernium, they had sometimes played a game to relieve the tedium. Being young men, and soldiers, and bored, it was obviously a dangerous and irresponsible game. One of them reached up as high as he could with a dagger in his hand and dropped it. It was the task of another to catch the dagger by the blade before it could hit the ground. Money was placed on the outcome. It was a stupid game, and had led to a number of visits to the valetudinarium to be stitched or bandaged, and the pain was often accompanied by a caning from the centurion's vine stick for affecting the fighting ability of the century. Silus had had something of a talent for it, and had supplemented his meagre income successfully in this way.

But this time he wasn't just contending with the natural force that impels all objects to the earth. He had to account for the strength of Aziz's arm as he thrust downwards. And he could tell it was impossible to stop the blow from striking home into flesh.

So he did the only thing he could. He put his own flesh in the way of the boy's. The knife went through the back of his hand, and the movement of his arm deflected the blow so it cracked into the boy's collarbone.

Avitus screamed and fell to the ground, clutching his shoulder. Blood welled up beneath Silus' hand, but not much, and it wasn't the bright scarlet that meant a mortal blow.

Silus stepped backwards, ripping the knife out of Aziz's grip, which remained impaled up to the hilt, the blade sitting between and parallel to the third and fourth metacarpal bones. He stared at his hand in disbelief. There was not yet any pain, or any blood, but he knew both would materialise at any moment.

Atius was motionless, uncharacteristically taken aback by the sudden action.

Soaemias fell to her knees at Avitus' side, clutching him, pulling the hand away from the wound, ripping his tunic away to see the extent of the damage.

Silus gripped the knife hilt and with a cry pulled it free and hurled it aside. Now the blood ran freely down his forearm from the holes in his palm and the back of his hand, and at the same time the pain hit, a searing agony. He stared at the damage in dismay, clutching at his wrist, fear that he would be crippled flooding over him.

Atius stared and whispered a word that Silus didn't understand at the time. 'Stigma.'

Then Aziz let out a high-pitched howl and threw himself onto Silus. Both arms wrapped around his upper chest, knocking Silus off his feet and onto his back, the air rushing out of him, losing his grip on his sword, which flew through the air and clattered to the floor. Momentarily he was stunned, but was brought back to awareness by a hefty punch to the centre of his face. He felt his nose break, and blood sprayed outwards in all directions like the splash of water from a stone thrown into a pond. It was agonising, and he roared and grappled for his attacker.

Atius, his brief spell broken by the assault, stepped forward to help his friend, but Gannys, also shocked out of inaction, lunged at Atius. Taken by surprise, he was unable to bring his weapon into play before Gannys had closed. They wrestled, Gannys gripping Atius' sword arm by the wrist. Gannys was no warrior, but he had bulk, and he fought with a desperate ferocity that shocked Atius.

Aziz was fighting with a similarly passionate intensity that Silus, supine, in pain, dazed, was struggling to match. Aziz straddled him, assailing him with blows to one side of his head and then the other. Silus held his forearms up to fend off the repeated blows that were raining down on him and the respite this brought him just allowed him to recover his wits. Aziz, seeing his left-right combination punches were no longer having enough impact, sat up straight, lifted his fist up high, and punched straight down towards Silus' face.

But this time, Silus twisted to one side, and Aziz punched the mosaic floor. The crack of his breaking knuckles echoed around the temple, drawing a gasp from the onlookers. Aziz screamed and clutched his half-closed fist with his other hand, staring in dismay at the crooked bones. Silus bucked and threw him to one side.

Slowly Silus regained his feet, wiping the blood splashed across his face away with his forearm. His nose was still radiating excruciating pain, and he felt it gingerly, noting that it had adopted an unusual new angle. He held up his punctured hand, tried to flex it, and had to suppress a cry at the agony that caused. But at least he could move and feel his fingers. That gave him hope the damage was not permanent.

Aziz was on his knees, staring up at Silus with loathing, cradling his broken fist with his other hand. Silus looked around for his sword, reached down for it with his good hand, picked it up, then straightened.

When he looked back, Aziz had retrieved the knife that moments before had penetrated Silus' hand. Silus lifted the sword wearily.

'Put it down, Aziz. It's over.'

A wild look came into Aziz's eyes, the sort that Silus had seen on the battlefield, when he was face to face with a Maeatae or Caledonian warrior, one who had lost all reason, and had surrendered to the blood lust. He braced himself for Aziz to renew his attack.

But Aziz turned the knife round, hilt facing Silus, blade pointing to his own chest.

'You understand nothing,' he hissed.

Then he tilted his head back. The sun caught his face, lit it up like some angelic scene from Atius' sacred book.

'Lord Elagabal,' he cried in a loud, clear voice. 'Accept my life, and let your reign on earth begin today!'

And with that, he plunged the dagger between two ribs.

His aim was good. He was a skilled assassin in his own right, after all. Bright cardiac liquid pulsed out around the hilt, and flowed in a river to the temple floor. Soundlessly, Aziz toppled forward, face first, and was still, a red lake spreading around him.

The great temple was silent. All fight left Gannys as he saw his co-conspirator's end, and he let his hands drop. Atius put his sword to Gannys' throat, and looked at the dead fanatic, then up at Silus. Silus looked back at him, breathing heavy and stertorous, with an irritating whistle through his wonky nose.

Then they looked around.

'Where the fuck are they?' wheezed Silus.

Soaemias and Avitus were gone.

–

Avitus had wanted to stay and watch the outcome of the fight in the temple. Partly from childish excitement, but also because he knew that the outcome was important to him. If Aziz won, he would be sacrificed and become a god. If Silus won, his life would be saved. Despite his deep devotion to Elagabal, he guiltily found himself rooting for Silus.

But Soaemias had grabbed his wrist and whispered to him to run. And for all that had been promised to him in recent days, an Imperial throne, godhood, he was still a young child who could no more resist his dominant mother's commands than he could resist a landslide.

He ran.

They fled the Serapeum, leaving the sounds of combat behind them, ignored by the onlookers who were fixated on the fighting. They burst out into the early morning light and ran through the temple complex, drawing mildly curious glances from scholars, priests and worshippers who ambled purposelessly or strode determinedly to appointments and destinations.

They ran down the slope leading away from the Serapeum and found themselves on the Serapic Way. The big north–south thoroughfare was now crowded with wheeled vehicles, laden donkeys and asses and many pedestrians. It was lined with shops, taverns, market stalls and small temples, and while the density of the traffic had not yet reached its peak, there were enough obstructions to impede their progress.

Despite being slowed, Avitus quickly found himself breathing fast, heart racing from tension as well as exertion.

'Mother,' he gasped. 'Where are we going?'

She didn't answer. He wasn't sure she knew. It was an uncomfortable feeling, to doubt a parent, one who had always been absolute in their certainty about the right course of action. But now he was seeing her in a new light. She was unsure. Even desperate.

They reached the large square at the crossroads between the north–south aligned Serapic Way and the east–west Canopic Way. Here she hesitated, looked behind her. Avitus knew that if they were running, she must be fearing pursuit, capture, and whatever followed that. He could see her brow crease, calculation behind her eyes. There was his mother, not panicking, thinking. Despite his uncertainty, he felt an inner relief as he watched her regain control of herself, of the situation.

She looked around her, down at the ground. Various animals and birds milled around, the sacred and the unclean, depending on your belief system, mingling together in the dirt. A pig snuffled, pushing muck out of the way with its nose to locate a half-eaten pomegranate. A small cat, not much more than a kitten, chased after a frog, which bounced around, attempting to evade the playful feline. Two ducks, a small group of collared doves and an ibis pecked at some grain that had spilled from a cart.

Soaemias looked around her furtively, then reached down and grabbed the surprised ibis, tucking it under her cloak.

'Stay here,' she hissed at Avitus. 'Don't move.'

She ducked behind an unmanned stall, the ibis just beginning to flap. She was briefly out of sight of the milling crowds. Avitus thought he heard a muffled squawk. Soaemias reappeared, the ibis still tucked away out of view but no longer flapping. A score of yards onwards was a temple with half a dozen marble steps and an open frontage. A statue of a woman, nude from the waist up and with the head of a cow, suggested to Avitus that this temple was dedicated to Hathor, goddess of music and dance, fertility and motherhood, of all things female and feminine.

Soaemias pulled the ibis from underneath her cloak. Avitus gasped. Where once had been its black head, with its long curved bill, there was now just a stump, oozing blood over its white feathers. As Avitus watched, Soaemias threw the decapitated bird into the temple, where it landed with a soft wet thud.

'Run,' she hissed, and Avitus did not need telling twice. She grabbed his hand, and they rushed east along the Canopic Way.

From behind them, a shriek pierced the morning air, cutting through the hubbub of daily life. Avitus looked back, then stopped, fascinated and horrified.

A priestess staggered out of the temple, her white robes stained with the blood of the dead sacred bird that she held aloft. Everyone at the crossroads turned to stare in disbelief.

'Sacrilege,' she screamed. 'Blasphemy. Murder!'

A murmur rushed through the crowds that became louder.

'It's the Christians,' shouted a man from the crowd.

'No, it's the Jews,' screamed a hysterical woman.

'It's the Romans with their cursed Olympian gods,' yelled another.

'It's a desecration. Death to the Christians and their false prophet.'

'Death to the Jews.'

'Kill the Romans.'

Soaemias tugged Avitus' hand urgently as the crowd erupted into violence behind them. Reluctantly, still amazed at the speed with which a peaceful street had become the scene of a full-scale riot, Avitus allowed himself to be led by his mother at a rapid trot.

'Where are we going?' he asked. He wasn't sure she knew.

But then, looming in front of them, was the Mouseion, and the Great Library it contained.

She pointed. 'There.'

'What about Gannys?' asked Atius as they ran to the grand temple doorway.

'Not important,' said Silus. 'We'll deal with him later.' He grabbed a temple slave who had barely moved since the moment they had first arrived in the temple, motionless, broom in hand, a pile of half-swept leaves at his feet.

'Where did they go? The woman and the boy?'

The slave gawped, and Silus shook him with both hands, trying to ignore the pain that shot up his arm from his damaged palm, and noticing he had left a bloody palm print on the slave's shoulder. He pointed down the Serapic Way, and Silus shoved him aside and set off down the wide street. Others he accosted as they ran said the same thing, pointing out the direction of the fleeing mother and son.

But as they approached the crossroads of the Serapic Way and the Canopic Way, the normal din of the street crescendoed to a tumult. And now others were running, some towards the crossroads, mainly men, angry, bearing sickles and hammers, others fleeing, mainly women, carrying or dragging children, pale-faced and terrified.

A pregnant woman with a young girl dragging behind her careered into Atius. Atius held out a hand to steady her. She fell to her knees and grabbed at the hem of his tunic.

'Please, sir, don't hurt me, don't hurt my daughter.'

'I'm not going to hurt you,' said Atius, trying to sound unthreatening, but coming across gruff. 'What's happening?'

'It's a riot, sir, a big one.'

'About what?' asked Silus.

'They say someone killed a sacred bird, desecrated a temple. They are saying it's the Christians.' She clutched at a chi-rho pendant, and Atius realised that she was a follower of the Christos herself.

'Did you see a woman and a young boy run this way?' asked Silus. 'Maybe before the riot started?'

She frowned, puzzled at the seeming non sequitur. Then she nodded. 'Yes, moments before the shouting started, a woman and a lad ran into the crossroads, and then turned east down the Canopic Way.'

Moments before? Was Soaemias responsible for this riot then? He didn't think he could put anything past her now.

'Thank you. Get out of here, find somewhere safe. I suspect things will get worse before they get better.'

She scrambled to her feet and rushed off. They headed on, towards the epicentre of the riot, but the nearer they got, the more crush, and the more danger. Clay pots and plates flew through the air, impacted collarbones and skulls, hammers swung, knives flashed. Roars of anger and screams of pain and outrage echoed all around. People were dying before them.

They pressed on, using their short swords sparingly. The blades parried weapons, while the hilts clubbed away the more lightly armed.

A large man with a huge blacksmith's mallet reared up behind Silus, the hammer behind his head, ready to be brought down. Silus turned, saw him just as Atius ran him through from sternum to spine. The big man toppled over backwards, dragged by the weight of the hammer.

'Juno's arse, Atius, this is serious. People are dying.'

'And a lot more are going to die when the legion marches out to restore order,' said Atius grimly.

A mad-eyed woman whose clearly well-coiffured hair was now loose and wild grabbed Atius' arm and bit it. He yelped and hurled her away forcefully.

'We've got to stop this,' he said.

'We've got to stop Soaemias,' said Silus. 'She was ready to see her son die. I think she still intends the same. Besides, what can we do to stop a riot?'

'Us? Nothing. But Origen could.'

'Origen?'

'You know what a powerful speaker he is, how respected he is in the city. Let me go and find him, bring him here. If he can

273

quell the riot before the legions arrive, think how many lives will be saved.'

Silus shook his head, torn between his duty to Marcellus and the moral obligation to stop the violence.

'Go,' he said. Atius gripped him by the shoulder in thanks, then retreated south down the Serapic Way to work his way around the riot to the house of Phryne.

Silus looked around him. The crowds were separating into factions, just like the riots he had seen before at the Circus, but instead of Greens and Blues, individuals were accreting into groups of Christians, Jews, native Egyptians and ethnic Greeks. They hurled insults and missiles, cursed and ducked as insults and missiles came back at them. Soon, inevitably, men were brandishing lit torches. A house known to be a meeting room for followers of Christos was the first to begin to smoulder, then spark into flame. Soon after, a small temple dedicated to Thoth was ignited, and then groups split up to roam the city, looking for targets – human, statuary or architectural – to smash, break and burn.

Silus worked his way between the cultural and religious combatants, avoiding confrontation where he could, facing it head on when he had to. He sidled around a native Egyptian and a Greek who were locked together in a wrestling hold, each trying to get the upper hand. He stepped over two middle-aged women rolling in the dirt, spitting and scratching like cats. He jumped sideways as a youth, barely more than a child, staggered backwards towards him, clutching at the knife protruding from his belly.

Abruptly the road east became unpassable, despite its expansive width, choked with rioters. Silus cursed and took a random north-leading side alley. At the end, he jogged right, and found himself face to face with three figures, two with clubs and one with an axe. They were beating a wealthy-looking citizen, a merchant probably, who was curled up on the floor, his hands fending off blows to his head, but unable to do anything about the kicks to his kidneys. These men weren't rioters, Silus realised instantly, but the ordinary criminals that lurked in the underbelly of every city, and they were taking advantage of the anarchy to make some money and have some fun.

They looked up as Silus came to a halt before them and turned as one.

'Let me through, lads. I've got no quarrel with you.'

The leader, whose wide ears protruded from under his curly hair, nodded at Silus' drawn sword.

'Nice weapon. Hand it over and you can go.' The accent was native Egyptian. He wondered if he could use the authority of Rome to make them let him pass.

'I am a centurion in the Roman army. Let me through, in the name of the Senate and people of Rome, and the Emperor.'

'He's a fucking Roman!' said the curly-haired leader. 'Get him!'

So much for the authority of Rome.

They rushed him all at once, three abreast. They were broad-shouldered enough between them to fill the width of the alley, leaving Silus no room to manoeuvre. They lifted their clubs and axe, and any one of them connecting in the right place with the right force would finish him. And he couldn't parry them all. He had no time to retreat, no way forward, no adequate defence.

So Silus ran at them, and as they reached him, he dropped to the floor. The axe and clubs descended through empty air as Silus rolled towards them like a stone from a catapult when it lands. One managed to hurdle him, while two went down in a tangle of limbs and weapons. Silus continued his roll to bring him to his feet, whirled and stabbed down, his sword passing straight through the back of one of the thugs who was prone on the muddy ground. The man arched his back with a cry, then collapsed forward onto his face.

The other two regained their balance and composure and faced Silus again. But now they were hesitant. They glanced down at their fallen comrade, then at each other and advanced on Silus slowly.

'Lads, I'm warning you. I don't have time for this. Fuck off.'

Why did they never fuck off?

The curly-haired leader was a step ahead of his comrade, and as he neared Silus, he swung his axe back.

It was a heavy implement, designed for chopping wood and felling trees, not combat. Silus took a quick step forward, and while the axe was still in its backswing, he thrust his gladius through the axeman's throat. Blood and air bubbled through the rent, the axe falling to the ground. The curly-haired man dropped to his knees, then slumped sideways.

Now the last remaining mugger hesitated. Silus swished his gladius around, hoping that the man would see sense and flee. For a moment it looked like he would.

Then a roar came from behind him and the merchant, who Silus had dismissed from his strategic view of the battle, came charging past him. The last thug lifted his club too late, and the plump merchant crashed into him. The thug flew backwards and the merchant landed heavily on top of him, and before he could regain his wind, the merchant started landing fierce blows onto his face and head, the power amplified by the considerable body weight behind them.

'Egyptian scum,' yelled the merchant, barely coherent, between punches. 'Poor, illiterate, barbarian pieces of shit.'

The thug struggled weakly against the first few blows, then was still. The merchant continued to pound him though, face red, breath hissing through clenched teeth between curses.

Silus shook his head. These Alexandrians were crazy.

He saw the axe lying on the floor, and looked at his sword. Certainly the gladius had shown its worth, its length making it much more nimble. But if he encountered another big group blocking his way, he wondered if the axe might look more intimidating, and make a fight less likely. For a moment he weighed up the merits of each, then thought, why not have both?

He sheathed the sword, picked up the axe, and with a final glance at the merchant, who was still assaulting and abusing the dead mugger, he ran on.

Sure enough, most people looking for trouble were happy to avoid the doubly-armed, blood-covered man who looked like he needed to be somewhere in a hurry. He passed groups of men brawling, two men dragging off a large, middle-aged woman down a back alley, and a child sitting on his backside and bawling loudly.

He gritted his teeth. It wasn't his job to save people. He couldn't. This would soon be a city-wide riot. What difference would it make if he stopped one woman from being raped, reunited one child with its parents?

The arguments rang hollow in his ears, contrasting with the all too solid screams coming from all directions. He forced his mind onto his problem. Where was she going? Did she even know?

And then he saw the Mouseion. The cultural and intellectual centre of the city, home of the Great Library. Before he had ever been to Alexandria, he had heard of two landmarks of the city, famous across the Empire. The Lighthouse of Pharos and the Great Library. The lighthouse was too far from this part of the city. But if Soaemias was planning on making some great statement about her god, and she had been forced to flee the Serapeum, then the library, with all its history, its irreplaceable texts, its place in the hearts of the elite of the Empire, would be a good substitute.

He put the axe over his shoulder and ran into the grounds of the Mouseion, heading towards the library itself.

He ran into the structure, the one that Tekosis had shown him. He remembered the priestess with a pang of loss, then pushed the thought from his mind. The library was huge, and he wondered where to start. There was no obvious disturbance. Just worried scholars and librarians, whispering their concerns to each other, casting anxious glances at the combustible piles of scrolls and even more anxious glances at the dangerous-looking man who had just appeared in their midst.

'What news from the city?' one of the braver of the scholars asked.

Silus shook his head. 'Chaos and widespread rioting. Have you seen a woman and a boy come through here?'

The scholar who had first spoken shook his head but another, emboldened by the first, spoke up. 'They ran past my desk. Heading towards the philosophy section.'

That would be where all the books on the religions of the world were, along with discussions of the various positive and negative traits of the different gods, how they should be honoured or even whether they actually existed. If she was going to choose a place to make a final stand, it made sense that it would be there, witnessed by the writings of the scholars on all the various pantheons of the world.

'Which way?'

The scholar pointed and Silus ran on, down a long corridor, at the end of which was a stout oak door. He hefted the axe, ready to break the door down if necessary.

He smelt burning just before he saw the tendrils of smoke sneaking under the door like demonic fingers. His heart sank. Was he too late?

–

Avitus watched in anxiety and confusion as his mother slammed and bolted the heavy door, then piled furniture up against it.

'Help me,' she hissed as she pushed a heavy wooden desk across the tiled floor. Avitus did as he was told, despite his misgivings. Mother had told him to. What else was he to do? Maybe when he was an Emperor, or a god, he could stop listening to Mother. But he doubted it.

The desk slid up against the door, and Soaemias put stools on top of it, and propped a heavy marble statue of a bearded philosopher that Avitus did not recognise against it at an angle.

When she was satisfied, she stepped back, chest heaving, and looked around. They were in a big room with shelves lined with books. Most were papyrus, though some were parchment, and most were in the form of rolled scrolls, though some of the newer-looking editions were in the form of codices. Rows of life-sized statues of philosophers looked down on them sternly over heavy beards. The room was windowless, and lit by multiple oil lamps placed strategically to maximise the light they shed, while maintaining sufficient separation from the books to reduce fire risk.

Avitus stoically assessed his environs. No exit. Barricaded in. Even for an eight-year-old, there was only one obvious conclusion.

'Mother, is this the end?'

Soaemias looked at him, and her face twisted in grief and uncertainty. He had never seen his mother unsure before that day, and it frightened him. But in a moment, a state of calm settled over her, and she appeared to be serene once more.

'No, Avitus, my dearest boy, most wonderful holy lord. This is the beginning.'

She walked around the room, gathering the oil lamps, blowing them out one by one, so the room dimmed, until only a single flickering lamp provided illumination.

'Lord Elagabal, thank you for giving us this chance to show you our devotion. Take this, my only son, into your arms, and embrace him in your godhead.'

As she prayed, she opened up each lamp and poured the oil over Avitus' head. It was warm, since it had just been close to a flame, but not scalding. Avitus was used to the concept of anointing in religious ceremonies, had anointed himself and others in various ceremonies with blood, milk, wine or perfumed oils. Mother was being very generous with the lamp oil though, and soon his hair and tunic were thoroughly soaked in the slippery fluid.

And now his mother picked up the remaining lit lamp, and carried it around the room, touching it to dry parchment scrolls, waiting for each to catch light before moving on to another.

In moments, the walls were alight, and smoke poured off them, some currents flowing downwards, most pooling around the ceiling like dark clouds. Soaemias stood in front of Avitus. The oil lamp she held in her hands lit her face from beneath, making it look strange and unfamiliar, like a ghostly vision. The room became brighter as the flames bloomed and spits and cracks came intermittently from all corners, making Avitus flinch.

'Mother, I'm scared,' said Avitus.

But his mother seemed not to be there any more. Just this terrifying woman who looked a bit like his mother, but whose eyes held no recognition or love, just madness.

She brought the lit lamp towards him, and he became acutely aware of the highly flammable liquid coating him. Terror froze him. He closed his eyes, fighting to find calm, acceptance.

'O Lord Elagabal,' he whispered. 'I don't want to die.'

And at that moment there was a crash, and the sound of splintering wood coming from the door. He opened his eyes to stare and Soaemias spun too. The crash came again, and an axe head protruded through. When it withdrew, he saw an eye appear in the small hole that had been created. Then a voice came. A man's voice, which he recognised.

'Soaemias, stop! Open the door.'

Silus.

–

The sight Silus beheld as he peered through the small hole that his axe had made in the door chilled him, even though he could already feel the heat from the fire. Avitus stood in the middle of a large room, lined with shelf after shelf of blazing literature. He was covered in some sticky liquid, and his mother stood before him, illuminated in the flickering light from the flames, holding a lit oil lamp.

It didn't take much imagination to work out what Soaemias was planning even if he couldn't comprehend it. She was preparing to immolate her son for some religious purpose that was beyond him, and she was prepared to die with him.

Thoughts of Sergia and Velua flashed through his mind. His wife would have done anything to save their daughter, give her life, and had had the tragedy of seeing the little girl die before her. This woman was preparing to kill her own son. It was unthinkable.

He threw himself at the door. It was solid oak, but he was a solid man. The lock should give way, or the door frame. But it just bowed slightly at the impact, then threw him back. He tried again, ignoring the pain it caused in his shoulder, but again the door remained firm. He peered in through the hole again. Now he saw all the furniture piled up against it on the other side. He could probably shift it, given enough time. But there was none. Even if Soaemias didn't ignite her son, the flames and smoke in the room would overcome them within moments. Already the smoke was descending from the ceiling to near the top of Soaemias' head.

'Soaemias, open the door,' he shouted through the hole.

'It's fitting, Silus, after all your efforts to thwart me, that you are here to witness the end.'

'Don't, please. Just open the door.'

'Be happy for us, Silus. We are joining our god.'

Footsteps came down the corridor behind him, three scholars, brave and curious enough to want to know what was happening. They gasped when they saw the smoke pouring out under the door.

'Get water, blankets,' hissed Silus. 'Quick, you fools.'

The scholars hesitated, then raced away. Silus put his mouth back to the hole in the door.

'You can't do this, Soaemias. Not to your own son.'

'It is the will of the Lord Elagabal.'

'But how do you know? It isn't possible to know the mind of a god. Maybe he hates sacrifice. Maybe he will reject your son, and you condemn the poor boy to an afterlife in the underworld.'

'You know nothing of the will of the lord of mountain and sun.'

'I agree. But what I'm saying is, how can you be sure even you know his will perfectly? We are humans. We are imperfect. If you have any doubt in your mind, you must stop this.'

There was a moment's silence, punctuated only by cracks and spits from the fire. He poked his eye to the hole again. The profuse smoke was filling the room, the flames reaching a peak, and he could feel waves of heat washing out through the little gap. Soaemias, facing the door, was perspiring. Avitus stood completely still.

'It's too late,' said Soaemias. But her voice no longer held that air of certainty. Her eyes no longer gleamed with religious zeal.

'It doesn't have to be like this, Soaemias. I can help you.'

'I didn't take you for a fool, Silus. How can you help me now? You know of my part in the plot. My husband will have me executed. And that murderer Caracalla will have my son executed for treason for the mere idea of him being Emperor.'

'They don't have to know. Only Atius and I know everything. I swear, by Elagabal, by Mithras, by every fucking god in the sky and under the ground, that I will keep your part in the plot secret if you just open the door.'

Soaemias' face creased in profound distress. She turned back to look at Avitus, and tears flowed down her face, partly from the smoke, but mainly from her agony.

'Soaemias. You are his mother. It is your job to protect him. As my wife could not protect my daughter. Live. Both of you. And maybe one day your dreams will become reality.'

Soaemias stared into Avitus' eyes, and he looked back, all doubt gone, just complete trust in his mother's decision.

Soaemias turned to the door, grabbed the statue, and heaved it away. Silus watched impatiently, helplessly, as the flames licked across the ceiling, and burning embers dropped alarmingly close to the flammable little boy. The smoke came lower, and now wisps reached Soaemias' face. Breathing hard with her exertion to move the barricade, she inhaled deeply, her chest filling with smoke.

Immediately she doubled over, coughing and spluttering. She bent down on her hands and knees, sucking at the pockets of clearer air lower down, but she needed to reach up to move the stools so she could lighten the desk enough to move it. She held her breath, her head now encircled in smoke, like a mountain covered in cloud, and threw the stools away, one, then two, then a third.

But anxiety and exertion made her gasp involuntarily and again smoke hit her throat and lungs. Short of air, she gasped, retched, inhaled more smoke, and dropped to the ground. Still conscious, she reached for the table with one hand. Then the smoke enveloped her, and her head dropped, and she disappeared from view.

Silus rammed his shoulder against the door again, and it gave a little, but not enough. He considered the axe, but it would take too long. He needed the door open, and the table was still obstructing him.

'Avitus,' he yelled.

The boy had been watching in terrified fascination. From his position in the centre of the room and with his short stature, the smoke had not yet engulfed him. 'I need your help,' shouted Silus. 'We need to move the table, together. You pull, and I'll push. Understand?'

Avitus remained motionless.

'Silus, your mother needs you. Your god needs you.'

Avitus said in a small voice, 'Will I still be Emperor?'

Silus paused, stunned by the question under the circumstances. But it just showed how deeply his mother had indoctrinated him.

'I'm sure you will, boy, but only if you help me now. Do we have a deal?'

Avitus nodded.

'Grab the table leg, stay low. I'm going to count, one, two, three, one, two, three, and every time I say three, you are going to pull with all your might and I am going to push. Ready?'

'Yes, Silus.'

'Now. One, two, *three*!'

Silus rammed the door with all his might as Avitus pulled, and this time he felt something give.

'Again. One, two, *three*!'

The table moved an inch and it was enough room for Silus' shoulder barge to smash the bolt through the door frame that held it.

'Again!'

The scholars had arrived now, with buckets of water and blankets soaked in vinegar. Fire was an ever-present threat in the library, and firefighting material was always ready.

'Help me,' cried Silus, and the scholars, weedy as they were, added their weight to the effort.

Three more times they rammed and Avitus pulled, and on that third attempt, the door opened enough for a person to fit through. Silus held out his hand.

'Quick, grab hold. I'll pull you out.'

Avitus hesitated.

'Hurry, child!'

'What about Mother?'

Shit. Letting her burn would solve a problem. But the boy wasn't leaving without her. Fuck it.

'I'll save her,' said Silus, 'if you come out first.'

'Promise?'

'Promise.'

Avitus reached out and took Silus' hand, and before the boy could change his mind, Silus yanked him out into the corridor.

He was hot and sticky, and Silus' suspicions that he was covered in oil were confirmed. He handed him to the scholars.

'Get him away from flame and put a blanket around him.'

'Save my mother, Silus,' said Avitus. 'You promised.'

Silus nodded. He grabbed one of the soaked blankets and wrapped it around his back and head, one end across his face. Then, head first, he squeezed his way through the crack in the slightly open doorway.

He was a lot wider than Avitus, though fortunately not as bulky as Atius, or he would have been in trouble. For one panicked, claustrophobic moment, he got his belt stuck, and struggled with the clasp before he was able to toss it away and slide into the room.

The smoke stung his eyes and his throat, even with the soaked blanket as a mask. He could taste the vinegar, and wondered why firefighters insisted it was superior to plain water in extinguishing flames.

Between the thick smoke and his own tears, he could see almost nothing. But he knew where Soaemias had fallen. So he got to his hands and knees and felt around, like a blind beggar searching for tossed alms.

Nothing. She should be right there, by the table. Had she moved? Managed to pull herself away a little? How far might she have gone? Already the heat was overwhelming, and he was fighting a coughing fit. He couldn't search the whole room.

But he had promised.

His fingers touched something soft. He probed. A foot. He groped around, eyes squeezed tight shut now against the acrid stinging atmosphere. Another foot. That was enough.

He gripped both ankles and heaved, still on hands and knees, slow awkward steps backwards. He expected to reach the door, and had another panicky moment when he thought maybe he had got turned around and was actually heading further into the room. Then his heels hit something solid. He found the gap between the door and its frame and manoeuvred himself backwards through it, heaving the inert body with him at every step.

The smoke entered his lungs and suddenly he couldn't breathe, couldn't stop coughing uncontrollably. His heart pounded as his body cried for air, and he felt dizziness encroaching.

Then several hands grasped him, ankles, tunic, shoulders, and pulled. He let himself be dragged the last few feet from the room, concentrating only on his grip on Soaemias' feet.

And then he was out, into the cooler, clearer air, and he gasped and coughed and spluttered until the smoke was gone from his airways, leaving behind a sting and a taste of woodfire.

He crawled over to Soaemias, who lay on her back, perfectly still. Her face was blacked with soot and ash, but there was otherwise not a mark on her.

She wasn't breathing.

He placed a hand on her torso. Her heart was beating, strong and fast. But her chest did not move.

He looked up at the scholars.

'What do I do?'

They looked at each other helplessly.

'I think,' said one hesitantly, 'that Hippocrates would suggest bleeding.'

'Don't be stupid,' said another. 'She needs a laxative.'

'You two are crazy,' said the third. 'First we need a kid goat, pure white, that has been blessed by a priest of Apollo, and then…'

Silus stopped listening and turned back to her. Was she even worth saving? Who was he to judge that? He wasn't a god. He killed people, yes, but that was his job. He had no orders to kill Soaemias. And so he did what he could.

He had saved the cat, applying his experience of seeing victims of drowning revived. He knew that pumping the chest forced the water out. Maybe the same would work for smoke. He pressed down on her sternum, and heard a hiss of air escape her mouth. And then when he released the pressure, he was sure a little air made its way back in. He did it again, harder. Then again, rhythmically, pumping up and down on her chest.

The stench of smoke came from her mouth, though his own abused nasal passages could only just detect it.

How long should he do this for? Until she woke or her heart stopped, he guessed. He kept pumping.

And saw her eyes flicker.

He didn't pause. He was aware of the scholars staring at him, at Avitus on his knees, praying to Elagabal to save his mother.

Soaemias arched her back and gasped a huge chestful of air. She let it out with a spluttering gasp, then inhaled again. Silus stepped back, and watched as the woman rolled onto her side, gasping, retching and coughing.

And breathing.

Chapter Sixteen

The city was in uproar. Greeks fought native Egyptians. Christians fought pagans. Romans fled. And everyone blamed the Jews, though there were few left in Alexandria since their revolt a century before.

Shops were burnt. Homes were robbed. Temples were looted and desecrated, their statues smashed, their walls daubed with blood and excrement. Men were surrounded by gangs and beaten to death on the merest suspicion of belonging to a different faction. Women were considered fair game for rape by men of all cultures and religions, as long as the culture and religion of the woman was different from the rapists.

Gangs gathered along the Canopic and Serapic ways, facing off across the great crossroads. They threw missiles – crockery, roof tiles, stones, and shouted insults, and worked themselves up to enough of a frenzy to be ready to charge at each other.

Then, marching along the Serapic Way, came the legion, fully armed and armoured, battle ready. A force against which a civilian mob, armed only with sticks and clubs, with no armour, and no discipline, stood no chance.

Nevertheless, belligerent Alexandrians of all flavours prepared to give battle. Their volatile tempers were fully triggered, and they were prepared to take on anyone.

The legions took position across the east entrance to the crossroads, shields to the fore, short swords drawn.

It was going to be a massacre.

And into the middle of the storm strode Origen. Right into the middle of the crossroads, between the factions, into the path of the oncoming legion. He was accompanied by just one man.

Atius.

Neither was armed. Origen had insisted that if Atius was to accompany him, he would have to leave his weapons behind. Atius had reluctantly agreed, realising that if Origen failed, then a sword would be unlikely to save him.

The legionary commander, Gratidius' deputy presumably, yelled an order to prepare to advance. Atius stepped forward.

'Hold,' he yelled in as loud and clear a voice as he could. 'Hold your positions, in the name of the Emperor Antoninus!'

The commander pressed forward so he stood behind the first row of legionaries.

'Who are you?'

'I am Lucius Atius of the Arcani. I work for the Emperor Antoninus, and I answer directly to Marcellus, and to Oclatinius.'

He hoped that dropping one of those names would be enough to give the legionary commander pause. Something seemed to have hit home. Atius suspected it was the name of the legendary Oclatinius that had had the most effect.

'Why are you stopping our advance?'

'Because I believe this situation can be resolved peacefully, without loss of life.'

'Bit late for that,' muttered a legionary.

'Silence!' snapped the commander. 'Tell me how, Lucius Atius.'

'This is Origen, respected scholar and religious leader. Let him talk to the crowd. See if he can calm them down. If he fails, you can have your massacre, and you have lost nothing.'

The commander thought for a moment, then nodded.

'Tell him he can speak. But if he does not disperse the crowds rapidly, then we will do it ourselves.'

'Thank you, sir.'

Atius nodded to Origen. The Christian leader turned his back on the legion and faced the mob.

Origen was a similar age to Atius, but physically much less imposing, a little plump, a little round in the face. And yet when he faced the crowd, his simple presence was enough to quell their angry shouts to no more than mutters. Atius, for all his martial prowess and physicality, knew he could never have held their attention the way Origen could.

For a moment, Origen said nothing, just turned his gaze in a three-quarter circle, so it took in the northerly Serapic Way, the westerly Canopic Way, and then back to the southerly Serapic Way. The moment stretched without him saying a word, and the muttering increased in intensity. Atius' stomach clenched. What was the man doing? Surely he must know the crowd was being held back by bonds the thickness of a human hair, which could snap at any moment.

But Origen was a consummate orator, and knew exactly what he was doing. When the tension had reached just the right pitch, he spoke, in a voice that cut through the muttering, without being raised to the point of shouting.

'We are all brothers and sisters,' he said. 'We share so much more than divides us.'

The crowd was silent now, straining to catch his words.

'You know me. I am Origen. My father was a scholar of literature, and he was murdered, along with many other followers of Christos, when the Emperor's father, Septimius Severus, ordered Christians in the Empire who openly practised to be executed. You know too, that I would have gone with him, had my mother not hidden my clothes so I would have had to leave the house naked.'

The story was indeed well known, and it drew a few smiles and chuckles from the crowd, despite the gravity of the situation and the tale itself.

'I am a scholar, a master of philosophy, religion and literature. I am also a devout follower of the Christos, and his father, the Lord God.'

This drew cheers from the Christians in the crowd, and angry retorts from the Greeks and Alexandrians.

'And yet I can make mistakes. Many of you here believe in gods of your own, deny what I contend is the truth of the coming of the Messiah. You believe in the gods of Olympos, or Mithras, or Serapis and Isis, or the gods of the river and the tree and the underworld. I believe you are wrong. Yet I am just an imperfect man.

'When I was a boy, soon after my father was killed, I was studying the holy scriptures. The writings of the apostle Matthew stated that there are men who have made themselves eunuch for the sake of the Kingdom of Heaven. I took this writing literally, and I visited a physician, in order that he could make me eunuch.'

And with that he lifted his tunic, and bared himself to the crowd. Atius gaped, as did everyone. Beneath his penis, small and wrinkled, was an ugly, red-grey scar which seeped and oozed. He held his tunic up, turning left and right so all could see. Then he let it fall.

'The wound has never healed, and gives me pain to this day. And I have come to realise that it was for nothing. Only an idiot would believe that the scriptures were literally urging man to self-castration. It is a metaphor, an exhortation to be prepared to sacrifice yourself for your god and your fellow man.

'And so I say to you, whether you are a master of philosophy or an illiterate freedman, whether you are a wealthy Greek or a poor Egyptian, whether you are a follower of Christos or Isis or Jupiter or Mithras, you can still be an idiot. But what you are also, is a neighbour. We are all one people, brothers and sisters. We all have families, desires, fears. We suffer hunger and pain, and we feel happiness and pleasure. We are the same.'

The crowd stood looking at each other uncertainly.

'You are each and every one my brother and sister, whether or not you ever come to know the love of my Lord. So embrace each other, and then disperse. Go back to your homes, to your shops, to your temples, and remember that we are all one.'

With that he strode over to where the legionary commander had been listening with surprise and suspicion. The legionaries in front of him stiffened, prepared to block his way.

'Let him through,' said the commander.

The legionaries parted, and Origen walked right up to him.

'Sir, your predecessors in Alexandria were responsible for the brutal beheading of my father. Yet I forgive you, and all your tribe. Will you shake my hand?'

The commander hesitated, and the crowd whistled and cheered.

'Do it!'

'Shake, shake, shake.'

The commander stuck out his hand, and with an uncertain half-smile, pumped Origen's hand three times, hard.

There was a moment of what next? The crowd knew something had changed, at least for that moment, but what should they do?

Atius took matters into his own hands. He marched up to a priest of Osiris, who was at the front of a gathering of Egyptians. The priest, in full regalia, and carrying a crooked staff, flinched as Atius raised his hand. But Atius simply grasped the priest's own hand and shook it enthusiastically.

Slowly others did the same, walking across the no man's land into the enemy lines to fraternise, like soldiers in a civil war who had no real reason for enmity. The ones who were first had friends or family in the other camps. A Greek pagan with a Christian brother. A native Egyptian with a Greek business partner.

Of course, it was not that easy. Not everyone was swayed. Many still grumbled. Anger still simmered, and many peeled away from the backs of the crowd to find trouble elsewhere in the city. Atius knew the criminal gangs would raid empty shops and homes, frantically attempting to maximise their gains before order was restored. There would still be beatings and assaults, robbery, looting and rape, until the legions had brought everything back under control, and the anger had burnt itself out.

But it was enough. There was to be no massacre. At least not that day. Not that year.

Of course Atius was not to know that he had merely brought a temporary reprieve, and that within two years, Alexandria would be mourning the loss of countless sons to a terrible slaughter. Despite that day's brief moment of concord, the city of learning and culture would soon once more see its streets flowing red with the blood of its people.

–

Marcellus wept openly as he clutched Avitus to his chest, his cheek pressed against the top of the boy's head. Avitus wept too. For all his strangeness, his belief in his mother, his religious convictions, he was still a little boy who had been through a horrible trauma, while separated for the most part from his mother, and for all of it from his father.

Soaemias had been taken to her bed and was being attended by Greek physicians. Silus hoped they were of more use than those scholars who had offered their advice when she lay dying. But in fact, she seemed relatively unscathed, suffering only a hoarse voice, a pale complexion to which colour was already returning, and a thick coating of grime that her chamber slaves would soon cleanse from her.

Gannys had returned to the palace, prepared for his fate, but had sensibly chosen to say little until he knew what had happened to Soaemias and Avitus. All he had said to Marcellus until that point was that Aziz, Avitus' kidnapper, was dead, and Silus was attempting to rescue the boy, and despite Marcellus' threats and entreaties, denied knowing more.

It came down to Silus to provide a story that would keep his promise to Soaemias.

After he had revived Soaemias, the scholars, reinforced by numerous academics, philosophers, priests and slaves, had managed to quell the fire. Elderly bearded men wept openly at the loss of irreplaceable texts, but actually the fire had been quite localised. The Great Library of Alexandria had known fire on multiple occasions, most notably the great destruction when Caesar had fired the ships in the harbour, and the flames had spread to the docks and thence the library. But the library had survived, and Silus hoped it always would. He couldn't contemplate a world without such a precious jewel in it.

With a small escort of academics, slaves, and some legionaries that Silus had rounded up en route, he had taken Soaemias and Avitus back to the prefect's palace, to a relieved and delighted Marcellus.

'Tell me again exactly what happened,' said Marcellus, after he had released his grip on his son.

Silus went over the story that he had rehearsed in his mind multiple times. He had told Soaemias and Avitus that this would be his testimony. Only Atius and Gannys could gainsay him, and he hoped they would have enough common sense to hold their tongues until they had learned the official version of events.

Silus told Marcellus how Gannys and Soaemias, desperate for news of the boy, had gone to the Serapeum to search for him themselves, that Atius and Silus had found Aziz and others in the conspiracy there, that they had fought and killed Aziz, and the other conspirators, who were only hired thugs, had fled. And that Soaemias had escaped with Avitus, but then got caught up in the rioting, and trapped in a burning building.

'And Silus rescued mother and me,' put in Avitus enthusiastically, happy to play his role in the make-believe.

Marcellus threw his arms around Silus and gripped him hard, and Silus was worried he would start to cry again.

'I owe you everything,' said Marcellus.

'Nonsense, sir. Just doing my job.'

'You went way beyond your duty. Thank you.' He indicated Silus' broken nose and injured hand.

'Family is everything, sir,' said Silus. Marcellus looked him in the eyes and nodded his understanding.

'And you, Gannys. Who would have thought you were a fighter?'

'Not a good one, as it turns out, sir,' said Gannys.

'That makes you all the more brave. Now both of you, get yourselves to a medicus and get your wounds and bruises tended.'

Gannys and Silus bowed and made to leave.

'Oh, Silus,' said Marcellus. 'What was it that triggered this riot?'

Silus gave a wry smile. 'You know these Alexandrians,' he said. 'Seems like anything can set them off.'

—

'This is the place where Marcus was martyred. Author of one of our sacred gospels, founder of the church here, and first Bishop of Alexandria.'

They stood at a point just outside the eastern city walls in front of a little altar on which had been placed flowers and offerings of fruits and cakes. Atius had insisted on walking Origen home, but Origen had refused to return to safety, preferring instead to walk the city and attempt to reduce tensions where he found them. They met with mixed success. Christians in particular recognised Origen and heeded his words, melting away shame-faced with bowed heads. Others were more belligerent, but none actually offered violence – Atius' presence was sufficient to dissuade them of that, even unarmed.

Slowly the pockets of disorder they encountered reduced in size and frequency, until, as the sun was dipping to the horizon, way off to the west behind the Serapeum, they had reached this spot, and Origen had halted.

'I've read the good news of Marcus,' said Atius.

'He came to Alexandria just a few years after the crucifixion of our Saviour. As he entered the city, one of the straps on his sandals broke. He took the sandal to a cobbler, pleased that the Lord had given him a simple means of getting in contact with the local people. But as the cobbler repaired the sandal, his awl went through his hand, and he cursed, "O, the one God."

'Mark talked to him about the true one God, and that cobbler became the head of the Christian community in Alexandria after Mark's death.

'Mark himself was dragged to this spot through the streets by an angry mob as he preached to them about love and truth and was killed here. This shrine is sacred to the faithful.'

They bowed their heads for a moment in silent prayer, and Atius felt something settle over him, a peace that he thought maybe he had never experienced. Until now, Atius' religion had been something he had been born into, something tribal, as immutable as the place of your birth or the colour of your skin. Now, in the presence of this inspiring preacher, on the spot of the death of a man who had walked with the apostles, he felt something much deeper. He reached for it, but felt it was just out of his grasp.

'What should I do, brother?'

Origen looked him in the eye.

'The scriptures have many commandments for you, brother. But I can say to you no more than the words of our Lord, the Christos. "Love the Lord your God with all your heart and all your mind and all your soul. And do to others what you would have them do to yourself."'

Atius nodded. It would be hard. He didn't think life was that simple. But he thought he would like to try. He noticed a tear had formed in the corner of his eye, and he wiped it away, embarrassed. Origen had noticed, though, and smiled sympathetically.

'Thank you,' Atius said, and they held hands in a two-handed grip, and Origen whispered words of blessing.

–

It was all one big pile of donkey shit, Silus decided. A load of excrement, crawling with dung beetles. All the religions were the same at the end of the day. Offering you one thing or another – glory, salvation, retribution on your enemies, a happy afterlife. But whether you followed Christos or Jupiter or Mithras or Elagabal, it was all a big swarm of lies, designed to manipulate the gullible. Maybe the gods didn't even exist. If they did, they certainly didn't give a shit about the likes of him. He sighed and entered Soaemias' bedchamber.

'You kept your word,' she said. Her voice was croaky, like an old woman with a chest complaint. She had asked to see Silus as soon as the physicians had finished fussing with her. Now they were alone together.

'Yes,' he said. 'I tend to do that. It's a weakness.' His thoughts drifted back to Tituria, in her exile. What had it cost him, keeping his promises to her?

'You must hate me.'

He should. She had tried to usurp the purple for her son, then tried to kill him when that had failed. She had schemed and lied. She had started a riot that had caused untold destruction, suffering and death. His shoulders slumped.

'I don't.'

Soaemias let out a humourless laugh.

'Are you trying to forgive me?'

Silus shook his head. 'I'm not Atius. Forgiveness isn't in my philosophy. I'm just too tired for hate right now. Give me a few days. Maybe I'll summon up the energy to hate you then.'

This time she seemed genuinely amused.

'You are an unusual man, aren't you, Silus?'

'If you say so.'

There was a moment's silence, which started to become uncomfortable.

'I suppose I am now in your debt,' she said eventually. 'You hold my life in your hands. You could tell Marcellus what you know and he would have me cut down on the spot.'

Silus said nothing.

'What do you want from me now?' she asked, voice loaded with suspicion. 'Money?'

Silus shook his head.

'Something else then.' She pulled down the collar of her gown, exposing one breast.

Silus took a step backwards in surprise. After what he had been through, and after the death of the first woman he had slept with since the loss of his wife, nothing could be further from his mind than sex, and in fact the idea nauseated him.

Soaemias looked insulted at his reaction, but covered herself up again.

'Not that. Then what?'

'I want nothing from you, Soaemias. Well, maybe one thing. Something I shouldn't need to ask of a mother. Look after young Avitus. He is a good lad.'

Soaemias looked chastened. Then she said, 'Thank you, Silus. Not just for saving me and my son from the flames. But for stopping me. In that moment, everything seemed so clear. I just knew that it was what the Lord Elagabal wanted. Until you spoke.'

'Certainty is a dangerous state of mind, I always feel,' said Silus. Then he said, 'You're welcome.'

Another pause, then Soaemias said, 'We depart for Numidia soon. No doubt Marcellus will want the former governor executed. Your job?'

'No doubt,' said Silus.

'And then what for you?'

Then, thought Silus, I am going to go to Lipari. I am going to stay with Tituria, indefinitely, well away from riot and murder and treacherous court politics.

The door burst open and Avitus rushed in. He was wearing an ankle length blue stola, a matching palla draped over his head. A delicate gold chain with a ruby pendant dangled around his neck, and he was clean and wafting a fragrance of delicate rose perfume.

He threw his arms around Soaemias, and hugged her tight, then stood up straight.

'Silus,' he said, his voice formal, as befitted the son of an important man, notwithstanding his feminine dress. 'I wish to thank you for your service.'

'Think nothing of it, my lord,' said Silus, with the hint of a smile.

Avitus smiled broadly back at him.

'Mother, Silus, I have come to a decision.'

They looked at him expectantly.

'I no longer wish to be the Emperor.'

Silus felt relief wash over him. It was short-lived.

'I want to be the Empress.'

Epilogue

"'And thus ends my report. Gaius Sergius Silus, Alexandria.'"

Oclatinius closed the wax diptych and looked up. Caracalla was looking off into the distance. Oclatinius wasn't sure if Caracalla had really been listening, but he didn't suppose that mattered. He was sure half of the report was fictional. Soaemias and Gannys in particular had appeared to come out of it with unblemished reputations, when Oclatinius was convinced they were up to their necks in the whole plot. When he got Silus on his own, he would find out the truth.

Festus, who was also present in the Emperor's chamber, had stayed rigid throughout the reading of the report, face expressionless. Oclatinius had watched carefully for any tells, any ticks or twitches that might have revealed Festus' inner thoughts, but the Commander of the Sacred Bedchamber remained inscrutable as always.

'Alexandria,' said Caracalla wistfully. 'I want to visit one day. See the city that was founded by the greatest general that ever lived. But first, I must make my own reputation. I will do what all the previous rulers and generals of Rome have failed to do. I will conquer Parthia. Already there is civil war there between the brothers Vologaesus and Artabanus. A war I helped incite when I received their ambassador here.'

'Yes, Augustus,' said Oclatinius. 'But before we can deal with the Parthians, we must secure our own borders. The confederacies of Germanic tribes are growing in number and strength, just as happened in Caledonia. The Alemmani and others in the region between the rivers Albis and Rhenus in particular are a concern, and I fear that we must confront them soon.'

Caracalla nodded. 'I am a young man. I have time. We will defeat the German tribes on the Rhenus, and then the Parthians. It is time to start planning. We prepare for war.'

Oclatinius and Festus both bowed their heads sharply in acknowledgement.

'Should I have Avitus executed?' asked Caracalla, forcing the topic of conversation into a tight loop back on itself.

Festus spoke first. 'There is really no need, Augustus. From this report, it sounds like he was just an innocent bystander in the whole enterprise. As were his mother and father.'

'Nevertheless,' said Caracalla. 'He could become a focus of resistance to my rule. Maybe someone else will have the idea of elevating him to the purple. His mother is certainly ambitious enough. What do you think, Oclatinius?'

Oclatinius hesitated and met Festus' eye. Festus gave the slightest shake of his head. Oclatinius paused a moment longer, mainly out of malice to his old friend.

'I agree with Festus. The boy and his family seem blameless. And you will find no more loyal a follower than Marcellus. Outside this room, of course.' He gave a nod to Festus, which he subtly overemphasised. It was lost on Caracalla, but not on Festus. 'But perhaps they should stay in Numidia for the foreseeable future, once Marcellus has installed himself as governor. It's far enough from Rome that little trouble should come from there, provided the province remains pacified. Far too from Syria, and supporters of Geta, and much nearer to your own supporters in Africa, who can keep an eye on the situation and step in if necessary.'

Caracalla considered, then nodded assent. 'It shall be so. The boy can live.'

Festus looked relieved, and gave Oclatinius a half-smile. Caracalla though had drifted off into a reverie. Oclatinius waited for a moment to be dismissed, then said, 'Shall we take our leave, Augustus?'

Caracalla waved them away airily with one hand. They bowed again, and left the throne room together. Once they were out of earshot of the bodyguards and Praetorians guarding the Emperor, Oclatinius said in a low voice, 'Aziz was one of yours, wasn't he?'

'Do you really expect me to dignify that with a reply?' asked Festus.

Oclatinius said nothing, and they walked on. Festus let out a sigh.

'Thank you,' he said. 'For speaking up for the boy.'

'Why do you care what happens to the boy? Still have plans for him?'

'No, no. Not that I ever did, of course. Anyway, that bolt has been shot. He won't be a figurehead for revolt any time soon.'

'Well the boy was innocent, and I am quite fond of him, in a way. He is different, and daring to be different is so rare in Rome.'

'He may also be the Emperor's son,' said Festus.

Oclatinius nodded. 'Maybe one day that will be important. But not while he suns himself in Numidia with his mother and father, forgotten by all.'

Festus looked at Oclatinius, worked his lips as if testing out some words before uttering them, then spoke.

'Why did you protect me?'

'You know why.'

'Still, after all these years?'

'Still. But don't push it, Festus. There are limits to my gratitude. My debt to you is not boundless.'

Festus sighed. 'I feel old.'

'There is no time for indulgences like that. We have an active young Emperor on the throne, and he wants to be the new Alexander. He will need us in the wars he is embarking on. He can't win everything he wants by sheer weight of arms. There will be a necessity for… other methods.'

'The methods in which we excel?'

'Just so. Maybe, for the first time in a long time, we might pull together, not against each other?'

Festus considered. 'It would certainly be less effort.'

They reached the palace entrance.

'I'm going home,' said Festus.

'As am I.'

And they turned their backs on each other and walked in opposite directions.

Bibliography and Further Reading

I have consulted too many texts in the research for this novel to list, but some of the principal books I have relied on are listed here:

Bowman, A. K., Garnsey, P. & Cameron, A., (2005) *The Cambridge Ancient History: Volume XII, the Crisis of Empire AD 193–337*, 2nd edition, Cambridge University Press, Cambridge

Grant, M., (1996) *The Severans, the Changed Roman Empire*, Routledge, Abingdon

Haas, C., (1997) *Alexandria in Late Antiquity, Topography and Social Conflict.*, The John Hopkins University Press, Baltimore and London

Levick, B., (2007) *Julia Domna, Syrian Empress*, Routledge, Abingdon

Lindsay, J., (1963) *Daily Life in Roman Egypt*, Frederick Muller Ltd, London

Lindsay, J., (1965) *Leisure and Pleasure in Roman Egypt*, Frederick Muller Ltd, London

Lindsay, J., (1968) *Men and Gods of the Roman Nile*, Frederick Muller Ltd, London

Macleod, R., (2004) *The Library of Alexandria*, I. B. Tauris & Co Ltd, London

Nixey, C., (2017) *The Darkening Age. The Christian Destruction of the Classical World*, Macmillan, London

Parson, P.,(2007) *City of the Sharp-Nosed Fish*, Weidenfeld & Nicolson, London

Pollard, J. & Reid, H., (2006). *The Rise and Fall of Alexandria, Birthplace of the Modern World*, Penguin, New York

Southern, P., (2001) *The Roman Empire from Severus to Constantine*, Routledge, Abingdon

Swain, S., Harrison, S. & Elsner, J., (2007) *Severan Culture*, Cambridge University Press, Cambridge

Sylvänne, I., (2017) *Caracalla, A Military Biography*, Pen & Sword Military, Barnsley

Historical Notes

Alexandria is one of the most extraordinary cities of ancient times. Founded around 332 BC and named after what many people believe was the most successful general of all time, Alexander the Great, Alexandria was a city of philosophy and learning, a cultural melting pot that spawned philosophers, inventors, politicians and religious authorities, as well as stunning architectural feats, intricate and cunning invented devices and new philosophies and religious denominations. After the death of Alexander the Great, Ptolemy took the Egyptian part of Alexander's empire for himself, and used its riches and trade to turn Alexandria into, for a while, the largest city in the world. For centuries after the emergence of Rome, it remained the world's second biggest city. Ptolemy and his dynastic successors successfully promoted Alexandria as an intellectual powerhouse, soon eclipsing its cultural mother city, Athens. Its Great Library hosted such luminaries as Euclid, the father of geometry, Hipparchus, the astronomer, and Eratosthenes, who calculated the circumference of the earth to within less than 0.2 per cent of its actual measurement, and this nearly two hundred years before the birth of Christ. Hero, who lived in Alexandria in the first century AD, besides various contributions to mathematics and physics, also invented a forerunner of the windmill, the first combined steam engine and steam turbine, and the first slot machine, described in this novel, which automatically dispensed holy water.

The Great Library was the ancient world's internet, with most of the world's knowledge housed within its walls. The

Ptolemies bought and stole manuscripts to fill its shelves. Any ship that docked in Alexandria was searched for books, and those that were found were seized and copied before being returned to their owners. The library and its associated Mouseion were among the major attractions to scholars from around the world.

I have chosen to include the Great Library in my third century Alexandria, despite the uncertainty of the date at which it burnt down. Some blame Julius Caesar for this event, and it is likely that many scrolls were destroyed in the fire that Caesar's troops set on the docks during the siege of Alexandria in 48 BC. However, some think it may have been a warehouse containing scrolls that burnt rather than the library itself, and it is recorded that around a hundred years later, the Emperor Claudius expanded the library building. A building full of flammable material such as this may have experienced multiple fires, though undoubtedly the scholars that worked there would have been aware of this risk. If the library still existed in the late third century, then this is likely to have been the date of its final destruction, when the Emperor Aurelian fought Zenobia, destroying the quarter in which the library was situated, or possibly a few years later when the Emperor Diocletian laid siege to the city in 297 AD.

Other extraordinary architectural sights would have included the famous lighthouse, an enormous structure nearly four hundred feet high, and ingeniously designed with a mirror that could reflect the sun's rays out to sea during the day, or the light of a great fire at nighttime. The Serapeum was another wonder, though unlike the lighthouse, not one that made the official list. Situated on a rocky plateau, it dominated the city's skyline. It was dedicated to the god Serapis, who had been invented or modified by the Ptolemies as a figure around which the Hellenistic city could unite. Serapis was a syncretism between the Egyptian gods Apis and Osiris, but was modified to appear anthropomorphic, in contrast to the commonly seen animal heads of Egyptian gods, in order to appeal to the Greeks of the city. The cult of Serapis survived in Alexandria until the Serapeum was destroyed by a Christian mob in the late fourth century, and Serapis was venerated throughout the Empire, not least by emperors such as Vespasian, Septimius Severus and Caracalla himself.

Alexandria's population consisted of a volatile mix of ethnicities and religions, and while a similar diversity could be found in Rome, religious and racial conflict seemed to be far more common in Alexandria. Jews, Christians, Greeks, native Egyptians and Romans lived cheek by jowl, and riots were frequent. The Jewish community had been sizeable at one stage in Alexandria, but various rebellions had led to many of them being expelled or murdered, so by the time of this novel, there were few remaining, although no doubt the Jews took the blame for most things that went wrong, as they have throughout history.

St Mark the evangelist is believed to have brought Christianity to Alexandria, and he was martyred in the city. The new religion found fertile ground in the city, and Alexandria became one of the great centres of Christianity in the world. Great Christian thinkers included Clement, Origen and Didymus.

As described in the novel, Origen's father was killed in the persecution of Septimius Severus, and Origen would have joined him if his mother hadn't hidden his clothes, his modesty preventing him from going out. He is thought to have castrated himself after a literal misreading of Matthew 19:12, an act he came to regret later in life, although some believe this event was actually malicious gossip spread by his enemies. Origen's numerous works were highly influential in the early Christian church, although in the years and centuries after his death, his work was condemned as heretical. He died a year after being released from two years of imprisonment during which he was repeatedly tortured in an unsuccessful attempt to force him to renounce Christ.

Incidentally, it was rumoured that Gannys was also a eunuch. This may have been a detail invented by Gibbon, but I have chosen to have him pretend to be a eunuch to conceal his affair with Julia Soaemias.

The religion of the god Elagabal is not Alexandrian, but originated in the city of Emesa, modern-day Homs in Syria, although he was probably worshipped as a major deity throughout Syria. Although he represented the sun, his name was thought to mean the god of the mountain. He was venerated as a black conical rock, with a rounded base and a pointed top. Ancient sources suggest that this stone was a meteorite, and it would not be surprising for a stone that in ancient times fell from the sky in a blaze of fire to be venerated or worshipped.

Varius Avitus Bassianus, the Avitus of this novel, who was later to become the Emperor Elagabalus or Heliogabalus, was descended from the royal priesthood of Emesa, and was the grandson of Julia Domna's sister, Julia Maesa. As such he had royal lineage. His mother later claimed that Caracalla was his father, although this may have been invented in order to give extra validity to his claim to the purple. There is speculation that Avitus had an older brother, since he is named after his mother's father, and an older brother would have been named after his father's father. Moreover, the tombstone of Avitus' probable father, Sextus Varius Marcellus, was dedicated by his wife and sons. However, it is reported that Julia Maesa had only two grandsons, who were cousins (Avitus/Elagabalus and Severus Alexander), and if there was an elder brother, why did Avitus take precedence when being elevated to the throne? I have therefore concluded it most likely that Avitus did have a brother, but like so many children of the times, he died young.

Avitus himself is a fascinating character. Although more roundly vilified than any Emperor, even those habitually demonised such as Caligula, Nero, Domitian, Commodus and Caracalla himself, most of the criticisms, accusations and smears of his character and his reign centred around his sexual behaviour and his religious zealotry. That he wished to introduce his god Elagabal as the supreme deity into Rome is no worse behaviour than that of the only Roman Emperor to bear the title 'Great', Constantine, and in fact Avitus probably believed profoundly in his god, while Constantine likely introduced Christianity for cynical political purposes.

As for the sexual scandals, Avitus became Emperor unexpectedly at the age of fourteen, a role he had had no preparation for. A hormonal teenage boy with gender identity issues, whose father had died a few years before and who was brought up by a manipulative and overbearing mother, suddenly being given supreme and absolute power over the entire civilised world – what could go wrong?

I have tried to write the young Avitus from a sympathetic point of view, taking into account both modern sensibilities towards gender identity, while not glossing over the reaction that Avitus' contemporaries would have had towards his behaviour. Avitus, of course, will become a much more important figure in Rome's history a few years after the point at which this novel ends, and perhaps if both reader and writer have the stamina to reach that far, we will see what sort of ruler he becomes!

Historical Texts

Herodian on the death of Septimius Severus and the co-reign of Geta and Caracalla

Transl. J. Hart 1749. Adapted from Herodian's history of his own times, original book IV, chapters v–vi.

Antoninus thought it was proper to stay the night in the temple of the camp, to bind the army firmly to his interest and to make them his own by distributing large sums of money. The next day he went to the Senate house, attended by all the Praetorians, more heavily armed than usual when they only attended the Emperor in State. After the divine service was performed, he ascended the Imperial throne and delivered the following speech to the Senate.

'I am not ignorant that every domestic murder is no sooner heard than detested, that the very name of parricide, the moment it strikes the ear, raises indignation and calumny. The unfortunate are always objects of compassion, the powerful of envy. In these cases, the vanquished party is thought to be injured, and he that gains the victory is always accused of having done wrong.

'But if anyone will consider the case with reason, and not form his judgement from affection for the fallen person, and to maturely weigh and examine the motive and intent of both parties, he will see that it is sometimes not only reasonable but necessary for a man to defend himself, because to fall by injustice carries with it a strong suspicion of cowardice, while repelling violence with success has, besides the defending his safety, the added glory of a bold and manly spirit.

'What frequent snares have been laid for my life, by poison and every other kind of covert treason, it is in your power to find out by torture. For I have ordered his ministers and servants to be present, that the truth of this might be discovered. Some have already been examined, and you may presently hear their confessions. In the meantime, let me inform you of his last wicked attempt on my life. He came to me in the presence of my mother, attended with armed men, with the intention of murder.

'But having previous suspicion of his villainy, I boldly defeated his attempt and I viewed him not with the affection and nature of a brother, but as an avowed enemy. To punish such traitors is undeniably just, as shown by numerous examples. Romulus, the great founder of this city, would not bear his brother vilifying and deriding his work.

'I pass over Germanicus and Titus without comment, the former being the brother of Tiberius and the latter the brother of Domitian. Marcus himself, that sage and meek philosopher, would not bear the arrogance of his son-in-law Lucius, but cut him off by secret treachery.

'So too, I, while poisons were being prepared for my food, and the sword was already lifted to my throat, struck the blow and revenged myself on my enemy, for his actions sufficiently justify that name.

'And therefore you should give thanks to the gods who have saved at least one of your emperors, and to cease henceforth your animosities and pass the remainder of your days in security and peace, looking only to one sovereign for protection. For as Jupiter reigns sole monarch of the gods, so he now gives the government of men into the hands of one supreme.'

These words were uttered with a strong and stern voice, after which having cast a look full of wrath and terror upon Geta's friends, he left most of them trembling and pale, and returned with haste to the Imperial palace.

Here he soon let loose his fury against all in his brother's service, whether ministers, counsellors, friends, officers or servants. Neither age nor sex was spared. Children and even infants were massacred, and their dead carcasses were thrown into carts with all the marks of indignity and contempt, and carried out of the city, burnt in huge heaps in the order they arrived.

No one who had the least familiarity or acquaintance with Geta escaped death. Wrestlers, charioteers, players, musicians, dancers and everyone he kept for the diversion of his eyes or ears shared the same fate. And those of the senators most distinguished by blood or wealth were, upon the weakest evidence or even surmise or hearsay, condemned and executed as sympathisers of Geta. He even put to death the eldest sister of Commodus, now an old woman, who was held in honour by all the former emperors, as she was the daughter of Marcus. He alleged, as a heinous charge against her, that she was found weeping in his mother's apartment, and consoling her for the loss of her son. Plautian's daughter, his divorced wife, who was now an exile in Sicily, his first cousin, named after his father Severus, Pertinax's son, the son of Lucilla, Commodus's sister – all the descendants of the former emperors, and those of the most illustrious families in the Senate, he cut down, as if he designed to extinguish the very relics of Imperial and patrician blood.

He then sent assassins to the provinces, and put to death the governors and procurators who were friends to his brother. Not a night passed without the frequent murder of men of every nation. The Vestal Virgins were buried alive for violating their oaths of virginity. And to complete all this, he committed an action so strange that it was almost without parallel. Some of the crowd at the races in the Circus mocked and laughed at one of his favourite charioteers. He took this to be a personal affront, and ordered the army to fall upon the spectators and to murder those who had the impudence to abuse the charioteer. The

Praetorians, having being given the power of doing mischief, did not spend much time investigating who had so impudently affronted the Emperor, and it was impossible to find the persons among the numerous crowd of people, nor would any dare to confess the truth, so they seized all they could lay their hands on and either cut them to pieces or stripped them of all they had on them as a ransom for their lives, after which they reluctantly allowed them to escape.

Dio Cassius on Caracalla

Transl. Earnest Cary PhD, 1914, Adapted from an English translation of Dio's Roman History, Epitome of book LXXVIII iii–xi.
Source: the Lacus Curtius website: http://penelope.uchicago.edu/Thayer/E/Roman/Texts/Cassius_Dio/78*.html

Antoninus, although it was evening, took possession of the legions, after crying out the whole way, as if he had been the object of a plot and his life were in danger. On entering the camp he exclaimed: 'Rejoice, fellow-soldiers, for now I am in a position to do you favours.' And before they heard the whole story he had stopped their mouths with so many and so great promises that they could neither think of nor say anything to show proper respect for the dead. 'I am one of you,' he said, 'and it is because of you alone that I care to live, in order that I may confer upon you many favours; for all the treasuries are yours.' And he further said: 'I pray to live with you, if possible, but if not, at any rate to die with you. For I do not fear death in any form, and it is my desire to end my days in warfare. There should a man die, or nowhere.' To the Senate on the following day he addressed various remarks, and then, after rising from his seat, he said as he reached the door: 'Listen to an important announcement from me: that the whole world may rejoice, let all the exiles who have been condemned, on whatever charge or in whatever manner, be restored.' Thus did he empty the islands of exiles and grant pardon to the basest of criminals; but before long he had the islands full again. Of the Imperial freedmen and soldiers who had been with Geta he immediately put to death some twenty thousand, men and women alike, wherever in the palace any of them happened to be; and he slew various distinguished men also, including Papinianus.

When the Praetorians accused Papinianus and Patruinus of certain things, Antoninus permitted them to kill the men, saying: 'It is for you, and not for myself, that I rule; therefore, I defer to you both as accuser and judges.' He rebuked the slayer of Papinianus for using an axe instead of a sword to kill him.

He also wished to take the life of Cilo, his tutor and bene- factor, who had served as prefect of the city under his father, and whom he himself had often called 'father.' The soldiers who were sent to Cilo first plundered his silver plate, his robes, his money, and everything else of his, and then led him along the Sacred Way with the purpose of taking him to the palace and there putting him out of the way; he had only low slippers on his feet, since he had chanced to be in the bath when arrested, and was wearing a short tunic. The soldiers tore the clothing off his body and disfigured his face, so that the populace as well as the city troops began to make an outcry; accordingly, Antoninus, in awe and fear of them, met the party, and shielding Cilo with his cavalry cloak (he was wearing military dress), cried out: 'Insult not my father! Strike not my tutor!' As for the military tribune who had been bidden to slay him and the detail of soldiers sent with him, they were put to death, ostensibly because they had plotted Cilo's destruction, but in reality because they had not killed him.

Antoninus pretended to love Cilo to such a degree that he declared, 'Those who have plotted against him have plotted against me,' and when commended for this by the bystanders, he continued: 'Call me neither Hercules nor any other god' – not that he did not wish to be termed a god, but because he did not want to do anything worthy of a god. He was naturally

315

capricious in all things; for instance, he would bestow great honours upon people and then suddenly disgrace them quite without cause, and again he would spare the lives of those who least deserved it and punish those whom one would never have looked to see punished.

Julianus Asper, a man by no means to be despised either on account of his education or of his intelligence, was first exalted, together with his sons, by Antoninus, so that he paraded about surrounded by ever so many fasces at once, and then was suddenly insulted by him outrageously and sent back to his native town with abuse and in terrible fear.

Laenus was another whom he would have disgraced or even killed, had not the man been extremely ill. Antoninus before the soldiers called his illness wicked, because it did not permit him to display his own wickedness in the case of Laenus also.

He also made away with Thrasea Priscus, a man second to none either in birth or intelligence. There were many others, too, formerly friends of his, that he put to death.

'All could I never recite near the names number over completely' of the distinguished men that he killed without any justification. Dio, because the slain were very well known in those days, gives a list of their names; but for me it suffices to say that he made away with all the men he wished without distinction, 'both guilty and guiltless alike,' and he mutilated Rome by depriving it of its good men.

Antoninus belonged to three races; and he possessed none of their virtues at all, but combined in himself all their vices; the fickleness, cowardice, and recklessness of Gaul were his, the harshness and cruelty of Africa, and the craftiness of Syria, whence he was sprung on his mother's side.

Veering from murder to sport, he showed the same thirst for blood in this field, too. It was nothing, of course, that an elephant, rhinoceros, tiger, and hippotigris were slain in the arena, but he took pleasure in seeing the blood of as many gladiators as possible; he forced one of them, Bato, to fight three men in succession on the same day, and then, when Bato was slain by the last one, he honoured him with a brilliant funeral.

He was so enthusiastic about Alexander that he used certain weapons and cups which he believed had once been his, and he also set up many likenesses of him both in the camps and in Rome itself. He organised a phalanx, composed entirely of Macedonians, 16,000 strong, named it 'Alexander's phalanx,' and equipped it with the arms that warriors had used in his day; these consisted of a helmet of raw ox-hide, a three-ply linen breastplate, a bronze shield, long pike, short spear, high boots, and sword. Not even this, however, satisfied him, but he must call his hero 'the Augustus of the East'; and once he actually wrote to the Senate that Alexander had come to life again in the person of the Augustus, that he might live on once more in him, having had such a short life before. Towards the philosophers who were called Aristotelians he showed bitter hatred in every way, even going so far as to desire to burn their books, and in particular he abolished their common messes in Alexandria and all the other privileges that they had enjoyed; his grievance against them was that Aristotle was supposed to have been concerned in the death of Alexander. Such was his behaviour in these matters; nay more, he even took about with him numerous elephants, that in this respect, also, he might seem to be imitating Alexander, or rather, perhaps, Dionysus.

On Alexander's account, then, he was very fond of the Macedonians. Once, after commending a Macedonian tribune for the agility with which he had leapt upon his horse, he asked him first: 'From what country are you?' Then, learning that he was a Macedonian, he asked again: 'What is your name?' And hearing that it was Antigonus, he further inquired: 'And what was your father's name?' When the father's name was found to be Philip, he declared: 'I have all my desire,' and promptly advanced him through all the other grades of the military career, and before long appointed him a senator with the rank of an ex-praetor. Again, there is the incident of a certain man who had no connection with Macedonia but had committed many crimes and for this reason was being tried by the emperor on an appeal. His name changed to be Alexander, and when the orator who was accusing him kept saying, 'the bloodthirsty Alexander, the god-detested Alexander,' Antoninus became angry, as if he himself were being called these bad names, and said: 'If you cannot be satisfied with plain "Alexander," you may consider yourself dismissed.'

Now this great admirer of Alexander, Antoninus, was fond of spending money upon the soldiers, great numbers of whom he kept in attendance upon him, alleging one excuse after another and one war after another; but he made it his business to strip, despoil, and grind down all the rest of mankind, and the senators by no means least. In the first place, there were the gold crowns that he was repeatedly demanding, on the constant pretext that he had conquered some enemy or other; and I am not referring, either, to the actual manufacture of the crowns – for what does that amount to? – but to the vast amount of money constantly being given under that name by the cities for the customary 'crowning', as it is called, of the emperors. Then there were the provisions that we were required to furnish in great quantities on all occasions, and this without receiving any remuneration and sometimes actually at additional cost to ourselves, all of which supplies he either bestowed upon the soldiers or else peddled out; and there were the gifts which he demanded from the wealthy citizens and from the various communities; and the taxes, but the new ones which he promulgated and the 10 per cent tax that he instituted in place of the 5 per cent tax applying to the emancipation of slaves, to bequests, and to all legacies; for he abolished the right of succession and exemption from taxes which had been granted in such cases to those who were closely related to the deceased. This was the reason why he made all the people in his Empire Roman citizens; nominally he was honouring them, but his real purpose was to increase his revenues by this means, inasmuch as aliens did not have to pay most of these taxes. But apart from all these burdens, we were also compelled to build at our own expense all sorts of houses for him whenever he set out from Rome, and costly lodgings in the middle of even the very shortest journeys; yet he not only never lived in them, but in some cases was not destined even to see them. Moreover, we constructed amphitheatres and race-courses wherever he spent the winter or expected to spend it, all without receiving any contribution from him; and they were all promptly demolished, the sole reason for their being built in the first place being, apparently, that we might become impoverished.

The emperor himself kept spending the money upon the soldiers, as we have said, and upon wild beasts and horses; for he was for ever killing vast numbers of animals, both wild and domesticated, forcing us to furnish most of them, though he did buy a few. One day he slew a hundred boars at one time with his own hands. He also used to drive chariots, wearing the Blue costume. In everything he was very hot-headed and very fickle, and he furthermore possessed the craftiness of his mother and the Syrians, to which race she belonged. He would appoint some freedman or other wealthy person to be director of the games in order that the man might spend money in this way also; and he would salute the spectators with his whip from the arena below and beg for gold pieces like a performer of the lowest class. He claimed that he used the Sun-god's method in driving, and plumed himself upon it. To such an extent was the entire world, so far as it owned his sway, devastated throughout his whole reign, that on one occasion the Romans at a horse-race shouted in unison this, among other things: 'We shall do the living to death, that we may bury the dead.' Indeed, he often used to say: 'Nobody in the world should have money but me; and want it to bestow upon the soldiers.' Once when Julia chided him for spending vast sums upon them and said, 'There is no longer any source of revenue, just or unjust, left to us,' he replied, exhibiting his sword, 'Be of good cheer,

Mother: for as long as we have this, we shall not run short of money.' Moreover to those who flattered him he distributed both money and goods.

Julius Paulus, a man of consular rank, was a gossip and jester, sparing not even the emperors themselves, and Severus caused him to be placed in free custody. When he still continued, even under guard, to jest at the expense of the sovereigns, Severus sent for him and swore that he would cut off his head. But Paulus replied: 'Yes, you can cut it off, but as long as I have it, neither you nor I can restrain it.' So Severus laughed and let him off.

He bestowed on Junius Paulinus a million sesterces because the man, who was a jester, had been led to crack a joke at the emperor's expense without meaning to do so. For Paulinus had said that Antoninus looked as if he were angry, the fact being that the emperor was wont to assume a somewhat savage expression. Indeed, he had no regard whatever for the higher things, and never even learned anything of that nature, as he himself admitted; and hence he actually held in contempt those of us who possessed anything like education. Severus, to be sure, had trained him in absolutely all the pursuits that tended to excellence, whether of body or of mind, so that even after he became emperor he went to teachers and studied philosophy most of the day. He used to be rubbed dry with oil, and would ride on horseback as much as a hundred miles; and he had practised swimming even in rough water. In consequence of these pursuits he was vigorous enough in a fashion, but he forgot his intellectual training as completely as if he had never heard of such a thing. And yet he was not lacking either in ability to express himself or in good judgement, but showed a very shrewd understanding of most matters and talked very readily. For, thanks to his authority and his impetuosity, as well as to his habit of blurting out recklessly everything alike that came into his head and of feeling no shame at all about airing all his thoughts, he often stumbled upon a happy phrase.

But this same emperor made many mistakes because of the obstinacy with which he clung to his own opinions; for he wished not only to know everything but to be the only one to know anything, and he desired not only to have all power but to be the only one to have power. Hence he asked no one's advice and was jealous of those who had any useful knowledge. He never loved anyone, but he hated all who excelled in anything, most of all those whom he pretended to love most; and he destroyed many of them in one way or another. Many he murdered openly; but others he would send to uncongenial provinces whose climate was injurious to their state of health and thus, while pretending to honour them greatly, he quietly got rid of them by exposing those whom he did not like to excessive heat or cold. Hence, even if there were some whom he refrained from putting to death, yet he subjected them to such hardships that his hands were in fact stained with their blood.

Strabo on Alexandria

Transl. Jones H.L., Loeb Classical Library 1917–1932. Strabo's Geography, XVII.1.6–10.
Source: http://penelope.uchicago.edu/Thayer/E/Roman/Texts/Strabo/home.html
Lightly edited by the author.

6. Since Alexandria and its neighbourhood constitute the largest and most important part of this subject, I shall begin with them. The sea-coast, then, from Pelusium, as one sails towards the west, as far as the Canopic mouth, is about 1,300 stadia – the 'base' of the Delta, as I have called it; and thence to the island Pharos, 150 stadia more. Pharos is an oblong isle, is very close to the mainland, and forms with it a harbour with two mouths; the shore of the mainland forms a bay, since it thrusts two promontories into the open sea, and between these is situated the island, which closes the bay, for it lies lengthwise parallel

to the shore. Of the extremities of Pharos, the eastern one lies closer to the mainland and to the promontory opposite it (the promontory called Lochias), and thus makes the harbour narrow at the mouth; and in addition to the narrowness of the intervening passage there are also rocks, some under the water, and others projecting out of it, which at all hours roughen the waves that strike them from the open sea. And likewise the extremity of the isle is a rock, which is washed all round by the sea and has upon it a tower that is admirably constructed of white marble with many stories and bears the same name as the island. This was an offering made by Sostratus of Cnidus, a friend of the kings, for the safety of mariners, as the inscription says, for since the coast was harbourless and low on either side, and also had reefs and shallows, those who were sailing from the open sea thither needed some lofty and conspicuous sign to enable them to direct their course to the entrance of the harbour. And the western mouth is also not easy to enter, although it does not require so much caution as the other. And it likewise forms a second harbour, that of Eunostus, which lies in front of the closed harbour which was dug by the hand of man. For the harbour which affords the entrance on the side of the above-mentioned tower of Pharos is the Great Harbour, whereas these two lie continuous with that harbour in their innermost recess, being separated from it only by the embankment called the Heptastadium. The embankment forms a bridge extending from the mainland to the western portion of the island, and leaves open only two passages into the harbour of Eunostus, which are bridged over. However, this work formed not only a bridge to the island but also an aqueduct, at least when Pharos was inhabited. But in these present times it has been laid waste by the deified Caesar in his war against the Alexandrians, since it had sided with the kings. A few seamen, however, live near the tower. As for the Great Harbour, in addition to its being beautifully enclosed both by the embankment and by nature, it is not only so deep close to the shore that the largest ship can be moored at the steps, but also is cut up into several harbours. Now the earlier kings of the Egyptians, being content with what they had and not wanting foreign imports at all, and being prejudiced against all who sailed the seas, and particularly against the Greeks (for owing to scarcity of land of their own the Greeks were ravagers and coveters of that of others), set a guard over this region and ordered it to keep away any who should approach; and they gave them as a place of abode, Rhacotis, as it is called, which is now that part of the city of the Alexandrians which lies above the ship-houses, but was at that time a village; and they gave over the parts round about the village to herdsmen, who likewise were able to prevent the approach of outsiders. But when Alexander visited the place and saw the advantages of the site, he resolved to fortify the city on the harbour. Writers record, as a sign of the good fortune that has since attended the city, an incident which occurred at the time of tracing the lines of the foundation: when the architects were marking the lines of the enclosure with chalk, the supply of chalk gave out; and when the king arrived, his stewards furnished a part of the barley-meal which had been prepared for the workmen, and by means of this the streets also, to a larger number than before, were laid out. This occurrence, then, they are said to have interpreted as a good omen.

–

7. The advantages of the city's site are various; for, first, the place is washed by two seas, on the north by the Egyptian Sea, as it is called, and on the south by Lake Mareia, also called Mareotis. This is filled by many canals from the Nile, both from above and on the sides, and through these canals the imports are much larger than those from the sea, so that the harbour on the lake was in fact richer than that on the sea; and here the exports from Alexandria also are larger than the imports; and anyone might judge, if he were at either Alexandria or Dicaearchia and saw the merchant vessels both at their arrival and at their departure, how

much heavier or lighter they sailed to or fro. And in addition to the great value of the things brought down from both directions, both into the harbour on the sea and into that on the lake, the salubrity of the air is also worthy of remark. And this likewise results from the fact that the land is washed by water on both sides and because of the timeliness of the Nile's risings; for the other cities that are situated on lakes have heavy and stifling air in the heats of summer, because the lakes then become marshy along their edges because of the evaporation caused by the sun's rays, and, accordingly, when so much filth-laden moisture rises, the air inhaled is noisome and starts pestilential diseases, whereas at Alexandria, at the beginning of summer, the Nile, being full, fills the lake also, and leaves no marshy matter to corrupt the rising vapours. At that time, also, the Etesian winds blow from the north and from a vast sea, so that the Alexandrians pass their time most pleasantly in summer.

–

8. The shape of the area of the city is like a chlamys cloak; the long sides of it are those that are washed by the two waters, having a diameter of about thirty stadia, and the short sides are the isthmuses, each being seven or eight stadia wide and pinched in on one side by the sea and on the other by the lake. The city as a whole is intersected by streets practicable for horse-riding and chariot-driving, and by two that are very broad, extending to more than a plethrum in breadth, which cut one another into two sections and at right angles. And the city contains the most beautiful public precincts and also the royal palaces, which constitute one-fourth or even one-third of the whole circuit of the city; for just as each of the kings, from love of splendour, was wont to add some adornment to the public monuments, so also he would invest himself at his own expense with a residence, in addition to those already built, so that now, to quote the words of the poet, 'there is building upon building.' All, however, are connected with one another and the harbour, even those

that lie outside the harbour. The Museum is also a part of the royal palaces; it has a public walk, an exedra with seats, and a large house, in which is the common mess-hall of the men of learning who share the Museum. This group of men not only hold property in common, but also have a priest in charge of the Museum, who formerly was appointed by the kings, but is now appointed by Caesar. The Sema also, as it is called, is a part of the royal palaces. This was the enclosure which contained the burial-places of the kings and that of Alexander; for Ptolemy, the son of Lagus, forestalled Perdiccas by taking the body away from him when he was bringing it down from Babylon and was turning aside towards Aegypt, moved by greed and a desire to make that country his own. Furthermore, Perdiccas lost his life, having been slain by his soldiers at the time when Ptolemy attacked him and hemmed him up in a desert island. So Perdiccas was killed, having been transfixed by his soldiers' sarissae when they attacked him; but the kings who were with him, both Aridaeus and the children of Alexander, and also Rhoxanê, Alexander's wife, departed for Macedonia; and the body of Alexander was carried off by Ptolemy and placed in Alexandria, where it still now lies – not, however, in the same sarcophagus as before, for the present one is made of glass, whereas the one wherein Ptolemy laid it was made of gold. The latter was plundered by the Ptolemy nicknamed 'Cocces' and 'Pareisactus,' who came over from Syria but was immediately expelled, so that his plunder proved unprofitable to him.

–

9. In the Great Harbour at the entrance, on the right hand, are the island and the tower Pharos, and on the other hand are the reefs and also the promontory Lochias, with a royal palace upon it; and on sailing into the harbour one comes, on the left, to the inner royal palaces, which are continuous with those on Lochias and have groves and numerous lodges painted in various colours. Below these lies the harbour that was dug by

the hand of man and is hidden from view, the private property of the kings, as also Antirrhodos, an isle lying off the artificial harbour, which has both a royal palace and a small harbour. They called it this to show it was a rival of Rhodes. Above the artificial harbour lies the theatre; then the Poseidium – an elbow, as it were, projecting from the Emporium, as it is called, and containing a temple of Poseidon. To this elbow of land Antony added a mole projecting still farther, into the middle of a harbour, and on the extremity of it built a royal lodge which he called Timonium. This was his last act, when, forsaken by his friends, he sailed away to Alexandria after his misfortune at Actium, having chosen to live the life of a Timon at the end of his days, which he intended to spend in solitude from all those friends. Then one comes to the Caesarium and the Emporium and the warehouses; and after these to the ship-houses, which extend as far as the Heptastadium. So much for the Great Harbour and its surroundings.

–

10. Next, after the Heptastadium, one comes to the harbour of Eunostus, and, above this, to the artificial harbour, which is also called Cibotus; it too has ship-houses. Farther in there is a navigable canal, which extends to Lake Mareotis. Now outside the canal there is still left only a small part of the city; and then one comes to the suburb Necropolis, in which are many gardens and groves and halting-places fitted up for the embalming of corpses, and, inside the canal, both to the Sarapium and to other sacred precincts of ancient times, which are now almost abandoned on account of the construction of the new buildings at Nicopolis; for instance, there are an amphitheatre and a stadium at Nicopolis, and the quinquennial games are celebrated there; but the ancient buildings have fallen into neglect. In short, the city is full of public and sacred structures; but the most beautiful is the Gymnasium, which has porticoes more than a stadium in length. And in the middle are both the court of justice and the

groves. Here, too, is the Paneium, a 'height,' as it were, which was made by the hand of man; it has the shape of a fir-cone, resembles a rocky hill, and is ascended by a spiral road; and from the summit one can see the whole of the city lying below it on all sides. The broad street that runs lengthwise extends from Necropolis past the Gymnasium to the Canobic Gate; and then one comes to the Hippodrome, as it is called, and to the other streets that lie parallel, extending as far as the Canopic canal. Having passed through the Hippodrome, one comes to Nicopolis, which has a settlement on the sea no smaller than a city. It is thirty stadia distant from Alexandria. Augustus Caesar honoured this place because it was here that he conquered in battle those who came out against him with Antony; and when he had taken the city at the first onset, he forced Antony to put himself to death and Cleopatra to come into his power alive; but a little later she too put herself to death secretly, while in prison, by the bite of an asp or (for two accounts are given) by applying a poisonous ointment; and the result was that the empire of the sons of Lagus, which had endured for many years, was dissolved.

Acknowledgements

Thanks to Michael Bhaskar and Kit Nevile at Canelo for their support and encouragement in the writing of this series, as well as the excellent job they have done with presenting and marketing the work, not least the lovely covers. Thanks as always to Nome and Abbie for their support, and to my little dog Ivy, who has wormed her way into these books as Issa.

The Imperial Assassin

Emperor's Sword
Emperor's Knife
Emperor's Axe